To Lead

Reborn in the Perfect Fantasy World

ISBN: 978-1-959098-07-2

Fantasy.Productions L.L.C.
4601 E. Douglas St.
STE 150
Wichita, KS 67218
For serious business inquiries only,
contact cristoph@fantasy.productions

REBORN IN THE PERFECT FANTASY WORLD

Thank you, to my wife, for supporting me through this series.

And to my daughter for brightening every day.

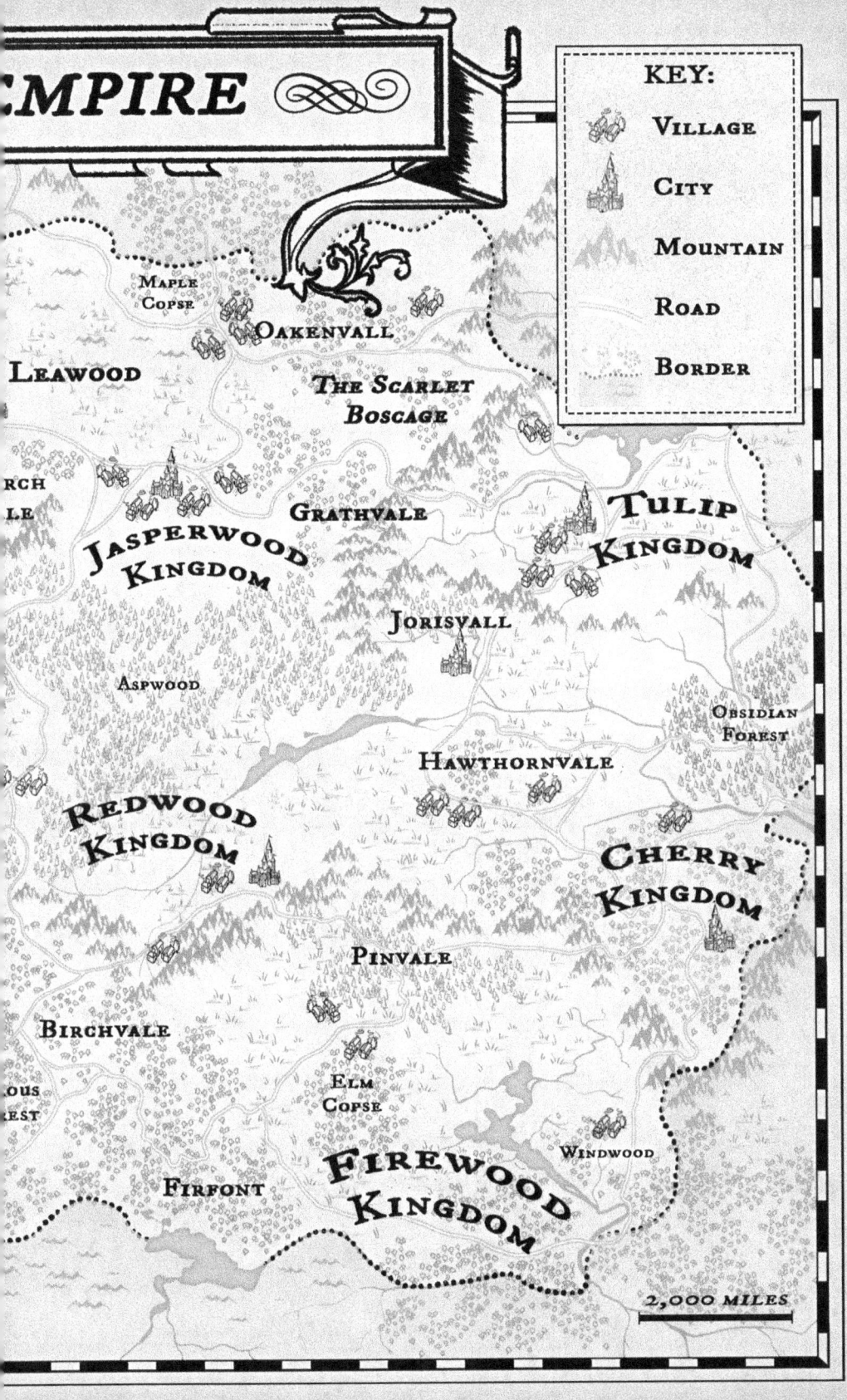

CHAPTER ONE

A PIVOTAL ANNOUNCEMENT / IT ENDS BEFORE IT BEGINS

Hexoday, Runariae 1st, 1739

AS A REINCARNATE from Earth, I learned that death was a dirty liar when my story didn't end. If there's a goddess of irony, I'd have a bone to pick with her. But the only deity I've met is the Goddess of Death itself, Eloria, who chose me to be her True Champion.

"What do you think?" said Sarah, my lady's maid, holding up a mirror.

With a half-grin I said, "You ask this every time. My hair style is always the same." Before she could pipe up I rolled my eyes and added, "Yes, I know." Interlacing my fingers in mock prayer I said, "I can thank Her Goddess Eloria for that." Patting the gigantic hoop skirt around my waist it rebounded exasperatingly. "Now, is this entirely necessary?" I thought to myself, *This makes me look like I have a huge booty.*

"Yes, ma'am," my other lady's maid Tania said. "You are one of the main attractions tonight, so you must look the part," she looked up at me from adjusting the light purple skirt she'd just sat over the frame, and added, "So says Her Imperial High Grace, Lily, your mother, at least."

"Yeah, but what about Gideon? Is his outfit equally attention-getting?"

When I met Marion Gideon Varn, I was only four years old. Our acp hoth, or child pact, was a decision made by our parents. I recently decided to change our child pact into a formal engagement. I'd viewed the child portion of the pact as a sort of play engagement. In the seven years that we'd known one another, we'd become even closer. A formal engagement seemed like the logical next step, despite my age.

Sarah's voice gained some levity, "Oh. He'll have plenty of attention on him."

"What do you know?" I said flatly.

"Nothing of note," she said innocently.

For a moment even Tania flashed a smile, which made me suspicious.

"I mean, I get that this is my public engagement announcement, but why is there such a stink about it? When Oliver announced his intent to marry with Mina, there wasn't nearly as much fuss." Wondering to myself, *Is it because he was three years younger than I am now at the time, or because I'm a girl?*

His situation actually gave me the clarity to do what I needed. He was my twin brother, and almost died a month and a half ago. Our uncle, the emperor, granted Oliver credit for my efforts in uncovering deep corruption in our empire. He was poisoned by someone who wasn't happy with what I'd done.

"Oliver wasn't planning on granting Mina a boost to her standing, whereas you chose a marriage of equality. That means Gideon will be promoted now and again, once you marry. Tonight, the focus on him will be equal to the focus on you." She carefully attached a bejeweled pin to the end of my already-tied braid. "The creation of a new high noble, an Imperial Marquess no less, is a *big* deal."

"Gideon is from a baronetcy," I said. "He would've been a morganatic spouse if I'd left his status as it was, wouldn't he?"

Tania nodded. "He would likely not even have lived with you in the future, if that were the case. His family would only have received the initial dowry."

Sarah cinched my lavender-colored kirtle, making my breaths a bit shallower.

Controlling my breathing was something I had to remember to do with each breath. Otherwise, my Cultivator strength would shred the garment. Cultivators like myself naturally use Essence, or the energy of the world, to empower themselves. It was taking me time to get used to my passive rapid increase in strength. Tearing my dress wasn't something I wanted to do in a room full of people, but it would be an effortless endeavor.

She picked up my gilded hairbrush and sat down the jewel-encrusted mirror.

Seeing them made me bemoan the excess that filled my life. *Ever since I told Mom that I was serious about Gideon, they replaced everything with* more *in every way.* Last week they'd even replaced my bathtub with one made, I swear, of solid gold. Despite my enhanced strength, I couldn't even make it budge. Admittedly, I couldn't dent it either, so I guessed it wasn't pure gold.

Tania fixed my brooch with our family coat of arms in the center on my chest.

Though, the changes might be because I'm now the heir apparent of our Imperial Duchy.

The pain in Oliver's face as he fought the poison that changed the course of his life came to mind. He survived, but the poison stole my brother's strength and future. He was destined to be the paragon of our generation. Now he was lucky to be alive.

Remembering my brother's cheery smile, I wondered, "Why wasn't Oliver going to boost Mina's standing, anyway?"

"It wouldn't be typical to grant an Imperial noble a boost," explained Tania. "Her position in the Imperial caste was already secured. With Oliver's status being higher than hers, the Honeybur Nation's future was bright."

Her *"was"* comment made me frown. *It's not his fault he was poisoned. At least he wasn't critically injured.*

Tania spotted my frown and quickly curtsied deeply in apology. "I'm sorry if I've misspoken somehow."

"Tania," Sarah smiled, "Something you'll learn about Lady Anessa is that she is not the type to chastise or punish us for speaking our mind. As unusual as that is."

Fluttering in my stomach made me swallow my nerves. Patting my garment again I asked, "This is such a big fuss, why do I have to go through this again?"

"If I recall, you extended the engagement offer to him," Sarah teased. "Something about it being easier to protect him if he were closer?"

Remembering the purple mosaic pattern beneath the sheet when Gideon was attacked by the Blackwood brothers years prior, I clenched my fist. *The thought of losing him makes my heart ache.* With my breath bottoming out, to avoid ripping my kirtle, the weight of the hoop skirt and the several layers of adornments, I thought of his smile and relaxed. *He's worth the trouble. Even if I have to rule in the future.*

"Still," Sarah said, "Her Imperial High Grace, Lily, approved your request for equality." Her eyebrows arched. "Also most unusual."

I said, "Y-yeah. Unusual."

"The Varn family must've had something valuable to trade," Sarah said with a crooked smile.

Knowing she meant well and was just curious, I wanted to let it slide, but I had to say sternly, "Sarah."

My tone got her attention and her smile faded.

"I promise you that I won't say this often, but…" I sighed. "Do not pry into that topic any further. Okay?"

She pursed her lips and nodded as her face blanched.

Sorry Sarah. Even Mom was afraid of that site. The very reason my child pact was formed in the first place was some archaeological site connected to an even greater paragon, Undine, who long predated my brother. The site was significant enough that Mom wondered if even the empire itself could safeguard it. Mom hasn't even said a word about it.

Thinking to myself, *Oh well, my focus on Gideon has moved far past that stupid pile of dirt.*

A knock at the door brought Gideon's voice. "Can I talk to Anessa?"

Sarah walked around me twice, giving my outfit a final once-over, before nodding and replying, "You may enter, my lord."

"My lord?" I thought, *That will take some getting used to.*

As he rounded the corner of the privacy screen, our eyes met. A vexatious fluttering hit my stomach and forced me to look away. *He's as tall as Dad, and almost as broad.*

In his hands was my named sword, Rufus. It has a name because it's sentient.

Seeing it brought a deeper smile to my face. When my hand touched the scabbard, a faint voice entered my mind. *"Hello Anessa."*

"Hello Rufus, feeling better?" The thought of a sword feeling sick made me chuckle to myself. Rufus was hurt, however, and it was partly my fault.

"Yes! They patched my hilt up quite nicely. I'm still surprised you took a bite out of it though, such a strange thing to do. You should watch what you eat."

His words made me sigh. *"Rufus, I didn't take a 'bite' out of you. It was an accident anyway."* A week ago, I'd been training with Rufus and it suggested that I use it to channel some of my essence. Somehow I'd managed to damage the hilt when I did so, making it cry out in "pain." They'd sent him to a master sword smith named Harold for repairs.

"Should I come back later?" Gideon said while grinning.

"Oh, sorry," I said meekly. "Rufus was just telling me they did a good job fixing its hilt."

Tania took Rufus and sat its baldric on my shoulder, making sure to cinch it so the hoop was unbothered by Rufus's presence.

Holding my left hand at my side, I heard it say, *"I haven't been worn like this for a while. A few masters at least."*

Gideon patted my head, which I leaned into and closed my eyes.

At least, until Tania spoke up. "My lord, I apologize, but I was informed by Her Imperial High Grace, Lily Carlyle, that such informality shan't be permitted any longer." She dipped her head to the floor. "At least not so long as you two remain unwed."

He withdrew his hand and took a step back.

Looking down at Tania who had taken to her knees to fix how Rufus sat on my hip, I asked, "Why the change, if I may ask?"

"Her Imperial Grace said it was due to the formality of your engagement. Close friends, and even those with a formal acp hoth are held to gentler standards."

Her words made me slouch. *I have to wait seven years for head pats?* I thought, then blushed deeply at how silly that was.

"So, I've been wondering," Rufus said into my mind. *"I've heard this word engagement several times. What is it, and is it an opponent we can beat together?"*

His comment made me snicker, drawing a few raised eyebrows.

Gideon gave me a deep bow and said, "Apologies my lady, I must excuse myself. There are some final preparations I need to make before I join you."

After his departure, Sarah and Tania were in a tizzy around me making sure nothing was out of place.

Guess it's time to go face the music, my shallow breaths from the restrictive kirtle, and nervous sweaty palms in thinking of the future made me add to my thought, *and get this over with.*

I had a flashback to a similar situation in my previous life. Walking onto the dance floor during prom was difficult for me on Earth. My Earthen body, unlike my current one, was tall and toned, instead of a petite bruiser. I'd been tall all my life, but as a junior I was gangly. The fact that I was four inches taller than my date made me stick out like a sore thumb. It might have been that moment which made him stand me up the year after.

Entering the room where I was effectively the de facto prom queen, all eyes turned to me at once, as silence settled over the room. Four trumpets, two on either side of the entrance, began to blare.

As they stopped, the herald said, "Presenting Her Imperial High Grace, Anessa Jean Carlyle, Imperial Princess of the Q'Tar dynasty!"

They'd even rolled out the gilded carpet, something I had only seen them do once before, at Oliver's similar engagement announcement to Mina Aramon.

Taking my first step made me reflect on the absurdity of it all. Controlled breaths, the weighty sway of my hoop skirt, and the drag of the cloth train behind me. *It's like I'm some prize pig in a parade before auction.*

A familiar face in the crowd, Yukirei Truval, made me smile. She's a girl who also fancied Gideon. In a polyamorous world, I'd come to find such a notion normal.

Arriving at my spot beside Yukirei I turned. Sarah and Tania busied themselves by positioning the cloth behind me, then retreated to a place along the wall. What looked like an entire orchestra began to play soft music as the dozens of people went back to talking amongst themselves.

My nerves made it difficult at the time to focus on who was around me, as I walked down the aisle that they'd made for me. However, once I'd taken my place, I recognized some familiar faces. There were at least five kings or queens from our nearest neighbors. In all there were no fewer than forty adults in attendance. *Twenty kingdoms, two representatives each?* I didn't see any markings from the northern territories of Westwood, though.

"Nervous?" Yukirei asked quietly.

A light laugh escaped and I said, "What do you think?"

"You'll be fine," she said and smiled. Her eyes darted to the side before she asked, "Have you given any thought to my request?"

"Not now," I chided. "We discussed this." I sighed. "Look, I'll agree to an Accord, but I can't promise more than that right now." An Accord was an informal "date." It meant I had to enter a brief acp hoth to permit the action, but it was far easier to break than an engagement.

I assumed she would be my future metamour, or another of Gideon's spouses, but her and I would just be friends. Like a sister wife, but not quite. She seemed happy with my comment and smiled with a nod.

If we go on a single date, perhaps she'll see that we don't mesh beyond friends. I hope I can let her down easy.

A few minutes passed, and the "band," if you could call a full orchestra that, died down.

Then things took a turn for the awkward. I'd been talking to Yukirei when the herald said, "Presenting Gideon Varn, of the Varn Baronetcy, Imperial Low Presumptive Duke Consort of the Carlyle Dukedom."

Everything I was thinking fled my mind as I turned to him. It wasn't his brilliant green irises, firm jawline, broad shoulders, or towering stature that caught my attention. Instead, I locked onto the vibrant red, upturned and tasseled codpiece that he was wearing. That shook and shimmered with every.

Single.

Step.

You'd be hard-pressed to tell which was redder: the garment or my face.

Yukirei laughed brilliantly and she began to fan herself. "That certainly sends a message," she whispered in amusement. "Anessa?"

"Hm," I said absently and turned to her. "What?"

She grinned and offered up her fan. "Need this?"

I swiped it in a flash. "Thank you." Covering the offending item from my view, I sent up a prayer to bless Yukirei's generosity. It was only then that I noticed the fashion choice was not his alone, though his *was* the only one that was so prominent.

Before I knew it, Gideon was almost standing right next to me.

Yukirei's fan was a welcome treasure that blotted the blight out.

Then my parents were announced, first Mom, then Dad. Based on my father's equally peacock-esque attire in that regard, I concluded that he was most likely to blame for Gideon's development.

Gods Dad, what were you thinking!

Mom took to the crowd and mingled like the professional high-born noble she was.

Whereas Dad approached us, with a solemn, measured pace, and held up a hand to silence the hall once he was within spitting distance. "It is with great pleasure that I announce today, by proxy of Imperial edict, that Marion Gideon of the Varn Baronetcy is hereby conferred an honorary title of Imperial Marquess."

He gestured forward in front of himself. Gideon stood in front of Dad, then formally dropped to a knee.

Dad said, "Marion Gideon, do you hereby swear an Oath to His Imperial Majesty, Jorin Q'Tar, and to the Westwood Empire, that you will henceforth protect our lands," Dad looked to me for a fleeting moment. "And uphold our laws so long as you shall live?"

Mom at some point had woven her way to the front and was standing nearby.

Gideon placed his hand in front of his chest. "I so swear, and I shall."

"Heard," Dad intoned.

Mom chimed in clearly, "Witnessed."

He took a sword from his storage ring and tapped Gideon on each shoulder, then on his head.

"Then by His Imperial Majesty's decree, you are no longer Marion Gideon Varn, but His Most Honorable, Marion Gideon Ignotus, in care of the Carlyle family. May Westwood prosper."

Everyone in the room, including myself, repeated, "May Westwood prosper."

Dad grabbed Gideon's hand and helped him to his feet. "I present to you His Most Honorable, Marion Gideon Ignotus!"

The room erupted into a brief cheer.

Despite my embarrassment I found myself smiling at the newly appointed young Imperial noble. Until he turned toward me and his choice of attire became impossible to ignore.

Now comes the fun *part.*

"Now then," Dad said and the room once again grew quiet. "This young man," he patted Gideon on his shoulder, "has been hosted by our Imperial Carlyle Duchy for seven years."

Dad then hemmed and hawed ad nauseam about my soon-to-be betrothed. However, halfway through his speech the doors to the great grand room opened unexpectedly. A soldier made a beeline for Dad, marching precisely but quickly. He bowed deeply before him and held a small scroll up toward him.

I barely caught Dad whisper angrily, "This better be important."

He unrolled the top portion of the scroll but stopped when a single gigantic letter was uncovered. It was either a "W" or a "V." Hastily re-rolling the scroll, he abruptly left the room with the soldier.

What is that about?

"That was father's handwriting," Yukirei said by way of explanation.

I blinked. Her father, Eugene Truval, was the Grand Master–General of the Empire, so it seemed the interruption *was* important.

Murmurs in the crowd were focused on the interruption.

This had better not disrupt the announcement, glancing over the top of my borrowed fan, toward the unsightly beast, I continued my thought, *I'd really hate to have to do this all over again!*

As the chatter escalated Mom chimed in. "Now, everyone. I think it would be a good time for us to change gears. Perhaps a dance or two would be in order?"

At her words, everyone in attendance parted and gathered around the edges of the room. Gideon held out his hand and said, "Shall we?"

Looking straight up at his face I said, "Sure, but keep your eyes on me, so I can do the same."

He raised an eyebrow but said nothing as we drew to the center of the room. Gideon towered over me. We must've looked like a child dancing with her father, because many of the comments filtering in to my ears were about how cute I was.

Great, not exactly the message I wanted to send, but… I'll take it.

"Are you okay?" he asked softly.

With a nod I said, "Yes, it's just a little awkward."

"What is?" He genuinely seemed puzzled.

I huffed. "We'll talk about it later."

Whenever the dance should have drawn me closer, I resisted getting within striking range of that jiggling crimson monstrosity. He ended up having to bend forward a little to compensate.

"You're mad about something, aren't you?"

"No." I said flatly, "I'm fine." Thinking to myself, *He should really learn to read the room,* I shook my head. *Except he'd think I meant that literally.*

After the second "dance," Yukirei approached and said, "May I?"

Gideon turned to her and offered his hands.

She took mine and said with a smile, "Sorry, I think you misunderstood."

Does she want to talk about Gideon?

He laughed and turned to Mom, "May I have this dance?" as I spun away with my new dance partner.

Yukirei asked quietly, "Is this better?"

It echoed a memory from my past life. Trish had done the same thing on my junior year. My boyfriend at the time was being a jackass, and had obnoxiously decried every mistake I made on the dance floor. Taking pity on me, my friend cut in and asked me to dance, with the very same lines Yukirei had used.

"Yeah, it is," I said as my eyes found hers. It was the first time I'd given them a good look. They were an olive color. For a moment, I got lost in the sparkling swirl of gold, green and brown. When I realized I was staring, I turned away and blushed.

"I noticed you were doing everything in your power to avoid looking below Gideon's neckline." She laughed. "Not that I blame you."

"It's a bit much, isn't it?"

"Mhmm," she dropped to a whisper, "It reminds me of an animal's nature."

Her words were lost on me, until it hit me. *Gods she is describing what amounts to "red rocket."*

The blazing fire of blood rushing to my ears and cheeks made me gently bump my forehead against her collar bone. "That was too on point."

She whispered, "I suppose an accord isn't too bad an idea, after all, huh?"

"Quiet, you," I said, my tone a mix of equal parts playful and cross.

For a second time the doors opened and Dad marched back in. His face was expressionless. He approached me and dipped in to tell me quietly, "Please follow me, Anessa." He then offered his arm for me to take. This left Yukirei in the middle of the floor alone. As my father led me away I noticed Gideon approached Yukirei, but she promptly walked off without him.

I must've made her mad. Sorry Yukirei. Though at the same time, I was thankful for the interruption.

CHAPTER TWO

DECLARATION

AS THE DOORS closed behind us, I asked, "So, Daddy, what was so important it required us leaving the room early?"

Dad's eyes stayed forward. He didn't say a word. While he had always been a man of few words, he didn't usually ignore others.

"Daddy?"

He glanced at me and shook his head before we continued. Our main estate was gigantic, and wherever we were going it was taking a while. After five minutes my mind was abuzz with several very scary things that might be wrong, though I didn't have a lot to go on.

Did someone die, or was there a riot of some form close by?

We finally entered the same room I'd first met our late butler in, Mr. Morris. That vile man had rubbed me the wrong way from the moment I met him, and it seemed there was a reason for that. He physically attacked me when I thwarted his treasonous efforts. Yukirei put him down and saved me.

Deep brown hardwoods lined the walls and in the center of the table was a large red cube. It was an S-ROB, or short-range obscuring barrier. The biggest I'd ever seen.

Dad closed the door behind us and a dim red flash flickered from the cube.

Was that flash indicative of higher security? Something's definitely going on.

That's new. Up until this point I'd never seen any visual effects from these "barriers."

"What's this about?" I asked.

Dad sat at the table and gestured for me to join him on the opposite side. "I almost forgot to invite you. A missive came through from His Imperial Majesty, Jorin Q'Tar and the Grand Master–General, Eugene Truval. You're my successor, so it seemed appropriate for you to join in."

Looking around the room I arched a brow. "Join in for what?"

As if on cue, the wall on my left at the end of the table chirped, and then blinked a few times. That most certainly got my attention.

Dad pressed a button on top of the cube, that I hadn't even noticed, which transformed the wall into a video conference screen.

Seriously? This medieval standard of living is nonsense. We're using horses and carriages, but have a television!?

Then the heavily blurred image resolved and I tensed. A very bored man on a throne came into view. With sun-kissed skin and eyes that looked to have seen it all and was done with all of it, the emperor of our empire, my uncle, was sitting cross-legged with his hand on his cheek.

Great, so my first experience with Anfang-Zoom is with the bloody emperor! Giving Dad a glare I thought, *At least warn a girl first!* Taking stock of my situation, I hastily adjusted the lopsided garment beneath me and gave uncle Jorin my best smile, though I'm sure I looked like a frazzled fool.

"Thank you all for joining me," he intoned. There wasn't an ounce of joy in his delivery.

I guess there's more than just us on this call? Glancing at the screen I noticed there was a seventy-nine in the bottom-left. *Exactly the number of imperial nobility in the empire, plus one, Jorin. He's talking to everyone of importance.* Remembering there were five monarchs in the hall we'd come from, I realized some of them must've been representatives.

"As of twelve hours ago," Jorin said, "we are officially at war."

Dad and I looked at one another, but didn't say a word.

We were the exceptions, however. Though we couldn't see or directly hear any of the other listeners, it seemed the clamor they raised was enough to cause feedback. The only thing that was clear was they were surprised. Often commenting about the Tanis Region.

My uncle's face remained unchanged. It seemed he was nonplussed at their reaction. Jorin took the scepter at his side and slammed it down on the tile beside him.

The chatter silenced.

"The aggressor is the Redwater Empire."

Instead of an uproar, there was silence. It was no wonder. This was like Canada attacking the USA. Redwater has always been touted as the sister Empire to Westwood, since both ruling dynasties are the Q'Tar family.

What the hell?

Jorin pulled out a metal tube with a scroll in it. From my not-sister Veronica's dealings with the emperor years ago, I recalled the insignia on it as belonging to Evan Q'Tar.

Great, that's the scary idiot that executes any wife of his that doesn't bear him a son.

My uncle continued, "We are certain the message declaring war is genuine. We took the time to confirm it, twice, before calling this audience." Returning the scroll to the tube, he used it to pat his hand. "The specifics of this declaration will remain sealed for now as there are details we still need to confirm." His tone hardened, "Effective immediately, Westwood Empire will shift into a war state. All industries will focus on supporting the war effort. As you all know, Redwater is in many ways our equal, and that includes their conviction once hostilities begin. This will be a long one."

Chatter once again flooded back onto our side, even louder than before.

He once again struck the ground and straightened in the chair. "Imperial lords and ladies. Calls like these are expensive. This isn't the time for questions. Field them with your superiors, unless that's me. There will be a messenger that will deliver information to you all later." Nodding to someone, I'd assumed was outside our view, the call ended.

"This is kind of scary, Daddy," I said in a shaky voice.

"I know, don't worry," he said.

Dad's the main striker for Westwood. He'll surely be on the front lines. I looked back at him.

He gave me a reflexive, fake smile, although after a moment the smile finally reached his eyes. "I'll do everything in my power to make sure you're safe." I caught his whisper to himself, "That everyone's safe."

Wait a minute… I'm the heir apparent, could I be called on, too?

Dad paced around the room before returning to his chair in a huff.

"What's this mean for school?" I stood with my hands on the table. "I'm expected to return in–"

Before I could say more, the wall once again flashed.

Dad gestured for me to sit and motioned with his finger to be quiet.

I sat.

He pressed the same button again, and my uncle reappeared.

His demeanor this time was much more relaxed compared to before. While there was still a touch of boredom in his face, it was livelier.

Dad said, "How may I be of service to you, Your Imperial Majesty?"

Jorin stepped right over Dad's question and said, "It is nice to see you niece. Well met."

Nodding to him I said, "W-well met." Hoping he wouldn't focus on my fumbled words, I smiled.

His reaction was to grin. "I won't hurt you, little sprout."

All I could do in response was tilt my head in confusion. *Sprout?*

"You really do wear your emotions on your face. When your mother Lily was a child, I used to call her flower." He chuckled. "She hated it."

Ah, flower because her name's Lily, and sprout because I'm her daughter, I guess?

He dropped his smile. "Now then. Anessa, when you return to school, you will be enrolled in their Martial Core program. Your work over the last few years shows," he tapped his temple, "you have the smarts for Civilian Studies, but right now we need you to reinforce your cultivation fundamentals."

I knew this day would come, I just hoped I could round-out my studies on history before it did. It wasn't so much the war that I knew I'd be forced to shift gears, I'd only just found out. It was becoming the heir apparent. My decision to stay out of martial studies was also tied to my penchant for aggression when I got worked up. Though some of my frustration might have been directed at the ruling class. Most of them, in fact, were assholes.

Jorin continued, "As a cultivator, failing to sharpen your martial skills is a disservice to the empire at this point."

"Yes sir," I said and focused my eyes to the floor.

"Don't feel bad," he said, "even the civilian studies are retooling for war efforts. I'm sure you're not terribly interested in agriculture, supply chains, communication and logistics."

Returning my eyes to him he added, "Don't get me wrong, you'll still receive a basic education there, but your main focus should be on getting stronger."

I turned my thoughts inward and disconnected from their conversation. *Get stronger, so I can protect myself. Probably on the front lines.*

My attention flickered back to uncle Jorin when his tone dropped. "Roland, you already received a message from Eugene on this, but I'll say it again. When you arrive in Lormaw, set an example." The call ended there.

Dad asked with a sigh, "Anessa, please leave the room."

That room had a full map of the Westwood Empire. Along the top was the border between us and the Redwater Empire. In the northeast, southeast for Redwater, was the city of Lormaw.

"That place is kind of large, isn't it?" I said, hoping Dad would say something before he shooed me out of the room.

"A hundred square miles," he said.

Turning to him I asked, "What is it you're supposed to do?"

He looked away. "You don't want to know."

"Like sneak in and capture someone, or take out their defenses?"

Dad pursed his lips but didn't say anything.

I prodded, "Lay siege?"

He breathed through his nose and closed his eyes.

It was my cue to leave. As I neared the door, Dad said, "I'm to go alone tonight." He paused and I'd nearly given up on him continuing, "And destroy the town."

CHAPTER THREE
CAUSE / CHOICES

DAD'S WORDS LEFT me a bit numb.

Destroy the town? How is he going to do that alone?

As I was closing the door to the room, I caught the faint noise of yet *another* call coming in. Curiosity getting the better of me, I all but closed the door, and listened in.

This is stupid. It reminded me of when I overheard my stepmothers arguing about Oliver and me. Eavesdropping was almost certainly a violation of some protocol or other. *But I'm tired of being in the dark on everything.*

It seemed Uncle Jorin still had unfinished business. "Do you understand the goal of your mission tonight?"

Dad's voice shook, "I do, Sir."

"Are you certain it's something you *can* do?"

"I've lost too much in the past to indecision. If that's what our tacticians decided is the best opening mo—"

"That wasn't what I was asking, though I'm glad you've found your resolve. My question is strictly about capability. It's not an easy task. None of the plans are. Are your reserves up to it?"

What are they asking Dad to do? How does one person destroy such a large town?

"Yes, sir. I've decided to go with the flip option, it's a little more demanding, but…" He hesitated. "I agree that its impact on Redwater's morale would be more significant. I might be a bit winded afterwards."

Uncle Jorin said, "Then drop by Aspwood and pick up a Greater Earth essence stone. Use it to power your efforts. Do not put yourself at risk. We need you for what lies ahead."

"Yes sir," Dad said. There was an awkward pause. "Do we know what caused this?"

"It's funny you asked that. That is my next order of business with you."

"Oh?"

Jorin's next words made my breath hitch. "The declaration we received mentioned your daughter, Anessa, by name. Apparently you rejected his marriage proposal, several times. I'd like to hear why my sister's daughter is worth what we're about to be dragged through."

Holy shit. What?! My mind reeled at this news. It didn't make sense. *Why would rejecting a proposal lead to war? More importantly, why wasn't I told they'd rejected him,* multiple *times?* It wasn't that I was complaining, by all accounts, the man seemed loathsome.

I'd often wondered about the Emperor of Redwater. When I was three years old, I'd heard he wanted to take my not-sister Veronica as a wife, if she didn't awaken as a cultivator, and I'd be joining them. Though I'd never heard anything about it since. As though it were forgotten.

I closed my eyes to control myself. Part of me wanted to object loudly to being left out of the loop. But they would both be livid with me if I burst in there and started yelling at Dad for not involving me in something so important.

"About that," Dad said. "There is a very good reason."

Jorin said, "Do tell."

"Anessa is Her Goddess Eloria's champion."

My uncle's voice turned cross. "I know about that already." A loud thunk sounded out. Jorin had slammed the staff at his side into the ground, I guessed. "That's simply not a good enough reason!"

Dad's voice grew meek. "Your Imperial Majesty. I'm sorry to have kept this from you, but Anessa is Her Goddess Eloria's True Champion."

"Meaning?" Jorin said, his tone made it clear his patience was wearing thin.

"She's not just her True Champion of Craft. She's also her True Champion of Death."

There was a brief pause, during which I could only imagine that Uncle Jorin was wasting some of the expensive call gathering his thoughts. "That's not something you keep from the Your Imperial Majesty, Roland. You'd better follow up with a very good reason."

"I'm sorry Your Imperial Majesty, it wasn't for the purpose of deceit, but for fear that it could be overheard."

Jorin breathed through his nose. "Okay. I get it. Any other secrets about her you've been hiding?"

Dad was silent.

"Roland?"

"She has access to all elements."

"Are you kidding me?" Jorin asked in disbelief.

"No sir," Dad replied, "Her Earth resonance alone is on par or greater than my own."

"Then when you asked me to ignore that, what was his name," Jorin said, and snapped his fingers a few times. "Renault the Sensor those years ago, he was telling the truth?"

"Yes, sir."

Oh, I barely remember that man. He was a jerk. Then the person Dad mentioned sending a letter to, all those years ago, was Uncle Jorin?

Uncle Jorin chuckled, "Next you'll tell me she has seven dantians."

Once again there was silence.

Are seven dantians really that unbelievable?

"Roland, if you're joking about any of this, now is the time to tell me. This isn't the time for tomfoolery."

"Everything I said is true. Part of the reason we didn't say anything is up until she awoke, she's been very weak. Even now, she's far below where Oliver was at the age of two."

"Her being a messiah," Jorin laughed bitterly, "is a longer discussion we *will* pursue later."

I didn't put much thought into being called a messiah, since he laughed about it. But I made a mental note to look into it myself, later.

"Your decision to reject His Imperial Majesty, Evan Q'Tar's proposal was correct," Jorin admitted. "That bastard executes any wife that doesn't bear him a son. If he were to execute a True Champion of both of Her Goddess Eloria's monikers… My gods. Remember her warning that she would burn the planet to the ground if they didn't purge the ethereal beasts and monsters?"

Dad said in a frightened voice, "The Purge of Evil might start again."

There was another pause.

"How much of this should we tell Anessa?" Dad asked.

"I think she already knows," Jorin said, then my skin prickled when he added, "Don't you?"

Crap!

Seeing as the jig was up, I opened the door slowly. Then I promptly bowed deeply toward where I knew Jorin's image would be. "I'm really sorry, Your Imperial Highness."

"It's fine," Jorin said. "Enter the room and shut the door."

As I complied, he added, "Don't make a habit of listening in though. I'm letting your transgression go because this matter directly concerns you."

I looked up at him in time for him to narrow his eyes.

"If it did not concern you? I would be *very* cross." The emphasis he put on very was not lost on me.

Bowing a second time I said, "Thank you for your understanding and generosity."

"Don't repeat the details of what we've discussed," Dad warned me. "Not even to Lily."

"Okay." I said as I moved to retake my seat across from Dad.

He held up his hand.

Got it. I should probably leave.

Moving to a curtsy to them both, I made my way back to the "party," though I was not really in a party mood any longer.

A war started in my name. I laughed at myself. *Most girls would find it flattering. It's terrifying, how many people will die?* Shaking my head I cleared those dark thoughts and a smile crossed my face. *Even if it was out of their own fear. I'm happy my family stood up for me.*

On Earth, my family had been very wealthy. After my mother of the time, Naia Rovenal, died, I was assigned a minder named Julie. She managed my mother's, estate. I'd never gotten the feeling that Julie cared one bit for me, other than the very handsome check that the estate paid her quarterly. Her mood would wax and wane, waxing each time when the check cleared.

Come to think of it, I'd asked for a car around when the serial killer, the Richmond Ripper, was active. She declined my request, explaining that it would affect her performance review if she approved it. Is that why I died, because I was stuck walking to my dormitory apartment?

Back in the great grand room, the mood of the party had changed. There was a cloud of unease over the gathering. People were whispering to one another more than talking jovially. Eyes darted in my direction but quickly darted away again.

"Everything okay?" Gideon asked as he approached.

I said, "Not really, but the news will likely be announced to everyone later." Waving my hand I continued, "Daddy didn't say if I can talk about it. So I'd better not."

"It's war, isn't it?" Yukirei said in a whisper.

"How…?" I said slack-jawed.

She tittered, "Consider who's in attendance. Everyone received a call almost at the same time and then the room got all serious."

Right. Almost everyone here is a representative of a nation. Eying the actual monarchs I amended the thought, *And others are the real deal.*

She said, "Her Imperial High Grace, Lily stepped out a few minutes before you arrived. I take it she isn't entirely in the dark."

"I'm surprised none of our guests have left," I said.

Gideon shook his head. "That would be bad for appearances. Although everyone's in the know, how people act after news can say as much as the news itself."

Oh… wow, what was that called? Op-sec? Operational security, I think it was. It was something I hadn't ever really thought of seriously. *What was it, where even the pizza guy gleans that there's a war coming because the Pentagon orders a hundred pizzas right before a military operation?*

His comment made me smile at him and I took his hand in hopes that we could have another dance. *I'm glad I'm marrying such a bright man.* Looking into his eyes put me at ease. *That he is nice to look at helps.* A bright red annoyance made me correct myself. *Attire aside.*

Before we could get too far, Dad reentered.

"Imperial Lords and Ladies, I thank you all for attending tonight. We have rooms prepared for each of you, and we would welcome your return home tomorrow." With his hand on his chest he said, "I will even personally help expedite your return home if you so wish." Clapping his hands a few servants entered carrying a few barrels. "Please enjoy the food and drink for this evening. This here," he patted one of the barrels, "is one-hundred-year aged wine."

Our Imperial guests cheered and promptly made a beeline for the booze.

Their genuine appreciation for alcohol over the intent of the evening, my engagement and Gideon's promotion, made me frown. *I suppose a young noble girl's announcement is only so interesting to them.*

"Strange," Yukirei said.

"What?"

She whispered to me, "Wasn't His Imperial Grace supposed to announce your betrothal?"

Gideon handed me what seemed like alcohol, and I downed it in one gulp. To my dismay, it was only grape juice.

▼ ▼ ▼

A marvelous headache was my reward the next morning. Midway through the adults' alcoholic delight they offered me a single glass, and suggested that I nurse it slowly. Now I knew why. They didn't fool around with their adult beverages, and it knocked me flat.

Rubbing my temples I thought, *I wish I were still a hundred and ninety pounds and six feet tall.* The toned figure I had before made such lightweight drinking easy. On Anfang I was a sixty-five-pound featherweight. *I suppose I'm only eleven. That they gave me any at all is surprising.*

Rays of light filtered in from outside hitting me in the eye, making me wince. *On Earth I could drink four beers before getting even a buzz! This sucks.*

Sarah came forward and offered me a cup of tea, though just a whiff of it made me wrinkle my nose. She whispered, "It should help. Despite the taste." Raising a finger she continued, "Take this one as fast as you can, it'll go down easier that way."

Plugging my nose, I picked up the offending item, closed my eyes, and gulped it in one go. Imagine socks soaked in kerosene, menthol and spoiled eggs wrapped into one. Then double it. That was how wretched her offering was. Choking back the urge to expel it at once, I was astonished to find that the pain was gone. Despite the magic in her concoction, it earned her a glare.

She smiled and winked. "Now then, let's get you dressed. You have a meeting in the solar with Their Imperial Graces, your parents, and our lord His Imperial Most Honorable, Gideon Ignotus."

"Solar?" I asked, as Tania entered.

Eying my younger Lady's maid I sighed.

She curtsied and moved to putting a few layers on me so they could "safely" change my shift.

This level of modesty is so stupid.

"The Solar is where meetings of high import take place." Sarah held up her hands in a rectangle focusing on me through it. "I think there's a remote viewing box that can be used in emergencies."

"Oh, I know where you mean now."

Both Sarah and Tania looked at me in disbelief.

Their gazes made me uncomfortable and I huffed. Crossing my arms I said, "I mean, I'll still need help getting there, but I know what room you mean."

They both smiled.

Yeah, yeah. I get lost easily.

"You two caught what was going on last night at the party, right?"

Tania pursed her lips and looked down, busying herself with her task.

Sarah nodded but didn't say anything.

"Are you not allowed to talk about it?"

"We can," she said cautiously and paused. "But it wouldn't be a good idea. If we heard something you didn't know, and were responsible for telling you, punishment would be likely."

"Oh," I said, and realized I hadn't thought of it that way. *Gossip among staff is a big no-no. I suppose if I tell them the obvious, they'll be able to talk about at least that.*

"We might hurry, Lady Anessa," Tania said. "His Imperial Grace, Roland Carlyle, said this discussion is of grave importance."

Her admission earned her a "spill it" glare.

She dashed my hopes of learning more by adding, "I don't know any more than that, I'm afraid."

▼ ▼ ▼

As the door clicked behind me, I found everyone else had already arrived.

Gideon's fidgeting with his hands told me all I needed to know about how he was feeling.

I'm right with you!

Mom gave me a melancholic smile and she nodded towards my seat.

Gideon apparently felt the need to rush up and pull out the chair, almost bowling his own over in the process.

Dad smiled at his clumsy eagerness. "Now then," he started. "The war changes things."

What things does it change? I wanted to say aloud, but Dad's tone didn't leave much room for discussion.

He pursed his lips and considered his words. "If you hadn't decided to announce your engagement, this discussion wouldn't be necessary."

"What discussion?" I said flatly.

Mom stifled a smile.

This isn't funny! I thought and gave her a glare. Her reaction was to narrow her eyes at me, and I backed down quickly. Turning my attention back to Dad, I thought, *I'm not prepared to take her on just yet.*

"A discussion about your future," Dad said and motioned between Gideon and me. He placed his left hand on his chest. "I'm sorry to ask this of you, but you have two options." Motioning with his hand he said, "Marry Gideon as soon as possible, or wait until after the war."

Dad held up his hand to stop me from talking, and he said, "Now, you might think waiting is the obvious choice, but…" He stood from his seat. "The Redwater Empire is strong. As strong as Westwood." Shaking his head he added, "If we let the war take its natural course, it would take years, and we may well lose."

A chill ran down my arms. *If we lose, the previous ruling families tend to not fare well. Especially at our level.*

"Anessa already knows about this, but let me be clear: this doesn't leave the room. Last night my task was to travel to Lormaw at the border to the Redwater Empire." He held out his palm and made a fist. "And destroy it."

For a brief moment Mom gave Dad a look of disbelief, but she smoothed it out almost as quickly.

Dad shook his head. "While there was no real resistance for me, there was plenty of opposition."

Mom pursed her lips, but said nothing. Her closed off body language told me they'd be discussing this later.

I do not want to be around for that.

His tone firmed. "The goal was to send a message. That if they continued with the war, it would be hard fought." Shaking his head he added, "Instead, the attack had the opposite effect. It rallied the Redwater Empire."

Looking down at the table he said, "Early this morning we received word that the Queen's estate in Rhinebur was destroyed. We've also confirmed that the capital city of Rhinebur has burned."

Mom gasped. "And Lady Fleure?"

Dad put his hand over Mom's and shook his head.

She grew quiet and looked away.

I can't believe queen Fleure is gone. It hit me in the chest. *War's a lot scarier when you're not reading about it on the couch.*

Gideon asked quietly, "And my mother?"

Dad raised an eyebrow. "Your family's lands are a hundred miles out. Redwater's goal seemed to be reprisal, nothing else."

An awkward silence fell over the four of us.

Mom shuffled uncomfortably and leaned away from Dad, who was clenching his fist while closing his eyes.

Seeing her discomfort I reached across to take her hand, and I immediately felt uneasy as the hairs on my arm stood up.

"Daddy," I said crossly.

"Yes?"

"I know you're mad, but please calm down. You're making Mommy uncomfortable."

He looked over at her and his eyes widened. Closing his eyes and relaxing his fist, he breathed for a solid minute, during which, nobody said a word. Then he whispered to Mom, "Sorry, I let it get away from me."

She shrugged away from him. "It's fine, but please give me some space." Her hand went to her stomach. "That immediately made me nauseous."

Mom isn't pregnant, is she? Shaking my head I thought, *Can't be. The energy released by cultivators can make mortals uncomfortable or even ill. That's all it is.*

Nodding he stood up and backed away from the table. Turning his attention to me, he said, "Thank you Anessa."

"What does the war, Lormaw and all of this have to do with me marrying Gideon?" I asked and motioned toward my not-quite fiancé.

Dad said, "This is the early days of the war. We're High Peers." He nodded to Gideon, "As is he, now. Any and all marriages at our level require His Imperial Majesty's direct approval." He walked over and put his hand on my shoulder, he continued in a whisper, "In your case you also require ecclesiastical blessing. It's a little more involved since His Imperial Majesty, Jorin needs to petition Her Goddess Eloria."

Oh. Crap. It hadn't even occurred to me that Eloria would have a say here.

Pursing my lips I said, "That still doesn't answer the timing part of my question."

Dad sighed and stood and returned to his seat. His voice went back to a normal volume, "Once the war gets into full swing, His Imperial Majesty won't have the time to focus on dynastic marriages."

Narrowing my eyes at Dad, I said, "This feels like a false dichotomy. Meaning you're forcing me to choose here and now." Crossing my arms, I added, "Why can't he approve our marriage in advance, allowing us to wed when I turn eighteen?"

"The Redwater Empire is called our sister empire for two reasons," he held up a finger. "The dynasties that control them are related by blood," he held another up and continued, "And we are equal in might."

Standing away from the table I walked around to Dad. "This entire thing seems far-fetched."

His response was to stare at me for a few full minutes.

Needless to say it was uncomfortable, but I didn't back down and kept my arms crossed.

Mom's contribution here was to give a half grin, until she noticed my gaze, then her expression flattened out.

With a sigh he said, "I get it, but this will be a war of attrition. Again, we don't know how long this will take *or* if we'll win."

"How long do they estimate it will take, *if* we win?" I asked.

"At least a decade, probably longer."

My eyes widened and I took a step back. "That long?" It made me realize, *I'd be at least twenty-one or older.* Placing a hand on my stomach I amended my thought, *Cat-kin have shorter lives, as mortals. I don't know how being a cultivator affects fertility and whatnot. It's not really a question I want to have with my Dad of all people. Men generally don't have the same kind of fertility issues as they age as women do.*

Dad was a full-blooded cat-kin who nonetheless exhibited none of their feline traits, due to a unique genetic quirk of his own. He had full control over what parts of his cat-kin traits he expressed. It seemed I'd inherited the same ability, but none of the traits would show for me until I was with child in the future. At least several years, I'd hoped.

"Yes, based on how thorough they were in decimating Rhinebur," he made a fist. "His Imperial Majesty, Evan, is not a kind ruler. There are signs that several of his own men were... discarded when they implemented their plan."

What the f–

"It sets a grim tone for the war," Dad admitted. "Tyrants rarely give in for simple means, and even if you offer them what they want," his eyes lingered on me before saying, "they don't back down."

That makes it seem like they floated the idea of handing me *over to him, to end the war.* It made the light chill in the room a bit more evident, despite the formal wear I was in. *I'm very glad they didn't, or we wouldn't be having this discussion.*

Swallowing my nerves, I cut to the chase. "Hypothetically, if we decide to marry, will there be any pressure to ensure–" my next words caught in my throat, and my voice cracked, "–dynastic continuity in the near-term?" I pointed to him, and said sternly, "Again, hypothetically."

Dad laughed and his smile finally reached his eyes. "No," he placed his hand on my arm. "There is no such expectation for one so young." Removing his hand he shrugged. "If it were to happen, though? As a legally sanctioned couple, no harm nor disgrace would befall either of you or our families."

I gave a fake laugh. "Yeah you wouldn't have to worry about that," I said and waved my hand. "Too many risks at my age."

He shook his head. "There are no risks for you."

"Huh?"

"You're a cultivator. Not that I want you to go through the experience, but remember that you can lift several tons, and run faster than a thunder ox."

Shit.

He added to my discomfort by saying, "Your body's not as fragile as a mortal's. You could have triplets and there'd still be no risk." His smile said he was teasing me.

Mom's smile reinforced it.

Gideon was white as a sheet.

Yeah, I'm right with you bub!

Dad's tone shifted. "You have until the end of the day. I was serious about Jorin's availability. Without his approval," he pointed to Gideon and me. "You get married to no one."

CHAPTER FOUR

DECISION

HOLDING MY HAND to my face, my emotions roiled. Taking a breath I moved to Gideon and pulled on his hand.

"We have some things to discuss," I said, and we left the room.

We made our way to my bedroom, with Sarah as a chaperone, and I pulled my own S-ROB from my storage ring and sat it between us at my tea table.

"Why were you silent for all of that?" I asked.

His eyes went to the floor. "I'm sorry. His Imperial Grace, Roland, told me to not say anything unless spoken to."

What the hell?

"My noble situation is tenuous, at best. With them canceling the engagement announcement, it makes me wonder if they'll also rescind the Imperial Marquess title if we don't marry." His eyes found mine, but his voice was barely a whisper. "I'm a small fish in a big pond."

His admission that he had been silenced by my Dad made me want to find him and scream at him, but that would not go my way, especially today. *I'd be lucky if all I get were a spanking.*

I grabbed his hand which got little more than a raised eyebrow from Sarah. *He's never been the type to go against the grain, but that needs to change.* Giving his hand a slight squeeze I said, harshly, "Gideon, you're an Imperial Noble now."

He nodded.

"You need to learn to speak up for yourself. Especially if I'm not around. There are few who can tell you what to do now. Even those who can need to have a good reason to counter you."

REBORN IN THE PERFECT FANTASY WORLD

He knitted his brow.

"Do you understand what I'm saying?"

All he did was nod.

Releasing his hand I crossed my arms. "Do you understand what I'm saying?" I repeated.

"Yes ma'am, I think so."

His use of "ma'am" made me huff. "I don't think you do. For one, I'm not your ma'am. Two, you should use something more appropriate. In private you can say something a little less formal." I patted my chest. "Try saying what feels right, and we'll go from there."

His shoulders slumped as he relaxed. "Okay, my love."

My jaw fell open and I took a moment to compose myself. Coughing, I said, "B-better, but you should leave that one until we are wed, whenever that is." His choice of words made my ears burn, though I couldn't help but smile.

"My Imperial Grace?" he said expectantly with a small grin.

Nodding I held his emerald gaze for a second before breaking it. *Gods his verdant eyes draw me in. I could get lost in them, and hearing him call me his makes my stomach flutter.*

"What do you think we should do, though?" I asked. "If we wait, and the war drags out, would it bother you?" Knowing he was still not used to asserting himself I added, "I am asking you, Gideon–" I squeezed his hand, "–what do you *want* to do?"

"I'm really not sure." He shook his head. "My gut says to tell you to follow your gut, but that's not what you asked me."

"If we wait, it could be problematic," I admitted. "Do you want to wait ten or twenty years?"

"No." He covered my hand with his. "That would be too much to endure, if I'm being honest."

Using my free hand I pointed at him. "Now, to be clear, I would still be off-limits until I'm eighteen, okay?"

"Understood. That's when we would have officially married anyway." He pulled his hand away and scratched his cheek. "Though some things would change, of course."

I smirked. "Yeah, they'll let you call me kitten again."

"No, I mean our living arrangements," he said, and pointed at my chest. "You're also worried about your estrus." He held both of his hands up and away from me. "I won't cross any lines," he gestured towards my Lady's maids, "you've also got Sarah and Tania to look after you."

The reminder that I would lose myself three days of every ten made me groan. I'd only started to gain a semblance of awareness, and if I were honest, I wish I could forget entirely. As a cat-kin, the cycle I went through drastically affected my brain. When on my cycle, I was basically a bundle of hormones with the simple mind of a housecat.

Coughing into my hand I said, "Yes, let's set that aside entirely for a later discussion." A sharp breath out helped push the embarrassment down so it didn't go beyond my collar bone, or so I'd hoped. "Doesn't it feel like we're being coerced? They didn't even ask *you* for your input. That doesn't seem right. You don't hold a low station anymore. Once we marry, you'll have a rank equal to my own, which means they should respect you, even before you're an Imperial Duke in your own right."

Looking around himself, Gideon finally nodded. "It does seem that they are pushing us into marriage, doesn't it?"

"It does. I think we need to confront them about it, and find out their real motives. I don't know about you, but I'd much rather know the truth."

"I'm with you," he said and smiled.

"Okay, so here's what we'll do—"

Later that evening my parents approached us. We'd made up our minds hours earlier, but used the situation to our advantage, and hung out for a while. During classes, we didn't get many opportunities besides lunch to talk.

Back in the solar, Dad said, "Have you come to a decision?"

We nodded, and once we'd all taken our seats, I said bluntly, "Tell us the real reason."

"The real reason for what?"

"The reason that you're trying to manipulate us," Gideon intoned. "You avoided Anessa's question earlier on why the Emperor cannot just approve our marriage to take place in just under seven years. We'd like that answer now."

Dad looked at Gideon and while Dad was suppressing his smile, it was evident he was amused that Gideon was speaking up, despite his prior directive.

"I know you told me to stay silent earlier, Your Imperial Grace, but I do not think that was appropriate." He put his hand to his chest. "Our decision to wait, or marry in the near-term very much involves me."

"It's also wrong to try and manipulate our emotions," I added.

Mom snickered. She shook her head and looked at Dad. "I told you she'd see through it."

Dad sighed and gave Mom a look that just made her smile broaden.

"Anessa," he said. "Do you remember why your engagement was set, seven years ago?"

"Yes," I said and looked at Gideon. "Are we able to talk about it now? No one has so much as mentioned it in seven *long* years."

Gideon's lips thinned out and he said nothing, although he did lean onto the table. He came down with a convenient case of amnesia right after our acp hoth was formalized. The secret ruins, a site so wildly important that nobody was allowed to speak of its existence. It was the very place our engagement had been secured for the Imperial Carlyle Duchy.

"If we were to approve your marriage for seven years in the future, when you are eighteen, what would happen if the Redwater Empire secured *that* site before then?" Dad asked.

Pulling absently on my braid I said, "I don't know. Would that be bad?"

He nodded. "What would happen is your engagement would be annulled, and you two would *never* marry. Unless we were lucky enough to regain that site at some point."

Gideon raised his hand. It seemed he wasn't quite used to being confrontational. "What are you two talking about?"

"There's an archaeological site on your family's land, that–"

"Anessa," Mom interrupted, and shook her head. "No more than that."

I clamped my mouth shut. The glare I was getting from both of my parents said that topic was still forbidden.

"Okay," Gideon said, "I won't ask about whatever *that* is, but can you tell me why our marriage is so important here?"

"That I can do," Dad said and motioned to me. "With your hand in marriage, we're allowed to actually secure the site, instead of just… look at it."

Patting Gideon's hand I said, "Alright then. We've discussed it. If we're given the real reason that you're pressuring us, *and* a suitable apology, we'll marry as soon as possible."

Dad nodded and Mom smiled.

"However," I said crossly. "Do not try to coerce Gideon like that again."

Dad waved his hand dismissively and said, "Yeah, yeah."

"I mean it, Daddy. He looks up to you. If his first few interactions with you, as a near equal, do little more than tear him down, what will that do to him?"

Dad pursed his lips. "Okay, message received. I will take it under advisement. Though I expect you to refrain from correcting me in public, is that clear?"

"Yes, sir."

Mom clapped her hands, and said, "Now then, once the request goes through to Jorin, the Imperial Royal Council will put in their opinion. Only Helios, the chancellor knows about," she paused as if searching for the right words, "that site. But Jorin will make sure the others approve it." She smiled. "As to your other requirement," she pressed a button on the cube and the wall chirped.

An indifferent Jorin appeared on screen once again.

Gideon's jaw dropped for a moment, he picked it up and gave a deep nod to the emperor.

"Yes, Lily?" said Jorin.

Mom explained the situation and added that we had agreed to wed if we received an apology.

Shit, heat gathered around my collar, but not from embarrassment. *I wasn't expecting uncle Jorin to apologize, just Dad.*

"Hmm," Jorin said and a faint smile fell over his face before he smoothed it out. "Very well. I'm sorry for manipulating you. Though, do know if the empire needs it, I might do so again in the future." He chuckled. "Feel free to call me out then, too." His grin faded again and he looked pointedly at Dad.

This made everyone else follow suit.

"Ah, right," Dad looked at Gideon and me. "Sorry Gideon, Anessa. I often forget you are wiser beyond your years. I'll endeavor to do better in the future."

Jorin nodded at Dad's apology. "With that, little sprout, I acknowledge receipt of your intent to marry. May our dynasty grow, and Westwood prosper." The call ended.

He's abrupt.

Mom rolled her eyes and sighed. "Sprout. Sorry Anessa, he thinks he's funny."

All I could do was blink at her. *Him calling me a sprout was a joke? His apology wasn't very genuine, though. He even admitted that he'd do it again!* Shaking my head I realized that I likely wouldn't get more than that, and asking for more would be a bad idea.

"We'd like to have a public ceremony when we're adults though. My original aim was to marry Gideon when I turned eighteen, which he had agreed to. Is that okay?"

Mom beamed. "It's more than okay. That would've been our suggestion anyway. Since we never announced your engagement, it works in our favor." She rushed to our side of the table and pulled me into a hug. "My little girl's getting married!"

Her excitement made a slight wave of realization hit me and my heart rate increased. *Crap. I'm not ready for this.*

She pulled away and her finger went to her chin. "I'm a little concerned about your age." She pointed at me, "Even if there is no risk of complications, waiting is apt." Whispering to herself, I caught, "Though grandkids might be fun."

My eyes widened and I waved my hands. "I'm waiting!" I basically yelled, "You don't have to worry about that!" With my hand on my chest I continued, "One thing at a time, marriage is happening seven *years* earlier than I planned."

Taking my hand she began to pull me out of the solar.

Sparing Gideon a glance, he waved my way half-heartedly. It seemed he was just as stunned as I was.

Sarah caught up with us in the great room, and we all entered a study.

Yllia was nearby and Mom called her over.

"Are you alright, Anessa?" Sarah asked.

"Yeah, I guess," I said with a sigh.

Turning toward Mom who was gushing to Yllia, Sarah said, "What's got Her Imperial High Grace in such a tizzy?"

Waving Sarah closer I whispered, "I'm getting married."

She arched a brow and said, "Yes, in seven years."

I shook my head. "No. Sooner than that."

Mom sat across from me at the long table in the room. "Now then, let's talk colors. I was thinking teal, orange and white."

Sarah said, "Oh, a lot sooner."

"Ma'am," Yllia said, "We oughtn't get too far ahead of ourselves. His Imperial Maj–"

"Don't be such a stickler. Jorin was right there and already knows about it. All that's left is the council, and they'll fall in line."

A knot formed in my stomach but after breathing with my eyes closed for a few seconds, it faded. "Can I have a white veil?" I asked, hoping to have at least a little say in my own wedding.

I didn't know if white veils were a wedding tradition on Anfang or not. But to me, with a whole Earthen life tucked away in my memory, it somehow seemed right.

CHAPTER FIVE
THE MARITAL TRACK

A WEEK LATER, Gideon and I had returned to school, Maaka Institute for Cultivating Juniors. For the past five minutes I'd been dithering in front of Dean Xandra's office.

How's this going to go, anyway? "Hey, I'm moving to the Martial division, see ya!" Shaking my head, I realized I was being silly. *I'd never say it like that.*

Pulling on the ring hanging form the door, I swallowed my nerves. *You're not doing anything wrong, Anessa. You were given an order by the emperor himself!*

Xandra's secretary saw me and froze, just like the first time I saw her, six years ago. In a flash she jumped up and peeked in on the dean.

"Go on ahead," she said.

As the door closed, the dean said conversationally, "It's been a while, hasn't it?"

Nodding my head slightly I said, "Far too long." I thought to myself, *Only five years.* I'd stopped visiting her after they'd finalized my monthly donations were handled. When I started classes, the students had been sharing books that were tattered, broken and out of date. It seemed silly for a place of learning, so I remedied it in the most rich girl way possible: with a lot of money.

Her office was as Spartan as I remembered. A simple set of chairs and an ugly excuse for a coffee table that was in even worse shape than I remembered.

"I hear you're leaving me," she said.

"Yes," I said. "His Imperial Majesty, Jorin, informed me himself."

Her eyes widened but she otherwise didn't respond.

"Nothing will change regarding my gifts to the school." Taking a seat in front of her desk I added, "Too many students rely on the Carlyle Tuition Trust, from what I'm told."

Xandra smiled. "I'm glad to hear that." She tapped the top of her desk. "Would it be too much to ask for that in writing?"

We sorted out a letter stating the conditions would not change, and I signed it. Perhaps I was imagining the hint of relief on her face, but probably not.

"Who is my new Dean, anyway?"

"Dean Donovan," she said simply. "All I can say is he is fair." I caught her whisper, "Even if he is an ass."

"Will I still be able to meet with my friends?"

She tilted her head. "What do you mean?"

"Won't my schedule change?"

"Ah, not so much that your friends will change. The two divisions align their schedules specifically to facilitate fraternization." She waved her hand. "And your dormitory will not change either, since you're in the Imperial Royal Dormitories. They're the same for either division."

Neither Gideon nor Oliver have ever talked about Donovan. Remembering Oliver's hit first and ask questions second, I realized, *Though I doubt either made an effort to meet their dean.* Gideon wasn't much for conflict, so he likely didn't *want* to meet his dean. *Let's hope he gets a bit more of a backbone.*

"How have things changed since being named the heir apparent, anyway?" Xandra asked.

Arching a brow I said, "They haven't changed much. They've changed a few of my amenities…" My voice trailed off. *Oh.* It reminded me that Oliver had been getting a much larger allowance than I was before our roles switched. I didn't track my money very closely, but I unquestionably gained more disposable income.

Once I figured out what she was getting at, I asked, "Why Dean Xandra, was there a shortfall in what I'm offering the Civilian division each month?"

The half smile she'd been giving me turned into a wolfish grin. "It is quite expensive to host two hundred Martial students per month in the tuition program your family offers. I've had to ask Donovan to help cover some of their expenses. He's demanding that we reduce our Civilian sponsors to make up for it."

So he's telling her: funnel funds away from the division that secured the Trust in the first place to the Martial division. He is a greedy bastard.

"I'll triple the monthly offering, but that is as high as I'll go. If you find yourself at a loss after that," I leveled out my tone, "you risk the Trust *drying up*."

She coughed. "Understood." With a smile she finished, "Have a good day Your Imperial High Grace."

Standing to leave, I paused as I reached the door, and cast a neutral look at the shabby furnishings. "Please buy some furniture for your office. It wouldn't cost much."

▼▼▼

"You're what!?" Portia yelled, drawing the attention of everyone near us in the lunch hall. Once she realized her mistake she looked around and whispered, while bowing her head, "Sorry."

"You don't need to cause a scene," I said, then sat down an S-ROB to provide us privacy.

"That explains why they canceled the school engagement announcement, it's happening even sooner!" She grabbed my hands. "I'm so happy for you, are you nervous?"

Giving her a shaky laugh I said, "Of course I am. It's seven years earlier than I expected!" Though I'd placed a device to avoid others eavesdropping, I was nervous because some people were still giving us reproachful glares at her outburst.

"Please keep quiet about it, though. It's not a public thing. It won't be until we were originally supposed to wed."

She held her hand over her mouth. "My lips are sealed," she mumbled, then repeated it as a whisper between her fingers.

Her silly antics made me chuckle. I decided to get back at her for making a scene and asked, "So then, tell me: have you reconsidered Max's request to elope?"

Portia's mouth opened and closed a few times. Then she huffed. "We talked about that. I won't let him elope." She stroked a stray strand of hair at the side of her head. "I'd be lying if the offer weren't tempting. He renews it every month at least."

"If you ever managed to gain a gentry status," I wondered aloud, "would you change your mind?"

She smiled and lightly smacked the table. "In a heartbeat!"

"I'll be honest," I said and shook my head. "I can't imagine something like status stopping me from marrying someone I love." With a shrug, I added, "Though I'll admit I'm coming from a privileged view."

Interlacing my fingers, I closed my eyes and sent up a prayer. *Please, if anything can be done about Portia's situation, help make it so.*

▼ ▼ ▼

"Portia said you're going to practice your forms now?" Max said as our last class ended for the day.

"Yeah. I have a meeting with Dean Donovan tomorrow. I'm not sure what to expect, but I figured I should at least get a head-start on being a Martial student."

Max flexed his arm, which was almost as wide around as my waist, and tapped his bicep. "Mind if I join you?" He laughed and deflated. "I, er, forgot to book a training room for myself."

"Sure," I said, and looked at Portia. "Want to tag along?"

She perked up. "I'd love to." Her eyes landed on Max, telling me my call was correct.

As we neared the building that housed the training rooms, a familiar voice yelled angrily, "I don't care if others have booked rooms. I'm the Imperial Prince of the empire. I expect a room should always be available to me!"

We slowed our approach. It seemed I wasn't the only one curious about the train wreck that my cousin Lukas was involving himself in.

"I'm sorry Your Imperial Highness, but I've been instructed that the rules apply to everyone," the attendant firmed their voice, "including you."

"Explain to me why I shouldn't just clear the room out myself, and use it anyway?" Lukas said.

"N-now, that would go against the school's rules." The once-stoic attendant faltered, "I'd b-be forced to report it to my superiors."

Once we'd rounded the corner I saw my cousin was *floating* in the air, looming over the man.

Max whispered to me, "Maybe we should offer our room?"

Nodding I said, "Yeah, probably. Sorry Max."

I approached my cousin who turned his steel gray glare to me.

Giving him a light curtsy I said, "If it would please Your Imperial Highness, we have booked a room you could use."

He dropped to the floor and approached. "No need. I've lost interest. I'll go to the forests and hunt instead." As he walked past, he body checked me, almost bowling me over.

Six years ago, I'd allowed myself to hit the ground when he did the same thing. Although he used several times the force as last time, and I skittered down the hall a few feet, this time I remained standing.

He scowled at me when I merely gave him another curtsy. This earned me a derisive snort, but he left me alone.

Max and Portia pushed themselves against the wall while giving him a bow and curtsy accordingly.

When the building's door closed, we checked in with the attendant.

"Damn it," I said inside the room, and rubbed my shoulder. "He didn't have to hit me so hard."

"Are you okay, Imperial Lady Anessa?" Portia asked.

"Yes, I'm okay, it just hurt more than I thought it would to resist him."

Pulling Rufus out of my storage ring, I winced as I raised my arm to place its shoulder harness over my head.

Portia seemed to notice and helped me get my sword settled.

"Thanks, luckily he hit my off arm."

"Hit? Someone hit you?" Rufus asked.

Yes, my cousin bumped into me on purpose. I'm fine. Knowing Rufus's personality I added, *No I'm not going to get revenge.*

"Rina is a butt head, isn't he?"

Rufus's mistake had me wondering, *"What do you mean? Rina is a girl, and the one who bumped into me was my cousin Lukas."*

There was a pause. Sometimes Rufus would do this, making me wonder if he actually thought things through. *"Right. Sorry. I've known of a few hundred Rina's. It's sometimes hard to keep them straight. So this Lukas, does he have a last name?"*

Lukas's last name is Q'Tar. The oddity of it made me ask, *Exactly how old are you Rufus?*

"No clue," it said cheerfully. *"Unless I'm being directed, talked to, or held in some way, I have no real way to tell what's going on around me."*

Tracing my finger along the flat of Rufus's form. "I'm sorry," I said aloud.

"That tickles."

Its admission made me stop.

"Anyway, I'm excited about your future with Lady Gideon."

Its flub made me laugh. *Gideon is a boy, and I am excited about our future together, too.*

"Everything okay?" Max said.

He and Portia were both giving me an *"Are you insane?"* look.

"Right, this is Rufus." I held up my sword and added, "It's a sentient sword, so I can hear its voice. It confused Gideon for a girl, which made me laugh."

"Ah," Max said, looking at my sword with interest. "Amazing. The method to create sentient swords is long forgotten. I've never actually seen one in person. Rufus is probably over a hundred millennia old."

Looking down at him I asked, *Rufus, are you really over a hundred thousand years old?*

He didn't respond.

Rufus?

A clearly synthetic, almost robotic voice replied, *"Access denied."*

Furrowing my brows at it I went from a different angle. *How many distinct people do you remember, anyway?*

The same voice replied in my head.

After that, no matter what question I asked Rufus I received the same answer.

Great, I broke it. If it's like anything from Earth maybe leaving it alone for a while will reset it? My stomach churned. *I really hope so, at least. I'd hate to tell Oliver I broke Rufus.* Ever since Rufus said it doesn't identify as male or female, and the simplistic responses I received from it, I'd stopped viewing Rufus as an actual sentient being. I thought it was more akin to a chatbot than a living thing, especially with how it confused people's genders.

I put Rufus away, afraid that using it in its current state would be detrimental to it.

Though I'd only gone through my forms once, Max said, "Would you like to spar?" He held up his fists.

"Sure, but I won't hit you directly."

With a huff he asked, "Okay, why not?"

"Imagine what happened to the shield, the one that the Blackwood brothers used against me, happening to your arm."

Five years ago, when I was only six years old, the school had sanctioned a dual duel against two impertinent bratty princes. The older of the two, Wyn, probably could've beat me himself, but his arrogance led to his defeat when he wasted time posturing and I shattered his shield with my dangerous, though barely controlled, power.

Max looked at his arm and nodded. "Good point." He turned toward Portia, "Would you do the honors?"

She raised up her hand. "Ready." Then swiped it down, "Start!"

Despite his height of six feet and width of three, his frame moved forward at a blistering speed. He was every bit as strong as Wyn was when I fought him, if not more.

"You're a lot quicker than I remember!" Max said as I dodged an attack to my midsection. He had to use an uppercut to accommodate for our height difference, or he'd have knocked my block off. "Have you been keeping up with your training?" he asked, as his fist all but grazed my nose.

Cripes!

Using my elbow I batted his fist away from me. Though if I were honest, I moved my own body midair more than his arm did. *Got it, keep my feet planted. I've been kind of lazy. Here's hoping Dean Donovan won't pick up on that tomorrow.*

Over the next few minutes, we danced around the arena. Portia cheered as we went.

"All you're doing is dodging!" Max complained. "You need to do more than pepper me with taps if you hope to gain any advantage."

He's right.

I stopped, wanting to see how much my cultivator body could bridge the gap in his training and size versus my own.

Using a wide stance, I attempted to take his next upward strike head-on.

The next thing I knew I was looking at the ceiling and there were four people standing above me. Moving my hand over one of my eyes, I realized it was only two. *Great I'm seeing double.* Blearily I asked, "Did anyone get the plate number on that [bus]?"

The two looked at one another and Portia asked, "What's a buss?"

Groaning I slowly sat up and used the arena floor to steady myself. "Never mind." I rubbed my face. "What happened?"

"Max," Portia said irately, giving him a glare, "didn't take it easy on you."

The giant prostrated himself and said, "I'm very sorry Your Imperial Lady, Anessa."

"Oh," I said and waved my hand as the idiocy of my prior action came to the fore. "It's not your fault. I tried to take that head on, all on my own."

A tile fell from the ceiling and crashed onto the floor, drawing my gaze up. There were three clear impressions on the ceiling close to one another.

"Did I do that?" I was perplexed as to why there were three impressions.

Portia dropped to a whisper, "Yeah, you hit the ceiling and bounced off the floor," she paused then said, "a few times."

No wonder my head's spinning. It made me laugh at myself. "And here I thought I could take it." Attempting to stand, I fell onto Portia.

"Could you help me back to my dormitory?" I asked Portia. Looking to Max I said, "Rain check on the rest of our sparring session?" Giving him a smirk I said, "I think you won this time."

"Sure," he held out his fist which I tapped with my own.

Back at the Imperial Royal dormitory, the guards let us through without trouble. Gideon stood at my dorm's door.

Portia whispered in my ear with a laugh. "Seems you have a late night visitor."

CHAPTER SIX

I SHOULD HAVE EXPECTED...
A DRESSING DOWN

GIDEON CAUGHT SIGHT of me and rushed forward, picking me up in a princess carry. It was the second time he'd done so in my life, and neither time did I mind.

Before Portia pulled away she teased in a quiet voice, "Good luck."

I swatted at her playfully as she dodged, then winked at me.

"I'm only eleven, you goof!"

She curtsied as she left and said, "And I'm only kidding."

Looking up at my proverbial prince I smiled. "What brings you around so late?"

He walked me inside my dormitory making my face flush a deep crimson. Though we weren't married yet, it made me think of a husband carrying his wife over the threshold–an Earth custom that likely had no meaning on Anfang.

Upon entering, Sarah rushed to us and helped me to the floor, then into a nearby chair.

Repeating my question to Gideon, he said, "I'm moving into the dorm suite next to yours."

His admission made me blush even more.

Sarah coughed. "Though that's for public appearances. Our lord will be staying in your guest room." She held up her finger. "That is, of course, only after you are wed in the near-term. For now," she looked to him. "He *is* staying next door."

Getting the hint, he bowed. "Yes, it is rather late, My Imperial Lady. Before I go, may I ask what happened?"

I sighed. "I tried to tank an uppercut from Max when sparring."

Both Gideon and Sarah winced at my words.

"I'll have a bath started," Sarah said, then paused. "Where does it hurt?"

"Everywhere," I said. Patting my shoulder, I added, "Though His Imperial Highness, Lukas, bumped into me pretty hard here earlier. This area seems to hurt the most."

"Now then, onto the topic of your," she cleared her throat, "heats. We need to figure out how to manage those."

"W-why would anything need to change?!" I asked, alarmed. "Aren't we handling them just fine now?"

She nodded. "We are, but once you marry, it's not *strictly* necessary for me to get in the way."

Gideon's ears and cheeks looked like they were on fire.

"Should our lord stay in the guest room on such nights, or–"

"There's no 'or' there!" I said and pointed to the guest room. "That room works fine for Gideon, and you playing interference on those days is *very* helpful."

"My lord?" she asked.

His voice cracked, "Yeah?"

"Your opinion?"

Sarah asking Gideon made my stomach churn.

He held up his hands. "I'm okay with things as they are."

She bowed at his words. "Very well. I was tasked by Her Imperial High Grace, Lily to make sure the status quo was acceptable." Then she bowed to me and added, "For both of you. I am sorry for overstepping my usual bounds."

Sighing, I waved it off. "It's fine. Thank you for telling me. Did Mommy say why she wanted to make sure?"

Sarah pursed her lips. "Grandkids."

Letting her word hang in the air, I replied finally, "You can tell her that she can wait several years!" Breathing out I remembered her saying waiting was apt. *She's teasing me, like she always does.*

A bell rang.

Sarah said, "My lord, your Imperial Lady's bath is ready. If it would please you to retire to *your* dormitory for the night?"

He bowed his head to me. "Of course." He smiled. "Good night, My Imperial Grace."

As the door clicked behind him she asked, "You smile every time he calls you that, you know?"

Covering my mouth I said, "Really?"

"Mhmm." She helped me into the bathroom, where Tania was busy checking the water.

They helped change me into a silly garment, then into the oddly cool water. The cloth spread out and covered the surface of the water in my bath.

"This modesty stuff lately is silly," I complained and leaned back.

"Maybe so," Tania said, "but it is entirely necessary. It is vital to keep your purity unblemished, not just in the eyes of others, but in the eyes of the gods."

Her words about the gods made me almost choke on the water.

"Are you alright?" Sarah asked and leaned in.

"I'm fine. Purity aside," I snorted, "sometimes I forget the gods are literally watching everything we do."

Tania corrected herself. "I don't mean the gods would look upon your bare skin, but that they would want to be sure you're never seen by those unworthy of you."

That earned Tania an arched eyebrow from me. "Unworthy? I'm no goddess–" my voice faded and I remembered Mom telling me that I would indeed become a goddess of death someday. *If I live long enough.*

"Perhaps you aren't a goddess," Tania said and closed her eyes in prayer. "But Eloria, High Goddess of Craft has set her eyes on you, and aims to guide you in the future. While she has not given you a mission yet, we must make sure we've done everything we can to make sure you remain worthy of her notice."

Turning to Sarah, I was about to ask her input, when I noticed she, too, was sending up her own prayer.

What's it mean to be a goddess's champion? I'd been wondering since I first received the dubious "honor." Despite asking many, including Mom, no one had a clear answer for me. *Would my two Lady's maids view me the same way if they knew I was Her Goddess Eloria's True champion of both Craft and Death?*

The two women helped me dress, after a belabored process of drying me off in layers, to ensure modesty, of course.

Their choice of attire was an odd one, a mostly sheer garment that was only opaque where it counted.

Holding up my arm and looking at the translucent fabric, I asked, "Isn't this a bit contrary to our prior discussion?"

Sarah motioned around us. "There are plenty of privacy screens around us. I need to make sure you don't have any broken bones. With this, I can see any swelling or asymmetry." She clapped her hands, and Tania entered with a thicker garment and put it over my shoulders.

"What, that's it?"

Sarah nodded. "You do not appear to have any broken bones. Bruising, yes, but nothing is broken." She shook her head. "You know, Max weighs over three *hundred* pounds. From the last time we weighed you, you aren't even sixty. To top it off, he's a middling Ascended Realm cultivator."

Heat gathered around my neck in the idiocy of my behavior. "Yeah, that meeting didn't go as planned."

She put her hands on her hips. "What was your plan? He made you into a pallone, I bet."

Pallone, a big ball? I'm not familiar with it, but I can even see what it looks like in my head.

"It's a sport played in the Tanis Region, they use a ball of the same name." She smiled, telling me my confusion was written on my face. "It's struck with a wooden bracciale."

Bracciale, or bracelet. Despite never hearing it before, I could even visualize the object. Shaking my head I occasionally marveled at the odd translation art that allowed me to speak from the day I was born. *I'd say I was more of a billiard ball than a Pallone, though I doubt that'd make sense to Sarah.* I laughed at the thought, which I instantly regretted, as pain erupted from my ribs. *Ouch.*

They then dressed me the most modest night gown I'd ever worn. When I walked back into the lounge, I realized why. Gideon was sitting on the couch and waved in my direction.

Oh, he's back. Without waiting for an invite, I sat next to him and rested my head on his side.

To my surprise, he did something he hadn't done before: he actually put his arm over my shoulder.

Fearing reproach, I glanced towards my Lady's maids, but they did nothing.

I closed my eyes.

He said, "I wish I were stronger, so I could've protected you."

Humming in contentment, I said, "It's okay. I got myself hurt all on my own. You stepping in wouldn't have stopped me from being stupid." My tone shifted and I looked into his emerald eyes. "I just hope my own inexperience doesn't get me killed, if I'm sent to war."

"Enter," a monotone voice said.

Unlike Xandra, Dean Donovan did not have a secretary.

Opening the door to his office, I realized that instead of spending for an assistant, he'd splurged on the decor. The walls were decorated with weapons from the martial path: a sword, a glaive, a pair of cestus combat gloves, and others I didn't recognize.

Behind his desk was a simple plaque that with the word "work" above "talent" with a bold line between them.

Dean Donovan looked up at me for a second before saying, "Sit down."

Hello to you, too, I thought as I sat. *Why do I get the feeling we'll butt heads.*

"How are your efforts as a cultivator, Your Imperial High Grace, Anessa Jean Carlyle?" he began without preamble, shuffling through papers on his desk.

Ugh, stuffy, I thought, then said, "I haven't had any formal training as a cultivator, so I'm not really sure how to answer that."

He stopped shuffling the papers, and his eyes looked up at me over his thick brass glasses.

"Let me get this straight," he started in a harsh tone, "and please correct me if I'm wrong," he held up a hand to stop me, "when I'm done. The heir apparent to the Imperial Carlyle Duchy, with access to a fairly sizable, nation-state level income as her monthly *petty* cash, has made no effort to hire someone on her own time?" His eyebrows rose and he said, "Hmm."

Each word hit me like a hammer blow. When he mentioned that what I had was *petty* cash, it made my stomach churn. *Holy crap I don't like him!* Looking down at his desk I had to admit, *but he isn't wrong.*

"I have hired some people," I said defensively, "to help with my martial studies." Taking a breath out, I added, "I honestly was a little scared of advancing my cultivation after my dantians came in. Early on I was too aggressive, and it wasn't a fun thing to go through."

Dean Donovan sat up and turned his attention to me. "Alright. Hiring someone for martial support is better than sitting in a corner. Barely." He sifted through his paperwork again and pulled out a page. "You've been a proper cultivator for," he circled something on the page in front of him, "three years now, is it?"

Pursing my lips, because I had an idea of where he was going, I nodded.

"You're *still* in the Nascent Realm, correct?"

"Yes."

"That's 'Yes, sir,'" he corrected.

I repeated, "Yes, *sir*," with a glare.

The trace of a smirk bit at the corner of his mouth.

"Do you know what stage or step are you in of the Nascent Realm?"

"No," I said and looked down, getting a sense of his personality, I added in a quiet voice, "sir."

"How many dantians do you have? I know that's a personal question, but if I'm to help you as I've been tasked, I need to know." He put down his quill and held up his hands. "I won't write it down," he tapped the side of his head, "but I will remember it. I also need to know your elemental affinities, and level of resonance in each, if you know them." He held up more fingers as he listed off more things he needed to know, most of which was foreign to me.

When he was done, I replied, "I have seven dantians, and possess an affinity for every element. I don't know my resonances, other than Earth, which my Daddy said was higher than his."

He did not react with shock or surprise as so many people did. Most cultivators resonated with one or *two* elements, not ten. Instead, he proceeded to repeat questions about the things I was oblivious to, though he didn't delve further into them. From his demeanor, this was obviously not a time for me to ask questions.

"Okay. That's about all I need on your cultivation background. I will be honest: I'm disappointed in your focus as a cultivator." He huffed. "Before your fiancé's, His Imperial Most Honorable, Gideon Ignotus's final awakening, I would've expected him to have difficulty advancing to the Ascended Realm."

Dean Donovan gestured toward me. "You're His Royal Majesty, Oliver Sil Carlyle-Aramon's sister. He had *three* dantians, and was our peak student in every way, save for his civilian studies. Your late awakening, by the whims of the Gods, is not something you can control of course. However, once you were blessed with an awakening, how you go from there is up to you.

"At the very least, I expected you to be in the Ascended Realm. Naturally, your brother's innate talent to advance unhindered is a gift all of his own. It's no excuse."

Throughout his lecture, my stomach went from churning to uncomfortable as a heat spread through my chest. I was done looking down and placating him with "sirs." As I stood, I put my hands on his desk. "Before Eloria told me I was a cultivator, when I was four years old, I was stonewalled on everything to do with cultivation. Even after that, I was limited to scriptures which mostly said nothing more than the fact that it's a gift from the gods. It was deeply frustrating. My inaction afterwards may be no excuse, but it's not that I'm lazy."

"I know," Dean Donovan said in a softer voice. "I never once called you lazy." He stood and while he wasn't a tall man, he towered over me. "Perhaps I pressed too hard over your inaction, but you need to know that I am not your enemy. I'm here to help. Those information bans no longer applied when you awakened as a cultivator." He crossed his arms. "Afterwards, as a cultivator, what did you do?"

Thinning my lips out I stared at him and exhaled. "Focused on my martial pursuits, mostly on hitting things."

He nodded. "But as a cultivator you did *nothing*."

Opening my mouth to retort, he held up his hand as a palm up to the ceiling.

"Cultivation," he held out his other hand as a fist, "And martial prowess are two different things." Lowing his palm, he held up a finger on his fist. "However, you are a cultivator first." He slid a piece of paper over to me. "According to the people you hired to train you, they say you're having a great difficulty adapting your forms effectively. Do you regularly face challenges in getting the feel for the same movement day to day?"

The fact that he had looked into me and the training I did after school surprised me. "Yes, sir."

"Essence," he started, making me look up, "has a great impact on your muscles. If you don't understand how cultivation affects your body, you're fighting a losing battle."

Holding one of his hands over his eyes, he continued, "Based on what I see, with my essence vision, the essence within you is chaotic and unbridled. Tell me, what would that mean for your ability to advance, martially?"

He'd made his point, and I was frustrated, with myself above all else. Sitting down in the chair I folded my arms and looked away from him. "It would make it difficult to make any appreciable progress."

"I'm sorry, could you face me? I didn't quite hear you."

Closing my eyes I suppressed my urge to yell at him. Aggravating as he was, he hadn't said anything that was an outright insult, or even untrue. Though by now the heat had reached the sides of my head, making checking my temper difficult. Turning back to him I repeated myself.

"That's right," Dean Donovan said. "I may not be your father…"

His statement made me arch an annoyed brow at him.

"…but with my guidance, you'll have a better understanding of how to regulate your strength," he paused to smile, "and aggression. Mistakes, like those you made with His Royal Highness, Wyn Blackwood, will be a thing of the past. Now then, do you meditate often?"

I shook my head.

"Your encounters with His Royal Highness, Wyn, were fortuitous, for you that is. During your duel with him, he should have won. You know that, right?"

"Yes, sir. It occurred to me in the middle of our fight." As I remembered the way he toyed with me I made a fist. "It's part of what amped me up to strike his shield to the point of failure."

"If that brat hadn't focused on demoralizing you, he would've won in seconds." Dean Donovan shook his head. "His biggest failing is his pride." He pointed to me. "Yours is fear. You have the intelligence to go far, but you know that it won't be easy."

He took a small flared glass jar with a pale yellow marble in it and sat it on his desk. Following that he presented a wooden box with pearl inlay.

"This pill," Dean Donovan said, and pushed the tiny cruet forward, "is a foundation establishment pill. Store it."

I tapped it, and it vanished into my storage ring.

He opened the box. Inside was a colorful array of what I'd guessed now were pills that almost sparkled in the room's light.

"Those are pretty," I said, before remembering my audience.

"See the white pill?"

Looking them over I pointed to the one furthest to my right.

"Any others?"

Furrowing my brows, I said, "No, should there be another white one?"

"Just checking," he said with a smirk.

"For?"

Shaking his head, he said, "You really are ignorant."

"Sorry," I said, glumly.

"These are essence condensation pills. They make it easier to collect essence of a specific element. Including neutral," he added and tapped the mini silver sphere.

Remembering that I had several elements that weren't common to Anfang, I asked, "What happens if a student takes these, but doesn't get all of the elements they have?"

"We would make sure that didn't happen. As early a cultivator as you are, it might be fine for a while, but eventually it could affect your future development. You might end up with an uneven, or worse, cracked foundation." He pointed to me. "Even with that pill I just gave you. It can help smooth out issues due to poor focus, but it cannot fill in what's missing."

He pushed the box forward.

"Based on what you said." I held up my hand and closed the box. "I shouldn't use these."

Waving his hand in a circle he said, "Because?"

"There's some missing."

Telling him about my time with Sir Orris, when I was a toddler, he nodded and put the box away.

"That is a problem. I'll look into it, and if I can resolve the issue I will, though I can't guarantee we'll find pills to as yet unknown elements. Setting that aside, let's go into your new itinerary…"

After we discussed my new class lineup I noticed an omission, I said, "There's nothing on leadership."

"Leadership?"

Clearing my throat I said, "Yes. I'm supposed to be the heir apparent to the Imperial Carlyle Duchy. While, in theory, I would not assume the ducal throne for some time, I worry that with the war, it may happen sooner than I think."

"I'll talk to His Imperial Grace, Roland Carlyle about it. I'm sure he has some ideas in mind already, and I don't want to step on his toes, so to speak."

A knock came at his door.

Dean Donovan looked at the hourglass clock to the side. "Seems our time is up for today. Focus on the classes I've given you and we'll work through your fear." He started shuffling through his files again, preparing for whoever was next.

I stood to leave and thought to myself, *I don't like him, but I have to admit, part of me wants his respect.*

CHAPTER SEVEN

AN UNEXPECTED DATE

I'D BEEN BOTTLING up the pain from Max's attack all morning. I blamed the tension I'd been under leading up to my meeting with Dean Donovan. When I closed the door behind me, I finally relaxed, and slouched as the pain came flooding back. I rubbed my neck wearily and sighed.

A cough to my side made me look over at one of my guards of the day.

It must've been they who coughed, because there was no one else around. They rarely ever interact with me unless needed.

She briefly mirrored my posture, then straightened out.

Right, appearances. Though I wanted to roll my eyes at her, she was right and I knew she was only trying to help.

As I stood properly again, my spine popped in the process. A light grunt slipped out before I stopped it. *That hurt.*

Dean Donovan had said my classes didn't start for a few days, so I returned to my dorm suite. Inside, I collapsed onto the couch.

Within a minute, Sarah said at my side, "Anessa, that's not a proper place to lay down."

"Nnnn," I replied, not moving.

Out of the corner of my eye, I caught her rolling up her sleeves and her hands going to her hips. "Do I need to carry you into your room?"

Lifting up my head a hair I mumbled, "Suit yourself."

Sarah groaned. "This is the only time I'm doing this. You aren't heavy, Lady Anessa, but you're more mature than this."

She put her arm under my collar bone and in the middle of my thigh and lifted.

Staying horizontal required me to basically plank, and was actually more effort than walking, but I was too embarrassed to admit it halfway through. *Why am I being such an idiot?*

After she gently laid me on my bed I was startled awake a few minutes later when she placed cool compresses on my back, shoulders, hip, and legs. Despite the initial shock, I fell back asleep almost immediately.

"Anessa," Sarah called, waking me.

Lifting my head up, I found the compresses had been removed, but my skin was cool where they had been. "Yeah?"

With a smile, she handed me a handkerchief. She whispered, "You're drooling."

Taking care of it with as much dignity as I could manage, I sat up in bed. "How long was I asleep?" My stomach growled, making me blush.

"Twelve hours." She gave me a curtsy. "I'm sorry to wake you, but you have a visitor."

"Gideon?" I said expectantly.

She shook her head. "Her Imperial Right Honorable, Yukirei."

Slumping down again, I said, "Oh." I thought to myself, *Why is Yukirei here for me? I know she doesn't want to talk about Gideon. His classes didn't change; neither did hers, for that matter.*

"Would it be possible to ask her to come back later?" I asked in a deflated tone.

"Are you still feeling unwell?" Sarah asked.

"Not so much that, but I'm just not feeling like company right now."

In response, Sarah pulled something out of my closet. "Yukirei did make a special trip to see you."

"Oh?" I replied, and found myself smiling.

When I exited my bedroom a short time later, she rushed over to me and took my hand. "I heard from Gideon you were hurt, and I just wanted to see how you were doing."

"I'm fine, Gideon isn't here though. He has martial training until second dinner."

Yukirei puffed out her cheeks. "Yes. I said I'm here to see how *you* are doing."

Grinning I asked, "Don't you have classes?"

"Hmmph," she said and turned her head away. "I'm a Martial Core Scholar, I'm allowed a little more flexibility." Opening one of her eyes at me she sighed. "In any event, most of my Civilian study classes have been canceled, or rolled into my Martial classes." She lifted up my hand and I winced. "How did you get hurt, anyway?"

"When I was training, I tried to–" I paused as she leaned in intently. Pulling my head back I said, in a quieter tone, "–tank one of Max's hits head-on."

"Ouch," Yukirei said. She shook her head and put her hand to her chest. "I wouldn't try that if I weren't in the Sky Realm."

"Why's that?"

Tapping her finger on her chin she said, "I suppose I can demonstrate." She tapped her shoulder. "Push me."

I arched a confused brow at her and said, "I'm not going to push you."

She smiled. "Humor me."

Shaking my head I said, "I feel we're getting off topic. But since you insist." I very lightly pushed her shoulder, and she nudged back as I expected she would.

Yukirei cleared her throat and stood on her tippy toes. "Now then. Try again."

What's she trying to do here? I thought, as I repeated my gesture. It was completely different this time. She didn't give an inch. It was as though I were pushing into a steel plate.

She raised her eyebrows at me and smiled. "You can do better than that."

With a huff I pushed far harder to no avail.

She tilted her head up a little, looking down on me. "What, is the baby too weak?"

I put my hands on my hips. "Really? You promised to stop calling me that."

She batted her eyes at me and tapped both of her shoulders. "Trust me. I'm going somewhere with this."

Placing my hands on both of her shoulders I pressed. That is, until I slipped forward, Yukirei catching me in her arms.

"Err, sorry." I said and stood back. I almost slipped again as the tiles beneath my feet were now fragments. *Crap.* In righting my posture, I winced in pain. *Taking on Max's attack was really stupid.*

Turning to Sarah I saw she was shaking her head. "I'll prepare a change of clothes," she said, and muttered, "and contact a mason."

Her comments on my clothes made me realize I'd shredded the back half of my dress when I slipped. My ruined shoes also fell away from my feet as I walked forward a couple steps. *Great, this outfit didn't last me five minutes.*

Yukirei and I moved to a different spot and the maids scrambled to clean the area. I'd not only broken one tile, but eight, and cracked the subfloor as well.

Why do I get the feeling I'll hear about this? I sighed. "What was the point of all of this?" Pointing to the area I'd damaged on the floor, I whispered, "I hope I don't get in trouble."

"To show you how silly it was to try and take Max's attack." Her hand went back to her chest. "Without Reaction, it wouldn't matter how sturdy I am. An attack that shoves me, places me at the mercy of physics, and would render me powerless. It's the difference maker."

Her bluntness made me laugh nervously. "Yeah. That's about exactly how it happened, too. I remember thinking I'd absorb the hit, then I saw a white blinding light. Apparently I smacked into the ceiling three times. Is that what a bouncy ball feels like?"

Though I was trying to make light of the situation, since after all I had survived, her brows were furrowed and she'd retaken my hand.

"Don't do stuff like that," said Yukirei, in a concerned tone. Holding my hand in both of hers, she said, "How about we go into Ersta to take your mind off of things?"

Ersta was the town built around Maaka, a castle school built into a mountain.

"A walk would do you good, Lady Anessa," agreed Sarah, and she sighed, looking at the mess I'd made. "We should have this fixed by the time you return."

I shrugged. "Sure, why not?"

She added, "Be sure not to stay out too long, though."

Tilting my head to the side I asked, "Why not?"

With a cough she said, "It's getting to be around *that* time. It tends to rear its ugly side around fourth ten."

Heat graced my cheeks and I said, "Got it. We'll be back before then."

Yukirei asked, "Ugly side?"

"Never mind that," I hurriedly said.

"Anessa," Sarah said sharply.

"What?"

"Change."

Looking at the back of my ripped dress, I said, "Right. Some new shoes would be good, too."

As we headed out, I asked Yukirei, "How does Reaction work?"

She giggled. "I'm honestly not exactly sure, but I do know it's natural to cultivators. The reason it's limited to cultivators in the Sky Realm is control."

"Okay. Control over what?"

"Essence." She gestured toward me. "As you are in the Nascent Realm, your control is poor because you're just starting out." Holding up her hands she clarified, "It's not that you're trying to be bad, but it takes a lot of practice to get better at it."

"Right, but there has to be some way to think about using it, or you wouldn't be able to do so at all."

"Okay," she said, and pointed to a small field of grass to the side. "See that flower?"

I nodded.

Flicking her wrist, the head of the flower twisted and lifted from its stem, levitating into the air. "You imagine that you have an invisible hand. That's a form of remote Reaction." Patting her shoulders, "When I apply it to my body, it's as simple as thinking that I don't want to move. It takes energy to accomplish it, but that's something I have in spades."

"Is it something I could do?" I asked thoughtfully.

"Hmm," Yukirei said. "Normally, I would say no, because your control is several orders of magnitude lower than mine, and the cost would be too high. But the only way to see is to try it."

Moving the flower head so it was floating between us, she said, "Try and reach out with your essence and take this."

Scratching my head, I wondered, *Ok. How?* Trying to visualize the essence within me, I thought of forming a hand with its fingertips pointing toward the sky, which would come underneath the flower and lift it up.

The first couple dozen attempts did nothing. But I kept at it. On the thirtieth try, I swore the petals fluttered. *Weird.* I touched my fingertips with my thumb. *For a moment, it was almost as if I could actually feel the bottom of the petals.*

Yukirei by this point was filing her nails in an ostentatious display of mild boredom.

She's being really *patient and doesn't even need to try to keep that flower head afloat.* Trying to expand on the sensation from before, I tried again, except this time, the petals all fell away from the receptacle. "Whoops."

"Yeah, that same thing happened to me at first," she said with a smile. Putting away her nail file, she added, "It takes some practice. Though, you used a *lot* more essence than I do." She whispered, "But I have to say that you also grasped that concept much faster than I did."

My stomach growled.

"See? It took you lots of essence. Should we catch a bite to eat? I know of a place with great food that is well-suited to cultivators."

"That sounds fine," I said and we walked through town at a leisurely pace. "How long did it take you to get the hang of Reaction?"

"A few years to get a real handle on it. I stepped into the Sky Realm at the age of seven, and from there it was a real trial." She let her shoulders slump. "My Master was a total slave driver."

"What was he like?"

"Mmm, well, you know how I don't really need to sleep, right?"

I nodded.

"Every day, for every moment, I was required to either meditate, cultivate, practice martial forms, or memorize Arts from a Manual they chose for me."

"Manual?" I blinked.

"It's a collection of Arts, that usually guide you along a Way."

With a sigh I said, "Maybe Dean Donovan was right."

"About what?"

"I had plenty of time to learn more about cultivation, and so far I've just been…" I shrugged. "I don't know. I didn't even know what a Manual or a Way are."

"There's nothing wrong with that," Yukirei said. "Do you know why I'm here, instead of staying at the sect?"

I shook my head.

"The focus on cultivation was too much. I was acting out, and getting into trouble," she said and held her hand out, studying her fingernails.

"Heh," I said. "I can see that."

She sent a glare my way. "Hey, I'm being honest. Don't make fun of me."

"Don't call me baby," I said, and stuck out my tongue to prove my maturity.

"Fair," she said and grinned. "Father implored my Master not to expel me from the sect. Master agreed, but at the same time, I had to take some time away." She held out her arms. "Which is when I came here. And I'm glad I did."

"Oh?"

She nodded. "I met Gideon," she beamed, and bumped my side with her hip, "and you."

"Yeah, yeah," I said dismissively. We'd stopped and I frowned at the sign of the café.

Nora's Essencial Goods. Whereas I'd been born as a cat-kin, and have to deal with estrus instead of menstruation, Gideon was part lupine. It gave him an exceptionally good nose, which was the reason why being around me during a heat was impossible, unless he had an "outlet."

"Please tell me this isn't the place," I intoned.

Yukirei had reached for the door handle and stopped. "Yes, it is. Are you not fond of it?"

"Do they really serve food here, or," I leaned in toward her, "something else?"

Her face flushed in an instant. "Um… I've heard it's a little bit of…" her eyes evaded mine, "both."

She knows about Gideon coming here, doesn't she? I narrowed my eyes at her.

Instead of responding to my non-verbal provocation, she hid behind the door and entered.

Okay. She's embarrassed. I suppose that's fair.

Upon entering, the hostess, Nora I'd assumed, glared at me, then focused a polite smile on Yukirei. "How can I assist you two ladies today?"

"A table for two, please?" Yukirei asked.

Nora smiled. "Of course." The hostess showed us to our table. "Your server will be with you shortly."

After the woman shut the door, Yukirei said with mild surprise, "She doesn't like you, does she?"

"No, I had a run-in with her a while back," I said and sighed. One of the other workers here, a succubus named Io, had taken on my physical appearance. The memory came to mind. Her version of me as an adult, which I understood was probably accurate, showed the only asset I would gain was a little bit of junk in the trunk and a free lifetime membership to the itty bitty committee. "I don't want to talk about it." Hoping to change direction, I asked, "You mentioned Manuals and Ways earlier from your sect. What was it you were studying?"

Yukirei smiled. "I can show you."

Looking around the room I said, "It won't break anything here, will it?"

She ignored my question and cupped her hands on the tabletop. Inside, a teal pony appeared with a long red mane and a hammer emblem on its posterior. It pranced around the table, each of its hooves making an adorable tinny clop.

"Oh, that's really cute!" I said and leaned in.

"My Way is that of the Real Illusionist," she said as the pony pranced toward me and climbed onto the backside of my hand.

Each of its tiny steps was like a Q-tip pressing on my skin. When I went to pet it, the animal leaned into it, and it shook its head and neighed, showing it enjoyed the attention. I grinned.

A click at the door made it go up in smoke, as though it had never been there.

"You were right," I said as we neared my dorm suite some time later.

"About?" she asked.

It had been an hour since our meal, and I finally admitted, "The food from Nora's was excellent. A bit pricey, though."

She was crossing her arms and had turned away. "Yes, and I told you I'd pay." Her face turned to me briefly as she said, "I invited you, after all."

The server had slipped me the bill, which I'd paid automatically, before Yukirei could do so.

Holding up my hands I said, "Okay. My mistake. You can pay next time, okay?"

A smile bloomed and she rushed ahead a bit. "I'll hold you to that." Yukirei basically skipped the rest of the way.

What's gotten into her?

When the door closed behind me, she said, "I need to go freshen up, if that's okay?"

"Sure," I said.

Sitting down on the couch I leaned into the cushions and relaxed. "I'm stuffed."

"How was your date?" Sarah asked politely.

I snorted. "It wasn't a date. We just went out for a bit."

Sarah raised a brow. "Are you sure? Her Imperial Right Honorable, Yukirei Truval made a special trip to see you. Then she invited you out to the town beneath the school. It appears you went to eat, which you seem to have accepted gladly. The smile she had as you returned said she really enjoyed herself." She paused to let her words sink in. "Not to mention, you *did* previously agree to go on an Accord with her."

Pursing my lips I fidgeted with my fingers. Revisiting things in my mind from a different perspective, I noticed she smelled of honey and cinnamon. Her lips had gloss on them; she was even wearing eyeshadow and mascara.

Heat spread through my chest and I fiddled with the end of my braid. *Crap.*

Yukirei sat across from me and smiled.

When we first met, she'd been a standoffish tsundere who I believed was there to steal Gideon away. Turned out she was also mildly interested in me, but she was so abrasive that it made it difficult for me to see her in a positive light.

"Y-Yukirei, did we just go on a date?" I asked. *Please say no. I'm not sure how I feel here.*

"Yes, and I look forward to the next one, where you let me pay."

Double crap.

CHAPTER EIGHT

ECHOES FROM THE PAST

WHEN MY CLASSES started a few days later, I was enduring physical training first thing in the morning. Watching my steam-like breath helped keep my interest at first, but after a while it grew old.

Although I'd run over two hundred miles an hour in the past, when you're running with a sense of urgency, or at dark, the effects of over one-hundred-ninety-degree breath are just an afterthought.

My mind drifted to other things. *How did I miss that was a date!? I feel so stupid, and even agreed to another Accord!*

On top of the burning sensation from my run, another warmth settled over my cheeks. Yukirei had held my hand most of the time and dragged me from store to store after our meal. Anyone watching us would've easily seen what was going on.

Did some of my ASD carry over from my past life? I should have noticed we were on a date. Recalling the sparkle of the glitter in her lip gloss made me shake my head. *Why can't I stop thinking about her perfume?*

As I finished my third lap around Ersta's major track including its fields for agriculture, I wondered more about Yukirei. *She's older than I am, but so is Gideon.* Though the steam on my arms from my sweat was cooling me off quickly, I still managed to blush despite that. *I entered an acp hoth with her to satisfy the expectations Mom and Dad set. While I've always assumed that it would be easy to break it off, I'm wondering now if it will really be that easy. I have Gideon, he's* all *I need, and we're getting married soon.* Remembering the *soon* part a chill suffused my neck chest, and shoulders. *Gods, I'm getting married soon!*

Slowing to a jog to the gymnasium, my teacher approached me. He had the physique of a retired sports star turned commentator. Every so often, I swore he flexed his pecs for no reason, other than to show he could.

"Imperial Lady Anessa," he said with a bright smile. "Great job! Though you're sweating; that's something most cultivators only do to avoid combustion. Your breath is steady and you do not appear to be harmed in any way. Starting tomorrow, I want you to push yourself harder. Your speed puts you at the top of your age group for your Realm, but it's not until you push yourself that gains are truly in reach."

He paused as I cooled further.

Did he just casually say that cultivators would combust *if we didn't sweat literal steam?*

"Do you think you could go ten percent faster tomorrow? You'd still complete three laps, but I think it should take you just under four hours instead of over four."

"I'll try," I said.

"That's Sir to you, Imperial Lady Anessa," he snapped.

"I'll try," I said and intoned, "*sir.*"

"No need to be cheeky," he said, smiled, and flexed. "Now then. If you're able to complete it tomorrow while being only lightly winded, you go harder. We'll keep doing that until we find your breaking point."

I groaned, and he just winked at me.

"Okay, sir," I said, then sighed. "Sounds like a plan."

"Great!" he said enthusiastically.

Walking away from him I shook my head. *That guy's weird.*

"Yeah, but he is quite the beefcake," said a familiar voice.

Darting my eyes around, moving my head I looked all around myself.

I asked, "Who said that?"

"You tell me," replied the voice.

"Gods, is that you Trish?"

"Ding, ding, ding!" Trish said.

"What the nether…"

"You might want to stop answering me aloud, people are starting to stare."

Taking stock of my situation, I looked around. My teacher was standing there with both eyebrows raised, as though he was wondering about me. He followed with a left, and then right pec pop.

"Ahh… beefcake," she said.

Stop that, I chastised. *You're making me look.* Hearing a voice from my past life, one I'd only had dreams about up until now, was disconcerting.

"I don't mind looking," she admitted.

Face-palming, while taking one last glance, I thought, *Well, I do! Since when do you have a thing for "beefcakes" anyway?*

"Since ever. You weren't the only thing that caught my eye in our past lives. It's something we share in common."

Yeah, sure. My stomach churned. *I do somewhat like boys and girls, don't I?* Power walking towards my dormitory I thought, *But I don't need this right now! Who cares if I'm bi.*

Trish's teasing voice said, *"I never said either of us were bi."*

What? I wondered, *What the hell else is there?*

"Pan," she said nonchalantly.

What, you're saying that I'm cookware?

A sense that she drew her hand over her face came through whatever connection we had together. *"No, pansexual."* She sighed audibly, a neat trick for someone with no lungs or body. *"Seriously, cookware?"*

Excuse me for not being up on terminology I haven't heard in over a decade! With magical gender-switching rings, the very notion of sexuality here is that people just "are" and there's no judgment.

"Yes, that part of Anfang is freeing, isn't it? It helps you get a feel for what matters, and who you are, without fear of persecution."

Nearing the gate to the Imperial Royal Dormitories, I nodded to the guard as he opened the gate for me.

I could do without the polyamorous part, though.

Trish laughed and it echoed in my head. Instead of reassuring me, a chill ran down my spine. *"Come on. You have been thinking about it more seriously lately. Despite Gideon's loyal nature, Yukirei's face, with special emphasis on her glossy lips, keeps running through your head."*

"Hey!" I shouted, drawing a few eyes to me. *Damn it.* My cheeks burned and I opened the door to my personal dorm suite.

"*What?*" Trish said as I entered. "*If you're so curious about them, why not try them out?*"

Gods Trish, don't make me think about that. I took a seat on the couch and put my hands over my face to calm down. *I haven't even kissed Gideon yet!*

"*But you* have *thought about it,*" Trish teased.

Interlacing my fingers I held my hands to the sky. *Eloria, I've been granted a spiritual companion, and instead of helping me along my journey, she merely taunts me about kissing. Please help me keep my thoughts pure.* Despite being Eloria's designated champion, I wasn't so much religious as looking for a way to silence the new voice in my head.

Standing, I sought out Sarah to clear my mind. She was in my bedroom holding up a fairly ornate, sheer shift with a low neckline and an intricate embroidery pattern.

As I entered, she smiled and folded the garment. It was so transparent that I could see the outline and skin tone of her hand through the front and back.

Huh, she has odd tastes. Though it's a bit short for her.

Then, to my horror, she placed the garment into a small trunk at her side which already contained some of my clothes.

There's no way that was mine! Heat licked my collar. *I'd never wear that!*

"Good morning, Anessa," Sarah said. "Did your run go well?" Before I could respond she continued, "Tania will be in shortly to assist with your bath. After you're done, we are headed to the Imperial Carlyle Estates." She let that sink in. "After which you and Gideon will be wed."

Shit. Her words ablated everything I was worried about, replacing them with a far more immediate issue. *I'm getting married today.* Hope rose in my chest and I looked to Sarah. "It'll take about sixteen days to get home, right?"

She shook her head. "If time weren't of the essence, that would perhaps be true." With her hand on her chest she added, "But I will be escorting you and our lord Gideon to the estates personally. We should arrive four hours after we depart."

Dang, she's still faster than I am.

"It would be faster, but their Imperial Graces have said it was necessary for me to be able to attend to your needs, so I'll be traveling at a more leisurely pace."

A lot faster. Her admission that three hundred miles an hour was her "leisurely" pace made me scowl.

As I took my bath, I said to Tania, "I thought today was going to be further away." I blew bubbles at the water's surface in my frustration.

"I understand, Lady Anessa," she said softly. Gently scrubbing my arm, beneath the modesty cloth, she said, "Her Imperial High Grace, Lily was excited, I hear, and has pushed things along somewhat briskly."

"I get it, she's excited because I'm her only daughter, but I think I'm too young for this," I said and dunked my head underwater for a second.

When I came back up, Tania said, "You're plenty old enough, my Imperial Lady." She smiled. "Perhaps it's best to not think about what ifs and focus on what is?"

That earned her a tilted head as I processed her words. "Yeah, maybe so. I'm mostly worried about what happens right after we're married. I know Mom's said there's no pressure, but is that actually true?"

"Probably not," Tania said to my surprise.

My voice cracked, "Oh?"

"There's the conjugal duty by law."

"Yeah, that." I sat up and pooled some water in my hand. "That's what I'm worried about."

"There's the Imperial Oversight, from His Imperial Majesty, Jorin. And the Dynastic Oversight by the Imperial Royal Council."

With wide eyes I stared at Tania. "That's... not helpful."

She bowed. "My apologies. I was merely answering your question. While there are pressures involved, Her Imperial High Grace's own view has always been to leave it up to you." She held up a hand. "They are the what-ifs." Then held up the other, "Your choice and your mother's acceptance are what is."

Dropping back with my chin in the water, I said, "Thanks."

"It is my pleasure," Tania said and ushered me to stand.

Sarah called out, "Anessa, our lord is already waiting in your joint carriage." She curtsied, stretching the cloth on her form-fitting pants.

I stared.

Her outfit was something I'd never seen her wear before. Her shirt hugged her frame and showed almost no skin. Even her hair was tucked into an odd cap that covered her eyes. The outfit reminded me of long-distance running gear mixed with swimwear. "I am not saying this to pressure you to hurry, but I did want you to know he is ready to go."

I smiled trying to not laugh at her. Changing topics, I said, "I look forward to seeing him on our trip."

"Sorry, but a joint carriage has an air-gap between two different cabins," she said. "It is usually customary for the husband-to-be to arrive under his own power, but we are on a strict schedule, so he will need to ride with us."

Slouching, I said, "That sucks." A particularly pretty face entered my mind's eye. "Will Yukirei be coming?"

"No," Sarah said. "This is intended to be a private event. Most likely Yukirei doesn't even know about it." She bowed her head. "I requested that our lord keep the details from her."

Pursing my lips I said, "Um, I may have mentioned something about it to Portia. I didn't know it was such a secret."

Sarah's eyes darted up to me. "That presents a problem. I'll see to it she joins us for our trip." She paused. "To show her support."

Arching my brow at her I wondered, *Yukirei, one of my possible future metamours and an Imperial Lady herself, isn't permitted to join us, but Portia, a commoner, can?*

Before I could ask her any follow-up questions she darted off.

Crap. Part of me was saddened that Yukirei wouldn't be there, though at the same time I was a little glad.

"Polyamory is normal here. It'll take a while to get used to," Trish piped in.

Great, I was almost *convinced you weren't real when you went silent for a while.*

"Hey now, I'm very real." An image of Trish crossing her arms entered my head. *"And don't you forget it."* She opened an eye and "looked" my way. *"Monogamy just isn't normal here. If anything, there's going to be pressure for you to seek others beyond Gideon. It's okay to be confused."*

This version of you is better, I thought. *You don't always have to tease me.*

She gave me a wolfish grin. *"But I do enjoy it."*

Within ten minutes I was ushered into my cabin in the shared carriage. It looked like your usual stretch carriage, with a section missing from the center. As I stepped inside, I saw that Portia was already inside, white as a ghost.

"Hey," I said.

"Hi!" she said exuberantly.

"Are you okay?"

"Yeah, just nervous."

I laughed. "Isn't being nervous my job?"

"Yeah, I suppose so," she grinned.

"I'm getting cold feet, I think."

She looked down at my feet with an expression of concern. "Should we tell your Lady's maids?"

"No," I laughed, "That's a figure of speech. Telling them wouldn't do anything. I just mean I'm nervous about going through with this. Despite it being something I cannot avoid."

Portia nodded in understanding.

Tania entered as Sarah popped her head into the cabin.

Sarah said, "Are you ready?"

I gulped. *If I said no, would it matter?*

Knowing the answer, I just nodded.

CHAPTER NINE
THE VEILS OF CHANGE

FOUR HOURS LATER, as we approached the Imperial Carlyle Estates, I felt a little saddened that there was no outward indication that we were getting married – no decorations whatsoever. It drove home that this was really a private event.

Looking over to Portia, I saw that she'd been dolled up during our trip.

Tania had changed her entire outfit. As a commoner, she was sadly not afforded the privacy I was. The only small mercy I could grant her was to look away as my Lady's maid unceremoniously stripped away Portia's modest, layered garment.

She was being remarkably gracious about the process, considering that she had been dragged into the carriage on just a few minutes' notice.

"Sorry about earlier," I said to her.

She held up her hands "It's okay! The fact that you're permitting me to join you is enough. I can't imagine going through all *that* on a daily basis, though."

Giving Tania the stink eye, she turned her head away.

"What you just went through was a little more aggressive than I am used to, but yes, getting used to this kind of service was a change."

Portia asked, "A change? Haven't they done this for you all of your life?"

The fact that our family took over for the Greensbaro Imperial Duchy isn't a secret. Is our original station not widely known?

Tania came in with a save. "What Imperial Lady Anessa means to say is, when she was younger her mother, Her Imperial High Grace, Lily Carlyle," she held out a hand toward me, "had our Lady do many things for herself. As a means of experiencing life from a lower's view."

What? I thought then realized her "assistance" could paint the wrong picture.

"Ah!" Portia said and held up a finger. "Is that why you act more like a commoner than an Imperial Lady at times?"

"Do I act that strangely?" I asked with an arched brow, taken aback.

With widened eyes she held up her hands. "Oh no, I didn't mean it in a bad way. Your manners are impeccable. It's just that–" She paused, and her eyes darted around the cabin as though she were desperately trying to find the words. "You're rather candid with me," she said hesitantly. "I appreciate it, but from my limited dealings with other nobility, that is quite uncommon."

"Oh, I suppose you're right. I can be a bit too honest."

Our carriage door opened, and Sarah greeted us. There wasn't a drop of sweat on her, despite having moved far faster than I could hope to without a break.

Show-off.

"Please follow me, Lady Anessa," she said.

Before Portia could follow, Tania stepped out and said, "This way, miss," guiding Portia firmly.

Sarah led me through the main estate into my bathroom. They'd already prepared a bath for me, which smelled of strong minty lilac.

After we entered, she exited, leaving me in there alone. A few minutes later, my Daughter Envoy, Daughter Hy, entered.

Giving me a deep curtsy she said, "We shall see to your bath." She stood and clapped her hands, before I could wonder about her phrasing of "we." A trio of daughters from the church's Scripture's Children entered.

They worked so quickly that by the time I was in the water I was almost dizzy from their flurried efforts. They left just as quickly as they'd arrived.

Goodness, this is moving too fast.

"Now then," Daughter Hy said. "You relax while I perform the ritual of bonding." She pulled out a folding fan and held it to the ceiling, then flicked it open.

What the heck is she talking about?

She started to pace around my bathtub, caught in a dance to a silent rhythm, wavering the fan erratically, yet in a way that seemed purposeful.

After a while I lost interest, and tried to relax. Until I noticed flecks of light rising from the surface of my hand. On it was a white chrysanthemum, almost humming to the same flow of my Envoy.

She stopped, and the symbol faded.

Reversing directions, she continued to yet another unheard beat. After an equally long and drawn-out moment, my right hand did much the same, in the shape of a gray hammer. Despite the reverence they had for Eloria's moniker of death, her crafting persona almost buzzed with energy.

As Daughter Hy's rhythm slowed, another fan joined hers, made of light. It followed her moves impeccably. Another minute passed, and another fan joined in. By the time she finished, there were seventeen of them, eighteen if you counted the first in the Envoy's hand. Two of them were hard to see, flickering in and out and somewhat hazy.

The spectral fans spiraled around the tub, each higher than the last. Before they vanished, it hit me: each one was a different color, and there was one for each kind of essence, even neutral. It made me wonder, *What does Daughter Hy's fan represent?*

She snapped her fan closed, and the copies dissipated like wisps of steam. Her hand grabbed the edge of the tub. She was drenched in sweat from her hairline to her collar. Letting out a shaky breath, she said, "That takes a lot out of me, my apologies Your Imperial High Grace."

"It's okay," I assured her, not really understanding what was going on or what it did to her.

In a minute she had leveled out her breathing and stood. She gave me a curtsy. "I'll send in your attendants now."

I guess if the "ritual" is any guide, Daughter Hy knows about my connection to Eloria's moniker of Death.

Before she could leave, I asked, "You said that was a ritual of bonding. What does that mean?"

"Champions have key moments in their lives. Shortly before or after those events, it's important to reaffirm your connection to your Patron." She closed her eyes and prayed. "These include the beginning of a union, where two merge, and your yin is lost. When you have a child," her tone gained a hint of sorrow, "or after the death of a loved one. At these critical junctures, these rituals ensure that your bond with your patron is at its peak. To give you strength, and guide you on your way."

What I didn't tell Daughter Hy, was that despite a lingering sense of wonder over the light show, I didn't really *feel* any different. She was the last person who I would want to hear that.

Also, what's a yin?

▼ ▼ ▼

As Sarah and Tania were helping me dress, I asked, "What was that whole thing about, Sarah?"

"The ritual?" she asked.

I started to say, "Yeah. There was a glowi–"

She held a gloved finger against my lips. "Sorry, but what happened during the ritual was for you alone." Shaking her head she added, "Unless Her Goddess Eloria grants you permission, you must not talk about it. We can talk about its purpose, though, in a general sense."

"Okay, so what's the benefit of reaffirming my connection to Eloria?"

Tania answered for her while applying the base layer of makeup over my face. "The most important connection in your life, is that between you and Her Goddess Eloria."

"Wait, even more important than my connection to Gideon?" I asked.

"Certainly," Tania said.

I shook my head. "It's difficult to believe my connection could be that strong."

"Close your eyes," she said. "This might tingle."

As I complied, she tapped my nose with the fixing agent and the makeup base she'd used went through some kind of chemical change. It was difficult to avoid twitching or scratching the stuff off. But I knew that if I did, we'd have to all start over.

When I was a baby by most standards, my not-sister Veronica applied this very makeup to my face as a practice run. It might seem like an odd thing to do, but I'd been speaking since day one, so she treated me like the little adult I was.

At the time, she was planning for her future marriage to the very same emperor who started this dumb war. That marriage never took place. Since she had finished with her makeup, she practiced further on my face, but was interrupted by my step-mother, Julilah. She took over and did a wondrous job, but it did little to ease the tension between us.

"Okay, you can move," said Tania finally.

"Thank the gods," I said and opened my mouth, hoping to scratch an itch without actually doing so. It didn't really work.

Thinking back to the ritual, I asked Sarah, "Can I ask you what a yin is?"

Tania stopped and looked at her, before picking up additional paint to apply to my cheeks.

"Depends on the context," she said cooly.

"Something was said about the beginning of a union and my yin being lost."

Tania, in the process of drawing a curl on my cheek, jerked the brush all the way to my ear in an abrupt motion.

Pulling away I looked at her with a quirked brow. "That didn't feel right. Is everything okay?"

A faint pink bit her cheeks and she coughed. "Yes, everything is fine, but that was indeed a mistake." She looked at Sarah, "She was about to answer your question."

When I had asked my question, Sarah had been brushing my hair, and her hand had stopped cold. "Well… a yin is something you hold to yourself, unbroken since birth. Once a union is formed, you share it with your new kin."

Tilting my head to my side I said, "Like giving my heart to Gideon?"

"Something like that," Sarah said slowly.

"Would Gideon give me his yin, too?"

She stifled a smile. "No, not exactly. He would give you his yang."

A word that rhymed with yang made the intent clear. *Gods, are they talking about my "first time?"*

I blushed from my collar bone to my ears. "Could you confirm if this gesture is what you mean?"

I started to make the usual motion with both of my hands, but Tania quickly covered them with her own. "Your Imperial High Grace, Anessa Jean Carlyle. That is *not* behavior fitting of a lady of your station!"

Her chastisement made me blush deeper. "Sarah, was that what you meant?"

"Mhmm," she replied.

In the mirror I could tell she was choking back a laugh.

She likes bawdy humor, I take it?

"Tania," I said calmly. "If I had used a specific word in asking, would that have been more becoming of a lady?"

She sighed. "Not exactly, no. I suppose being indirect in every scenario isn't always helpful, especially if you are unfamiliar with a term. However, a vulgar display like that is not acceptable. Whispers only carry so far, but that was visible to everyone in the room."

Taking a second to look around, I confirmed that there was no one here but us. "I think we're fine, it's just you two."

"But remember that Her Goddess Eloria is watching."

Recalling Eloria's comment that I was "interesting," when we first met seven years ago, I countered, "I think she'd probably find it funny."

Tania curled her lips over her teeth and closed her eyes.

Uh oh, she did not *find that amusing.*

"If you were anyone other than her champion, I would ask that you pray for forgiveness, and likely even tell Her Imperial High Grace, Lily about that comment."

Furrowing my brows, I said, "I was being honest based on my interactions with her. Please do not use the threat of tattling on me to my Mom as a deterrent. If you feel the need to tell her, you should do so."

Her anger and defense crumbled. She bowed, and said, "I'm sorry, I will not do so again."

With a sigh I said, "I'm not that mad, but I didn't feel that was a nice way to go about expressing your concern. I may say and do things at times that are strange, but if Her Goddess Eloria is upset with me, I'm sure she would tell me."

"Understood," Tania said. "You are right."

"I don't know if I'm right," I said thoughtfully and put my hand on my chest. "But when I talked to her, she didn't seem that scary. Deeply remorseful, but not vengeful."

All Tania could do was nod, then she went back to painting my face.

Damn. The spark in her eyes I'd started to see in her was gone. *It's going to take a while before she opens back up to me.*

Instead of being walked into a chapel or something similar for a ceremony, they led me to a bright room with several people I didn't know.

Oddly, there were several easels set up, ready for artists. The canvases were smooth, despite the grainy texture.

What are these for?

Off to the side, one of the people was holding up their hand, but lowered it and looked away when I noticed.

"Sarah, what's going on?" I asked quietly.

She whispered. "The master painters are setting up to capture their subjects from multiple angles."

"I can see that," I said flatly. "Am I here to literally watch paint dry as they capture their study?"

"No," she drew the word out. "Not exactly."

I glared at her.

Gideon rounded the corner, and I briefly panicked.

"Wait," my voice pitched. "Am I allowed to see him now?"

"Yes, why?" She seemed slightly puzzled.

With a huff I thought, *I almost asked about an Earthen tradition of Gideon not seeing me before the wedding. If it weren't for Trish and my connection with her, I'd almost think my memories of my time on Earth were a dream.*

"Anessa," Gideon said, shocking me out of my inner turmoil. He fidgeted with his collar and our eyes met for a moment.

"Hey," I said and smiled.

For a moment I admired his outfit, a brilliant teal shirt with a vibrant gold inlay down the center that was mixed with fire-orange accents. The broad swoop that went over his shoulders and collar gave the impression that he had been blessed by a sun god. *I wonder if there even is a sun god on Anfang.*

"Sarah-Knecht von Anessa," Gideon said, "what was it we were doing here, again? No one has told me anything."

Though the manner in which he chose to address Sarah was correct, I narrowed my eyes at him. There were more than a few people in the room that started to whisper at the Knecht marker.

Before Sarah could answer him an elderly man wearing a black square top cap approached us. His maroon outfit was impeccable, despite his hunched shoulders and overall bad posture. "Good, you're both here." He gestured forward in front of us toward a six-inch pedestal, or a miniature stage.

It was then that the dynamics of the room's arrangement became apparent. Their subject of study was us, and I was instantly glad I was wearing makeup to hide my embarrassment at not noticing. *Okay, great job missing the obvious.*

The older man stroked a long handlebar mustache that extended beyond his chin and looked between us. "Which one of you is the Carlyle child?" His eyes stopped on Gideon. "Are you that Oliver boy?"

"No, I am Gideon V-," He stopped himself and cleared his throat. "Let me start again. You may call me Lord Gideon Ignotus, sir...?"

"Henfield. I'm the grandmaster painter," he waved over at the others, "in charge of these lumps."

His comment got a few chuckles, and a couple of shaking heads among those moving to their easels.

"Ah," Henfield said and turned his attention to me. "You must be Anessa, then." He then looked between us once more. "Equals, subordinate, or as he was?"

It took me a second to figure out what he was asking and I tilted my head, then answered. "Equals."

He sighed. "Huh, equals. Right." Walking off and muttering I caught him say, "The new generation and their equality. Such drivel." Pulling out a stepstool, he pulled it up onto the platform and said, "Sit." Shaking his head he amended, "No, strike that. Stand."

His admission that I was too short to sit on a step stool while Gideon sat made me frown.

He's not wrong, but I hate reminders that I'm so... vertically challenged.

Henfield mumbled, "I suppose such a little woman needs a protector."

That comment made me groan. "Really?" I whispered.

"What?" Gideon asked.

"Nothing, he seems to think I need protecting." I crossed my arms.

The old man smiled. "What, are you saying that you protect him?"

I'd been looking at Gideon, not realizing that Henfield could hear me. With a fake smile I merely nodded.

"Sure, sure." Henfield waved his hand at me. "Now then, Lord Gideon, please sit down and place your legs over the edge."

Over the next five minutes the grandmaster painter directed us into position on the podium. He was exacting on where my hands would go. How high my head would be above Gideon's. Despite stating we were equals, because I held a High moniker and he would become a consort, I had to stand with my chin above his head.

The next four hours were grueling. Throughout the entire process, I pondered the irony that Anfang had what amounted to twenty-first-century video calls, but had not figured out nineteenth-century camera technology.

It took sheer force of will for me to make it through without moving. Stretching afterwards I said, "Thank the gods that is over." I shook my right hand that had long since gone numb. *If I were a normal eleven-year-old, that would've been impossible.*

"Yeah, an eleven-year-old can't sit still that long. They'd be twitching to run around after half an hour." She paused, then added, *"It's a shame though."*

"What is?"

"That Yukirei couldn't be here. Your mind drifted to her more than a few times."

I sighed. *Sometimes you are a bit of a dick, you know?*

"But I'm a fun dick."

Her comment made me chuckle aloud. *True, but don't make me laugh when others are around. They'll think I'm crazy.*

"Girl you so crazy, you hear voices in your head."

Rolling my eyes, I peeked at Henfield's easel. Despite running around like a chicken with his head cut off, his rendition was indeed a masterful, almost lifelike depiction of us. What's more, he didn't use oils or pastel but *chalk.*

"Wow," I said, then looked around at the others. Theirs were barely actual studies that focused on parts of Gideon and me.

"Yes, wow," Henfield said. "These lumps will use this to refine their compositions."

Curiosity about part of the image poked at me until I asked, "Why is my face so... pale?" Motioning over my makeup I added, "The pattern is all different, too."

He snorted. "If you walk through the Imperial Royal archives, what do you think you'll see?"

"Treasures?"

"Portraits," he retorted and tapped the canvas on my face, "with faces that are this color. While what you're in an azure paint mask, it wasn't always so."

"And the elemental markings on my face?"

He raised one immaculately-cut caterpillar eyebrow at me. "Well... information is power. Want to kill a noble?"

His words made my stomach churn and I pursed my lips.

"You study them. The information on your face would be priceless intel for someone who wished you harm." He placed a long, but neatly-trimmed, nail near my cheek. "At least that would generally be the case. If I painted this accurately, they would know you could handle everything they threw at you."

I don't know about that.

Gideon stood at my side and asked, "How long until they will be done?"

"Hmm," he stroked his pencil-thin beard on his chin. "Two months?"

My eyes widened. "That long?"

Henfield smacked Gideon's hand, which I now saw was reaching out to touch the canvas.

"Yes, that long. If we had more time with you, it might be less, but–" Henfield shook his head and motioned over his work, "four *hours* is barely enough for this mess." He gave us a shooing gesture. "Now run along. You two have some marrying to do, don't you?"

Awful humble for such a great artist. A bit prickly, though.

▼ ▼ ▼

"This way, Imperial Lady Anessa," Tania said, gesturing forward with one hand and her other on my back.

Gideon had already been hustled away by his own manservants.

Great, now what are we doing? I thought. Tania led me until we stopped near the entrance to our medium-sized great room.

"Can you believe our college apartments could both fit inside that one room?" Trish asked.

Yeah, noble life has kind of skewed things. Though only this main estate was as large as Naia's home before it sold. To help me frame my prior life from my current life, I'd started referring to my previous mother by her name. After all, I was, technically, no longer related to her.

"Man, this is so awkward. We're in your own home, yet it's like waiting at your graduation ceremony for your name to be called."

I snickered. She was right. The small gesture drew a few glances from the servants milling about, so I turned my attention elsewhere.

Remind me to not react to you, no offense.

She said, *"None taken, looks like you're up."*

Sarah approached from behind and said, "Are you ready?"

How the heck did Trish know about that? I wondered.

Once the doors opened, the low chatter in the room silenced and a music I'd almost missed continued unabated. There was no tradition of procession music on Anfang. My Dad walking me down the aisle was also simply not a thing.

I wish he could have been here.

"Yeah, war is stupid," Trish agreed.

The first few steps were easy, no different from when I entered the room on what would've been my betrothal announcement. After that however my stomach started doing somersaults and a bitter taste developed at the back of my throat. *I feel like I'm going to be sick.*

"Hold it together!"

There were fewer than fifteen people in attendance. To my left was Una Varn, Gideon's Mom. She looked a bit gaunt today, a striking difference from seven years ago. My Mom and her latest spouse, my half-sibling Nicole, were whispering to one another on Una's left. My half-siblings were in the second row. Lana, Julilah's daughter, was fixing Lom's bowtie in the second row. His bristled cat tail shot straight up behind him.

Kristine and Julilah, my step-mothers, sat in the front on the right. Despite their contrasting temperaments, they carried themselves much the same. Not a speck of dust on either, nor a stitch out of place. Behind them were my step-siblings, Veronica and Marcus. An old man who reminded me of the Colonel from a chicken restaurant chain on Earth sat next to an oddly weepy Portia.

Taking my place, I finally stood next to Gideon. Swallowing my concerns I steadied my breathing.

A very ornately dressed man from the Scriptures Children stood in front of us. His vestment and octagonal hat were both trimmed with gold.

"Thank you all for coming today," he started. "Marriage is a sacred bond. A…"

The man droned on for at least a quarter hour explaining the institution of marriage as though none of us knew what it was. By the end of it, my nerves had calmed. So despite the bore he was, I was thankful for the reprieve from my thoughts.

"At this time, Daughter Envoy Hy will come forward to showcase the bond of elements and bless this union."

What is this? The details for the actual marriage were obvious to me, but there had been no mention of a "bond of elements" ritual or a blessing.

A few Scripture's Children daughters came into the room, carrying a series of candles. Each girl was wearing the same style of robe and wore a thick opaque veil over their faces. They placed the candlesticks throughout the room and departed just as quickly as they'd arrived.

Man, it's like being part of the Scripture's Children is all about efficiency and being unseen.

Daughter Hy waited for the doors to close before breaking out of her statuesque pose. Her fan was back in her hand, and she had a far more graceful and deliberate dance to perform this time around. In no particular order, she would approach each of the unlit candles and wave her fan across them. Without any other effort, they would ignite.

Once again, each matched the color of the elements, except instead of a normal flame, a stock-still figure of light bloomed out of their wicks: me.

The brown, gray, and black candles each had a pair. A smaller, yet still accurate depiction arose in the form of my groom.

"Wow," Gideon whispered. "Those flames are kind of large, aren't they?"

"I see images of you and me in them," I said succinctly.

He squinted and rubbed his eyes. "I guess so, it's not very clear for me."

Glancing around the room, I saw that probably most others couldn't see what I saw either. Nonetheless, there were a few in attendance that reacted to the candles. Mom's face bore a frown whereas Julilah looked bored. The others in my family, who we knew to be mortal, were praying.

I bet they can't see it at all. Acting on my hunch I asked Gideon, "What do you see in the blue fire?"

"There's a blue one?" he said, slowly panning his eyes over the room.

For whatever reason, people on Anfang could only see elemental light they were attuned to; having every element made me a stand-out. *I wish everyone could see what I do. If even for just today, it's uncomfortable being alone.*

A loud, almost booming voice, filled my head, "So it shall be."

The sound made me cover my ears.

The gasps around me made the origin of the voice clear, *Crap, that was Eloria.*

All of the Scripture's children, save for Daughter Hy, had prostrated themselves to one of the candles in their immediate vision. Julilah's boredom had been replaced by what was either anger or concern. Mom was gripping her hierogram for Eloria, placing it to her forehead in prayer.

Double crap. I had to go and send up a request during a bloody ritual. Of course Eloria would hear it!

A faint, almost ghostlike giggle traipsed through my head, giving me a chill. This was not the voice of Trish, which seemed to live in my head. It was a stark reminder that even my thoughts, beyond prayers, were open to the goddess.

In a handful of seconds, the candles all winked out, leaving a rich colored soot to trail out of the candles. Despite the wonder in Gideon's eyes, there was something deeper, shared by everyone present.

Fear.

Are they afraid of Eloria's show? Or since I was the image in the flames, me? I've been her champion for seven years. What's changed, and why now of all times does she make such a show. Surely it's not as simple as me asking for others to see, is it?

Daughter Hy approached us and handed Gideon and me a small fan each. "May this union be forever, and bright; only through death and reincarnation should you part." She then wrapped the handles of the fans together above the parts where we held them.

Thanks to Eloria's display, my nerves were once again a mess and I bit back the bile in my throat. When Kristine came up to officiate the *actual* marriage, it seemed rather anticlimactic by comparison. Though it was still awkward to hold Gideon's hands in front of so many others.

"Your Imperial Most Honorable, Gideon Ignotus, will you…"

After we both affirmed our intentions and provided our verbal consent to marry, Kristine said, "May the Ignotus become Carlyle, and our Westwood Empire grow strong and prosper." Up to this point she'd been her usual stoic self. Before she continued, she smiled. "You may now seal the marriage before these witnesses."

As Gideon lifted my veil, my heart raced. First he kissed my left cheek, then my right, and finally my forehead. I closed my eyes as he went in for my lips, but to my mixed relief and chagrin he merely gave me the briefest of pecks.

"I present to you," Kristine said and held our hands up for the small group to see, "Anessa and Gideon Carlyle!"

Despite her enthusiasm, a wet blanket had definitely been thrown over the evening by the goddess' intervention. Even Mom was subdued in her reaction.

Great. Note to self: don't ask Eloria to pipe in. Remembering she could literally hear my thoughts, I added, *Err… no offense. Their reactions are just awkward.*

▼ ▼ ▼

At the meal afterwards, Portia and I were finally able to connect for the first time in almost ten hours.

Her eyes were puffy from her emotional overflow during the ceremony.

"What's gotten into you, anyway?" I asked with some surprise. "You're not usually like this. Got a weakness for weddings?"

She ushered me forward. When I leaned in, she whispered, "I can get married to Max."

Pulling away I blinked a few times, and asked, "Can you give me a little more than that?"

This time she leaned in towards me. "I have promised to take the date you really married Gideon to my grave. And in exchange for my silence," she dropped her voice further, "I'll be confirmed as gentry next month!"

Taking her hands I smiled. "Congratulations!" Hugging her I added, "That's great news. Promise you'll invite me?"

Portia pursed her lips and paused to consider her words. "If I'm allowed, I will."

I said, "Okay." I couldn't ask for more than that.

"May I borrow her?" Gideon asked Portia.

"Of course," she said, and smiled.

Waving I said, "We'll talk later."

"I have something for you," he said after I sat down at our table.

"Funny you should say that," I said, and pulled out my necklace with Eloria's hierogram. "Mom gave me this a few years back." Dropping it into his hand I continued. "It used to be hers, but she's since replaced it. Since we're connected now, I want you to have it."

"Thank you," he said gravely. He held his hand over it and put it around his neck. Then he pulled out a trinket of his own. Its edges were roughed up and its threads faded with the passage of time. "This was my Mom's. It's called the moon's calling. As near as I've been able to tell, it's been around for a few thousand years."

"Ah, is that why it's red and blue intertwined?" I asked.

Gideon nodded. "It's intended to be passed to your true love." Fastening it around my wrist he added, "Mom took hers back from Dad when he attacked me years ago."

True love, huh? I thought and blushed. His eyes drew me in, as I brushed my thumb over the bracelet.

The moment passed when Mom coughed and said, "Anessa, we need to talk about this evening."

"What about it?"

She looked pointedly at Gideon. "Alone," she added and nodded to him as he stood without hesitation. Once we were alone, she took out an S-ROB and activated it to give us the privacy we needed. "After your reception, we will move onto another ceremony involving you and Gideon."

"Yeah, what's that one involve?" I asked, then patted my palm with my fist. "Right, vows?"

Mom gave me a sad smile. "No honey, not vows. That's between you two. Your Daughter Envoy Hy will bless your bed, and–"

Before she could finish my eyes widened and I shouted, "I thought you said–"

She sighed and covered my mouth, out of instinct, I guess, because no amount of shouting would escape an S-ROB's field. "Quiet down please, and let me finish."

When I reluctantly nodded, she removed her hand.

"Now then, I will continue. You will change your clothes. Daughter Envoy Hy will remain in the room until both you and Gideon have sat on your bed. After this, she will then retire and you two will be alone for the night."

Leaning in, Mom whispered, "The intent of the ceremony is obvious, but once you two are alone, what happens is your call. That is all I can say."

Got it. She's saying that whether I give Gideon my yin is up to me.

"Do know that due to… the rejection we gave a certain imperial royal, we must follow every detail of this process by the book."

All I could do is nod as my cheeks heated up.

Not long after that Tania and Sarah guided me out of the dining hall to my bedroom in the main estate, though I didn't expect our entourage to also include Mom, Kristine, and my half-sisters Nicole and Lana.

We all entered my bedroom and the ladies changed me into the sheer outfit Sarah had packed. I was given a robe, or houppelande, that opened in the front for modesty.

Then, to my surprise, Lana and Nicole took my arms and legs and lifted me up.

"What the heck!" I laughed.

They carried me to my bed and I was in a fit of giggles at how silly it all was.

Once they'd sat me down, Lana, Nicole each gave me a hug and departed.

Kristine tarried for a moment and when I held open my arms she rushed forward and gave me a bear hug. "Good night little kit," she whispered.

Kit?

Mom's parting words after her hug were, "May this union bring never-ending joy. Don't worry about anything, okay?"

I nodded.

Daughter Hy was standing at the edge of the room.

"Woah," Gideon said shakily, from just outside the room.

My bedroom door opened on its own, and Gideon floated in. The gentleman who reminded me of a certain Colonel hobbled in with a cane. Using his free hand, he gestured and moved Gideon toward the bed.

Once he was in place, the man waved his hand and Gideon dropped like a sack of potatoes.

Colonel whoever then shuffled out of the room without a word.

Now that both of us were on the bed, Daughter Hy bowed to us. "May Eloria bless you both, now and into the future." With that, she left.

As though he were trying to act cool, Gideon blew the disheveled hair out of his eyes and looked at me. "Hey."

I couldn't help but laugh. With a smile I said, "Hey yourself." With his hand in mine I added, "So what would you like to talk about?"

CHAPTER TEN

A SOFT WIND BREWS A STORM

OUR RIDE BACK to school was at a much more measured pace than the hasty dash that had spirited us away to the secret wedding. Everything had moved so fast, that I forgot they'd nicely aligned things with my weekly estrus cycle. I realized that this was the entire reason the date we were married was set.

To my immense relief, it was also the first time I was in partial control of my mental faculties and was fully aware during my cycle, though it was *quite* awkward.

"Are you okay Lady Anessa?" Tania asked.

"I'm fine," I said and looked out the carriage window. "Just a little upset at my parents, is all."

Tania shuffled a bit in her seat but didn't say anything.

When she didn't respond, I continued, "Do you know how embarrassing it is to yowl someone's name?" With my hand on my chest, I looked at her.

She looked away for a few seconds before saying, "No, I do not."

A hand landed on my head. "I didn't mind," Gideon said. He smiled brilliantly at me.

"Maybe you didn't," I said, and turned away. *Gods, his smile drives me crazy, especially days like today.* I was acutely aware of the fact that it was at least another thirty hours before the heat would pass. "But having to struggle every minute I'm around you stinks."

"Here," he said, then put his hands around my waist, lifting me easily. "This might help."

"Hey!" I was wholly unprepared for that and held onto his wrists until he sat me back down in his lap. He earned a glare for his efforts.

He gently nudged me to look forward. I was blissfully unaware of what happened after that, as he started to knead my scalp with his fingers.

His touch blew my frustration out the window. It was as though I took flight. Something about being part feline meant that head rubs felt like a gift from the gods. He'd done something similar the night before to help us through the night without any accidents.

When my senses returned, I found myself nibbling on the muscle near his thumb. As quickly as I could I removed it from my mouth and said, "Sorry." Then wiped the edge of my mouth and his thumb dry, which was impossible to do with any grace whatsoever. *Gods that's so embarrassing.* Our carriage hit a particularly large bump, needing Gideon to steady my shoulders with his hands.

That bump made me quite aware that I wasn't the only one facing difficulties, and I politely removed myself from my husband's lap. *Not as embarrassing as "that,"* I thought. I noticed that he was beet red from his ears through his neck.

I shouldn't be too mad at him. It's not like he's attracted to the bean-pole I am today. He's seen the grown-up version of me at Nora's. Remembering that the heat comes with its own awkward aspects, I amended my thought, *Then there's my* smell. *At least he said it's intoxicating and not nauseating.* Thinking about it did little to help my situation and only deepened my blush.

How many hours now? Twenty-nine? Gods above it can't pass soon enough.

Within the hour our carriage came to a halt. Gideon gallantly held out his hand after he stepped out to help me down.

As we walked to my dorm suite, I thought, *I can't believe I'm an eleven-year-old bride. Why did that idiot emperor have to go to war over me? It's so stupid.* Looking between those with me, a tingling bit at my nose. *I suppose my saving grace is that I'm surrounded by people who treat my age and our status with the seriousness it deserves.*

Shaking my head I realized, *If I didn't have all these memories of a past life, who knows how different things would be. Would Her Goddess Eloria even care about me?*

I thought back to my first meeting with the goddess, and I realized the answer was: probably not. My life on Anfang was largely due to her, since she'd let it slip that I was there in the first place because of her.

Upon entering our room, Gideon walked towards my bedroom, making me seize up.

"My Lord Gideon," Sarah interrupted him, "That is our Lady Anessa's room. If it would please you," she gestured towards the guest room, "may I show you to yours over here?"

He nodded and followed her.

Exhaling I whispered to myself, "Thank the gods. I'm not ready for that."

When Tania's voice broke in, practically at my ear, I jumped. "Do not worry Lady Anessa. Until then, please come to Sarah or me if you have any questions. No matter what they may be. Including those about your yin, should you choose to give it."

I wanted to scream at her for nosing in, but I also didn't want to alienate her like I'd done a few days ago, so I settled for, "Thank you Tania, I'll keep that in mind."

She curtsied to me while nodding her head and went off to do something else.

Before she could get too far, I said, "Could you please help me get ready for bed?" Slouching I added, "I'm beat."

She blinked. "Our Lord Gideon didn't hit you, did he?"

Opening and closing my mouth a few times I sighed. "No. It's an expression. I just meant that I'm tired." Her misinterpretation made me realize, *Earthen phrases are more and more vexing. More often than not, people misinterpret my words. I wonder how often I'm giving people the wrong impression without realizing it.*

Ten minutes into trying to sleep, I sat up in bed, sending a thought to my new invisible companion. *Did you have to put a bug in my ear about Gideon?*

"No, despite my efforts," Trish said, *"he won't leave your mind. Your imagination is getting stronger, too. Remember the way you'd imagine him used to be self-censored? Now you think of the full Monty. You dirty cat-gir—"*

Stop. I thought sternly. *Seriously. It's bad enough that I have to deal with those kinds of dreams. It's entirely another to have you remind me of that, especially since that hasn't passed yet.*

Trish smiled. *"Okay. I'll lay off. Remember though, he's just in the other room. He'll be around you every day during each of your heats. It might get a bit hard to deal with, and I'm sure he'll continue to visit Nora's regularly."*

Buzz off, Trish. You're starting to piss me off.

She did as I asked, and the silence finally allowed me the peace I needed to sleep. As I drifted off, I wondered, *What are you really, Trish? You ought to have my back.*

"Sorry," She said softly. *"Being trapped here without a body of my own has me a bit bored. I was just teasing you."* Her voice quavered and faded as I fell asleep. *"Remember how I used to do that when stressed? I–"*

▼ ▼ ▼

"Get out of my way!" Lukas yelled, then bowled through a few students.

I was headed to the training rooms to get some practice in and was curious at the throng of students tarrying at the entrance.

Lukas stormed away from the training room, and the other students sensibly parted for him.

When he passed me, he did little more than glance before snorting and continuing on.

A soft murmur broke out in the crowd. "I hear someone died."

"No way!" whispered a girl loudly.

Then a shaky voice confirmed, "I saw it. There was blood everywhere." The other voices silenced. "The entire side of the room was just a big smear of red."

One of the attendants tried to run after Lukas, but his personal guards stood fast in his path.

The taller of the two said, "State your business."

"I–" the man took a moment to find his voice. "I need to get a statement from His Imperial Highness about the inci–"

"Then you can get one from his manservant, Li. Make an official request." The guard's tone soured. "In the future, run after His Imperial Highness at your own peril." His hand went to the blade at his waist.

Sheesh. Even his guards are assholes.

The attendant cowered away and bowed, before jogging back to the training rooms.

A bell tolled in the distance, marking the hour. *Crap. Why did I think I had time for a little training? I have a new class today.*

Hurrying through the campus, with a little help from my own guard, I found the semi-spherical building I was supposed to report to.

Inside was a tall room with a single window on the far side near the top. In the center was a single rectangular woven mat.

"Hello?" I said, hoping I wasn't so late as to be unwelcome.

"You're late," a cross voice replied. A man barely my height stepped out from behind an almost unnoticeable privacy curtain.

Giving the man at the far edge of the room a curtsy I said, "Sorry. I wasn't sure how to get here."

He sighed. "Yeah. Sit down," he said and pointed to the mat. "And draw in essence as you usually would when you meditate." The man then stepped back behind the paper screen.

It's been at least two years since I meditated, I thought and took a seat. *Guess Donovan's pushing me to make up for that.*

"This isn't my dime," said his voice from behind the screen. "You wouldn't normally be permitted exclusive use to such a gathering array, but someone clearly pulled some strings."

I closed my eyes.

"It's expensive as the Nether to operate, so until I'm confident you're ready, it stays off."

Drawing on the essence around me, the cloth on my arms fluttered lightly as a cool breeze pushed in from outside.

The screen clattered to the floor.

"Damn it. Who activated the array?" he complained. He muttered to himself, "Did one of the kids place an activation rune somewhere?"

His nattering broke my concentration, and I looked over at him.

The squirrelly man was tracing something on the wall that looked something like a circuit. "No, it's not active. What was that then?"

Looking over at me he asked, "Tell me what you see when you meditate."

"Um…" I said and realized it hadn't changed since I was a child. "Static?"

He stared. "What does that mean?"

Right. Static is something specific to earthen video transmissions. I haven't seen enough of the video conference calls to know if they're subject to the same sort of interference. And it's possible he's never seen such a call. I scratched my head and tried again. "An explosion of color that changes rapidly?"

"Oh. How many colors?"

"All of them?" I said, unsure to how he'd take it. *Also the colors were a lot more chaotic than I remember, though I doubt I should say that.*

"Right," he sighed. "Great," his voice dropped. "They gave me another weird one."

"I wasn't able to weave it into a cord like I used to. The colors came far faster than I remember." Looking around I said, "Maybe it's this room?"

"Right then. Your focus should be on that, first. Though I'm impressed you've already made it to the elemental stage. Have you mastered creation yet?"

"Huh?" I said and stared back at him, slack-jawed.

"Could you maybe…" I laughed ruefully. "Give me some pointers about what you're talking about?"

"Alright," he held up his hand with his fingers out and his thumb folded in. "There are four steps to the elemental stage. Essence, Coercion, Control and Creation." He held out his hand and a ball of water manifested above it. I'd seen Master Kile do the same thing a few years ago. I noted that this man's sphere wasn't quite as stable as Master Kile's had been.

"Yeah…" I said and pointed to the bluish sphere. "I can't do that."

The instructor in front of me cleared his throat. "Well, most don't *weave* essence together into a cord until they've mastered this, or what is known as Control. Have you created your Will yet?"

Arching an eyebrow I thought, *What, like my last will and testament?*

As usual my tendency to wear my thoughts on my face made the man sigh. "Guess not. For now, focus on drawing in essence. Since you seem to have a knack for it, regain your feel for weaving essence into 'cords' as you called them."

I caught myself before I could raise my hand to ask what they were actually called. *He's a bit temperamental.* Instead, I closed my eyes once again. There'd be time for a vocabulary lesson later, I was sure.

Ten minutes later he spoke up. "Time's up. These rooms are rented by the hour. If you want more time, you'll need to pay up beyond what your sponsor has already. Normally there would be five others in here with you. So if you want exclusive use," he rubbed his fingers over his thumb. "It'll cost extra."

Standing I stretched and smiled. "Should I come back tomorrow like I'm supposed to, or wait until I can weave essence together?"

He waved his hand at me. "Wait until you can 'weave.' I never even turned on the array. Until you're at a certain point, this field array isn't that useful."

▼ ▼ ▼

Octday, Totharae 21st, 1739

Cultivation is weird. You know that sensation when moving your arm through a pool of water and there's a drag against your arm? Meditating is similar to the pressure of water, except you're pulling the water *into* your body.

It'd been three weeks, or two Earth months, since I'd meditated in the room with the field array. It took that long to once again weave essence together into cords. Watching them rush forward towards my dantians on their own was a remarkable spectacle. Magical wavering bands of energy would just dance in place on their surface like a plasma lamp. It looked surreal.

Though I was indeed able to create "cords," I was only able to manage a few dozen at a time per dantian. The remaining essence just rushed forward on its own and bounced off my dantians. Watching all seven in tandem was quite the light show, if you knew how to see it.

Stopping my efforts, I sighed and slumped forward in my bed, glad to stop the exertion. "This is tough," I said to no one.

"Done meditating?" Sarah asked.

"For now," I said and stood.

She then proceeded to open the windows and placed a small vase of flowers back onto the desk. She'd moved it into the closet when I started.

"Why do you always shut everything up when I meditate, anyway?"

She smirked. "You probably don't notice because you do get a bit absorbed in it, but you generate an essence draft when you meditate. It's part talent and part lack of control."

"Aren't those two things the opposite of one another?"

Shaking her head she said, "Not exactly. An essence draft is exactly that. The essence you're pulling in is charged," She pointed at me, "…because of you. That charge triggers other essence to draw forward in turn. And so on."

"What, are you saying that if I had better control it wouldn't become charged?"

Nodding she continued, "I'd guess you're pulling in at least fifty lines at once to create a draft like that. Which is why I mention talent."

"Two hundred fifty, or so," I corrected her, absently.

She cleared her throat. "Right. I guess your control is better than I thought. But it requires even more control to smooth out the draft."

As I changed, or more accurately was changed, I asked, "Is it such a bad thing to create a draft, though?"

"Yes and no. If you're in a safe place, the draft doesn't really matter." She pursed her lips and added, "But cultivators are rarely safe when they use their power. A draft does one thing that would be bad."

Thinking for a moment I said, "It gives you away, doesn't it?"

She paused, as though waiting for me to say more.

"If you're in an unsafe place, and need to stay hidden," I continued, "a draft would be a beacon saying 'Here I am.'"

"Exactly." She nodded. "There are times when you might want that, though. When setting traps, or to frighten someone."

"Frighten?"

Her grin gave me a chill. "Yes. Cultivators who deliberately grab at essence to create a draft send a message depending on how much they pull in."

Right, they're broadcasting how strong they are. Realizing the issue I said, "And if you're up against someone stronger than that?"

Tying my braid off she said, "Run. Or be prepared to fight if you used that as a form of trap."

"Ugh, that sounds an awful lot like applied psychology."

"War can seem that way sometimes."

Avoiding her gaze for a second, I asked tentatively, "Have you fought in a war?"

"Anessa," she said carefully. Her tone made me look closely at her.

"Yeah?"

"Are you asking, or ordering me to answer?" she asked with knitted brows.

"Asking," I said instantly.

"Then I would prefer not to answer," she said briskly.

So the answer's most likely yes, I thought. "Okay, that's fine. But would you be willing to talk about it if I'm ever…" I pointed to the floor, "…called into this war to some capacity?"

She gave me a hug, holding my head against her chest. "Absolutely."

"I'm nervous about seeing Eloria again," I said, my voice muffled.

"Hm?" Sarah asked, looking down at me.

I repeated myself and she said, "There's nothing to worry about. If the display from your wedding is anything to go by, you most certainly have Her Goddess Eloria's favor."

"But why me? What makes me special?" Holding my hand to my chest I said, "Oliver is… I mean was, special before he lost his cultivation base, and she didn't pay any attention to him whatsoever."

"There are several possible reasons. One might be she saw Oliver's fate," Sarah said.

That made me frown, *Wouldn't that mean she could've stopped it?*

"Or your talent might be greater than his," Sarah said and held me at arm's length. "You said you crafted over two hundred and fifty strands, right?"

With a nod from me, she continued, "Oliver was a natural, through and through. He was naturally meditating at all times, without any effort. But do you know how many strands he was capable of weaving?"

"More than me, I'm sure."

Shaking her head, she said, "Two per dantian. He couldn't actively meditate and draw in more." I was shocked. "It's why he didn't use the pills most cultivators do," she continued. "It flooded him with more essence than he could handle. He would likely have hit a wall at the end of the Sky Realm, since he was unable to do more on his own." She tapped the side of her head. "He just didn't have the mind for it."

My eyes burned at her words. I whined, "Why does everyone seem to think he's stupid?"

"Sorry," Sarah said and hugged me again. "It's not that Oliver is stupid. For a mortal, he's a genius, no doubt. But for a cultivator..." She let her words hang in the air. "He's pretty normal mentally."

"What's that make me, then? I struggle with things Yukirei finds easy. If I'm supposed to have all this talent, why doesn't it feel that way?"

"Experience, and time," Sarah said.

"What?"

Guiding me over to the mirror, she started to fuss with my outfit, making sure every detail was just so. "Yukirei is a genius for a cultivator. And she most likely uses her cultivation base to bolster her natural intelligence even more." Sarah paused and held her finger up at me, "Do not try and figure out how to do that. You are *not* ready for that. It requires being in the Sky Realm, at a minimum, due to the essence control required. Anything earlier could risk brain damage." She moved to putting makeup on my face. "I personally like Anessa as she is, and would prefer you not be a vegetable."

Yikes, message received. She didn't completely answer my question though.

"You draw in a lot of essence for a Nascent Realm cultivator. Oliver was stronger than you back when he still had his abilities. But even at his peak back in the Ascended Realm, Oliver didn't compare to how you are now," she said and pulled back to review her work. "There's a qualitative difference between the Ascended Realm and the Sky Realm. If you were to match him in the Sky Realm, as you are now, you'd likely have an entirely different, and much scarier, life."

"Scarier how?"

"Hmm," she said and moved onto my lip gloss. "Imagine someone from another world stealing you away against your will." She grinned. "Though, if I'm being honest, I'm a little surprised that hasn't happened already."

I puffed my cheeks out and crossed my arms. "Real funny."

"I'm only half kidding. You are something of an enigma, though. The favor Her Goddess Eloria shows you really is striking."

"Yeah, it's almost like I'm her daughter," I joked.

"That is one possibility, yes."

Her serious response to my joke made me pull away. "That's not funny." My tone soured, "Definitely not funny."

Dipping her head to me she said, "I meant no ill will. Though it is not *entirely* impossible. Gods and goddesses have been known to meddle in such ways, though it is exceedingly rare. You *do* share her unusual hair color, however."

At her words I picked up my braid and gripped it tightly. *I haven't seen* anyone else *with this hair color.*

Sarah continued, "Though you would be, most certainly, Lily's daughter as well. Her Imperial High Grace has told me that they checked."

"It's not possible to have two sets of parents," I said flatly. "I'm Lily and Roland's daughter, and no one else's."

Sarah started to open her mouth, and I said harshly, "No one else's!"

She pressed her lips together and nodded.

I don't care what fantasy bullshit Anfang has, but having more than one set of parents isn't genetically possible. That entire line of thought is not even the slightest bit amusing. Even entertaining the thought scared the hell out of me. It was one thing to be favored by a goddess, entirely another to be the actual daughter of the Goddess of Death. That was the day I started to hate the color of my hair.

My brooding was interrupted by Tania knocking and entering.

She curtsied, "Imperial Lady Anessa, you have your cultivation class in ten minutes. You told me last evening that you were going to attend today."

"Thanks," I said and smiled. "Sorry Sarah, I'm not mad at you, just…" bunching up the cloth of my dress I added, "think of it from my perspective." Seeing Tania in the room made me choose my words, "That's really scary, you know?"

"I know. You never have to apologize to me, Anessa," Sarah said.

Tania coughed and glared when Sarah gave me another hug.

"She's like a grandchild in my eyes," she said defensively to Tania.

"I still can't wrap my head around you being over seventy!" I said.

"That may be so, Sarah-Knecht," Tania chided, "but a sl–" she regarded me for a moment.

Sarah's breathing hitched and her eyes went to the floor.

Tania continued, "a servant should not be overly familiar with their charge, regardless of the circumstances," her tone firmed, "or their past titles."

Seriously, why is Sarah constantly the target of Tania's needling about the pecking order? I know she was about to say "slave." She was there when I put that damned collar on Sarah's neck myself! Her words made me fume, remembering that my uncle had given me no say in the matter.

It pained me that I held Sarah's prior role, and it was now my turn to be stern. "Tania, we've talked about this. I know you are a stickler for protocol, and in general I appreciate it, but mind what you say about Sarah. Continued failure to remember that can and will result in your *immediate* dismissal."

I didn't even give Tania time to respond and simply walked past her.

Sarah kept looking at the floor and gripped her skirt, clearly not wanting to get in the middle of our discussion about her.

Something about the click of the door as it closed behind me felt right.

▼ ▼ ▼

My encounter with Tania lit a fire under me. It brought the issue of enslaving Sarah to the fore, and with it, the memory of Oliver's poisoning. There hadn't been much pressure on me to advance from either Mom or Dad when Oliver was still the Heir Apparent. It was part of why I hadn't focused much on cultivation. But when I was in front of Dean Donovan, none of those excuses mattered.

The teacher for my meditation class was pacing as he waited for me. When he saw me, he snapped, "About time."

Looking around for a clock I said, "I'm on time, aren't I?"

"Two minutes late," he said crossly. "You don't get to slide past the end of your class, either." He waved toward the mat. "Sit. This would be much easier if they'd tell me more about my students. Always shrouding things in mystery." He stomped over to the wall that I'd assumed controlled the array.

Before I could offer up information about my circumstances, he complained further, "It's impolite for me to ask what Realm you're in, your resonances or even how many dantians you have." Gesturing with his hand toward me, he said, "I get it, during war, information is king." Waving his arms wildly he said, "But it makes my job a lot harder!"

My frustration with Tania was still fresh and my eyebrow twitched. *Don't let him get to you.* I said, "I had to slow down my gathering to get the hang of making the cords again."

He nodded. "You'll need to try harder then. For today, just focus on getting a feel for the gathering array's effects."

Closing my eyes I did as he asked, but didn't pull any essence in. For a few seconds nothing changed. Then without warning, or any effort, essence began to pour in without me doing anything at all. *Whoa.*

"Feeling" around myself with my nexus's natural draw, I found that my usual reach had been expanded at least a hundredfold. Stranger still, I could even "see" the teacher with my eyes closed as a black void. *Okay, do I just grab at the far edge and pull?*

Following that thought, I "saw" the professor fall over and he let out a little squeal. Then my world went sideways and I hit my head on the floor.

"Ouch," I said and shook my head, holding my hand over my right eye with my eyes closed.

"What did you just do?" he said, his shrill tone laced with ire.

Opening my eyes, I saw that the concrete floor was cracked and disheveled. *Oh crap.* Despite being reinforced with rebar, bits were sticking up here and there.

"Actually, no," he chided. "Don't tell me. Just follow me outside." He grabbed my wrist and pulled me to my feet then out into the courtyard.

"Please let my wrist go," I said.

"Excuse you?" he said, maintaining a firm grip on my arm.

Nodding at my guards, I said, "I would much prefer it if you removed your hand."

My two personal guards both began to critically assess the teacher and had tensed for action.

If he doesn't let go soon, I might not be in this class much longer.

The teacher took stock of the situation and released me, then bowed to my guards. "Sorry."

Neither one said a word, but they removed their hands from their weapons.

"My problem is that they have a Sky Realm student taking a class for the Nascent Realm," he said, then pointed back at the ruined array. "Look at what you did! That costs more than I make in ten years!"

"But I *am* in the Nascent Realm." Jumping in place a few times with my arms held up, I said, "See, I couldn't fly if I wanted to."

A light feminine chuckle made me turn toward one of my guards. She had been smiling and looked back to the teacher instead of at me, returning her face to a neutral state.

Coughing into my hand I said, "Anyway. I'm sure my family will pay for the room. I didn't do that on purpose. I've never used such an array before. It was definitely weird being able to reach out that far."

The short man looked at me thoughtfully for a moment, then took a pill from his storage ring. He promptly handed it to one of my guards to inspect.

They exchanged a few hushed words and she nodded, handing the pill back.

"Take this," said the teacher, and he placed it in my palm. "It should give me an idea of what I'm dealing with, so I'll know how to move forward." He gestured toward a small clearing in the courtyard.

One of my guards laid down a blanket they retrieved from their storage ring.

"*I wouldn't take that,*" Trish warned me.

Why?

She sighed. *"Trust me. For you, right now, it's bad news. You aren't ready for it."*

"Well come on then, we don't have all day." He looked back to the room and sighed. "Well, I suppose *I* might have all day. It's not like that can be used as is."

Taking a seat I sent up a silent prayer. *This shouldn't be too bad, right?* Hearing nothing I popped it in my mouth. Nothing happened.

Not so bad.

Then a peal of thunder caught my ear and I looked up. A rainbow-colored cloud swirled above.

Then it felt like a fistful of daggers lanced through my chest.

Gods, what the hell!

CHAPTER ELEVEN
BOTTOMLESS PITS

THUNDER CONTINUED TO boom out, drawing everyone's eyes up. The funnel that had just detached from my body had already started to rise, although the storm itself didn't seem to be going anywhere.

"What the Nether is that?!" my teacher said, appalled.

Holding my hand to my head, I asked, "I think the real question is: what did you just give me?"

"Um," he said while staring at the sky. "A minute-to-second pill."

"Hardly," a familiar stern voice said. "That was at least an hour-to-second pill. Check your stock."

"Dean Donovan," the man said in exasperation, then rifled through an unseen screen, his storage ring, I presumed. "Damn," he muttered. "It was."

"It goes without saying, Cal, that you're suspended for a week," Dean Donovan said briskly. "We'll discuss the specifics in my office, but for now this class is over." The Dean then waved his hand at the storm above, wiping it from the sky as though it were barely worth mentioning.

"Yes, Sir," Cal said and bowed. His fists were clenched at his side. "With pay?" he asked, turning his head toward the Dean.

"If she were any less lucky than she is, she'd be dead right now. So Cal, you tell me."

This idiot nearly killed me?! I thought and glared in Cal's direction.

"Understood, Sir," he said, and his hands relaxed.

"Your Imperial High Grace, Anessa Carlyle," Dean Donovan said. He stood next to Cal and bowed, forcing the man's head down in a similar display. "On behalf of Maaka, I am truly sorry for his foolish display. Please take the remainder of today to rest in your dormitory."

Holding my hand to my chest I gave a half-hearted curtsy and excused myself.

As I turned away, I nudged my nexus for a blink of an eye. It responded by lancing pain through my sternum and a dull ache suffused my meridians. *Ouch. Don't use it for now. Got it.*

"Your Imperial Grace, are you okay?" asked one of my guards.

"I'm fine," I said through gritted teeth. "My nexus is just not very pleased right now. It hurts to use it."

"That cur is lucky you are unharmed," my other guard said. "I nearly cut him down after he manhandled you, then this. If Dean Donovan hadn't stepped in…"

"It's okay," I said. "Let Dean Donovan handle it." I smiled at her. "I'm thankful you feel that way."

She put her hand over her chest and bowed. "As you command."

It wasn't really a command, but there's no need to correct her.

As we walked off, Dean Donovan was tearing into Cal about how reckless his action was. How Nascent Cultivators should never be given hyper collection pills since they can fracture their foundations, and rupture their dantians. Or worse, the energy could've flayed or fried me alive.

I rubbed my sternum over my dress and stopped when my action drew a few eyes. *It's like heartburn on steroids.*

▼ ▼ ▼

It was a week before Sarah allowed me to return to classes. She and my parents were worried about the event, and Cal was let go. Mom probably had something to do with that. If he hadn't put me in potentially mortal danger, I might have felt bad for him.

"You know, there is some good that came from that pill," I said.

"Oh, and what's that?" she said while monitoring the other maids changing my bedsheets.

"Essence is easier to draw in for me now." I placed my hand over my nexus. "It's strange though."

"Hm?"

"My usual draw? The one that caused the wind a while back?"

"Mhmm," she watched their efforts, her focus unwavering.

"It happens automatically now. If I try to meditate, I can, but it's almost three times as much as before."

Sarah turned to me. "Really? That's…" Her tone became contemplative, "Most unusual."

"Yeah, I was worried at first when I noticed it just streaming in on its own, because of Oliver's issue. Maybe his problem was that he drew it in automatically from infancy, and he never could bridge the gap mentally?"

She nodded. "Perhaps, but I'll need to let your parents know."

"Is it a bad thing?" I asked, a little concerned.

"Not bad at all. However, essence homeostasis is blindingly rare. Oliver having it is largely what made him a paragon, after all."

"Crap," I said aloud and covered my mouth.

She only smiled and shook her head.

Pointing to myself I asked, "They're not going to apply that label to me, are they?"

"Probably," she laughed. "You were pretty close as it was. Do you still experience a draft when you meditate? I'm asking because I haven't had to shutter everything up lately."

Her comment made me beam. "You're right, I don't. That's weird!"

"Yes, weird is one way of putting it. Your parents may have to reevaluate the gravity of that incident."

"What do you mean?" I asked, then realized, "Oh, you mean about Cal?"

"He wouldn't get his job back, of course, but they might quietly make sure he has enough to float him until he finds something new."

Not wanting to think about someone's fate who I wouldn't ever see again, I said, "I hope they don't give me some silly title like that."

"Anessa, if I'm being honest, you've been a Paragon for a few *years* now." Her attention returned to the maids, who had stopped when she stopped directly supervising them. "What would change is you'd likely be called a Genius Paragon."

"Ugh, that's so... odd." I sighed. "I suppose I didn't even know about it, so there's no harm, as long as others don't treat me differently."

"Differently than they already do?" she asked, amused.

The other maids completed their task. They curtsied and left the room.

"I didn't like how you said that. What do you know?"

"Tania," Sarah said, "What can you tell us about Anessa's Acolytes?"

For the last week, Tania had acted distant, like I'd feared she would. Hearing her name, she jolted and gave a curtsy.

While she collected herself, I thought, *Acolytes, huh? Like Anessa's followers? That's odd.*

She replied in a quiet voice, "Right, they're a modest group of commoner students who gather bi-weekly to discuss your latest actions." She fidgeted a little and turned her face to the window. "Your guards have deemed them harmless, since they really only talk about what you do in your classes. None of them know about your," she paused and looked around the room, "marriage. Which is best. Though they do have a wild imagination."

"Such as?" I wondered.

She thinned out her lips and played with her fingers. "They suspect you're secretly involved with Portia."

That admission did little more than make me burst out laughing. "Portia?! Seriously?" But while I recovered, I realized, *She does visit my dormitory on occasion, maybe that's why?* After Sarah smoothed out my dress from my chuckle-fest, I asked, "Should I do anything to put that rumor to rest?"

"Probably," Sarah said. "Although, our lord's regular presence nearby *should* help balance it out." She then produced a small letter and presented it to me. "Since you are returning to classes today, your usual physical education class has been replaced with weapons training."

When I reached for the letter, she withdrew it and added, "Though you're supposed to see Dean Donovan before doing so." She winked. "That isn't in the letter. It was a message from the courier."

▼ ▼ ▼

A frown plastered itself on my face as I stood outside Dean Donovan's office. Last time I was here, I received a dressing down. This time was likely a response to Cal's misstep and what had happened afterwards.

Given Dean Donovan's personality, I feared he'd find something to needle me about.

"Enter," his voice called from within.

Great, he knows I'm here. I sighed. *Let's get this over with*, I thought and opened the door.

"Please, take a seat."

On his desk were three pills, each in its own little jewelry box, sitting on top of a black velvet cushion.

He motioned over the set. "If it would be okay, I would like for you to do a little test for me."

I looked at the pills, then back to my Dean. "Are they safe?"

"Yes, they're safe. These aren't like the pill that Cal gave you," he said and picked the one on the left up. He motioned for me to take it from him. "These have Will inside them. Any excess will spill out naturally."

"Excess?" I said nervously, holding the pill away from my body.

"These are Essence pills. Specifically, a Nascent pill," he tapped the center box, "Ascended pill, and a Sky pill."

"And you want me to take them?"

He held up a hand. "One at a time. We don't know your limits." Pulling the Sky pill back a bit he said, "It's highly unlikely you'll need this one, however."

Anything to say on this one, Trish? I asked my spiritual companion. Hearing nothing, I popped the pill in my mouth and swallowed it, mentally bracing myself.

"Anything?" he asked.

"What's supposed to happen?"

He smiled. "I figured as much." Holding out the next pill he said, "Try this next."

Asking my guide again, followed by silence, I repeated his experiment. Except this time a whirlwind of essence shot toward the dantian behind my navel and my eyes widened.

"Noticed that one, did you?" Dean Donovan chuckled. "How full are your dantians?"

Raising an eyebrow I shrugged. "No one's taught me how to check. Do I poke my dantian mentally or something?"

His half-smile vanished and he frowned. "I suppose if you've never been full, it would be hard to tell." He grunted and nudged the box with the Sky pill forward, but he didn't touch it. "Finally, this one."

Picking it up I noticed his eyebrow twitched. *Is this expensive?*

Dean Donovan sat a bucket out next to me. This was not a good sign.

Great, he's expecting me to throw up, and expel the excess, or whatever. Trish was still silent on the matter, and I took it like the others.

In a second I snapped up the bucket in a flash, and held it in my lap as a tsunami of essence buffeted my dantian. It was intense enough I swore the bucket would've been necessary.

Once it slowed I opened my mouth and breathed a sigh of relief.

"Breathe in deeply through your mouth," he commanded. As I complied, he added, "Good, now swallow that breath into your stomach."

Doing so another, far smaller, wave splashed against my dantian.

He let out a belly laugh. "Intense, was it?"

"That was awful!" I said and stood, sitting the bucket down, though not very carefully. "You could've warned me."

"Your dantians are full now, aren't they?"

Sitting down again, I closed my eyes to check. I wasn't certain what I was looking for, but I could tell that all of the essence had gone to the dantian behind my navel, and nowhere else.

"No. It all went to the same place."

He sighed and rubbed his forehead. "You're saying that you took all of that essence into *one* dantian?" His voice took on a rare pleading quality, "Is it at least full?"

"Um," I said and tried to check. I still wasn't sure what to look for, but I could at least compare it to my other dantians. "It's... more than half full, I think?"

Letting out a growl he placed six additional pill boxes on the table. They were all closed.

"What are those?" I said and pressed myself further into my chair.

"Sky pills, like you're thinking. Though..." he pulled out a small pill bottle with a handful of pills. "Take these, first, so we can make sure you're able to redirect them."

The pills all had a faint color to them. The Ascended pills were a pale blue-white. The Sky pills, despite being for the Sky Realm, were more of a ruddy-white, like a blush.

The Ascended pills helped a lot. It took two pills before I got the hang of redirecting them. It took fourteen in all before Dean Donovan was confident I could move on.

"Do I have to do this?" I asked with a bit of a whine in my voice.

"Yes. Your dantians are unbalanced. If you were further in your cultivation, I'd help you balance them on your own, but it would take a few months since you *really* don't know what you're doing."

His emphasis on "really" made me wince. *He's still kind of an ass, but he isn't wrong.*

Over the next hour I whined and pleaded to stop part way before I was finished. Several times my head hovered over that infernal bucket as I hugged it, but I never actually needed it.

"How do you feel now? You're scheduled for lunch within the hour. Feeling hungry still?"

I frowned and considered his words. "I'm actually not. Though I suppose I could still eat if offered."

He gave a fake laugh and his usual adherence to etiquette fell away, "Girl, you just *ate* seven times your yearly gift to the school."

"What!?" I stood. "Is that... after I upped it?"

He nodded grimly.

I collapsed into the chair and put my face into my hands. *That's over ten large black gold. That's a fortune!* Popping back up I took a breath and pulled out ten large and four small black gold and sat them on his desk.

"What is that?" he said in a sour tone.

"Payment for the pills. You didn't ask for it, but I could tell from how you acted you were bothered by it. All I ask from you in return is to send my dad a letter explaining why you're in possession of it."

He didn't argue, just nodded and promptly put them away.

Before I could excuse myself, he said, "Well, we did learn something valuable today." A smile graced his face.

When I didn't say anything in response he added, "Your limits. Though, I'm frankly astonished to see a Nascent Realm cultivator pulling at the Sky Realm. What's more, those pills were only neutral essence. The quotes I received for your *other* elements were higher than all seven of those Sky pills, for a single Ascended Realm pill. You'll need to spend your own time filling your bottomless pits with elemental essence."

As my hand touched his office door, he commented, "Incidentally, in a little over a month you'll begin hunting lessons arranged by His Imperial Grace, Roland. He has done so because you expressed interest in leadership training."

Hunting? I suppose that's better than being thrust into battle. A brief sense of dread gripped me and I amended my thought. *Gods, I don't want to fight and… kill people over a senseless war.*

CHAPTER TWELVE

CHRONOMANCER

ALMOST A MONTH later, my progress on balancing my elements was still slow. Opening my eyes I let out a groan. "This is so annoying," I said aloud.

"What is?" Sarah asked and once again put out the potted plants.

As I pushed my nexus harder, the essence wind had returned and she'd had to put away the breakables again on a regular basis.

"It's going to take me *years* to gather the elemental essence to match what Dean Donovan gave me. I'm only meditating four hours a day. Even if I pushed myself and meditated all day, every day, that's ten years!"

Sarah nodded. "You might find this surprising, but that's actually very fast."

"What? How?!" I complained.

"Without the use of pills, or essence stones, it can take *thousands* of years for some cultivators. Your father, Roland, would take twenty thousand. That's why he kept his mine quiet. Cultivator resources are very valuable."

"I can't use pills, Dean Donovan already told me they're too expensive," I grumbled.

Sarah was arranging one of the plants she'd placed and turned to me. "That's unusual. I know nature essence is one of the pricier elements at ten times neutral, but that's not beyond what your family can afford."

Crap.

I realized that she didn't know about my *other* elements. I thought for a moment and then said, "R-remember my wedding day, and the bond of elements?"

Sarah nodded.

"Do you remember how many groupings of candles there were?" I asked. *I hope this doesn't get me in trouble, she was there, so it shouldn't be too much of a stretch.*

For a few moments her eyes darted around the room. "Seventeen."

I nodded. "Right. Each of those corresponded to an element. Including neutral of course."

Her eyes widened and she looked around the room. She sighed in seeing no one but us were present. Rushing to the door she closed and locked it, then closed the shutters again. Afterwards she took to my side. After brandishing and activating an S-ROB, she said, "Be more careful about what you say, and who's around to hear it. Elements beyond Anfang are probably not something you should be speaking of so casually."

"Right. Well, now you know, and Dean Donovan knows. The rarer elements are over forty thousand times as much, for one pill." Shaking my head to correct myself I added, "Or to put it another way, an Ascended pill is worth seven Sky pills of neutral."

"That is far too high," she admitted. "Now I understand your frustration." Tapping her forearm she said, "You mentioned you've stopped sleeping, right?"

Though I knew where she was going with this, I didn't like it, and nodded.

"You might ask Dean Donovan if you can use the essence gathering array for Sky Realm cultivators at night," she said. "It would still cost... a lot, but I think it's something your parents would approve of, since it's more manageable than the alternative."

"How much is 'a lot?'"

"You probably won't get an allowance for a while. Since you'd be reserving it by yourself."

"Is that strictly necessary?" I asked.

"Do you want to run into His Imperial Highness, Lukas, or share it with Her Imperial Right Honorable Yukirei?"

Biting my lower lip I thought, "Lukas would find a reason to do something, and..." I sighed. "I'm not sure how it would go with Yukirei. Would using it with someone else reduce my efficacy?"

Sarah nodded. "Usually Sky Realm cultivators reserve the arrays for themselves. Part of the high cost includes construction. They'd have to build you one. Maaka only has two, and they built the second one for Oliver."

"What was Yukirei using before Oliver stopped using his?"

With a smile Sarah said, "She was sharing the array with Lukas. After he broke it the second time because he threw a fit, he was banned for a month," her smile widened, "by His Imperial Majesty himself. Needless to say, Lukas didn't cause trouble after that."

"Would you take care of the arrangements, then?"

"I will," she nodded. "Even with the array though," she opened the shutters. "It will probably take you a few years to catch your elements up. Worse, it may not even work."

"Why's that?" I asked.

"Those extra elements you referred to," she once again closed the shutters and activated the S-ROB. "We might have to ask Dean Donovan to seek... outside help to build your array."

"Right. If Anfang doesn't know of the other elements, then whatever makes the array work might not apply here. And probably nobody local would know how to build it."

"Exactly," she said and moved to restore the room to its open state. "Though the Dean does have good connections. In the end it comes down to cost."

I laughed. "At this rate, I might not get an allowance, ever again."

Sarah merely smiled.

Oh, I was joking, and she's serious. Crap. I asked, "Is it normal for me to not need sleep in the Nascent Realm?"

"Not at all. Lack of hunger rarely occurs in the Ascended Realm, and is usually only in the middle of the Sky Realm that the need for sleep fades."

Yet another reason I'm an oddball, or as Sarah put it before, a "Paragon." Shaking my head I realized it wasn't a title I wanted.

Hoping to change the topic away from me, I asked Sarah about something I'd been worried about. "Any word on the war?"

She sighed. "I think it's time we set up a permanently shielded room for these kinds of chats," she said and brandished her S-ROB once again. "What I'm about to tell you isn't for general discussion, so please don't discuss it with others." She paused and added, "That means don't tell Portia."

"Fair, I do tell her too much." I sighed and deflated. "I mean, there's a rumor we're dating, for crying out loud."

"Your father has pulled the front line away from Rhinebur," Sarah said. "As you know, they took the region a week after the war started, thinking it would be an easy location to manage. I'm not sure what's so special about the region, despite its destruction, but of course I'm not on the war council."

Her words made me tense up, because I had a pretty good idea of what was special about that region, but I said nothing. *Yeah, Undine's site is likely what Westwood is trying to keep safe.* For a moment, I wondered if my footprint on Anfang would be remembered by a similar location, almost forgotten yet coveted nonetheless.

Sarah's voice broke me out of my thoughts. "With the frequency of their clashes, it's wearing both sides pretty thin."

"With how long cultivators take to regain their energy, how's Daddy's reserves?" I asked. *Weird how I return to calling him "daddy" when I'm worried about him.*

Sarah pursed her lips. "He's likely taking a Sky pill daily."

"Is that bad?" I asked.

"It can be, but with him being the main striker, they're keeping an eye on him. There's no word about him getting a pill from a bad batch or suffering backlash from consuming it prematurely." She patted my hand. "Overuse can also burn your meridians."

Pointing to myself I asked, "I took seven of them in rapid succession, is there no worry about mine?"

"Do your meridians ache?"

"No."

"Then you're fine. It's the first time you've taken them. It usually only causes issues if it exceeds your limits and rebounds off of your dantian."

"Ah," I said. "Like that essence storm. My meridians ached after that."

"Right. Now, you have lunch with our lord in a few minutes. While you are doing that, I will seek out Dean Donovan on your array." As I checked myself in the mirror Sarah said, "Remember your hunt will begin next week, have you mentioned it to our lord yet?"

▼ ▼ ▼

After my lunch with Gideon, I found myself wandering Ersta idly. I had no sense of direction, but I knew my guard could help me return to the Imperial Royal dormitories. Despite being easily lost, I happened by the soothsayer. A lady Sarah introduced me to over four years ago.

I'm here already, and I'd likely not find my way back unless I asked Sarah or the guards that were with me that day. An image of me lying flat on my back, and someone with a large hammer hovered over me entered my mind. Since Sarah had told me about how worn down Dad was getting, I'd had no less than two waking nightmares of someone attacking me on the front lines. A chill went up my spine when the all too real image of a hammer came down on my skull.

Entering her shop at that point was easy, though I asked my guards to stay outside.

I really don't want them to hear anything awkward I might ask.

"Welcome once again," the woman said. As usual the pagan iconography was present.

I always get a darker vibe from this shop. It must be how media vilified paganism due to it sharing a pentagram with a darker religion. Looking back at the image above her, I was relieved that the point was still pointed up.

"I'm fine, kind of."

"Congratulations on your marriage," said the soothsayer.

"How–" I started then sighed. "Right, that is kind of your thing, isn't it?"

She smiled.

"I wanted to get a reading about the war," I said simply.

"Follow me," she said, and we entered a room on the side with a crystal ball. One that was most certainly decoration, if my last visit was any indication. The woman held her hands out toward me and closed her eyes. "Hmm, I see."

"What?"

Her voice turned sorrowful. "Such a grim future. I would avoid of mallets, if I were you."

Her comment made me lean away from her. *Either she's able to read minds, that was a prophetic memory, or that was a dumb lucky guess.* I asked, "Is there anything I can do?" I rolled my wrist to emphasize my words. "You know, to have a better outcome?"

She shook her head. "Probably not on your own."

"Who's help do I need?" I leaned forward. "Do I need my Daddy's help?"

She shook her head. "Your daddy wouldn't be able to help you, I'm afraid." With a smile she continued, "But I might know who can."

▼ ▼ ▼

Exiting her storefront, I handed the instructions of how to get to her friend's shop to my guard and we headed there.

Being directionally challenged sucks, I thought as we rounded two left corners and arrived at our destination. *I would've missed this, why would I have gone right?*

Through the inconspicuous door was a cluttered mess of a shop. Stranger still, it had no windows on the outside, yet was vibrantly lit by windows that presented a sea of stars and clouds.

Are those fake windows some form of tech like the Solar room at home that projected the Emperor's image to us?

The shelves were stuffed with books and piles of them sat around. Vials of unknown liquids sat haphazardly about with no labels or prices. Whoever this was collected a little bit of everything.

In the left corner was a strange blue box with the text "Son Aven" along its top, which was Estar for guard box.

Despite the space, and disarray every item had a strange well-kept yet timeless look to it.

Walking up to the counter a large furry mess of a cat, as big as or bigger than a Maine coon, lounged. There was no sign of the owner. I had no aims to touch the cat because despite my connection to them, this one seemed a bit creepy with its gigantic toothy smile. It gave the impression it could take my entire hand off at the wrist if it so pleased, and gave the impression that it was a greater threat than a room full of demons.

Despite that, its coloration was beautiful. A deep navy coat with frosted teal tips around its mane and covering its tail. Its ears were long and pointed like a lynx. Bands of blood red fur banded above its paws' joints. Its bright brown eyes drew me in.

After five minutes of waiting, my curiosity overrode my better judgment and I reached out for the beast. Hoping it wouldn't bite as I'd feared.

"I wouldn't do that, if I were you," came a voice in front of me.

"Ahh!" I shouted and jumped back a foot. "You startled me." I thought, *He was not there a second ago.*

"Sorry, I have that effect on people. Don't pet the cat, he'll erase you."

Taking the cat in for a few seconds then regarding the owner, I said, "Erase, not attack, bite or scratch?"

"Yep, erase. His fur isn't fur, but elemental fire," he said and dropped a book onto the cat. The item landed on the cat and was gone before I realized it was burning. "How may I help you today?" he said, despite his casual threat of a fire cat which didn't seem to affect the counter it was perched on.

"Um…" I paused then realized I couldn't remember the soothsayer's name. *I know she told me.* Instead of trying to remember her name I said, "The local soothsayer sent me. She's just around a few corners," I said, guessing where her shop might be.

"There's only one soothsayer around. You're pointing in the wrong direction," he laughed. "Bad with directions, are you?"

His pin-point accuracy at my flaw made me frown. "I'm here because she said you could help me. I'm worried about the war, though she said you're a chronomancer. I'm not sure how time will help."

"Time can *always* help, girl. It's all in how you use it," he said and vanished from my sight. "Pausing time can help you move unseen–" his voice came from my side.

Before I could catch up to him, his voice came from where it was, behind the counter, "Rewinding time just a little can do wonders," he said and held up the book he'd incinerated before. "There are other means of time control, like fate play, but it's a bit more complex, and hard to even describe, let alone show."

I sighed. "Yeah, I might be in the wrong shop," I said and turned to leave.

"Skeptical?" he asked.

"Well, moving fast is something most cultivators can do. For all I know," I said and pointed to the book in his hand, "You had two copies of that book."

"What, then you don't believe the claims?"

With a shrug I said, "Why would I?"

He nodded and snapped his fingers. "Then I'll give you a better example." Brandishing a mirror he offered it for me to take.

Crossing my arms I paused and regarded the mirror for a few seconds. *It doesn't look like anything other than a mirror, but he's super suspect.* Reluctantly I took it from him. Looking in the mirror there was an immediately obvious "change."

Within my reflection, my eyes were vibrant blue, almost to the point of emitting light.

The hell?

CHAPTER THIRTEEN

TREAD LIGHTLY

THAT'S SO WEIRD. Am I seeing this right?

The large cat stretched out on the counter behind me, its tail flicking back and forth in the reflection. Positioning the mirror to look at the cat showed its eyes were also vibrant blue.

Wait a minute. They were brown.

Turning back to the cat, I saw that its eyes were still brown.

Ah, this "chronomancer" is trying to pull one over on me.

Checking the reflection again, the cat's eyes were blue.

This mirror must be an artifact of sorts? Beguiling, or using illusions?

Flipping it over in my hands, it seemed to be a pretty ordinary item with a flower engraving on its wooden back. *Weird. It doesn't look enchanted; it's quite basic, even.*

"It's not nice to fool others," I said. Hefting the mirror up I said, "That cat's eyes are blue in the reflection, but you can see they're brown–" As I said that, the cat blinked and presented two differently-colored eyes.

The man gave me a smile behind his skin-tight mask. "Suit yourself," he shrugged. He lifted his arms and dramatically said, "For what is this god to a non-believer?"

God, huh? If you're a god, I'm the empress.

He winked at me just before I turned away.

Another chill ran up my spine as I exited his shop. *Yikes, he's just creepy. Don't try to flirt with me, weirdo. I need to go give that Soothsayer a piece of my mind, and find out why I can't remember her name!*

"Let's return to the first shop, okay?" I said to my guard.

They gave me a brief bow of assent, and we returned.

Before I could touch her door, I heard the chronomancer's voice from inside. "Madame Vira, the girl you sent my way was a difficult case." His voice once again became melodramatic. "She doesn't believe."

How did he get here before me? Then I remembered the communication system we had at home, and wondered if these two had something similar.

Vira said, "She'll come around. They always do. When she comes face to face with her fate, that'll be all she needs."

"Yes, Eloria is most certainly meddling," the chronomancer said. "Her bindings of fate are everywhere, especially around that girl."

They're talking about me, obviously. Why would Eloria be messing around in the war? If I'm her champion, surely she's working with us!

Since Madame Vira was busy talking to the chronomancer, I decided against confronting her and to return to my dormitory. I passed by the mirror in the loft and stopped. Then I backed up. Within the mirror, my own eyes were an electric blue.

"Sarah!" I called in a panic. *Did he really change my eye color? How the hell did he do that? Is there anything else impacted by it?*

"Yes, Anessa?" Sarah said with a curtsy. "What is it?"

Pointing to my eyes I asked, "What color are my eyes?"

With a concerned look, Sarah said, "Blue of course, why? Are you feeling okay?"

I was stunned. "H-how long have my eyes been blue?"

"Always," she said and touched my forehead with the backside of her hand. "You don't have a temperature, but you are sweating quite a bit."

My eyes have always been blue? Bullshit! That doesn't even make sense! Sitting down on the couch in the sitting area I hugged myself. *This is bad; changing my eye color is one thing, but Sarah said they've always been blue. Worse, if I'm being honest, the simplest way to accomplish this trick would be to tweak my memories, and not the memories of anyone else.* I was distinctly uncomfortable with the idea of someone mucking about with my mind.

Placing my hands on my forehead, I hyperventilated a bit.

Tania a few minutes later said, "Your Imperial High Grace, I've prepared some calming tea for you."

Looking at it, I recognized the smell as the one Sarah had given me a few years ago to calm myself. Despite the fact that I knew it would knock me on my ass, I downed it anyway.

"Thanks Tania," I said meekly. "I'm going to go lay down. Please let my teachers know I'll be missing the rest of my classes today."

"Very good ma'am," she said and curtsied.

"Is everything alright, Anessa?" Sarah asked.

"Yeah," I said and sighed. I'd been staring at myself in the mirror for the past five minutes. *They're still blue.* Worse, if I put my hand next to my face, I could see a faint blue reflection on my skin. They didn't just look bright, they were actually emitting light!

She opened the shutters, making the luminescence my eyes exhibited fade with the extra light.

"Let's get you ready. You have some free time this morning to spend with both Gideon and Yukirei."

A smile came to me unbidden. "That'll be nice." I thought, *Not sure about Yukirei, but Gideon I don't mind seeing.*

"Haven't you been thinking about her nice pink lips?" came a sardonic voice inside.

What are you saying? I have not.

"Your daydreams seem to suggest otherwise," Trish said with a smile.

My smile turned into a frown, and I grumbled to myself. Despite that I played with the end of my braid after Sarah tied it off.

Trish said, "I was only kidding Anessa."

When I entered the common area, Yukirei was already there drinking tea, facing away from me.

"Good morning," I said, and gave her a curtsy. *Gods, what am I doing? I rarely ever greet her this way.*

"Hi there," she smiled, twirling a strand of hair in her fingers.

I sat across from her and we talked about my upcoming hunt. Heat suffused my neck and cheeks when I realized I was mirroring her pose, even to the point of playing with a lock of my hair.

Yukirei didn't talk about anything in particular, but she was all smiles.

The bug Trish had put in my ear made it impossible to *not* notice her lip balm, eyeshadow and mascara. Most of my focus was on her smile.

Damn it Trish.

"Sorry," she said. *"I wasn't trying to cause trouble."*

I'll admit, she does *seem to be flirting some, I think?*

Trish sighed. "You may still have the slightest bit of ASD left inside you. Yes, she's flirting, and so are you."

I am not flirting! I thought fiercely, with a frown.

"Is something the matter?" asked Yukirei.

Waving my hand I said, "No, nothing's wrong, just had a bad thought." My admission made me think to Trish, *Damn it, now you've made it weird. I'm not flirting.*

"There's nothing wrong with it. It's not like you're doing anything inappropriate." Trish paused then added, *"You're just enjoying one another's company, and that's okay."*

Her words calmed me a little, but my blush never left my cheeks. Focusing on my body language and tone, I had to admit that Trish was probably right, on both accounts. *Damn ASD. I have to try harder to notice things about myself.*

Gideon's arrival made Yukirei perk up when he sat next to her. They had soon locked eyes, solely focused on one another.

I smiled when they held hands, and thought, *Compersion is a feeling I never thought I'd have.* Laughing at myself, I realized, *On Earth, I didn't even know what the opposite of jealousy was! No one ever told me that I'd feel joy seeing someone I love, love someone else, too.*

Jealousy did weasel its way into my head when Gideon kissed Yukirei on the lips. Though it was brief and not really all that romantic, I thought, *Damn it. I haven't even kissed him yet! And he's my husband!*

Trish reminded me, *"You are not yet married as far as the public is concerned, and Gideon asked your permission to become betrothed to Yukirei a few days ago. You even approved. You technically did kiss him when you two married, though you were a bit flustered so you might have forgotten that part."*

A tear nipped at the corner of my eye. *I know, but that passive knowledge doesn't make seeing them kiss any easier!*

"True," Trish said with a nod. *"They're basically cheating right in front of you. You should set some ground rules."*

Don't be like that. Communication is difficult in any relationship, let alone in polyamorous ones, but perhaps you're right about setting rules.

I coughed to get their attention. "Yukirei," I said in a firm tone, "Gideon. We need to talk later about relationship boundaries, okay?"

They each looked at their connected hands and separated them. Then they went rigid and looked at me with studiously neutral faces.

Their clear concern about my opinion made me sigh. *Too stern, I guess.* I said, "Holding hands is fine," I said and held out mine to indicate they were okay. Closing my eyes and turning my head, I said with a pout, "But I would really like to have had Gideon's first k-kiss."

"Oh!" Yukirei said and stood abruptly. "I'm so sorry."

I opened one eye and looked at her.

She bowed, instead of curtsied, showing her remorse and deference.

"It's okay, but I think we need to talk more as a group. How would you have known that if we had never talked about it?"

"Good point," she said and sat back down. "We really should." Levity entered her voice. "So which of us gets *your* first kiss, now that Gideon's has already been taken?"

"I… I…" Words failed me, and I took a few seconds to find my voice. "Most likely Gideon," I said and exhaled. "You and I are in an acp hoth, yes, but we've gone on no more than one Accord."

She crossed her arms, still holding Gideon's hand, and huffed. "You haven't let me set another date yet."

"You don't need to set the date, I will," I said. *What am I saying? This is so confusing.* My mind raced a million miles an hour. *I'm acting like I know what's going on, but–*

CHAPTER FOURTEEN
THE HUNT BEGINS

TANIA HANDED ME a knife, which I strapped to my thigh. Sarah was off to the side preparing my backup outfits for the hunt. My outfit for my Awakening ceremony in a week's time was adorning a dressmaker's dummy nearby.

Even stranger was that she had also prepared Gideon's *and* Yukirei's outfits. Gideon I understood. However, since the two were betrothed, the task of preparing her outfit fell to Sarah, for some reason. An image of the brusque maid-guard that would tail Yukirei came to mind, and I realized, *Yeah, Aul is* not *really a maid. She's effective at being intimidating, though.*

She was so intimidating that my guards wouldn't even permit her inside my dormitory, or within ten paces of me.

Still weird that Yukirei doesn't have any staff of her own. Does her dad want her to be self-sufficient or something?

In my sitting area, Gideon and Yukirei were already waiting on me. Approaching them, I held out my hands and said, "How do I look?" Aside from my physical training sessions, this hunting excursion would be the first time I would be permitted pants for more than a few hours.

I did a simple slow pirouette, and I caught Yukirei whisper, "Eyes up Gideon."

He chuckled and replied, "You too."

Ignore them, I thought. *I don't want to think of Gideon having those kinds of thoughts just yet, and Yukirei's just being a troll.* It took a lot of self-control to ignore the fact that their eyes had drifted when I finished my spin.

The half grins they had when I glared at them told me they were *both* being trolls.

Their mischievous behavior was contagious, however, and I just giggled at them both. "You two are bad. But I appreciate the break in tension. I'm really nervous about this hunt."

Gideon nodded. "My first hunt was much the same. It was a bit shorter, but that's because my mom took me herself. Her game was mostly white tail deer and the rare rumble fox."

Rumble fox? I thought, but didn't ask further.

"On my first foray, I came close to snagging my first deer, but I missed and my arrow hit the tree right beside it." He sighed. "We never caught up with that one. The next few outings I mostly focused on gaining confidence." He smiled as he looked my way, he chuckled as he said, "I cried when I made my first kill. Mom had to give me a few minutes to recover."

Both Yukirei and I took one of his hands. "That's part of what I'm afraid of. Taking the life of an animal."

He removed his hand and placed it over mine, giving me a light squeeze. "The hunt is as much about you as it is the animal. Expect that your party will not waste anything. The biggest lesson is finding your resolve." With a light cough he added, "At least that's what my mom said. I'll be honest, I still have difficulties with it."

Sarah chimed in, "Your hunt is about more than respecting life. It's about discipline, order, rank, and finding your voice in the field."

"Yeah," I pulled away from Gideon and faced Sarah. "That's another big thing I'm uneasy about," I said and threw my hands in the air. "Who's going to listen to me? I'm all of sixty-five-pounds—"

"Sixty-seven," Sarah politely reminded me.

"Yes, sixty-seven," I said mockingly, then I mumbled to myself, "What's two pounds, Sarah?" Returning to Gideon I said, "Thanks for sharing, I'm glad to hear anything of your childhood..." I paused, realizing we'd known one another for a good part of it. "The parts I don't know, I mean."

He flashed me another smile. My chest heated up, and I thought, *Damn those pearly whites and emerald eyes!*

"I didn't learn any of that in my hunts," Yukirei said. "Since I can fly, it gives me an unfair advantage." She held up a finger. "Though the tracking skills are useful if I wanted to go on a ma–" She cleared her throat, "On a hunt."

Yukirei paused for a second.

"Hunting wild game will teach you the value of life. It's easy to say every life is valuable, but…" her voice quieted, "It's an entirely different thing to experience it."

Oh… she almost said manhunt, and then mentioned the value of life. Are the hunts she's had to go on, a far different kind? Despite my resistance to her feelings, I felt compelled to place my hand on top of hers. Patting it, I removed my hand and gave her a forced smile, which she returned.

I suppose her hunting beasts wouldn't be fair, to the beasts. The Mystic Beast Purge came to mind, and I wondered, *Did Mystic beasts cultivate like humans? Is that why they were seen as a threat? Would they have given Yukirei a challenge, or even been able to threaten her?*

Shaking those thoughts off, I stood to leave. "I'm supposed to meet the party at an Inn in Ersta." With a laugh I said, "I hope they're nice."

Standing near the exit, I said, "Gideon, please come here."

As he moved closer my heart rate increased. *Is this a good idea? We are married, so I suppose it's okay to indulge a little, but…*

My thought was interrupted by him patting the top of my head and saying, "What is it, little kitten?"

Damn it. I loved head pats, but I couldn't help but worry he merely viewed me as a little kid, despite the conversations that we'd had to the contrary.

Holding his wrist with both hands I gently pried his hand away. "Come closer," I said.

He leaned down and said, "Okay?"

"Close your eyes."

He smiled and did so.

I glanced over at Yukirei, who was watching intently from the couch, having turned around in her seat. She was smiling.

Despite my enormous embarrassment, I gave her a grin before cupping both sides of Gideon's face. *I told you Gideon would get my "first" kiss, I'm not sure I could kiss you anyway, Yukirei.* I gave him a quick peck on the lips and pulled away. My cheeks were burning as his eyes opened. "For good luck," I said.

Yukirei saw my display and sauntered over with a broad smile while humming. Standing next to me, she turned to Gideon and leaned forward.

Before she could plant her own kiss on his lips, I interposed my hand between them, and she kissed my palm instead.

"Hey!" she protested.

"We talked about this, just the other day!" I said and huffed.

"You just gave him a kiss, didn't you?"

Crossing my arms I said, "Yes. For luck. I said that. And you wanted one 'just because.'" I turned my head away. "You can kiss his cheek."

She gave me a wolfish grin. "Okay," she said and did so. Afterwards she turned to me and closed her eyes.

"What are you doing?"

Batting her eyes she said, "Don't I get one, you know, for luck, too?"

I growled, "No."

Her reaction was immediate, and she looked like I'd just kicked her puppy. It tugged at my heart and I sighed. Holding out my hand I said, "You can kiss my hand."

She pouted a little and said, "Fine."

Within an hour I was standing in front of the Inn where I was supposed to meet the hunting party. My guards entered first and held the door open for me. When I stepped through, the ruckus died down and almost all eyes turned to me.

It was a simple place compared to what I was used to, but it reminded me of a museum that had relocated a medieval tavern and used it as an exhibit.

The barmaid approached me and said, "How can I help you, little miss?" Her skirt came to just below the knee, which I knew, after eleven years living on Anfang, was rather scandalous here.

Man, I miss modern fashion. I'd never wear anything like that with this stick figure of mine, or without proper Earthen undergarments.

In response, one of the guards holding the door said, "Please know that you are addressing Her Imperial High Grace, Anessa Carlyle."

Great.

The barmaid smiled and gave me a curtsy. "Welcome, Your Imperial High Grace. Is there something we can help you with?"

"I'm supposed to meet someone here," I said. "They're the head of a hunting party."

"Oh, that'd be master Ban over there," she said, and pointed to a man standing at the bar.

Walking up to him, it was clear all eyes were still on me. *I suppose someone who can barely see the bar top is a little unusual. A noble girl at that.* I hesitated before speaking to him. Both sides of his head were shaved and his hair was in a mohawk, the first I'd seen.

When I hadn't said anything for a few seconds, he said, "Yeah?" and then bared his teeth. They were pointed as though he'd filed them, giving him an overall edgy look.

Charming, I thought. "Are you Ban?"

He grunted and stepped around the guy next to him. "You got a customer," he said then mockingly added, "*boss.*"

"Well met, Anessa," Ban said, without looking at me. His attire was clearly a cut above that of the man with the pointy teeth. It consisted of leather studded bracers and a nice black lace-up tunic with leather straps that seemed to be more decorative than functional.

He took a long drink of his ale and sat the wooden tankard down with a hollow clunk. Turning to me after wiping his mouth with his forearm, I suspected his move was intended to be discreet. He held out his hand.

It was calloused and he clearly worked hard for a living. Despite the expense he had invested in his outfit, I felt a little guilty knowing that a single piece of my hunting garb would likely buy his entire wardrobe several times over.

"Ask him if he uses a hammer," Trish intruded as I took his hand.

I'm not asking a man named Ban if he uses a hammer. The chat joke would be completely lost here. People already think I'm weird enough!

Taking his hand, I gave him a firm handshake. He asked, "Do you have any experience in hunting, or leading a group?"

I shook my head.

"Did you prepare for your excursion?" he asked in a steady tone.

Shit. His blunt question put me on the spot, with all eyes on me, I was uncomfortable to admit, "No sir. I wasn't aware I needed to."

"What *did* you bring?"

I reached for the knife on my outer thigh and hefted it up. "A knife."

He smirked briefly, but flattened his expression just as quickly. "A leader must take initiative. Don't rely on others to tell you what to do all the time." With a chuckle he continued, "I know that's usually what your privilege grants you, but imagine you were planning for a party next week, and showed up only to find a single person struggling to set it up. You might blame the poor soul who was there when you had the thought."

Knocking on the bar top, he said, "*Or,* you could make sure. Follow through. No one has enough pull to *will* something into existence." He winked. "Except maybe the gods. But neither of us is lucky enough to be one of those, now are we?"

Laughing nervously I thought, *Gods, I hope I don't become a goddess of death. Her Goddess Eloria said it's very likely, but that's a terrible role to step into.*

"I can tell it will be a pleasure to teach you, Your Imperial Grace, Anessa." Ban nodded to my guards.

It was clearly a signal they were expecting. They put their hands over their chest and bowed before departing.

I couldn't help but wave to them as they left. To my surprise they returned the gesture.

"Why do you say it'll be a pleasure?" I asked.

"You didn't try to immediately say you were in control." He sighed. "I've had a few fun cases. The worst was a boy who had just awakened his fire and just had to show it off to everyone." Shaking his head he added, "He got angry when I told him I didn't even notice his candle-sized flame."

His comment made me snort. *Gods, that was Rhis, I just know it.* Wiping the smile off of my face, I asked, "Who all is joining us?" Looking around Ban, I noticed the mohawk man give me a glare, so I used Ban as a visual shield.

He gestured around us to the patrons in the Inn's tavern. "Everyone you see here."

"Everyone?" I said, astonished.

"That's what I said," he said with a laugh.

Mohawk swaggered around Ban and put his hand on my shoulder. "Are you ready to go, little girl?" He edged closer. "Do you need me to carry you?"

"Please remove your hand," I said flatly.

Inching closer, he put his free hand to his ear. He cackled and said, "What was that? Is that an *order*?"

Turning to Ban, I saw that he was busy paying his tab, so there'd be no help there.

"I won't ask again, remove your hand."

His grip tightened on my shoulder, and I was finding I don't suffer fools gladly.

Taking his wrist in my hand I gently, for me, twisted.

He yelped. "Ouch!" His other hand scrabbled uselessly at my grip, and he shouted, "I give! Let me go!"

When I let go of his wrist he fell over onto his rear. He cursed under his breath, "Damn it Ban, you could've warned me that she's a cultivator!"

Ban knew he'd be doing this? Is this some form of hazing? Shaking my head I thought, *Why is it that putting him in his place seemed easy, but I have reservations about taking the life of an animal?*

CHAPTER FIFTEEN

A STONE'S THROW

WATCHING THE MEMBERS of Ban's party exit the inn, I followed him, being sure to match his pace. Seeing them all geared up made it clear I was woefully unprepared.

I don't even have a proper weapon for hunting. Ban had kept the knife I handed him, probably because it wasn't suitable. *What am I going to do, punch the animals?* Shaking my head, I realized, *That's too brutal.*

"Here," Ban said and placed something in my open palm.

"What's this?" I asked looking at the small rusty cube.

He tapped his ring finger. "It's a poor man's storage ring. Treat it like how you would a storage artifact and you'll see what's inside.

Doing as he asked, I saw that the cube held a tent, a rough blanket tightly bound around the tent… and nothing else. From my experience with storage rings, what little there was, it couldn't hold anything more, not even a tin cup. "Cool," I said. "Thank you."

He snorted. "Your father is paying us well enough."

While I want to ask what Dad's paying the party, it would be a rude question.

Westwood lived up to its namesake. Within minutes of exiting the town's front gates, we were surrounded by the thick of the forest. Since the trees were everywhere, regional forests didn't have individual names, and were often simply called the unclaimed forest.

Either Ban's party was quite good, or I was quite green, but it wasn't three minutes before they'd found tracks of a game animal.

A woman flagged Ban down, and I followed.

"Jackrabbits," he said.

"Oh?" Looking at the impressions in the dirt, I didn't know how he got that. *These are barely two bars in the ground and what look like paw prints. How can he tell they're from—*

"They're old though," he stuck his finger into the dirt, then ushered for me to do the same.

Great. The ground was a tad moist, but I had no idea what he was getting at.

He pointed at the edge of the impression. "Note the cracks around this impression. This was wet when the print was made, but has since dried out. This morning's dew is why it's tacky again," He shoved his finger a bit deeper until he got to some dirt, and said, "but the moisture only goes so deep."

I blinked at him. "You got all that from looking at it?"

"You can tell it's a rabbit, first, by the bars its hind legs leave; they're almost always in line with one another," he said and put his hand next to one of the tracks. "A jackrabbit because it's about as long as my hand to the finger. Your hand's shorter, so you'll have to think of it as a hand and a half or so."

Lining up his hand and arm with the track he closed an eye and pointed forward, despite how easy it was to see the next track. "Sighting," he said, "can help when you don't have the clearest or newest tracks." He pointed to the next track in the set. "The closest next imprint was actually a *different* jackrabbit. If I didn't sight it first, I would have had a hard time telling."

Ban gestured for me to do the same. When I did, he continued, "The second track is at just enough of a different angle that it's evident a different jackrabbit went by later, or maybe the first one circled back. The order isn't important." He smiled and pointed to the third impression. "We're tracking this line."

We followed it, and sighted a few times before it went ended abruptly.

"Damn. It went cold." He looked around and smiled, his eyes fixed on something in the distance. He stopped near something black, what I thought were berries. Picking one up he sniffed it, then smeared it between his fingers, smelling it again.

Motioning for me to pick one up, I did so. It was *warm,* and I instantly knew it was not a berry. I involuntarily stuck out my tongue.

"Go ahead, break it," he offered.

I groaned. "Do I have to?"

"What else are you here for?"

With a frown bigger than I thought possible, I squeezed my fingers like he had, and the little ball turned into a very gross jam on my finger. "Eww," I whispered.

"Get a whiff," he said.

My right eye twitched but I did so. The scent was almost bitter and I kept playing the texture through my head because I was bothered by it. It made me want to wash my hands immediately.

"Yuck, it's like hay and lemon with a bit of, uh, poo?"

Ban gave a belly laugh at my displeasure. "Well, the last one you'd expect, given what it is."

"Yeah, funny," I said with a disgusted look. "Ha-ha."

Calming himself, Ban produced a handkerchief which I accepted gladly and cleaned my hand.

"Now then. That's a cecotrope, and believe it or not, seeing these is a good sign. They're usually ingested shortly after they're produced. Given they were still here, we must've spooked the animal away."

His words made my impressive frown deepen. *They eat this?* I involuntarily shook my hand not wanting to think about it.

Standing he chuckled lightly. "To be young again." He wiped his finger and thumb on a nearby *tree*, then poured the smallest amount of water from his water skin over his fingertips before finishing by wiping his hand on his trousers.

Looking at the ruined handkerchief, a pang of guilt went through my gut. *Damn, I really am bad at this.*

Around the remaining "berries," I noticed a footprint and used the knowledge Ban had taught me over the last hour. He left me to my own devices and though it went cold, I did spot an odd, almost arrow-like burrow in the ground.

It's too big to be a snake, isn't it? I hoped. The hole that accompanied the spot was at least seven inches around.

"What'd you find?" Ban said, nearly making me jump out of my skin.

"I'm not sure, is it too big for a snake?"

"No, but I don't think there's any snakes inside," he said and pointed back to the earlier spot I'd prefer to forget. "I think you found the home of our earlier friend. Probably a cottontail warren, based on its size."

"How can you tell any of that?"

"If a snake had taken it over, our friend's little mess wouldn't be there. They would've been eaten or moved on. Jackrabbits don't burrow, so it's not the home of the first jackrabbit we were following. I'll explain more," he said and pointed to a tree a few dozen paces away. "Let's go wait and see if our friend pops out in a little while and I'll explain."

▼ ▼ ▼

Over the next *ten hours*, Ban droned on about tracking and the basics of hunting in a forest. My Earth knowledge meant jack-all in the wilderness here. Several times I asked him to slow down or repeat himself.

"Zev," he said, calling to the mohawk from earlier.

"Yeah?" Zev grumbled.

"Teach her to shoot," Ban said.

Stomping over to us, Zev asked sourly, "The Nether you choosing me for?"

Ban smiled. "Well, you so graciously volunteered earlier in the bar, remember?"

Clicking his tongue, Zev said, "Fine." He lazily gestured toward a rabbit cautiously sniffing around the burrow and added, "Rabbit." Pulling an arrow from his quiver and held it up. "Arrow." Without hardly looking he lined up a shot and let it loose. Turning to me he said, "Done."

Though he *had* nailed the rabbit just below its ears, I just stared at him. "What?"

Ban motioned for the temperamental man to join him off to the side for a moment. Though they were whispering, I had good hearing, though I had to *try*.

"Listen, Zev," Ban started quietly, as he put his arm over the lanky man's shoulders. "I'm trying to help your dumb ass. The last noble child you did your stupid act with was a baron's son. I had to give up half of our pay for that screwup." He shook the other man's shoulders. "I don't want to know what a highborn *Imperial* Duke might ask for if she tattles on you."

Placing his hand on Zev's neck Ban finished his lecture, "I would like you to keep your head where it's at, are we clear?"

Zev's voice cracked. "Crystal." Returning to me, he put on a fairly creepy smile and said, "Hey sweety, how about we try again?" Holding his bow out he said, "If you'd like you can use my bow, though you don't have to."

His one-eighty made me take a step back. "That's okay. I can use a different bow. But please stop smiling, you're making me uncomfortable."

Clinching his jaw he said through gritted teeth, "Great, give me a few minutes to get you a different bow. Okay?"

He dashed over to one of the other archers and all but begged them to borrow their bow and arrows.

As he did this, Ban handed me a set he pulled out of one of the "poor man's storage rings." Winking at me he said, "Thought I'd wait before giving you these. Watching Zev try to scrounge one up was fun."

I couldn't help but smile.

Zev stopped in his tracks as he rushed over to hand me "my" bow when he saw me already holding one. His knees knocked and his shoulders slouched. Groaning, he muttered, "Seriously?" Then he returned his forcibly borrowed weapon and put on his best smile as he approached a second time.

"Sorry for the wait, Your Imperial High Grace, Anessa. If it would be okay with you–" he turned his head and stuck out his tongue. "Gods above, I can't do this. I'm terrible at all this mannerly crap." He bowed. "I'll try to teach you properly, if you'll allow it."

"It's fine. I wasn't even going to mention you annoying me in the tavern earlier." Though I was being honest, I may have been a bit blunt when I added, "It's not worth the effort."

Once again his teeth ground and he gripped his bow tighter. "Glad to hear it."

Seeing the half grin on Ban's face made me snort-laugh.

Zev seemed to be seeing red at this point, so I offered him an apology of my own. "Sorry, I didn't mean that like it sounded. You're a very honest person, and I'm starting to see what people mean by being easy to read."

He sighed. "Fine, let's get this done. Take your bow, and nock an arrow."

Even though he demonstrated, my first four attempts had me picking the arrow up off the ground. Afterwards I still struggled when trying to pull back on the string; the tip of the arrow would veer away from the bow, and fall quickly to the ground.

After a few minutes of this Ban once again called Zev over and the two started to exchange words.

They're almost like an old married couple.

A few of the other hunters were grinning and shaking their heads.

It's not the first time those two have argued like this. Is Zev Ban's younger brother or something?

Trish decided now was the right time to noodle in on my thoughts, *"Maybe they* are *married. Who knows, on Anfang."*

Her intrusion made me shake and think, *Yeah that's not a thought I want to have.*

"I get it, Zev's not my taste either, but Ban I could get behind, or... well you know what I mean."

Eww, no. My thought leaked out of my mouth, "Seriously, stop."

More than a few eyes turned my way. Ban must've heard because the two stopped instantly.

Crap.

Zev approached and changed his tune again. Instead of just *repeat after me* without instruction, he tried to explain how I should hold the fletching and keep it in place.

"Now let's fix your stance, I would normally help guide your posture, but…" he held up his hands and shook his head. "I'd rather there be no misunderstandings like in the tavern."

I think Ban's getting through to him.

It took another hour before I succeeded in pulling the bowstring back. The instant I had, there was a tinny twang and snap as the string broke and the tension released on the bow's limbs. "Whoops, sorry."

"Must've been a worn string," Zev said and took it from me. In a minute he'd restrung the bow and handed it back.

"Thanks," I said. Then in less than ten seconds, we heard another pop. Closing my eyes, I sighed. "It snapped again, didn't it?"

"Yes, what's wrong with you?"

"How am I supposed to know how far back to pull it?" Holding the bow out for him I asked, "Do you want me to restring it?"

He snapped up the bow. "No."

"Why not?"

He looked thoughtfully at me and pointed to a roughly seven-inch thick tree. "Use half your strength and push on that tree."

That's an odd request. Shaking my head I complied, and quickly yelled out, "Crap, timber!"

After the tree was fully felled, I laughed to Zev. "Maybe we can start with how far to pull the string back? Seems pulling the string isn't what I struggle with, but knowing when to stop."

"Yeah. I guess so," he said and added, "Here's the bow, start by pulling back slowly. When it's reached its limit, I'll say stop, so don't go very fast."

He said slowly twice, guess he doesn't trust me, though the two snapped strings are a good enough reason.

Holding up his hand he said, "First, we might want to set up a target." He gestured toward his chest. "I don't want your arrows finding my ass as a target."

Setting up a makeshift target, he said, "Aim for the black dot I marked on the tent. That's five points. The rest of the cloth is one. Outside the cloth is zero."

"Okay," I said and tried to line up a shot, and promptly figured out I had no idea how to do so.

"Stop sticking your chest out like that," Zev chastised.

"It's not like it's in the way," I countered with a groan.

"Damn it girl, I'm not worried that your flat chest will get hit, it's a form thing."

"My what!?" I yelled and stomped toward him. "That wasn't nice!"

He backed up until he bumped into a tree and tried to press into it as I advanced. "Now, I didn't mean that as it sounded." Stepping around me gently he lined up his own shot. "Look, notice how my body's in line with the shot instead of opposing it? My chest is very slightly in." He slowed his breath. "Keep your hips and shoulders straight. When you anchor your shot, consistency is key." He turned to me for a second and added, "Which means pick a reference point and stick to it. So if you get used to pulling the arrow back to your chin, do it that way, always."

Going on for a few minutes, he gave me a clearer idea of what he was trying to convey.

Once he gets in the zone, he's much more like Ban in his thoroughness. Zev went through all this before, but having him show me is worlds different than me trying on my own.

"Now then, you try, and I'm sorry I pointed out your flat chest."

But he has the social grace of a frog.

On my first shot, by complete luck, it hit dead center.

"Beginner's luck," Zev said, mildly impressed. "Try again."

Following his request, I did, and it went so far off course that *everyone* in the hunting party decided it was safest behind me.

Great. It's not like I'm going to hit any of you.

Trish piped in, *"Not on purpose, anyway."*

Gee thanks.

My next ten arrows hit nothing but air. Well, more accurately the trees around the target. When I ran out, I went to fetch them.

A brisk *crack* told me I'd snapped the arrow's shaft off at the base of the trunk. The moment the sound hit my ears I ducked instinctively and peeked back at Zev.

It seemed he hadn't noticed, so I moved to the next arrow for retrieval. *crack*

"Seriously?" he complained.

"It's not like I did it on purpose."

He followed me to my next target and my right eye twitched as I heard a third break. This time, the arrow split straight down the center.

Breathing through my nose, I ignored the glare of the cranky man beside me. We collected the remaining arrows, with Zev retrieving most of them.

By the end of it, I'd ruined twenty. All the while he continued to gripe under his breath, but never quite loud enough I could hear exactly what he was saying.

Four hours. It was four hours before I could hit the *edge* of the target twice in a row from ten feet away.

"About time, isn't it?" Trish teased.

Real helpful, do you have any actual advice?

"Suck less?"

This earned her a snort and before I could line up my next shot, Zev said, "Alright, double your distance from the target."

"What?" I said and my eyes shot to him. "Why?"

He pointed down range, "You can hit it. So we make it more difficult. The goal is to make you competent, or at the least," he smirked and looked at the rest of his party who were all keenly watching me, "safe."

It was another four hours before I hit it dead-center, like the first fluke. Emboldened, I tried again and heard a snicker when it went so wide, I may as well have been blind.

Glaring at the offending party, he covered his mouth and after a moment he said, "Well, sometimes even beginner's luck strikes twice."

Turning, my foot bumped into a rock and I was quite annoyed. Picking it up I threw it at the target, ablating the lucky arrow in the center of the tarp. A dull thunk lightly shook the tree.

Figures, more beginner's luck.

Grabbing another I lobbed it in the same direction and a louder *crack* told me I'd hit the first stone that I had embedded in the tree.

By the fifth strike on the same spot, Zev whistled, "Looks like we have a natural stone thrower!"

I rolled my eyes at the comment, but was secretly glad he'd acknowledged me in some way. *Better to be good at something* odd, *than nothing at all.*

CHAPTER SIXTEEN
NO MATTER HOW SMALL

AFTER THE TENTH successful thud against the target space, Zev suggested, "Maybe we should move back some. When hunting you won't always be so conveniently close."

Once I'd moved back to fifty feet I had a nagging sense that something wasn't quite right.

"Let's fix your posture some," he said, then guided me into a vaguely familiar pose.

It clicked. *Holy crap. How did I forget this?*

"It has *been fourteen years since you played baseball,"* Trish said, and I could see her tossing a baseball in my mind's eye. *"Well, eleven of your new life, and three years before your demise on Earth at least. There's a bit of a gap, of course, between there and here."*

Sensing my body adjust itself, my pose and weight shifted. Despite having no glove, I patted the rock against my fist and heat bit my cheeks as I knew Zev likely found the gesture strange.

Taking a breath I cleared my thoughts and took aim. The sharp snap of the rock leaving my hand and hitting the tree in less than a blink of the eye made me jump a little. As a cloud of splintered wood burst from the tree, which shivered and fell, I realized that all the other noise nearby had ceased. I took a peek behind myself.

Everyone had stopped what they were doing. The forest itself had grown quiet for a minute before the sounds returned.

Breaking the silence, I laughed nervously, "Hehe, should I use a bit less force?"

Zev's response was pitched, "Ya think?" He cleared his throat. "Or at the least, hope your first shot succeeds. You won't get a second, not with that racket."

Running his hand through his hair he said, "Let's work on your approach a bit. That speed is unreal, but we have to make sure it goes where you want." He held up a hand to stop me, though I wasn't arguing. "We need to make sure your aim is perfect, or you're a liability, not an asset."

I nodded.

"Since you're so..." he pursed his lips, "...monstrously strong, perhaps you could add grooves to the rock yourself. Usually you'd take rocks to a blacksmith's apprentice for engraving practice, but I think you could handle it yourself, using another slightly sharp rock."

His admission that my strength was *monstrous* didn't sit well with me, but I didn't have a succinct comeback.

"At least he didn't say demonic... right?" said Trish, I assumed to try and console me.

Sure. I'm not a demon, just a monster. Repeating the thought made me laugh at myself ruefully.

Carving grooves in rocks without crumbling them to powder was another thing I was bad at. It took the remainder of the day to get a single passable specimen. Though to be honest, I think Zev only declared it okay because he was just tired of me at that point.

When I woke up the next morning, I lamented, *We've still got six more days of this, and I'm already bored. When am I going to learn anything about leadership?*

"What do you mean? Haven't you been paying attention? Watch Ban and how he directs others." Trish paused, then added, *"I know it doesn't take all of your focus to dig tiny trenches in those rocks."*

Her reminder that I tended to miss the obvious made me shake my head. *Of course.*

"Come on," Zev said. "Let's see what you've learned so far."

We walked for a few minutes, and I realized the entire hunting party was moving along with us. Every so often he would glance back at me. After five minutes, and his third brief pause, I realized he was trying to tell me something. Looking around, I saw the telltale signs of rabbits, like those we'd seen on my first day with their party.

Crap. I really am oblivious. Stopping myself, and noticing the others doing the same, I wrinkled my nose as I picked up what I thought was a cecotrope. It was warm, like the first time. Though I did not feel the urge to smear this one. The temperature and smell told me everything I needed to know. The passive smiles of those around me, said there was likely a less direct way to tell, but I decided to ignore them for now.

"Do you remember chemistry class?" Trish asked.

Vaguely. Why?

"Remember how our teacher hammered into us to waft the vapor instead of smelling it directly?"

Oh… shit. Well that's what it was, but yeah, I didn't need to sniff it. The admission made me shake my head at myself once again. *I should really stop and think about what I knew and apply it to what I know here on Anfang. Thanks Trish.*

Taking stock, I noticed the other signs that a rabbit had moved through recently. Based on the stride it was a smaller species. Seeing me continue, the party spread out. Though it was cheating, I watched where they avoided, which gave me a clue on where to look.

Zev gave a quiet click as he realized what I was doing.

Ban was trailing the furthest behind, and was directing a few of the members at our tail. It seemed he was confident in Zev's ability to teach.

He really has surprised me, not being as rash as before.

"Probably had something to do with Ban reminding him that pissing off high nobles was a bad idea." Trish sighed contently. *"Not that Roland would do anything, because of who he is, but we don't need to tell them that."*

Spotting a cottontail, I took a rock out of my storage ring.

Ban raised an eyebrow.

I guess he didn't see my tree hunting yesterday. Remembering the stares and the stark silence in the wood, I amended my thought, *Though he must have heard it.*

Before I lined up my shot, I closed my eyes and sent up a prayer. *I don't know if you want to hear this, Eloria, but I won't take this life lightly. Please help my aim stay true and make sure it is quick, and painless. … um, Amen?*

A whisper caught my ear. It wasn't harsh or judgmental, but it said, *"Instead of Amen, please ask me to 'guide this poor soul into your eternal embrace.'"*

Hearing Eloria respond to me made me smile, and at the same time, put a lot of pressure on me, I repeated my prayer, *Please help my aim stay true, and make sure it is quick, painless as you, my Goddess, guide this poor soul into your eternal embrace.*

"Good ad-lib, but if you want to use a title for me, call me Mother Goddess. Otherwise, so it shall be."

Mother Goddess? I thought. *A bit concerning, though I suppose if I take over her monikers she would be my progenitor of sorts, since she carries the titles today.*

I took aim and let loose, trying to keep the strength I used to the bare minimum. The small animal leaped and fell over, motionless.

Ban moved forward and brought it to me. "Not bad for a first time. Stones, though? Did the bow not suit you?"

"Not really," I admitted. In attempting to take the rabbit by its ears, the animal's carcass fell to the ground. It no longer looked like the cute little bunny it once was, and I was left holding two ears. Closing my eyes I breathed through my nose. *Don't panic.* Flattening my lips out I picked the remainder of it off the ground. It looked as if it had been hit by a car.

"So that happened," I said aloud.

"Yes," he said with a nod. "You'll need to watch how much strength you use."

"I thought I did," I said with a sigh. Then I made the mistake of lifting it, to look at where the ears had been attached, and found it was quite mangled. There wasn't a "face" to speak of. My stomach roiled and I held it away from myself, turning my face away. I had to hold my lips tight and breathe. *Don't puke, you'll just look stupid.*

Without missing a beat, Ban said, "Ready to skin it?"

Letting out a groan, I whined a little. "Sure, but... can you give me a few minutes? I'm not used to this." Thinking for a moment, I realized I didn't want to forget this moment. Despite the small size of the game, I knew the memory would stick with me. Then I had an idea. "Ban, do you think I could have one of the rabbit's feet?"

He arched a brow. "Sure, but what for?"

Before I said, *for a good luck charm,* I caught myself. "Just a memento of sorts." I thought, *They probably don't view rabbit's feet in any special way.*

Ban nodded. "I would usually say this would ruin the pelt, but…" he looked between the two parts of the rabbit in my hands and said, "that ship has sailed."

His commentary made me frown. *Sorry little guy… or girl.* I shook my head. *Not checking, I really don't want to know more.*

"You'll find out more anyway when you process it," Trish chimed in.

Great.

As we worked through the steps that followed, I had a chat with Ban.

"How has any of what I've done so far helped me learn anything about leadership?" I asked.

"Well, right now we're not focused on that part of your training. You need a bare minimum of survival awareness and hunting skills," he gestured around to our party, "before you'll be effective at giving anyone here an order."

All I could do is nod along. *That makes perfect sense. What would I even tell them? This isn't some fairy tale where I instantly know how to direct everyone.* Glancing between Ban and Zev, I added, *I don't even know but two of their names. It'd be the height of hubris to order them around with 'Hey you! Go do the… hunting thing!'* The thought made me chortle. *I know so little that my imagination doesn't even know what I'd say.*

Ban glanced at me with a wry smile and shook his head. "Now, to be clear, this lesson would apply to *any* leadership position."

His voice firmed, drawing my attention.

"Without situational awareness, you can't lead effectively at all. Out here I'm in charge, but put me on a horse in a battlefield? I'd be on the horse at the back, following the leader." He shrugged. "I've never been a commander."

Another member of the party brought Ban another, slightly larger and considerably less squished, cottontail. He processed it as he talked, making the work appear effortless. Holding the animal up he removed the rope around its neck. "Usually these are hunted with traps. They're small, nimble, and not really suited for arrow or stone felling. You can do it, as you've seen, but it's more work than it's worth."

With a smile he added, "So I was surprised when you had even a little success earlier. It was going to be a lesson in how *not* to hunt small game."

His smile fell. "Back to the battlefield. For you to lead there, you'll need battle experience. Don't fool yourself if you think the play fights you engage in at school are even a little like real combat. Out there, no one will try to demoralize you before cutting you down."

Dad must've told him about my bout with Wyn. His comment made me raise a brow since his story didn't add up. *If he hasn't been on the…*

"You and Zev are a lot alike," he added.

"How so?" I said crossly.

Ban smiled. "You are both open books." His motions with the rabbit carcass grew sharp. "When I was a child a group of bandits attacked my village. They paid no heed to rank or station, and just slew anyone they came across. Their luck ended because a wandering cultivator was in town and dealt with them for the crime of," his tone gained a hint of ire, "spilling his drink. It amazed me that he seemed ready to simply let the town burn until they messed with his wine."

"That's awful. Not all cultivators are like that," I said aloud.

"I envy your optimism. Many nobles are cultivators. Tell me, how do most of them act," he said and waved the knife in his hand around to get his point across, "you and your family notwithstanding?"

Wyn and Rhis came to mind, and my small circle of friends made me realize I didn't know many. I'd avoided those who seemed pompous, and once I thought about it, that included most of them.

"The ones I avoid are prideful, arrogant, and…" I sighed. "Not worth mentioning."

"I'm glad that someone of your nature is a highborn noble."

Thinking through our conversation, I realized that as a noble, my hands were already not completely clean. Despite the fact that it was the result of their own crimes, my part in helping Mina regain her kingdom had led to the deaths of over a dozen people.

Seeing the blood on Ban's knife, I grew cold looking at my open palms. It brought forth thoughts of hurting someone for real, face to face. Making two fists, I thought, *I hope the war doesn't last until I'm an adult by law. It may be helpful, but I'd much rather not have battle experience.*

CHAPTER SEVENTEEN
THE FOX AND ITS TAIL

BAN'S PARTY COOKED a mean rabbit stew, or so they thought. Since to nobody's surprise I'd never been taught anything about cooking, I was given the option to merely partake in the meal.

"You doing okay?" asked one of the female hunters as we ate.

"Yeah, why?"

"You're sitting as far away from the group as you possibly can without making Ban nervous. I just figured you needed some space. Did your first hunt bother you?"

Giving her a half grin I said, "Partly that, and partly thinking about the role I may need to play in war, in the future."

The toned woman tilted her head and asked, "War?" She looked fit, as everyone here did but me, though based on her attire's threadbare nature, she was either not the best huntress of the group, or she was so new as to not have made enough to buy new clothes.

Crap. My right eye twitched. "N-never mind. Daddy set this hunt up in the event that I need to lead in the future, is all."

"Are you worried you won't lead well?"

I shook my head. "Worried about taking a life of something bigger than an animal."

Her eyes widened and she nodded. "Right. Definitely not an enviable place to be." Her eyes lingered on me a second before she asked, "How was the food, anyway?"

"Great, thank you," I lied. It had little to no taste, and I suspected they hadn't added much, if any, seasoning. *I am very spoiled, I thought ruefully.*

Trish said, *"You are a bit, but it is one of the perks of being part of the noble class. The food you're served is on par with what you had on Earth, though probably healthier due to the lack of preservatives and ultra-processed junk food."*

"Right, anyway," the woman said. "Would you mind rejoining us? We're moving onto the next target."

Following her, Ban began speaking when I got close enough. "Our next quarry is the black fox…" He went on for a good twenty minutes, slowly transitioning to talking to me alone. We went over how to identify their tracks.

Our party spread out until the female hunter from earlier called us over.

"Good find, Sam," he said. "Hmm…"

"What?" I asked.

"What do you see, Anessa?"

Looking at the tracks, I wasn't sure what he wanted me to say at first. Then the oddness of the tracks dawned on me. "Oh. Is it missing a leg?"

He patted me on the back and said, "Good. It seems so. These are fresh, so we should track this one down."

I asked, "Even though it's injured?"

With a frown he said, "Especially because it is injured."

"For what, mercy?"

Nodding, he gestured forward for me to continue.

It took me over an hour to travel less than a football field's length. The fox had been around here a lot, so there were a lot of overlapping tracks the further we went. *It almost seems lost.*

When I spotted it, I instinctively held up my hand as I'd seen Ban doing. In the corner of my eye I saw the man smile and shake his head.

The animal was thrice the size of the rabbit I'd felled, yet it seemed a bit thin. Its wound seemed to have scabbed over, though based on the tracking we'd done, it wasn't having much luck hunting.

A pang of guilt tugged at my chest and I instantly understood Ban's sense of mercy. *Poor thing.*

Taking a golf-ball-sized stone from my storage ring, I took aim. Sending Eloria a prayer, I let loose, but I failed to notice the twig under my foot. The moment it broke the fox's head snapped to us. What would've been a clean dispatch ended up snapping its remaining front leg.

After that, all it was able to do was spin in place trying to escape.

"Shit." My eyes shot to Ban and I asked, "Now what do I do?"

He sighed and closed his eyes, pulling a knife from a strap on his chest. "Make it quick so it doesn't suffer any more, okay?"

The hunter was holding the knife by its tip, and I took its handle nervously. *Gods, not like this.*

As I approached it the animal cried out with what sounded like a mix between a dog whimpering and a monkey screeching.

Slowing my approach, the cry only added to my unease.

I guess it had tired itself out, because it was now lying there glaring at me.

Placing my hand firmly on its snout I desperately looked the animal over as it started to struggle once again, finding its second wind. It didn't have a chance at breaking free, of course.

Looking back to Ban, I said pleadingly, "I don't know what to do."

He joined me and motioned to the fox's neck. "Feel its neck. The point where the pulse is the strongest is where you'll need to cut."

Tears welled up in the corners of my eyes. I put the knife down and followed his instruction. Once I found the spot, I picked up the knife again and sent another prayer up to Eloria in hopes it wouldn't suffer.

In the longest moment of my life so far, I did what was needed. Despite the lack of danger to myself, I held it in place firmly because I was worried it would prolong its suffering. After thirty seconds I let go, as it faded.

Cliché as it was, I closed its eyes and sat with my back against a nearby tree. I didn't bawl aloud so much as cry. *That was horrible.*

Trish consoled, *"Don't be so hard on yourself, I'm here if you need me."*

After hugging my legs for a minute, Ban approached and said, "You doing okay?"

"No," I whined.

"You did the right thing," he said and crouched next to me. Holding his hand up to those around us he added, "Everyone here has been through that in some form or another."

Looking over the group, no one was smiling. Instead of looking down on the newbie who couldn't even kill a fox without crying, they all had somber looks on their faces. Even Zev was looking downtrodden.

"It's not easy to go through that," Ban said. He held out a waterskin. "Get yourself cleaned up." He gestured toward the fox. "I'll take care of processing this one, you take care of you." Before letting go of the container, he said, "Remember, it's as important to learn how *not* to hunt, as it is to learn what to do. Hold your head high, okay?"

Wiping my eyes with my sleeves I nodded and took it from him.

Probably due to my cat-kin heritage, my hearing was quite a lot better than average. As I washed my hands, I overheard Ban talking to Zev.

"She'll make a great Lady some day," Ban said quietly.

Zev asked, "Isn't she a bit emotional?"

Ban countered, "Says the man who cried last month when he made a similar mistake?"

"I did not," the mohawked man protested, "and you can't prove it!"

"Empathy, compassion, quick wit," the party leader continued. "Each great traits, and she has all three."

Zev sighed. "She's also quite humble, which is pretty rare for a noble brat. The Blackwood boy we trained up was a real piece of work. He almost reveled the suffering he caused."

So they did train Rhis Blackwood. It's a shame he's following in his brother's footsteps.

Trish jeered, *"He was the cuter of the two, too."*

I froze as that thought entered my head. *Gross, girl. It doesn't matter how they look if what's on the inside is rotten to the core.*

"True. It's a shame though, isn't it?"

I don't need you to go shipping me with other people, I have Gideon, that's all I need. Polyamory or no.

"Sorry, sorry," she laughed. *"Just trying to get your mind on brighter thoughts."*

I smiled, and frowned just the same. *Thanks. But I don't want to think about the Blackwoods any more than I have to.*

"Are you alright?" Ban said at my side.

The suddenness of his presence made me falter, "Y-yeah, just heard a name I wasn't too pleased to hear."

"Oh?"

Lowering my voice to a whisper I said, "Blackwood."

"You heard that?" he asked in surprise and laughed nervously. "I'll need to remember you have good hearing."

"Sorry. Rhis and his brother Wyn tried to force my hand in marriage several years ago. They aren't my favorite people." I sighed. "I only got out of it because Wyn toyed with me in a school-sanctioned bout when he could've won. If it weren't due to my own luck, I would likely be a Blackwood." That admission made me shiver thinking about it. "Gods, that's scary to think about."

"While I'm not really able to talk about previous clients," he smiled and continued, "I can say I am glad you are still a Carlyle."

Seeing the fox's pelt rolled up, I asked, "Would it be okay to ask for the fox's tail?"

"Of course. This is *your* hunt. It was also your kill. Is that all you'd like from the carcass?"

I nodded, wincing at the word "kill."

"Are you okay and ready to continue? I'll have the tail to you once its processing is complete. It needs a few extra steps besides field dressing. If you'd like, we could go over them together after the hunt is over. We don't have all of the materials with us to do a full job of it since we usually hold that off until a bit later out of the wood."

"Okay, I'd like that."

"Do you want to help with the steps to keep it fresh until the hunt is over every evening as we make camp?"

That's a thing? I thought and nodded. "Sure, there's a lot for me to learn. If I'm going to ask for something, I should at the very least understand what I'm asking of someone, even if I don't complete the steps myself every night."

He grinned. "Very good. Let's start on the next target: a whitetail deer."

Despite my willingness to continue, it took me half an hour to get back into the swing of it. Smacking my own face, I shook myself out of my funk and followed Ban. It seemed that was what the group was waiting for because the pace and movement of everyone else followed suit.

These guys are really good at what they do.

Trish said, *"Not just the hunting part, but managing their client as well. I bet they're expensive."*

Not compared to just a single trinket my family buys me, I bet.

"Well, if you want to go there, you'll work yourself back into a humdrum mood." Her voice hardened, *"So don't."*

Right, right, I thought and moved next to Ban. "What do we need to look for with whitetail deer?"

As he was explaining their diet and shape of their hoof prints, Zev motioned us forward and I followed along.

When the party became eerily quiet, I assumed there was something nearby. Indeed, after a dozen or so minutes, we spotted one.

"Now then," Ban whispered, "You're strong enough to take one out with a stone, so that's what we'll do. They're big enough that you can get an idea of what they're going to do by watching them. Notice the ripple of fur as it makes large movements. Let that guide your timing." As he finished his commentary its head perked up.

Just before it bolted, I saw what Ban was talking about. *Neat. I would've never noticed that on my own. But why'd he tell me that instead of having me learn it on my own?*

Trish said, *"You have how long with them? They'll only be able to teach you so much. If you notice an animal's about to run, you're less likely to... accidentally injure it."*

Oh... yeah, I thought, my mind remembering my previous mistake.

"Stop!" Trish yelled in my head. *"Don't do that to yourself. He wants you to avoid that. Remember, he's teaching you how not to hunt, too."*

Thanks. You've been really, really helpful Trish. I was afraid you were just some twisted memory I was hallucinating. Although you are sarcastic, annoying, and tease the hell out of me, it's nice to have some of what I remember of you back. I laughed at myself. *Even if I am just going crazy.*

CHAPTER EIGHTEEN
[KINDA] YOUR TURN

ALTHOUGH BAN'S PARTY was highly skilled, it took us the remainder of the day to find the next whitetail that didn't bolt. I was extra cautious, and more importantly everyone was very patient with me.

"Sorry that took so long," I said as I watched him start to clean the animal. My task was to hold the hide as he removed it with his knife. I did my best not to wrinkle my nose.

"It's alright," he said. "Starting tomorrow you'll be in charge of the hunt for a boar."

I took a step back at that. "Uh. I need to know a lot more, like hand signals and stuff. I've seen that you guys often communicate silently, without saying a word. Can you teach me that?"

He smiled. "And that's why you're taking point tomorrow. You're taking this seriously, and moving through my training faster than most." He held up his hand like I had the day prior. "You already figured this one out; it means to hold. We use it when we're stalking prey and everyone needs to come to a stop and pay attention."

He held his hand out to the side, slightly behind his torso. "This is stop; we only use it when we're dealing with sharp and dangerous prey. The two are similar, but stop should be immediate, and means you need to be mindful of even your breathing."

We went over several other signs, over two dozen in all. "The five you need most are hold, stop, you, me, and come here." He demonstrated them as he went. "If you do much hunting in the future, the rest will come in time."

"Thanks," I said and yawned.

"You're sleeping tonight. I know you don't really need it, considering, but I'm requiring you to do so, as the master of the hunt."

Giving him a nod, I found an empty area to set my tent up. When I took it out of what Ban had called a poor man's storage ring, I was bemused to see that the device crumbled in my hands once the contents were released. *Oh, I guess a poor man's storage ring means it's single use.*

Seeing the items scattered on the ground, I picked them up one by one. Each was more mysterious than the last. *What the heck do I do with this?*

Looking around, everyone else was setting theirs up so quickly and easily, it wasn't evident which piece went where.

Over the next ten minutes I tried, and failed, to set it up. When I finally thought I'd had it, I turned around and one of the poles smacked me in the back of the head.

In my mind I could hear Trish snicker.

You're not going to help, are you?

"It's not really something I can help with. Some things you have to see to understand," Trish said. *"No worries: here comes your knight in sarcastic armor."*

Sarcas… I began to think and noticed Zev standing beside me with his arms crossed.

"This is too difficult to watch." He held out one hand. "Would you like some help?"

I sighed. "Sure. I'd rather it not smack me a second time."

He stifled a chuckle and whispered to himself, "That *was* pretty funny."

As we set it up, I noticed that only ten single-person tents had been set up. Some of the party was clearly not planning to sleep. There were five people sitting in trees, and an equal number standing around our site.

Huh. Is this part of the forest particularly dangerous?

Zev, someone who I know isn't super fond of me, then placed the final anchor for the tent.

Right. I'm the reason. It's not dangerous out here, but if something were to happen to me, heads would roll, so to speak. The other nights, when I didn't sleep, the patrol duty was lax by comparison. Six at most. *Maybe I'm considered more vulnerable if I sleep?* Remembering my sleeping situation I asked Zev, "Can you ask Ban to come here?"

Once the master of the hunt was present, I said, "I might make a bit of noise when I sleep." Laughing nervously, I added, "Okay, a lot of noise."

Zev was in earshot and said with a snort, "What, does our little monster lady snore?"

Shaking my head I said quietly, "No. I have nightmares." I thought, *I can't tell them that I was murdered in my past life, since only my parents and Mama-Krissi know about that.* Placing my hand on my chest, I came up with what I thought was a believable lie, "A criminal in the Sky Realm pinned me down a year or so ago and tore through my bodice and shift." I closed my eyes. Despite believing it to be a lie, my voice quivered, "I don't think I'm over it yet." Clenching the hand over my chest into a fist, I wiped my eyes and thought, *Crap. Was that a lie?*

"Lady Anessa," Zev said.

Once I'd focused on him, he bowed. "Sorry." He didn't say anything more and instead went inside his own tent.

Trish piped up, *"I don't think you are over that. Your nightmares had mostly stopped until that bastard Mr. Morris attacked you."*

Maybe you're right. I still see his face at times when I close my eyes. Furrowing my brows, I continued thinking to Trish, *I didn't know my nightmares had returned. No one else had told me.* It was times like this that I was glad I didn't sleep very often.

"He didn't mean anything by it," Ban said.

"Oh, I know." I waved it off. "I just wanted to give you a heads up so you weren't concerned about the occasional scream coming from my tent."

His lips thinned and he merely nodded.

I'd better just stop talking. He's getting worried.

"Go get something to eat," he said, "and turn in for the night. I'll let the others know not to worry about you."

Nodding, I walked to the fire, and Sam served me some deer stew.

"You okay?" she asked.

Giving her a false smile I said, "Yeah, I just have something on my mind."

Ten minutes later, I'd barely taken a bite. Not that it was bad, per se, but thoughts of that memory I'd buried, and clearly not dealt with, had robbed me of my appetite. *Gods, Mr. Morris was going to kill me. I don't even want to think about what he was planning* before *that by tearing my clothes.*

"Mind if I join you?" Sam said, saving me from my own thoughts.

Gesturing to my side, I said, "Sure."

"Not hungry?"

"It's not that, though in truth I don't actually need to eat." I lifted my bowl. "Perk of being a cultivator, I guess."

Sam tugged at a pouch on her left arm. "Try this, it might help."

Accepting her offering, I noticed it was a small black ball. *Oh, pepper.* It wasn't an uncommon spice in my meals, but it was far better than the *nothing* they'd added to the meal.

Crushing it between my fingers, I spread half of it over my bowl and tossed the rest to the side.

Her mouth opened for a second and she reached out her hand hesitantly.

Oh right. I froze. *Pepper's expensive, isn't it? And I'm chucking half of it away.* Pulling a large copper from my storage ring, I handed it to her. "Sorry, no harm intended."

"This is too much," Sam protested, trying to return it to me.

"Don't worry about it." I shrugged. "If you give it back, I'll just toss it on the ground," giving her a wink I added, "and someone else will pick it up."

She gave me a smile and put it away. "I'll accept, but only because I don't want Zev to get it."

Oh man, I thought to Trish.

"What?"

I kind of understand Oliver now.

Trish gave an impression of confusion. *"That makes even less sense!"*

He always had a hard time telling the difference between ten pounds and a hundred. For me, I have the same problem with money. When it's given to you like it's worthless, your sense of scale is thrown off.

I added that to the list of things to worry about when I turned in for the night.

By the time I rolled out of my bedroll the next morning, the entire campsite had been packed and the hunting party was ready to go.

Great, and I was hoping I wouldn't hold them back.

"Morning sunshine," Sam said.

"Good morning," I said and yawned. Dropping my voice to a whisper, I asked her, "How long has everyone been waiting?"

"Only about five minutes," she said.

Ban motioned for me to come over to him and said, "What's our plan for today?"

Laughing nervously, I said, "To hunt a boar."

"And to do that we…?" he said, drawing out the final word.

"Remember why you're here, Anessa," Trish said.

Her prompting reminded me. *He hasn't taught me how to track a boar, or what the best approach to use is.* But glancing around, I realized I had the resources I needed, even if I didn't know exactly what to do.

"Zev," I said, then paused, thinking on my words. "Form two groups and go find us a target or two."

He laughed and said sarcastically, "What would I look for?"

Arching a brow at him I crossed my arms. "Does Ban tell you what to do in such detail when he gives you an order? Do you need him to hold your hand?"

The smile vanished from Zev's face. "No ma'am. That's not necessary." He turned to the side and gestured for five others to join him. They talked together for a while and split off.

"Ban," I said, and he looked to me with a half-grin. "Do you generally exhaust boars and go in for the kill then, or is there a better way?"

He rubbed his stubbled chin. "You *could* hunt boar that way, but we're not doing this for sport. Once we find them we tend to draw one away from the group, if it's not solitary, and set up an ambush."

He went on to explain that they use overgrowth, parts of the forest often trampled underfoot by animals. Something perfect to setup a trap.

Before he could go any further, I called, "Sam." Once I'd had her attention, I said, "Take a few people with you to find a suitable ambush site." Shaking my head, I corrected myself. "Make that two. We don't know where Zev will find our quarry."

She nodded and pulled someone else with her in the same direction Zev went.

"We might need to adjust our tactics based on what they find," I said to no one.

"And what should we do?" Ban asked.

"Stay put, I guess," I said and shrugged. "I didn't designate a rendezvous point, so I'm guessing they'll meet us... here?" I said, unsure of myself.

"You are the boss right now," he said with a bland smile.

"You're going to let me waltz right into a mistake, aren't you?"

With his hand on his chin he pulled it away long enough to say, "Maybe. Mistakes happen, everyone makes them." He winked. "Even me."

"Will you tell me when I make a mistake?"

He shook his head. "Not right away."

"Promise you'll make sure no one gets hurt or killed. If something happens you think warrants you taking over, do so."

His smile fell. "I don't need to promise that. Someone might get a light injury, but no one will die."

"Once we have an ambush site. How do we draw the boar?"

"Someone will act as a lure. They'll piss it off, and allow it to give chase."

I blinked. "Isn't that... dangerous?"

Ban's next words hit me in the chest, "If you're prepared to take a life, be prepared to lose your own."

"I..." my words caught in my throat as I thought of my Dad on the front lines against the Redwater Empire, "... suppose you're right."

"Aggressive prey," Ban continued, "come with risks. That's why we use traps or cunning when we can."

His change of pace helped me dismiss some of my stress. *I wish I could take notes. I'm learning so much it's becoming a bit difficult to track.*

"Don't worry," Trish assured me, *"I'm taking notes."*

Her words made me tilt my head to the side and scratch my cheek. *How, exactly? But her only response was a faint chuckle that echoed through my head.*

It made me question whether I really *was* descending into madness.

CHAPTER NINETEEN

ONE SHOT SURPRISE

WITHIN AN HOUR everyone had returned.

"We found two sounders about half a mile out that way," Zev said and pointed to the northeastern forest around Ersta. "There's five adult sows, and two, possibly three boars per sounder."

When he finished, I blinked at him a few times. "Now explain that as if I have no clue what you're talking about." Because I didn't.

He sighed. "A sounder is a group of wild pigs." Chopping the air he added, "Generally there are multiple generations in a group, around three, with a single top sow that keeps everyone in line."

I nodded.

"When a group is large enough, it attracts multiple boars. During…" he hesitated as though he was considering his words, then rolled his hand, "You know…"

"I don't know."

His cheeks flushed, and he said, "During mating season."

"Oh, right. Estrus."

"Yeah," Zev said, drawing the word out, "that."

"We're after the…" I thought for a moment, "a boar?"

"Right. The sows are needed to make more piglets. We usually don't fell them unless there's too many, and they're causing trouble." He motioned toward Ban with his head, "Then we'll get an official request to cull 'em."

Pursing my lips I realized that he likely meant the juveniles, since they wouldn't survive without their mother.

"Got it. Who's the best at being a lure?"

A few people looked over at Ban.

At their prompting, I corrected myself, "Who here needs the experience?"

Sam raised her hand. "That'd be me."

"You up for it?" I said.

She nodded.

I hope she doesn't get hurt.

"She won't," Trish said. *"I'm sure if she was too inexperienced, Ban would step in and assign a shadow or whatever the equivalent is for hunting."*

Good point. For all I know he'll do so anyway, since he said he wouldn't correct me.

We walked for a good fifteen minutes, pausing briefly at the ambush site for Sam to show the traps they'd already set up.

Zev called Sam and me over a few minutes later. He whispered, "They are about a hundred yards ahead."

"Got it," Sam whispered. "I'll wait five minutes for everyone to get into position, then I'll draw it out."

We nodded and hoofed it to the tiny clearing. It was large enough for us to comfortably hide several paces outside of the perimeter.

Before I could step into the clearing, Ban held his hand in front of me. He said in a low tone. "You almost stepped into one of the traps. Be careful."

I looked with chagrin at the spot. I hadn't noticed a thing. *How will Sam not trip it herself?* I wondered.

"Probably because she set the snares. I'm sure they have ways to remind themselves of where they're at when running for their lives. I would hope so at least, or we wouldn't be using this method," Trish said.

We surrounded the area. The worst part was the waiting.

"This is a weirdly-shaped area, huh?" She asked as we waited.

What do you mean?

"It's on the smaller side being about twenty foot wide, but it's so long."

Looking over to Ban showed he wasn't looking for Sam, he was also examining the clearing. His brows were furrowed.

Maybe there's something odd about this place?

Our attention turned as a whistle rang out.

She's here.

Her arrival involved a feat of athleticism that belied her form as she jumped a good fifteen feet without touching the ground. The moment she did, she bolted to the side.

It was accompanied by a clearly aggrieved squeal that sent a tiny shiver down my spine. The animal stormed through, and snagged its hind leg in the very snare Ban had saved me from.

The rope around its leg shot up off the ground and halted its forward momentum in one go, slamming it into the ground.

Ouch. That had to hurt.

Seeing no one else move to engage the animal, I pulled a rock from my storage ring and exited the trees slowly. The beast was a bit stunned and was struggling to make it to its feet. Based on its repeated failures, I suspected the sudden stop had hurt its leg.

Don't worry l… big guy, it won't hurt for long.

Taking aim, I nailed the boar right between the eyes. Without another peep, it fell straight to the ground.

A few others entered the clearing, giving the animal a wide berth.

"Uh, I was only trying to stun it," I said.

Sam approached the animal and struck its neck with a foot long dagger, causing a serious laceration.

It didn't react.

"Remind me not to piss you off again," Zev said shaking his head. "That was instant."

"Instant what?"

"An instant kill, no suffering, n–"

Ban clapped lightly and lowered his body into a crouch. He spread his arms out, pressing them both toward the ground, twice. Then he made several other hand signals I wasn't familiar with, and everyone retreated backwards and climbed into the trees.

Sam approached me and helped me up into one, since I had the strength, but not the finesse to do so quickly.

Before I could ask her what was going on, she clamped her hand over my mouth, and shook her head. It was then that I noticed the entire forest had gone silent.

After a little while, Sam removed her hand, and the next couple of minutes were awkward.

What's gotten everyone so concerned?

Seconds later the lightest of tremors went through the tree we were on, and then I heard a whooshing thump in the distance.

"Behind us," Trish warned.

Slowly, I turned my head. In between the gaps of the trees, I saw something *massive* moving. It was at least sixteen feet tall and equally wide.

What the heck is that even? I thought with alarm, and felt my fingers dig into the wood of the branch we were on.

As it emerged, all I could think was how it looked like a mix between a English Bulldog and a boar, only far, far larger. Its tusks were as wide as I was around, if not more.

Once it entered the clearing, which I then realized was just about exactly the width of its body, it lunged toward the boar at a speed I didn't think possible for such a massive beast. When it turned its body, the entire swath of trees in its way were merely shoved over like toothpicks.

It picked up the boar as if it were a chew toy and shook its head twice. This simple act severed the carcass into two, throwing the other half dozens of feet into the air.

That thing weighed at least six hundred pounds! Though my cultivator strength granted me a push force of a few tons, doing what it just did was well beyond me. My gut said it wasn't even trying.

I really hope it goes away once it's finished.

As that thought finished, someone sneezed.

All eyes snapped to the source. Zev. Who itched his nose.

Damn it, man!

Turning back to the beast, its eyes narrowed to pinpricks. A shiver ran through me as it seemed to be looking at me.

A lot of yelling came from Ban the moment the "Bull-boar" started to move.

Sam quietly said, "Sorry," and then shoved me from the tree. To my surprise I landed on my feet, and she landed next to me and pulled on my wrist.

As we ran, I could hear it behind us. I almost pissed myself when I felt a warm, moist blast of air on my back.

Despite my cultivator strength, and despite knowing I was far faster than Sam, her dragging me made it impossible for me to find my stride.

When the thought entered my mind to look behind myself, a massive splash of drool dropped on my shoulder.

I screamed.

Sam briefly turned and locked eyes with me, before yanking me forward and shoving me to the side. She stalled her momentum in that simple motion.

My world spun as a second impact orders of magnitude greater hit me, and I spun like a top until I crashed through a few trees before coming to a stop.

"*...t up.*"

It took a good fifteen seconds before my head stopped spinning and I could make sense of the words rattling around in my skull.

"*Get up!*" Trish screamed in my head.

Putting my hand on my head, I realized there was something in my other hand.

It was Sam's hand, and arm.

But only up to the shoulder.

Before I could process the reality of what I was holding, my mind went to releasing it abruptly and I took stock.

"It's coming back around!" Ban yelled.

It was making a beeline straight toward me.

I was suddenly *very* pissed.

Driven by that fire in my gut–to hit the bastard in the head–I took out a stone from my storage ring. *This won't do anything but appease my anger.*

Pushing my thoughts inward, I thought of all the times I'd used my cultivation skill to damage things by mistake. Leaving pock marks in steel even my brother Oliver couldn't dent at his prime, before he was poisoned.

If I can leave this thing with a reminder of our meeting today, maybe it'll think twice before approaching humans.

Based on its speed, I knew it would be on me in twelve seconds, so I counted down, giving myself three seconds to dash to the side.

I marked off the seconds in my head, holding the rock to my forehead as I did so.

When I reached one, I threw the rock as hard as I could, and watched as a shining pink object shot forward in an instant. In the very next, the center of the beast's head, all through its body in a straight line, sported a six-inch-wide hole. Clear enough to see skylight through its form.

My plan had been to move, but I stood there in shock, as its massive form collapsed, and slid to a complete stop, inches before my face.

Instead of cheer or smile, I fell to my rear and put my hands on my head, still sorting my feelings out. *How the hell did such a large beast get so close before we noticed?*

I thought about Ban's reassuring promise that nobody would get hurt, and looked bleakly over at Sam's dismembered arm. I no longer felt reassured.

CHAPTER TWENTY

KILL STEALER

TAKING A FEW minutes to collect myself, I stood. My eyes locked onto Sam's arm. *She…*

"Didn't make it," Trish said, solemnly.

Before I could process my grief, or look for the rest of her, someone spun me around by my shoulder.

Zev got into my face and picked me up by my shirt.

"If you could do that, why didn't you damn well do it in the first place!?" He yelled inches away from me, spit showering my face. "If you had, Taali, Leon and Sam would still be alive!"

No tears came. Instead, the accusation ignited a furious anger inside me. With an abrupt shove, I pushed him away. I remembered at the last second to pull my efforts, but I still used a bit too much, because he tumbled back several feet. His own grip was torn away along with a part of my top.

Once he'd come to a stop, I stepped toward him and yelled back, "If your dumb ass hadn't sneezed it wouldn't have happened, either! There's no point in worrying about what-ifs!" I stomped. "Seriously, if I knew I could kill that monster, don't you think I would have done so sooner!?" The admission made me turn my head to the sky, put my forearm over my eyes, and I cried. Without looking at the beast I pointed to it with my free hand and sobbed, "I don't even know *how* I did that."

Ban came over and placed something over my shoulders. He whispered, "Sorry, Lady Anessa, your chemise is torn."

One of the other huntresses rushed over and tied it off for me.

Ban pointed at Zev, who was clutching his chest with a grimace, but otherwise quiet.

Sternly, Ban told him, "You can go cool off."

At the break in tension, my tears flowed, and I hung to the unsuspecting woman they'd sent my way. She placed her hand on my back.

"Do you have a change of clothes?" she asked me calmly.

I nodded and wiped my eyes. Then I noticed why she asked. Zev's efforts had done the final bit of damage needed for my garment to basically start falling off. Were it not for the large cloak Ban had placed on my shoulders, I would have been exposed to the world.

"Clear the area," Ban hollered at the party. "Find our fallen," his voice gained an edge of sorrow, "Dress them with care. Leave the dire boar until then."

The huntress looked to Ban, who nodded. She then followed me over to the tree line and I pulled a few privacy screens from my storage ring. "Would you help me set these?"

She nodded.

Once we'd done so, she asked, "Do you need any help? You took a big hit earlier."

"No, I'm okay. Would you keep a lookout though?"

She smiled. "Sure."

Opening the cloak Ban sat over my shoulders, I took stock of my outfit. It was in tatters. All three layers of my top were torn. As I moved to remove the cloak from my shoulders, I realized that I wasn't as untouched as I thought. The effort made me groan.

"Miss?" I said.

"Yes, Lady Anessa?" she said behind the screen.

"Could you help me after all?"

"Of course."

As I changed, it was clear I'd be a purple mess later. "It really nailed me, huh?" I said to the huntress, trying to force a smile.

She pursed her lips and nodded.

Right. Several others, Sam included, didn't make it. I sighed at my social miss. *It wasn't the time for lighthearted comments, I guess.*

"I'm glad that getting hit by the dire boar didn't kill you," Trish said quietly.

Her words were like a cold bucket of water, and from my scalp down it was as though I'd been doused in it. *Me too.*

"So that was a dire boar?" I said aloud.

"Yes," the huntress said quietly. "It shouldn't be here."

"What do you mean?"

"They're from the Tanis Region, in the south. They usually don't travel this far out."

"I wonder why it was here," I said, then shook my head. "I guess that doesn't really matter."

"Lady Anessa," she said, then bowed once I turned to her. "You saved our party. Thank you."

Scratching my nose, I said. "I actually feel pretty guilty."

She gasped. "Why?"

"I was just mad and threw a rock at it. Sure, I wanted the rock to do damage," with a shrug I continued, "but I don't even know *what* I did."

"What you did is save our hunting party. Dire boars are known for being horribly aggressive, fast, and almost impossible to stop. The Tanis Region is known for its critical zone where such beasts are usually kept. It's closely guarded, and few manage to get out due to the damage they can cause." She gave a smile. "Let us be glad it was a juvenile."

My mouth hung open. "That was a *juvenile*?!"

"Yes, the adults are much scarier."

Scarier than that!? Taking a moment to imagine an adult Dire Boar made me shiver. "Yikes." I shook my head. "What was your name, anyway?"

She dipped her head. "This one does not have a name."

It was only then that I noticed the collar around her neck. Similar to Sarah's, it lacked the penalty engravings to harm the bearer at the owner's will.

"I didn't know. What should I call you, then?"

"Just call me Knecht von Ban," she said with a small smile.

She seemed almost proud to serve Ban. Stowing my privacy screens, I looked over at him.

"He isn't a bad guy," Trish said. *"You can tell that."*

"Can you tell me something?" I asked her, ignoring Trish.

"Yes?"

"Does he treat you well?" I asked quietly.

Her smile broadened. "Better than I deserve."

Though she was being genuine, it still broke my heart that such a system existed on Anfang. *Maybe I'll have the power someday to change it.*

Returning to the party, I paused and fought back the urge to bawl once again. Three makeshift stretchers lined the clearing on the side, bodies beneath cloth coverings. One of them had no more than an arm beneath it, making my chest clench.

"Begin assessing our latest quarry," Ban ordered, all business despite the tragedy. "We can't take everything, but we'll take what we can. Do not cut until assessment is complete."

The remaining members surrounded the massive collapsed form and a few even gave it experimental nudges, finding no luck against its tough hide.

They can't even move it a little.

One of the hunters examining the brute's head froze, then rushed over to Ban and they talked quietly. His face fell, and his stance shifted.

What did they find?

Trish said, *"You don't want to know."*

Yes, I do. Spill it.

"Sam really did save you, that's all I should say," she said quietly.

Oh gods. Her commentary made it obvious, and I rushed to Ban. "Is something wrong?"

He turned his head away and closed his eyes. "They found Sam," with a sigh he added, "What's left of her, that is."

Looking over to the Dire Boar, I could see that its mouth was partly agape. Though part of me wanted to approach and look for myself, a hand on my shoulder stopped me. "You don't want to do that."

"Can you retrieve her?" I asked.

"Not currently, no. It's too heavy. We could all try together and be no more successful than lifting its tail."

Trish.

"*Yeah?*"

Am I strong enough to open its mouth?

She said nothing for a good minute. "*Maybe.*"

Good enough for me.

I gently put my own hand over Ban's. "I'm not going to look. Have everyone gather near the front," giving him a smile I continued, "this monster lady is going to try to use her strength."

Instead of stopping me, he removed his hand and nodded once, then barked out a few orders.

During my approach, I caught a few words discussing how valuable its tusks and hide were. But it made me wonder how the heck we'd move the thing.

Approaching it near its snout I noticed the best place to find purchase was right beneath it, dripping with slobber, snot, and blood.

My stomach sunk when I said, "Ban, have them clean that area off," I said and pointed. "I'll have the best luck trying to lift from there, though..." my words caught in my throat as I saw the slow march of the goo continued to spill out, "it's not going to be fun."

As Ban's men cleared the beast's hide under its snout, they also cleared the slop from the stone where I'd soon stand.

"*Thank goodness for small mercies,*" *Trish said.*

What do you mean? I asked her.

"*If that stone weren't there, you'd be fighting against sinking into mud-ichor.*"

Reflexively, I curled my lip and wrinkled my nose at her comment. *Oh. Good point.* Before getting into position, I dropped to one knee and sent up a prayer to Eloria, *Please, Mother Goddess, give me the strength to succeed and give Sam the honor she deserves.*

Bracing my back and shoulders against the largest surface I was able to find leverage against, I was sourly amused to realize that if I were any taller, I'd be too big to help. *Ironic twist of fate.*

Clearing my mind I pushed, hard, only to find it didn't give even a little.

"You've got this," Ban said.

His words of encouragement made me smile, and I pushed harder.

Voices from the party joined in, cheering me on.

"It's moving!" Knecht von Ban called.

That gave me motivation to push yet harder, straining until I knew I was at my limit, and I couldn't give any more.

Their voices were drowned out by the rush of blood in my ears, and my vision swam as darkness creeped around the edges.

"They're done," Trish said calmly.

Her admission made me collapse to the ground in a heap of breaths. The ick covering my left side didn't matter, and I pulled myself away and fell onto the ground with my chest heaving.

"That…" I breathed and gasped, "sucked."

I took a few moments to recover my wits while the party continued their evaluation.

"We can't hardly carry any of this with us," Ban admitted. "If it would please you, Lady Anessa, would you mind carrying the tusks in your storage ring, should they fit?"

Sending my senses into my ring, I realized they would fit. Barely, but I could get them in there.

"That's fine," I said.

Before they could do anything about the tusks, a voice called out, "And just what do you feeble commoners think you're doing with *my* quarry?"

Everyone paused and turned to him.

I held up my hand for Ban to stop, since he was about to speak.

"To what do I owe the pleasure," I said and gave a light bow, "Your Imperial Highness?"

Along with my cousin was a pasty white man, the second son of the Juntaro Imperial Duchy, now the current heir. He had the faintest of green hues to his skin. His hunched posture and general demeanor reminded me why Lukas's much nicer sister, Rina, said he looked like a goblin.

"Did I stutter?" he snarled. "I asked what you were doing with my quarry. It's obvious *I* felled the beast since," he looked at the stretchers and disdain came from his lips, "everyone here is sorely lacking."

Zev yelled at the prince, "She killed the beast herself! You have no claim!"

"Excuse me?" Lukas said and glared at Zev, who took a step back.

The Juntaro heir clamored, "We lost sight of it a day ago. It's ours because we paid–"

Lukas's ire-filled glare swiveled to him. "Quiet, Gobza."

"What is it you need from the Dire Boar, if I may ask?" I said, hoping to diffuse the tension the two men had added. It took a lot to not grin hearing the Imperial ducal heir had a name like a goblin.

"It's best you don't smile, you'll only goad Lukas," Trish reminded.

"Sometimes I wonder if you are touched in the head, cousin. I require *all* of it." He motioned with his hand, and to everyone's surprise, its entire body lifted off the ground.

One of the hunters had been tying a rope to one of the tusks to help guide it once it was free, and used the rope to quickly reach the ground. He gave Lukas a dirty look that was fortunately ignored.

When the beast was just above my head, I worried as it stopped. Looking up was a mistake as my lovable cousin tilted the mass mid-air and a torrent of gross, of every variety imaginable, poured over me.

After five seconds the vile downpour finally subsided, and the laughter coming from my cousin and his retinue was all I heard.

Heat rose from my stomach and through my chest, and the back of my neck and cheeks. It was all I could do to not bum rush the arrogant fool.

"Ignore him," Trish warned me.

I seethed, *I would rather end him!*

"He would split you in two without lifting a finger. Leave it. For now."

Wiping your eyes off with equally slop-covered hands is nigh futile. Once I could see again, I noticed the Dire Boar vanish, the tell-tale swirl of particles spiraling quickly into his glove. It was evident he had me beaten in every way. Skill, power, rank, even the tools at his disposal.

Thanks for talking me down.

"Anytime."

Ban's party was glaring daggers. As one, they reached for their weapons.

"No one move," I said harshly, looking in their direction.

"It's good my cousin finally understands her place," Lukas said.

A glob of *something* dropped from the top of my head and fell to the ground in a wet splat. This only served to reignite their laughter as they walked away leisurely.

I wish I had control over whatever killed that dire boar. Shaking my head I realized pretty quickly, *No, even with it, I'd be no match for him.* As the sticky muck ran down my arms I added to my thought, *If I never meet him again, it'll still be too soon.*

I doubted fate would be so kind.

CHAPTER TWENTY-ONE
THE HUNT'S END

AS LUKAS'S LAUGHTER trailed off, I stood there, drenched with bile and who knew what. Shaking my hand to get some of it off, Zev cried, "Hey!"

"Sorry," I said. "I need to change," sighing I added, "again."

Nobody argued with this, and once I had done so, Ban approached.

"We're canceling the hunt." He gave me a bow. "I hope you'll understand."

"Of course," I said and shook my head. "If you hadn't, I would have myself."

"I wanted to extend a thanks from our party," he said and pursed his lips. "With what you did for Sam, that is."

I'd used my prior outfit to scrub off what I could of the dire boar, but despite my best efforts to turn a serviceable set of clothing into a scrub brush, a very distinct odoriferous *something* hung in the air around me. *I need a bath so bad.*

As if reading my mind, Ban added, "We'll be heading back to the inn. They could give you a bath, though I don't think it would live up to your usual expectations."

Waving him off I said, "No. I'm not really permitted to…" I paused realizing I was about to say, *"bathe around commoners"* and said nothing in its place. *Sometimes less is more, I hope.*

He merely nodded. "Understood."

We neared the stretchers, and a pang of guilt hit me. "Ban, would it be okay if I helped carry Sam's?"

With a faint smile he said, "She'd be honored, I'm sure."

Our trek back was solemn. Few conversations were started, and most were about the injustice of Lukas's actions. No one boiled it down to it being because he was nobility, I'd hoped it was because I was an example of what nobility could be.

Halfway through our trek the person behind me asked if we could switch, and they admitted it might be because of a certain smell.

Once we arrived at the inn, I almost laughed at its name, Boar's Head Inn. Ban rushed ahead to talk to the management; we couldn't just waltz in with our dead. He reappeared shortly. "They've agreed to let us use the cellar for two nights until we have the arrangements in order."

While moving them, I asked Ban, "Why aren't we taking them directly to a church?" I knew enough about Anfang not to inquire about coroners or medical examiners.

"They don't really follow the major pantheon in Westwood," he made a "money" gesture with his hands, and added, "because of that, they would require more than we will make from this endeavor as a donation."

My eyes widened and I automatically reached for my purse. Before I could offer anything, he held up his hand. "All due respect, ma'am, but that's not something I'd want you to do."

"Okay," I said quietly. "What's next for them?"

"The day after tomorrow, we'll hold a small ceremony. Then they'll be buried here, in Ersta." He looked down and away. "If we had the money, we'd arrange for them to be taken back home, but that's not a luxury we have."

Before he could say no, I pulled out a single large platinum. "Use this to pay for it, and I'm not taking no for an answer."

His eyes grew wide.

"If you have qualms, ensure Sam at the very least returns home." I gripped the coin tightly. "She saved my life, it's the least I can do."

Taking his wrist and opening his hand I added, "I wouldn't have closure otherwise."

Shaking his head he sighed, "Fine. But the rest I will see returned to you." He stood near Leon and Taali's resting spot. "These two were a couple, and didn't have any family to return to. They'll stay here."

Knowing they had no one but each other made my eyes burn hard as I teared up. *Damn that Lukas for covering me in this stuff.*

"What are your party's plans after that?" I asked.

Ban shrugged. "We'll move on. I'm sure everyone wants to put some distance between us and Ersta."

Wiping my eyes I cursed. "That reminds me. Can you send someone to the Imperial Royal dormitories and fetch one of my lady's maids? I would get in a lot of trouble if I were to walk the town like this. My usual guards aren't here yet, because we returned early."

"How bad would it be, exactly?"

Instead of giving him a direct answer, I said, "They put wraps on under my clothes to change my attire. I have to wear something when I enter baths. They take appearances seriously, even in private."

Raising an eyebrow, he said, "I take it you're saying you don't know yourself, but you're guessing bad?"

I nodded.

"If that's the case, it might be best if you just stayed here," he pointed to the floor, "in the cellar until your people arrive. I'd really prefer not to make an Imperial Noble mad." He chuckled and nervously rubbed the back of his neck. "I wouldn't even want to upset their attendants."

Within ten minutes both of my lady's maids were standing in front of me. Both looked displeased.

"You walked into town like this?" Tania asked and gestured from my head to my toes.

"From the woods straight here, yeah."

Sarah asked brusquely, "Roughly how many people saw you?"

"Maybe one?" I said. "We headed down here immediately."

They peppered me with questions on who saw me and their description. My maids had brought a handful of guards with them, and had a few fan out to find the witness and make sure they stayed quiet.

If my family were like Lukas, they'd disappear the witness permanently, but I knew my people were merely going to use money to solve the issue.

"Let's get you cleaned up," Sarah said and looked at everyone else present. No one moved, so she said, "Could everyone leave, please?"

"Not here," I said.

"What?"

Motioning toward the departed, I repeated, "Not here."

She curtsied to me. "Very good." Upon standing she turned. "Tania, secure the upstairs."

Sarah then gave a curtsy to Ban's party. "Please forgive my misunderstanding. If it would be okay, the Carlyle family will station a guard for the evening so that your party may retire."

"Acceptable," Ban nodded before turning to his team. "Let's go. Drinks are on me."

I'd expected to hear lots of boots entering the upstairs, but none came.

Once Tania returned, she gestured towards the stairs, which Sarah mirrored. "If you'd please, ma'am."

At the top of the stairs was a series of privacy screens reaching all the way around to the front of the building.

What the heck did they do?

Entering the Boar's Head Inn's main building, it was eerily quiet. The guards had moved every table and chair into a corner.

One of the soldiers broke several chairs' legs off, stowing one table atop another without minding what was in the way.

"Shouldn't we be more careful about damaging stuff?"

Tania turned to me. "Ma'am? What for?"

"The inn needs those to operate."

She smiled. "It's fine. The inn is yours now."

My jaw dropped and I reminded myself, *I often forget my monthly petty cash is more than the accumulated wealth of Melon Trusk from Earth. He was the richest man in the world.* Shaking my head I added, *This inn was probably no more than a cup of coffee to the average Joe.* I smiled at the humorous overlap in terms.

"Will you be giving the inn back to the owner, when we're done here?" I asked.

Tania curtsied, "If that is what my lady wishes, yes."

"I do," I said firmly.

Sarah walked in behind me and began tapping the floor with her foot. Though she did so hard enough to cause dust to rise from the floor.

After a while she stopped and placed the tub from my dorm suite.

The brought my tub to me? Isn't that excessive? Remembering that Tania just bought an inn to give me a bath, I sighed. *Maybe not.*

My Lady's maids rushed everyone but us out once the bath had been drawn. It seemed it heated itself through some kind of device I was unfamiliar with; I hadn't watched them prepare my baths since they replaced it with this newer gilded version.

"How's that work?" I asked, gesturing to the steaming water.

"An enchantment in the middle layers of the tub heats the water from beneath it," Sarah said simply.

An enchantment. So those things are real. It made me wonder, "Are enchantments how the, what was it you called it, 'remote viewing box' works in the Solar at home?"

"Exactly so," she said. "That device is a lot more expensive though due to the enchantment channels that must be prepared across long distances."

Oh. So it's not wireless. They enchant something like a wire over the whole distance? The cost must be staggering.

Sarah pulled out an S-ROB and pressed on its top. Giving us proper privacy.

"Now, Our Lady Anessa," Tania said. "What happened to get you in this state?"

"We encountered a dire boar," I said, and both of their eyes widened.

After describing what happened with Lukas, they were fuming.

Tania especially. "He should be publicly reprimanded for that," she said. "Dousing an Imperial Princess with such vile substances."

Wow, I'm surprised Tania is taking my side so strongly after I scolded her the other day for bullying Sarah.

"No punishment will come of that act," Sarah said simply. "They are of the same blood, and publicly announcing that he did such a thing would merely bring shame to both the Q'Tar and Carlyle families." She shook her head. "No, if anything, his biggest transgression was drawing such a beast in the first place."

I tilted my head to one side and raised an eyebrow.

"With the war ongoing, our strongest cultivators are afar," she explained. "If that beast had happened upon a town during their chase, and the prince was as far behind it as he seemed to be, the damage would've been catastrophic."

"He'd get in more trouble because of a 'maybe' than for humiliating me?" I wondered.

"Of course. It isn't always the outcome, but the optics and reception that matter," Sarah said. "Your humiliation," she added while my outfit was peeled away, then wrinkled her nose. "Is secondary, sadly."

Tania did her usual to make sure I showed as little skin as possible as they continued to prepare me for my bath, despite the circumstances.

The two gave me no fewer than *four* deep scrub baths before they were satisfied. The water was mostly clean after the third bath, but the smell lingered.

Once they had finished preparing me for our departure, I gave them both a light curtsy. "Thank you both. You can't imagine how dreadful it was to be covered in that," I said and took a breath. "And how nice it is to not smell like a rotting pig."

"Anytime, Our Lady," Tania said. "Our Lord Gideon was going over some cat-kin history with Sarah when word came in of your arrival," she said. "I believe he decided to wait for you."

Her news made me perk up and a smile came unbidden. "Really? Let's go then." A silly thought entered my head, *I wonder if they'll let him put his arm around me again.* I secretly hoped so.

Back in the dorm suites, Gideon was indeed waiting inside. The smile on my face dropped the moment I saw Yukirei sitting next to him.

"Come on, you don't hate her anymore, do you?" Trish asked.

It's not that I hate her, I just wanted to spend time alone with Gideon.

"It doesn't hurt that she's cute, right?"

Not now, I thought and rolled my eyes. Trish had just made my thoughts more complicated, and I noticed Yukirei's lip gloss and olive eyes as I sat across from the pair. *That's never been an issue.* It made me shake my head. *It's hard enough to focus on one person right now, let alone a second.*

"What happened little kitten?" Gideon asked, leaning forward to take my hand.

Once I'd explained the situation, I mentioned that I'd felled the beast, which prompted Sarah to start writing on some paper.

"Sarah, didn't I already tell you everything?" I asked.

She shook her head. "You didn't mention that you felled the dire boar. It was, by rights, yours. While it's not a transgression on the level of pulling it into our region in the first place, stealing someone's quarry, even if they were the reason it was there, is unjust."

Gideon continued for her and patted my hand. "It's undignified. If you saw that he was following it, and then you stepped in to kill it, that would be different."

Giving a light cough, Tania said, "There's also the possibility that His Imperial Highness Lukas sent it your way."

Sarah responded coolly, "The information in my report will include only facts, observed or otherwise," she regarded Tania for a moment before continuing, "not speculation."

Tania gave a light curtsy and exited the room.

Those two are still patching things up, I see.

"You mentioned a report Sarah, to whom?" I asked

"Your parents, specifically Her Imperial Highness, the Imperial Princess of Westwood, Lily Carlyle," she said.

Why does this feel like a bigger version of tattling?

"Because someone else is tattling for you, maybe?" Trish proposed.

Best not to think about it, I was going to ask Sarah to write a letter anyway. If he'd left it at taking the dire boar, I wouldn't have bothered.

"You mean being covered in that *made a difference?"* Trish jeered. *"I can't imagine why."*

"Haha", very funny. I just hope at the least he gets a tongue lashing. Given his station, I doubt much more than that will happen. He technically didn't hurt anyone himself. The loss of a commoner is... my heart clinched for a moment, thinking of Sam, *likely not going to move the meter much. Especially since he didn't harm her himself.*

Thinking of Sam made me say, "I just wish I'd acted sooner." A light burning tugged at my eyes as I teared up. "If I would've carried Sam, or attacked it more quickly..." my voice trailed off.

"Don't think like that," Yukirei said. "When Mr. Morris attacked you over a year ago, I froze up, too. If you hadn't called my name..." She shook her head and clenched her fist. "I can't imagine what would have happened."

An image of his face inches away from mine flashed through my mind and I shook my head and waved in the air to dispel his image. *Don't think about him. He's dead, that's all that matters.*

"How *did* you take down the dire boar, anyway?" Gideon asked providing a welcome digression.

"You know how I can damage that cultivator steel?" I asked and added, "The stuff Oliver couldn't even dent?"

He nodded.

"That." Though I didn't say more than that, my face bore a smile. *If there is a small mercy, it's that I might have figured something out about my odd skill.*

It didn't seem like much consolation.

CHAPTER TWENTY-TWO

LEND ME AN EAR

THE INTERMENT WAS simple. All of the deceased were covered from head to toe in cloth. Our family's coat of arms had been stitched into the burial shrouds, which were perfectly laid over their chests.

Sam's was far more ornate and included my own personal marker. They also placed a mask over her face to represent her. It was uncannily accurate, despite the circumstances, but still had that uncanny valley ick you'd get when something's just not right.

Afterwards, I approached her still form and had to take a few moments to breathe to avoid breaking down into tears.

I couldn't help but trace the edge of the mask with my finger. Doing so, though, made it infinitely more difficult to avoid crying. More than once, I had to dry my eyes, look away and calm myself.

Why am I feeling like this? I didn't even know her, really.

Trish piped in, *"Because you know the value of what she gave up."*

Ban's obituary on Sam was so brief. I know she was one of their newest members, but it's just sad.

With the ceremony over, most of the hunting party left.

"Lady Anessa," Zev called. Once I'd turned to him he said, "I'm sorry for how I acted. I've asked Ban to send my share of this hunt to Tim, Sam's husband." With a nod he added, "No hard feelings, yeah?"

I could only return Zev's nod. His small gesture made the frustration I'd been holding onto with him vanish, and I reminded myself that he was doing pretty well for someone with the social grace of a frog.

After spending a few more minutes with Sam, I headed towards the cellar's stairs.

Ban was waiting there with his hand on his neck, something I noticed he did when nervous. He did it a lot more often once things went sideways on the hunt.

"I have something for you," he said and held out his hand.

Accepting the item from him with my palms, I tilted my head in confusion. *What is this?* It was a purple pouch with a crude white flower on it.

Opening it up and turning it sideways had a handful of hard, black, wrinkled spheres tumble into my hand, along with an instantly recognizable whiff of pepper.

At that moment, the effort I'd made to hold back the tears failed in full, and I started cry silently.

Ban placed his hand on my shoulder. "I can't ask her to confirm, but I'm sure she would've wanted you to have it." He blew through his teeth. "She sent nearly every Wua back home to support her husband and daughter. But occasionally she'd splurge on herself and buy ten grams of peppercorns for her meals on the road."

Hearing that Sam sent back most of what she made, her threadbare clothes, and her rationale, made me realize she was exactly the kind of person who would make that kind of sacrifice.

"Anessa," Trish said. *"I can't do this often, but there's something I need you to see. Close your eyes."*

Following her instructions, I started to see a slow-as-molasses replay of the attack play out in my head. Before it could go anywhere, I opened my eyes and scowled. *Why would you show me that?*

"Just trust me. It takes a lot out of me to do this. Please, let it play out."

Breathing to calm myself, I did so, and closed my eyes again.

Right as Sam pushed me, she gave me a smile and closed her eyes, as though she knew what was about to happen and had accepted it.

It broke me, and I started to bawl uncontrollably, holding the small bag of peppercorns to my chest. *I'm so sorry, Sam.* Minutes later after I'd calmed down, I thought to Trish, *Thank you.*

Walking up the stairs in a daze, I thought bleakly, *I couldn't do that.*

"What?" Trish asked.

Give my life for someone else, I thought back, the bile in the back of my throat making my realization more palpable. *Does that make me a bad person?*

"Probably," Trish said, a bright note of levity in her voice.

That's not funny.

Upon exiting the cellar, the three guards acting as my liaison followed along, unaware of my inner dialogue.

"Sorry, I was just trying to break the tension. It doesn't make you a bad person." Trish sent me a brief image of her apologizing with her hands in a prayer, in front of her face. She continued, *"All it means is you've never felt that way about someone. Loved them so much that you'd give your life for them."*

But I'm married! I know I love Gideon, and want to protect him, but...

She sighed. *"Anessa, you're turning twelve in two days, and your 'marriage' is platonic at best because of your age. It's less how close you are to him physically and more emotionally. Not everyone develops such strong feelings that quickly."*

I found myself frowning. *Doesn't seem right, though.*

"Perhaps what you're missing is that deeper connection. Granted, some aspects of it require being closer to Gideon..." she paused, *"...physically, but that's only because you two don't have children together."*

Her comment made me snort. *You speak as though you have experience with it.*

"I don't, no, but I did have similar talks with my Mom ages ago when I was discovering myself, and my identity. It was difficult at first to figure out why I resonated with you as much as I did boys."

Her comment made me stop in place. *Oh. I can see how that would be difficult.*

After wandering aimlessly for an hour, I found myself at Nora's Essencial Goods. The very store Gideon frequented to keep himself in check during my weekly estrus. I reached for the handle and pulled my hand back several times before committing.

The bell above the door announced my entry, causing the hostess, who I learned was Nora herself, to look up from her podium.

"Is Io in?" I asked.

Nora flipped through the pages the book in front of her. "She's busy for at least the next five minutes." She whispered, "Maybe less." Looking up she added, "Would you be willing to wait a little bit?"

I nodded and sat on a small black leather bench to the side.

At first, during my wait, Nora kept glaring at me. But once she realized I wasn't here to give her grief, she just ignored me.

About five minutes passed and the tell-tale roll and smack of a sliding door being slammed open rang out. "Get out!"

Leaning slightly to my left to peer down the hall, I saw a man holding his trousers up by the waist. He was backing out of the room with a half-unbuttoned shirt. His other hand was up defensively.

Nora made a beeline for the open door and entered.

Seconds later the man's eyes widened, and he took a few steps back before trying to bolt down the hall. All while trying to fasten his pants.

Quickly catching up to him, Nora lifted him by his shirt as though he were a feather. She pulled him into a side-hall where light cascaded in, where I assumed another door to the establishment was. Her rough voice burst forth with a resolute, "And stay out! You know the rules!"

Nora returned, walking briskly as she reentered the foyer. Seeing me seemed to make her take stock and she pursed her lips, holding her hand to her forehead for a second. She said, "It seems Io is free. However, please give her a few more minutes. Her most recent customer put her in a bad mood."

What the hell am I doing, going to what amounts to my husband's brothel, to talk to the woman that takes my form to help relieve his pent-up s— tension?

I spent the moments I spent waiting for Nora to tell me Io was available in awkward silence. Blushing so furiously I got lightheaded.

When she was finally free, I walked down the hall without a sense of urgency, my stomach fluttering with each step. *What am I going to ask her, even?*

Rounding the corner, I came face to face with a carbon copy of myself. I wondered when Nora had told Io about me, but thought better of asking outright.

"Yo," she said nonchalantly in my voice.

The insolent carelessness in her posture, sitting with her legs wide and her arms up on the windowsill, had my hands on my hips sternly in seconds.

"Don't 'yo' me!" I started to say, but I deflated when I saw the cheeky grin on her face. She was clearly messing with me.

"What brings you here?" she asked.

Since I didn't really know why I was there, I said the first thing that came to mind. "How does that," I pointed at her and my finger drifted from her head to her toes, "work, anyway?"

"It's a trait of my people," she said with a shrug.

"Are you a… demon?" I blurted out.

"Haah?" She said drawing the word out, the ire evident in her tone. Crossing her legs and arms made it clear I'd asked a taboo question. "I'm not a *demon*, girlie. I'm a beast-kin, just like you. We're known as wood nymphs, though I was born with an unusual skin tone," she said and rolled her eyes.

"Sorry," I apologized. "I didn't mean any insult."

"People rarely do," she intoned. While her arms were crossed, she lifted one of her hands dismissively. "I get it, we use blood. We change shapes and are scary or evil." She sighed and shook her head. "It's tiresome, the number of times I've heard that. Most people haven't heard of pink-skinned demons in Redwood," her eyes narrowed. "So I'm surprised to even hear such a thing here."

So she's not from here, and I'm not the first person to call her a demon.

"I really am sorry for my ignorance," I said and gave a light bow. "I read a lot," I lied, "which is how I knew of such demons, or succubi." Giving her a half-smile I added, "I'm glad to hear you are *not* a demon."

"Do you have a thing against demons?" Io asked.

Furrowing my eyebrows, my stomach did a somersault. *Crap, are there good demons?*

She barked out a laugh. "Relax, I'm kidding. Wow, you really are easy to read. I could use that."

Raising an eyebrow I asked, "Use what?"

REBORN IN THE PERFECT FANTASY WORLD

With a smile she said, "Nothing."

My hands went back to my hips. "Just how often does Gideon come here, anyway?"

She thinned her lips and zipped a finger across them. "Can't say. But how often does your issue crop up?"

Oh. Once a week.

Leaning forward she continued, "Surely you already had a good idea about that, based on our last talk. So why are you really here?"

Her bluntness made me avert my eyes. "I don't know. Someone I barely knew recently gave their life for me. It made me wonder whether I could do the same for Gideon." Placing my hand on my chest I told her about my concerns with him.

"So, you wondered about the one girl who…" Io paused, and her eyes searched the room, as if trying to find the words in the air, "has a connection with Gideon that you don't, that you may want, but you cannot have?"

Damn she zeroed in on that so fast, I thought with my eyes closed. Her precision stung, but she wasn't wrong.

"I don't have your answer there, I'm afraid. Honestly, I thought you were here about the girl that visits me."

"Girl?" I said, startled. "Do you mean Yukirei?"

She winked. "Can't say."

"What does…" I smiled, "'Can't say' ask you?"

Tapping her chin Io said, "Hmm… She asks me to hold her hand and listen. Anything beyond that, I really cannot talk about."

"Oh." Her words, though simple, helped guide me. *I've been avoiding Yukirei the past two days. Is it the deliberate distance I'm putting between us that's causing her to visit Io?* Shaking my head, I said, "Thanks for your time."

I placed a small gold onto the counter inside the room.

Io swiped it between her fingers quicker than I thought she should be able to. Making a fist she placed it in her palm, presenting it with her hand open. In the time it took for her to close and reopen her hand, the coin had vanished. "You can visit anytime," she said. "If you bring a little of a certain boy's blood," her voice dropped an octave and she got closer than I wanted her to. "I might be able to—"

Before she could finish, I exited the room. *Nope, not going there!* I couldn't keep my thoughts pure after she said that, so I thought the simplest thing was to exit while I could.

As I scurried away, she chuckled behind me.

As we exited Nora's, one of my guards asked, "Is everything okay, ma'am?"

"I'm fine," I squeaked untruthfully.

At my dormitory, Gideon and Yukirei were still there, and she was about to leave.

Nice timing.

As I approached her, she avoided eye contact.

Her aversion made my chest tighten. *Have I been* that *inconsiderate?* I wondered, then asked, "Yuki, I was wondering—"

Yukirei's eyes snapped to me and she smiled. "You called me Yuki!"

It was my turn to avoid her gaze as my cheeks flushed. *Gods I'm acting like a child.* Turning back to her I asked, "I was wondering if you wanted to catch second dinner somewhere."

She pulled my hands into hers and bounced on the balls of her feet for a moment. "I would love to." In an instant she floated up to Gideon and gave him a quick peck on the cheek, then glided to the floor towards the door. "I need to go pick out something to wear, I'll see you later, okay Gideon?"

At the click of the door, I looked at Gideon, who said, "What came over her, I wonder?"

Remembering that she visited Io to talk to "me," I knew exactly what came over her. *I think my invitation was the right thing to do.*

Maybe.

CHAPTER TWENTY-THREE

GIFT OF A GODDESS

Octday, Lokandae 21st, 1739

ON THE DAY of my twelfth birthday, Sarah and Tania buzzed around me from the moment my eyes opened. I didn't really need to rest, but they made me sleep anyway, saying I needed to be my best for my third Awakening Ceremony.

Since the day happened to occur in the middle of one of my heats, the slightest sound or sight easily stole my focus.

I hope I get this under control someday.

"Arms up," Tania said.

Sighing as I did so, I complained, "I miss Oliver."

"Yes, it's a lot quieter without him around," Sarah said while changing my clothes. "He would usually be in before you could even get your head off your pillow to wish you happy birthday."

Tears fell from my eyes without provocation. "I know. Why can't he be here? Why can't I visit him?"

Tania immediately started dabbing my cheeks, trying to stop the waterworks in their tracks.

"If it weren't for the war, I'm sure you two would both be in the Redwood Kingdom with your parents," Tania said.

Rubbing my eyes with the back of my hand I found tremendous difficulty in reining in my emotions. "Estrus sucks," I grumped. "Being a cat-kin sucks. Why did I have to be born like this?"

"Now," Sarah chided, "Lady Anessa. Don't speak like that. There are plenty of benefits."

Furrowing my brows at her I said, "Name one. I'll have a shorter life. I started estrus at the age of seven years old, for crying out loud. It might only last until I'm in my mid-twenties. So whether I want to be a young mother or not, I'll have children by then, or I won't have any." I flailed my arms, then hung them at my side. "Every single week I go through a stupid weepy or s—" I thinned my lips realizing what I was about to say wasn't appropriate. "...crazed phase that serves no one."

"Enhanced senses," Tania whispered from the corner of the room, drawing my gaze.

"Greater strength," Sarah added. "Despite being a cultivator. Pound for pound, you'll out-pace your fully human counterparts." She held up her hand and splayed her fingers. "When you start to exhibit your cat-kin traits, you'll have claws that can tear through steel."

Her commentary made me look down at my fingernails. Even after the hunt, days of camping and physical effort in the woods, they remained perfect and unblemished. It was obvious they were *already* stronger than normal.

"Speaking of Oliver," Tania said with a smile. "Your letter to him went out this morning. He should receive it in about a week."

In a flash I replaced my frustration-laden frown with a brilliant smile. "Great, I'm glad to hear it."

Trish sent over a big yawn, one so large that it was contagious, making me do the same. *"Sorry,"* she said. *"I might be quiet for a bit."*

Oh yeah? I thought back. *Why?*

"I overexerted myself showing you that memory the other day. Us spirits need sleep, too," she said, and yawned again.

All I could do is arch an eyebrow. *Really?* It didn't make sense that a spirit would need *anything,* sleep included, but I didn't press her, since I guessed a happy spirit was better than one who was pissed at me. *I just hope it's not because I'm about to meet Eloria.*

Exiting my bedroom, I came face-to-face with Yukirei. She was wearing a sleeveless black and floral-gray dress.

Given the typically conservative nature of our attire, seeing her exposed arms made me blush, and I immediately felt silly for having such a thought. *Gods, they're just arms, get over it.*

After I had the thought, Tania promptly covered Yukirei's arms and buttoned on sleeves that matched the garment. I'd almost sighed at seeing the need.

Right, that makes more sense. Thinking back to what I saw, I thought, *Her arms have a lot of freckles like mine do. They're just a lighter color.*

On our ride to the church, she brought up a topic I wasn't prepared to discuss.

"Would you be willing to help Gideon and me with our future wedding?"

I squeaked out an answer, "Um… sure?" Hoping it was something we could share together, I dumbly said, "Only if you could help me with mine."

She reached across and took my hands. "I would love to!"

Giving her a half grin I thought, *She'll be pissed when she finds we're already married.* I sighed. *That's a problem for tomorrow.*

When she didn't release my hands, my Daughter Envoy from the church, Daughter Hy, coughed gently.

She wasn't as chatty with Yukirei around. I suspected that was because Yukirei's own Daughter Envoy was sitting across from her.

I never caught her name.

We were the last two to go this time around, without Gideon and Oliver.

When Yukirei created a divine link with Lokar, the lesser god of War, for almost the full minute, several of the onlookers began to murmur. She was then led off to the side to meet with him in person.

This whole thing is still so bizarre. That we meet with actual gods and goddesses should we create a link with them. At the time I didn't realize the "meeting" was only granted for those with a divine link lasting ten seconds or more. Since all of my links were with Eloria and lasted the full minute, I assumed that sort of thing was more typical than it was.

"Lady Anessa," the Father of the Scripture's Children said. "Please step forward onto the spot of awakening…" The older man explained the process yet again, as he clearly had dozens of times before.

As I stepped forward onto the marker on the floor, all feeling fled me, and per usual, I heard a gasp or two in the peanut gallery.

Dual-divine links are *unusual.*

Not everyone in attendance had been at my last Awakening Ceremony, so there were plenty of people seeing this for the first time.

Counting it down in my head, at the sixtieth second, a collective breath in caught my ear, and the room went silent.

Great, what now?

Opening my eyes I found myself bowing; my calves ached a little, as it appeared I had been on my tiptoes the entire time. Lowering my arms and lifting my head I almost gasped, myself. Standing before me was Eloria herself. Even in my limited experience, I knew this was something that Did Not Happen.

Crap. A look behind myself showed equal parts adoration and abject horror among the crowd. Some went so far as to prostrate before her. I could not blame them, all things considered.

She turned to the Father. "Would you lead us?" she said in a voice that seemed to echo off every molecule in the building.

As if a spell had been broken, he breathed out, "Y-yes!" He bowed hastily. "At once!" Then he stepped forward and led us to the meeting room.

Once the door was closed behind us, she snickered. "Sorry about that, sometimes I get bored. I don't make it a habit to descend in person."

"Where do you usually spend your time, anyway?" I wondered.

She smiled. "Oh, you know. Here and there."

Not really an answer.

"It is an answer, just not the one you wanted to hear," she said with a wink.

Right, she can read minds. It's so easy to forget.

She sat down in the lotus position at the base of the altar with the blank statuette.

"Now then. Let's get down to your gift." She held up her hands and showed they were empty. "It's not an item that I will give you; however, your senses will improve, vastly so." Waving forward for me to lean in, she touched my forehead with her right thumb.

At first, nothing happened, and I closed my eyes. After half a minute, heat that suffused my entire body radiated from her thumb. Once a full minute had passed, the warmth turned into a searing heat. I would not have been surprised if, when I opened my eyes, I found myself on fire.

Despite my best efforts, I was rooted on the spot, unable to pull away, scream, or breathe. By the end of it, if someone had told me I'd turned into a charred briquette right there, I would've believed them.

"That," I said and opened my eyes with a gasp. "Sucked." Though the pain was gone, the memory of it was not and my hands went to my forehead. "Why did it hurt so much?"

"God-given gifts are not really given by the divine," Eloria said bluntly. "They are gifts already buried within you. What I did now was condense eighty years worth of trials and tribulations into a few short minutes. The pain over those years was sadly not something I could absolve you of, since I used it to guide me." She put her hand under my chin, pulling my eye line up to meet hers. "Sorry about that."

"That's okay," I said. "Eighty years worth of effort? I didn't even know I had something like that in me."

She nodded. "Then that would be eighty years of 'I know what I'm looking for,' effort. The full effects won't be immediate. To avoid your body going into shock and instant…" she averted her eyes, "death, your senses will adapt over the next few years."

I could only blink at her and laugh nervously. "Thanks for avoiding the death route."

Eloria smiled and her eyes returned to mine. "Of course." She tapped her chin. "Your thoughts were quite chaotic when you were waiting for your ceremony. Outside these chambers they are a bit less clear to me, especially when they're in disarray. What's bothering you?"

Good to know she can't read everything, I thought, then realized it may have been poorly timed while sitting right in front of her. "What color are my eyes?"

She crossed her arms and tilted her head. "Blue. As they have always been."

"Well," I said and tapped my temple near them. "They *were* brown. I remember being born with them brown. And until a few months ago, they were still brown." I sighed. "I visited a soothsayer in Ersta and asked her about the War, because I'd been having nightmares about being attacked on the front lines."

As I completed the sentence, I found it very odd that since then the wakeful nightmare had vanished, and a chill nipped at my skin. "Madame Vira said she couldn't help, but knew someone who can. When I visited them…" I went on to explain the chronomancer and his shop.

Eloria didn't interrupt once.

"That sounds improbable," she said when I was done. "Timekeepers, or a chronomancer as you've called this one, are impossibly rare. Even I've only met one, and that was at a great cost." Holding out her hands to her sides she said quietly, "You must understand that the least of the timekeepers is more powerful than the entirety of all pantheons on Anfang combined, myself included."

For the briefest of moments, I knew what it was to have an outer body experience, as fear gripped my heart. *Holy crap.*

Holding up a finger she continued, "What is more likely is they tampered with your memory. But to be sure, let's check. The soul is the best kept source of memories. If they did mess with your mind, I'll know." Her hand moved forward toward me and paused. "This is very invasive. May I?"

I nodded, hoping the Chronomancer was indeed just the charlatan I believed him to be. I also hoped that her thumb wouldn't hurt again.

In less time than it took to blink, she tapped my forehead and was done.

That easy? It was concerning that she could scour my mind that fast, yet unlocking a sense took so much pain and effort.

"Troubling," she said and stood, biting her thumbnail. It was such a human gesture of anxiety that I was taken aback. With a breath she said, "If you ever meet this timekeeper again, be very respectful. I only even knew about them by happenstance in a very old archive. It came with a warning: 'Cross not the timekeeper, for the world itself might forget you.'"

CHAPTER TWENTY-FOUR

A "NEW LEAF"

ELORIA STOOD AND paced back and forth for a few seconds before stopping in place. Turning to me she smiled. "This is likely not helping you any. I can tell you're afraid, and… that's actually not a bad feeling to have right now." She crossed her arms. "To even *meet* a timekeeper in the first place…" Shaking her head, she continued, "It's unthinkable. Your memories about entering his store are nothing but static to me."

Her comment made me think of the store.

"Right. Your thoughts right now are a completely chaotic mess. It reinforces that a timekeeper–" she paused. "Or at least someone more powerful than I has meddled with you. In the Mysselhøj universe, that list is usually empty."

Our universe has a name? Wait… does that mean there are others?

She coughed. "Don't repeat that thought to anyone. Just as land can be bought and sold, so can continents, planets, galaxies, and yes, even a universe." She rolled up the sleeve on her robe. "In this case, I fought someone for my prize." Waving her hand, as though she knew what I'd ask she added, "It wasn't to the death or anything."

"You choose your words wisely," I said with a nervous laugh. *She didn't say no one died.*

With a grin she said, "And you notice too much." She sighed. "That said, your next Awakening Ceremony will be in six years instead of four. I have something I need to look–" A bell tolled in the distance. "It seems our time has once again come to an end." Cupping my cheek with her hand she said, "Until we meet again."

Despite her warm departure, I spent a few minutes sitting there reeling in my own abject horror. The goddess overseeing the universe admitted outright my eyes had always been blue, while also confirming they had been changed.

Someone beyond Eloria. My mind drifted to the book I'd chucked into the fireplace when I was seven years old. "The Accounts of the Day of Death," a book that described the atrocities committed by Eloria against beast-kin.

Back then, I'd thrown it into the fire because I was terrified. I'd just found out I was a beast-kin. Burning it was pointless though, because it reappeared shortly after, and someone or something wrote into the book while I was looking directly at its pages. The message seemed to be as much for me as it was for Eloria: *"You can deny what happened, but it doesn't change the past."*

It was when I told Eloria about that moment, during my second Awakening Ceremony, that I became her True Champion.

Reflecting on the memory made something click. *Gods, that very reappearing book trick is what the timekeeper did! Did they write that message in the book for Eloria, then show me the same trick later as a warning?* I was very uncomfortable with all this. It made me feel like I was just a pawn in some bigger game far above me.

Over the next five minutes, I just sat there and hugged my legs, until Daughter Hy entered to collect me.

"Are you okay, Lady Anessa?" she asked.

Standing I said, "Yeah, I'm just a bit spooked."

She smiled weakly. "We all are. I don't think anyone expected her to visit in person."

Yeah, I'm pretty sure we're scared for different reasons.

During our trip home, our Daughter Envoys stayed behind. Since neither Sarah, Tania nor Aul were with us, it was just Yukirei and me on the ride back. She chose to sit at my side.

I decided to look out the window while we were driven back to our dormitory.

"Did Eloria really just pop into the church in front of everyone?" Yukirei asked, pulling my gaze away from the scenery.

"Yeah, it caused quite the stir," I said and gestured to the empty bench in front of us. "I'm sure it's why we're riding back alone."

"There is a benefit to it, though," she said, and smiled.

"What's that?"

She didn't say anything and instead took my hand into hers and interlaced our fingers.

Though I wanted to pull my hand away, I merely squeezed hers back and turned my focus back to the window. *I'm not sure I feel that way, Yuki, but I won't say no to some comfort. Eloria admitting she was outclassed made me feel very small.* A simple flash of Eloria biting her thumbnail and pacing about made me wonder if the Goddess of Death was actually afraid. The thought made me grip Yukirei's hand a hair tighter. *Who saves you when death itself is afraid?*

Despite the imported cherry blossom trees being in full bloom going by, they offered me no solace.

She responded by covering the top of mine with her free hand and patting it.

Minutes later, we stopped in front of the Imperial Royal Dormitory. Yukirei kept hold of my hand as we exited the carriage. It was honestly a welcome distraction from my thoughts.

Entering into the commons area of the suites, we came upon the Empress of Westwood, two of my other cousins, and my "favorite" person in the world: Lukas Q'Tar.

Just what I need. An asshole incarnate.

Yukirei and I gave a short curtsy to the Empress and continued toward the center of the commons to head toward my dorm suite.

Lukas intercepted us first. "Ladies," he said with a curt bow, his hand on his chest. "I wanted to apologize for my boorish behavior the other day. If there's anything I can do to make up for it, please let me know."

The hell? Is he terminally ill? It took everything I had at the moment to not scream about the gallons of bile and blood he had poured onto me, but I bit my tongue. His apology alone was a miracle, and I could only imagine what kind of pressure or threats had led him to make it. I knew that, despite the performatively gallant nature of his offer, I had better not press my luck by asking for anything significant, so I asked for what I knew the party would need most. "Would you be willing to return the dire boar's tusks to the hunting party I was with the other day?"

His response was swift and cool. "I will make it a priority. They should have it within a week." Giving us another brief bow I caught the slightest hint of annoyance in his face when he narrowed his eyes at me as his head came back up. It was subtle, so it could've just been my imagination. But it probably wasn't.

"Thanks," I said with a raised brow. As we returned to my room, I couldn't help but turn to him a few times and wonder if he would attack me now out of spite.

Once we'd entered, most of the dread I'd been feeling vanished when I saw Gideon in our sitting area. I may have let go of Yukirei's hand and rushed to sit across from him.

Why did I need to see him so badly, but not realize it once?

"Is everything okay?" Gideon asked.

Without thinking, I pulled him into a hug. "No. Everything's not okay." Over the next few minutes, I explained what happened at my Awakening Ceremony, leaving out the parts that caused my deep existential dread. By the end of it I realized I was sitting in his lap leaning on his chest, but no one seemed to object despite the breach in decorum.

"That reminds me," I said and looked up at Gideon. "The Empress of Westwood is in the commons area. And Lukas is being oddly nice."

Turning to Sarah, I asked, "Do you think it's the letter you sent to Mom?"

"Possibly," Sarah mused. "Her Imperial High Grace was quite annoyed, judging by her return letter."

"She responded?" I asked, shifting my tone down to let Sarah know I was annoyed.

Waving her hand, Sarah said, "I was told not to mention it, since her response doesn't directly involve you. But since you are asking, she sent a letter to His Imperial Majesty."

"Hmmph, good. Lukas needed to be brought down a peg or two."
Remembering the cold and calculating stare he gave me earlier, I
wondered aloud, "I don't trust him, though. He's clearly faking it." The
chill that ran through me faded when Gideon placed his hand on my
shoulder. All I could do is rest my head against his chest. *I should enjoy
this while my Lady's maids permit it.*

Sarah held up a finger as though she were about to lecture me, and I
was right. "Be that as it may, unless he directly crosses a line, it is best
you not openly pronounce that you are suspicious. He is quite well-
versed in using even hints of dissent against dissenters."

"You know," Gideon said, his voice reverberated through his chest.
He shifted our focus away from the Imperial Prince. "I have martial
training in under an hour."

"Oh," Yukirei said. "Would you mind if I joined you?"

"Me too!" I said holding my hand up for no reason. My cheeks heated
up immediately after, for acting like a child. "If you don't mind, that is."

"It would be my pleasure for you both to be there," he said. "Room
302C." He turned to Yukirei. "Would you two go on ahead? I have to
fetch some things from my room."

Hopping off his lap, I said, "Sure."

Yukirei gave him a smile and then took my hand, leading us out.

As we exited, I heard Sarah ask, "Are you going, My Lord?"

I barely caught Gideon's response, "Yeah, I just need a minute."

Once the door closed behind us, I said, "Huh."

"What?" Yukirei asked.

"Wonder why he needed to stay behind. Must've had a cramp in his
leg," I said.

She just laughed. "Yes, I imagine he did have a 'cramp' in his 'leg.'"

Tilting my head I asked, "Why is that funny?"

She stopped and pulled the hair in front of my eyes, placing it behind
my ear. "You'll understand when you're older."

In a flash, my face flushed crimson. "Oh gods," I said and covered
my face with my free hand.

"So, you do understand!" Yukirei said and giggled.

"It's not funny!" I stomped.

Wiping a tear from her eye she said, "It is, just a little."

"Why didn't he say anything?"

She tapped her chin. "What could he have said that would've been *less* awkward?"

Biting my lower lip I hung my head. "Nothing." My clear miss made me think, *How did I not notice that?* The thought made my blush return with a vengeance. *Scratch that. Thank the gods I didn't notice.*

"You two ready?" Gideon said behind us, making me jump.

"Yes!" I shouted, eliciting a titter from Yukirei.

Gideon settled in beside us and he whispered to her, "Is she okay?"

She took his hand. "Yes, just the palpitations of a maiden's heart."

"Huh, okay," he said in evident confusion.

It took the remainder of the walk to the training arena for my embarrassment to subside.

Setting out one of my special steel training dummies, my first task was to try and repeat what I'd done with the dire boar. Trying to focus my frustration toward the boar in my fist, I smacked it as hard as I could. A second later I was crouching and holding my hand. "Ouch."

"What are you trying to do?" Yukirei asked.

Shaking my hand, I stood and looked critically at the spot I'd hit. "Trying to understand how I killed that beast that attacked us."

She looked at the dummy, with several marks taken out of it already. I'd had it for a few years already. When I could control it, I'd merely ablate a tiny surface area away, no thicker than a hair as wide as a small copper. When I didn't try to do anything, it was as large as an Earthen quarter and equally half as deep.

Looking at my latest effort, I saw that it was still as wide as a small copper, but instead of being a little fleck, the blow had bored into the dummy enough to put my pinky finger in up to the first joint.

Tracing the edge with my finger, I said, "Cool." Then I sighed, "But I was trying to go *through* it."

"There aren't even any burn marks or melting," she said in a calculating tone, and felt the edge herself once I'd withdrawn my finger. "What kind of Will are you imbuing the stone with?" she asked in a matter-of-fact tone.

I blinked. "What is Will?" I knew better than to ask, "Who is Will?" because nobody on Anfang would get the joke—Earthen idioms fly over their heads.

"It's the intent you include with your essence to make it do work."

"I'll admit," I said and scratched my cheek, "My training on cultivation hasn't covered that. I have heard the word before, but it's never been described."

Yukirei sighed. "That's probably what you're missing." Clasping her hands in front of herself, she asked, "Would you like me to help you with it later?"

I smiled and took her hands into mine without thinking. "That would be great!"

She turned her eyes to our hands, "Then we'll make an accord of it."

Oh. I blinked and released her hands making her pout. *It's not the same as going on a picnic or a concert. Is tapping into dangerous powers the sort of thing that actually makes for a fun date?*

CHAPTER TWENTY-FIVE

IF THERE'S A WILL

Deuday, Lokandae 24th, 1739

A FEW DAYS later, Yukirei and I entered a different building, which had its own training arenas.

"Why are we *here*?" I asked. *This reminds me of being a kid and visiting a high school as a child.* The rooms were far more ornate than the ones we used last time. And in place of the simple white tiles were hardwoods and a generally higher sense of polish. On top of that, the outer perimeter of the room included a series of ornately-crafted tiles that connected to one another, almost like a densely-packed circuit.

"You felled a dire boar. That shows significant strength. Even if it was a juvenile, they are powerful and would give me a difficult time. This room should make sure your power doesn't leak out or harm someone if you're successful in invoking it again." She shook her head. "I'm honestly surprised you killed it in one strike. Even with Reaction, I would have little hope of stopping it, let alone harming it."

She showed an illusion of a teeny tiny boar on her palm. "I'd probably need to lure it into a trap," the boar fell into a pit with spikes at the bottom, "and take my time whittling it down." A small image of her began attacking the animal from above. Tiny Yukirei was, I noted, just as stylish as the real deal.

Her admission made me frown. "Lukas lifted the thing like it were nothing. Is he stronger than you?"

Pursing her lips she nodded. "A lot. I'm closer to the early Sky Realm. He's in the middle. In comparison, your daddy's at the top." Patting the dummy in front of us she said, "Let's not think about that though. His family spends a lot of money to push him forward and advance his skills. Considering that you're doing basically nothing, and how far you've come regardless..." she smiled. "I have no doubts you'll surpass him someday."

When he bumped into me months ago, the gap between us was obvious. He was just *walking* and moved me several feet because I was in his way. "It seems like a tall order," I admitted.

"We best get started then." Yukirei said.

"What's so special about these rooms?"

Yukirei created a ball of blue fire the size of her hand floating above it. Since she used illusions so often, I wasn't sure if it were real or not. In a flash it darted forward toward the edge of the room and scattered midair as it met the perimeter created by the fancy tiles.

"This room has a barrier on it. Since you felled a dire boar in one strike, it seemed to reason we'd need to take a few precautions." Tapping the tile of the arena we were in with her foot, she said, "This is a high-spec room. As you can see, it absorbed one of my fire attacks with no problem."

Let's hope the high-spec room understands whatever the pink energy I'm using is. Since pink as an essence color was absent from Dean Donovan's box of pills. I shook my head to clear my doubts. I'm sure it'll be fine. I can't even replicate what I did anyway. Especially if Will is tangible, that "barrier" might just erase it.

"I'm sure Will is what you're missing," Yukirei continued. "When I try to use fire without it, I just get a chaotic jumble." By way of illustration, she held out her hand, and a sputtering orange flame sat there that petered out almost immediately. Her posture straightened and she coughed into her hand. "Now then," her voice took on a clearly fake pompous air, "Will as a concept is simple." She held up a finger and added, "It's the process of bundling up your intentions into a ball and moving that to meet your essence to form an attack."

I couldn't hold my laughter any longer and I busted out in response to her silliness. "Stop that," I breathed. "I can't focus." After I'd calmed down, I asked, "How do I bundle my intentions, anyway?"

Pursing her lips she said, "It is a simple concept, but doing it takes some getting used to. It's like when you tested with Reaction, you'll just need to try." She shrugged. "I don't know more than that."

I suppose my teacher is only four years older than I am. Let's hope practicing Will isn't as damaging as it was with Reaction. I shredded that flower head.

There seemed no danger of that. Over the next hour and a half, I tried and tried again. To no avail.

Yukirei was her usual patient self and sat down at the edge of the arena floor in the lotus position to meditate.

An hour later, I was starting to feel bad for making her wait so long.

That was when a familiar voice poked its way in. Trish said, *"You're thinking about this much too hard."*

Where have you been? I thought back crossly.

"Sleeping, like I told you earlier," she said.

All I could do is roll my eyes at the idea of a spirit "sleeping." Sighing I thought, *Sure. We'll go with that. What do you mean, I'm thinking about it too hard?*

"When you use your nexus, do you think *about doing so?"* she asked.

Not really. It just works.

"Right. When you asked your Dad, Roland, about holding his essence, the look he gave you was as though you'd grown a second head."

When I'd awoken as a cultivator at the age of eight, I understood what he meant implicitly. My body used essence of its own accord without the slightest effort.

Closing my eyes, her words clicked. Near my nexus I saw the teeniest sphere form. All I'd done is think about my essence boring through the dummy. Carefully guiding the pebble into my hand where I forced the pink essence, I guided both the essence and the dot into a stone I took from my storage ring.

Opening my eyes and looking at the stone, it had the faintest pink hue.

A grin came unbidden, and I called out, "Yuki!"

She opened her eyes and joined me. "Did you figure something out?"

Holding up the lightly glowing stone I said, "I think so, do you see the color of the stone?"

Arching a brow she shook her head. "It's just a dull brown stone."

Then she can't see it, I thought, deflated. Maybe I was just seeing things. I tossed the rock half-heartedly and missed the target entirely. It sailed right over it, through the "barrier" and the wall beyond it.

Yukirei and I looked at one another and approached the hole.

It'd gone through to the next room, and beyond. Since it was not in use, the tell-tale sign of light peeking in meant it'd found its way outside.

Crap!

We shared a look and laughed.

"Maybe we should–" I started.

She finished with a half-grin, "–leave?"

Tattling on yourself is never easy. We approached the attendant of the high-spec rooms and Yukirei told him what happened. He was clearly not sure whether to believe us. For most of our walk back to the Imperial Royal Dormitories, we were quiet, but busted up giggling once the door closed behind us.

"I can't believe your rock went through the barrier!" she said with a smile.

"Do you think we'll get in trouble?" I asked.

She shook her head. "No one got hurt, so I don't think so." With her fingertips touching she flexed them nervously and asked, "Would you like to go on the rooftop to watch the sun set?"

There's no harm in that, I thought, and said, "Sure."

When lifting a ton is second nature, flipping out of a window onto the rooftop is effortless. Even when I was seven, it was a cinch. Five years later, it doesn't even count as exercise. The only hard part was maintaining decorum in a dress when the world lacks proper undergarments.

For half a breath I almost forgot about that, and blushed deeply as I landed holding my dress down below my waist. *I wasn't planning on using my legs during practice, so I didn't think to wear my shorts. What was I thinking?*

Yukirei landed beside me with no issues. Her use of Reaction meant she had a natural ring around her mid-thigh without much thought on her part. Though it did billow out some giving her a temporary bulb appearance just below the waist. I was too embarrassed myself to find it funny.

If I'd used Reaction, my thought drifted to the flower and how I'd shredded the petals off in one swipe, *I'd have stripped myself.*

She pointed in the distance above the main dormitory that Lukas resided within. "That seems like a nice spot."

I laughed nervously. "Okay, let's hope we don't meet anyone who lives there."

We made our way over and sat on top of the cupola, which gave a great view of Ersta and the surrounding forest.

Despite knowing a fall from thirty meters would not harm me, I held onto what I thought was likely a lightning rod, just in case. *I'd probably just expose my bare rear to the world if I fell, knowing my luck and penchant for shredding garments.*

As we sat there, and Yukirei leaned against the metal rod towering above us, she asked, "How did you do that, you think?"

Remembering Sir Orris said I had access to sixteen elements made me cautious about what I revealed; he said it was good my parents followed the scriptures so ardently. Despite that, I didn't have a clue what the essence was called, other than recognizing it by its pink hue. *Is this tension I feel why Mom was always so quick to lean on the Church to say nothing?*

"I have some ideas," I said and shook my head. "But I'm not really sure if I understand it, or if I'm permitted to talk about it."

"Mmm," she intoned and nodded. "The gods do love their secrets."

Huh, I'll have to remember that. It's a better excuse.

As the sky's blue hues gave way to a fiery spectacle, Trish piped up, *"Yukirei isn't so bad, is she?"*

Cripes, you startled me, I thought with a light jump. *Do you just hang out waiting for the right moment to talk?*

She said, *"I don't have a whole lot to do, you know, with no body and all."*

Huh. I hadn't thought of that.

"So back to Yukirei," Trish said.

What about her? I replied harshly.

"You've thought about kissing her, haven't you?" Trish jeered.

Stop with trying to push things along. If anything like that ever happens, it'll be at my *pace. I'm only twelve. That's far too young to kiss regularly.*

"You've kissed Gideon," she countered.

That's different. We're actually married, even if it is partly political. My cheeks heated up thinking about our *two* kisses, which led to another thought of Yukirei's lips, which only made my blush worse.

"Okay. You're right, I'm sorry. But you should prepare yourself, at the very least."

Prepare for what? I thought.

"Anessa," Yukirei said.

Turning to her, the lower light and sunset brought out the golden flecks in her olive eyes. They almost seemed to twinkle.

My spiritual companion's intrusive thoughts made it impossible to miss her pink lip gloss.

Ah crap, Trish you're putting silly thoughts—

"Would it be okay if I kissed you?" Yukirei said.

Shit. I then realized that *I* wasn't the only one who had their own pace. *As usual, Trish is always more observant than I am.*

More than a few times, my eyes darted from her lips to her eyes. Each beat of my heart made my trepidation that much more evident. I was thankful for the sun's light hiding my crimson cheeks, or so I hoped it was.

"S-sure," I said, and gripped the finial tighter as Yukirei moved closer.

I closed my eyes a bit too soon, and it appeared she had too, because we knocked foreheads.

"Ow," I said and rubbed the spot. We shared a short moment of silence then giggled.

Yukirei was as awkward as I felt at that moment.

I was thankful for her inexperience, as her tongue never entered the fray, but she lingered longer than I thought she might.

"Um," I said when she pulled away. "That was a bit more than I was expecting."

"Sorry," she nodded quickly.

"It's okay," I said, then repeated the moment over in my head. *It's okay,* I reassured myself. My blush deepened as I repeated it again.

Why wasn't that as bad as I thought it would be?

CHAPTER TWENTY-SIX

THRUSENSE

Octday, Polarae 21st, 1739

NUMEROLOGY ON EARTH often tied the number thirteen to bad luck. Since I was never a big proponent of such a belief, I never thought twice about it. On Anfang, I wondered if the number really *was* bad luck; if gods and goddesses existed here, who knew what else might be true.

Of course, this was probably due to the world-ending migraine I woke up screaming to—on my bad-luck thirteenth birthday.

Sitting up in my bed made me immediately fall over in the opposite direction, folding in half. I couldn't make sense of what I was seeing. There wasn't a single straight line in sight. Every surface was curved and wrapped in on itself like the mirror mazes at carnivals, only it was one continuous surface.

What the hell! I thought, and my heart raced as I realized I couldn't see myself, despite waving my hand about. Rolling onto my back I could both see the bed sheets flattened by the head that *should* be there, and a lesser image of the tiled surface beneath the bed itself.

The stabbing pain in the middle of my nose, or the place it would be if I still had one, made it difficult to tell if I could really see the stuffing and springs in my bed or if I was losing my mind.

Righting myself again, it took both of my hands flat on the bed to avoid tumbling over again. Gently turning my head made it evident I was looking *everywhere* in the room all at the same time. Bile nipped at the back of my throat, forming a lump I couldn't swallow.

I'm going to be sick.

Knowing I didn't want to do so here in my room, I edged myself to the side of my bedpost, and lifted up. I made it no more than three steps before my world spun and a cacophony of noises assaulted my ears.

Gideon's light snoring in the guest room, the maids tidying up, our cook preparing for the day's meals—the rapid increase in sounds made my tumble to the ground come to a crawl. A thunderstorm of heartbeats kicked in from everyone in the entire Imperial Royal dormitory. In under a second it was more of a fluid-rushing than the slamming of drums. The crickets' usual sing-song harmony became a screeching chorus of torment.

A second after I hit the floor, I voided my dinner from the night before. I rolled away to avoid lying in ick and instantly regretted it as the acrid bite of my sick ratcheted up to eleven in both my nose and on my tongue, then went beyond. The tell-tale reminder that I was living in a world around the medieval time-period came in the form of the toilet I'd been inching towards. I knew whatever I was experiencing hadn't finished with me, and I was not going to hold onto my last lunch or breakfast either.

Inches from the bathroom floor I cried out again and fell onto my face when the shifting of the fabric from my chemise seemed to rip into my skin and my palms burned from the floor's smooth surface, the rock layer prickled pitting of the sub-floor and the tiny rocks digging into my palms despite them being between layers.

Gods, what's going on! Am I dying? My plea reminded me of a certain goddess's words that my senses would improve. She claimed she'd avoided the death route. The assault I was under made it seem otherwise. I rolled onto my side and curled into a ball. Tears came unbidden as I feared this was just the beginning.

"Sarah," I called out, surprised to find my voice boomed. It was likely an effect of hearing everything at once, but I didn't much care to dwell on it. "Help, please!"

Moments later my lady's maid rushed in and tended to my side.

"Anessa?" she shouted and knelt next to me.

"Too loud."

She whispered back, "I'm barely talking. Everyone in the dormitory heard you."

"I'm scared, what's going on?" I said as quietly as I could.

She asked me a series of questions, which I answered as quietly as I could. My lady's maid explained that she was using the barest whisper she could muster. Despite that, her voice, along with every other sound, was roaring in my ears.

Remembering Eloria's words, I explained that my senses were supposed to improve, though up until now I hadn't noticed anything too drastic.

Sarah helped me into the restroom and I emptied myself until there was nothing left. We then worked on making me presentable, and moved into the lounge.

Gideon had dressed himself in the least needed to be presentable, though when your vision is warped, and every sense is rebelling, it's difficult to smile.

As I approached with my lady's maids' aid, he stood and guided me next to him.

Sarah closed in on my dorm suite's exit and whispered, "I'm going to reach out to your parents to see if they know what can help."

"Okay," I replied.

Both Gideon and Sarah's eyes flared in surprise. It was quite unusual to see everything around me, and watch her depart through solid stone.

Man she's fast, I thought as she took two steps at normal speed then all but vanished.

Her sudden absence left a natural pause.

Gideon's warmth gave me solace, and I wrapped my arms around him the best I could.

Tania, my ever-zealous lady's maid, coughed. "Anessa, please be mindful of decorum."

Gideon had started blushing ear to ear to his chest.

It made me realize I could see through his shirt, and made a tremendous effort not to focus on his midsection, fearing it would push my estrus to rear its ugly head were I to see anything I shouldn't.

"What do you mean?" I asked.

"You're looking straight down," she cleared her throat again. "Very intently, I might add."

It was my turn to join him in his youthful shock. "Tania. Please correct my posture," I whispered, knowing full well that whatever was projecting my voice would let her hear me. "I cannot tell where I am looking."

"I heard you talking to Sarah," Tania said as she moved about me. Though I could sense she was positioning my head and neck, the relatively minuscule shift in sight made being unable to see my own body frightful.

Is this my new normal? People will think I'm blind, daft, or both.

"Why are you smiling?" Tania asked.

"Because Gideon's smiling."

She arched a brow, and he turned to me.

"He was facing away from you, though."

Weird, what was he smiling at? And was I able to tell because I can see through things?

"It's..." he started, "a nervous smile. I'm worried." Squeezing me he added, "This is different. Not bad," he cautioned. "Just different."

Tania then brought me a piece of paper with an inkwell along with a table to write on.

"What's this for?"

She covered her ears, and whispered, "So you can talk. You might not realize it but you're shouting throughout the entire Imperial Dorm Suites. Not just your own."

Oh. Crap.

For the first few moments that I held the quill, I giggled.

"What's wrong?" she asked.

Lifting my hand up and down, then side to side, I asked, "Don't you see–" I caught myself. "Oh," I whispered. "I suppose you don't. For me the quill seems to be levitating midair."

Tania came to my side and asked, "May I?"

"What?"

"You're hunched over and smiling like you lost your marbles last week."

"R-right," I said. "Please do correct my posture."

As I wrote, Gideon rubbed my back as a welcome relief. Despite the occasional tremors of tearing pain that would shudder through the spot, it was nice to not be alone.

"I was delighted to see you here," I wrote to Gideon, my eye twitched at the pitch the sound of scrawling on paper made. "Even if I didn't show it."

"It's my pleasure," he said and smiled. "Always is." Taking the quill from my hand, he repeated his words on paper.

It was a dorky, unnecessary move that merely made me smile.

He followed it up by placing his hand on my head and tousling my hair.

Resting my head against Gideon must've triggered something in my inner ear, because I instantly knew there was more of my prior day's meals inside.

"Gideon," I said in my haste and blanched, "Please help me to the restroom."

He did so and held my hair for me, just as Sarah had.

A while later I was nudged awake. It seemed I had mercifully fallen asleep.

"Anessa," Sarah said quietly. "Drink this, it should help."

Without question I snapped it up and downed it in an instant. Although it was easily two pints I thought, *If this magical liquid has a chance of fixing this, I don't care what it is or how much I have to drink.*

The moment I pulled the waterskin away from my face, I hiccuped. "What was that?" The taste of bile faded, along with the heart-ridden pulse of the dormitory and I was happy to report that Gideon now appeared to have a solid shirt on.

"I contacted your father, who contacted someone else, a 'Sir Orris.' He suggested the drink you just downed. It was alcohol."

Locking onto the drink my heart rate increased a hair. "Will I be okay? Isn't it poisonous at my age?"

She sighed. "That was very weak alcohol. Had it not given you relief," she produced two other similar containers, "I would've given you something stronger."

Her admission made me sigh. "So, nothing to worry about. Good."

"Your gift is called Thrusight, or so I'm told. Every time it manifests for the first time, the simplest way to resolve its overwhelming nature is to relax the gifted patient. I was told alcohol is a seda-teeve."

Looking at the waterskin again I handed it back. "Yeah, it did do that."

When Sarah took the item from me, the parts of "me" I would usually see returned to my sight. I spent a few moments looking at my hands and flexing my fingers in relief.

"Everything alright?" She asked offering one of the stronger "sedatives."

I waved her off. "I'm fine. It's nice to be able to see my hands again."

"This 'Sir Orris' I'm told should be crafting you a less poisonous draught to help you along. He said you'll also need…" she paused, "I'm not sure of the words, but it's something that goes on your eye so you can see where you're looking."

"Ah, contact lenses?" I asked.

She nodded. "Yes. That does sound right."

It strikes me every time, there's a word for something that others don't know, but I don't say it in English, so I know it's a word. Translation arts are bizarre. Thinking on the need of contacts I chuckled to myself, imagining a room full of old people who forgot them looking in random directions. Then caught a brief shiver as I could see myself right there next to them if I failed to follow etiquette.

"Strange that it's called Thrusight," I said.

"It's possible the adviser your father talked to is only versed in the vision. Difficult to say," Sarah added.

"I'm surprised how quickly you got all that information."

"You've been passed out here for two hours before Sarah-Knecht von Anessa arrived," Gideon said.

"Oh," I said with a laugh. "Awkward."

"Thankfully I was able to get a hold of your braid before you…" he paused and rolled his wrist toward his mouth, a gesture for getting sick, I'd guessed.

Giving Gideon a hug I said, "Thanks for holding my hair while I puked my guts out."

Sarah coughed. "Lady Anessa, you're looking straight down."

I groaned. *Great. I can see roughly where my nose is, but not where I'm actually looking. I hope Gideon doesn't think any less of me.*

I was fairly sure he didn't. Not yet, anyway.

CHAPTER TWENTY-SEVEN

LETTER

LEARNING TO WALK when you're a baby and having the wherewithal to know you'd done it all before was a treat. It didn't bloody help me learn it faster, but knowing that the skill wasn't impossible helped.

However, having your senses rebel and learning how to do everything all over again was not my idea of a good time. It took a full month, as long as two Earth months, to not chuck my cookies after taking three steps.

"What's going on with Lady Anessa?" a female voice asked.

Turning my head toward where my gut said the voice was, I peered forward above me in the kitchen, through the floors, and found the target.

"I'm not sure, but she seems very sick," another girl said.

A third gossip piped in, "There are also rumors that people have heard her voice late at night *yowling* her betrothed's name."

That they heard what amounted to a literal cat-call when I was in heat made me flush from my neck up. "Oh gods," I said aloud, by mistake.

The three gabby girls stiffened, and their eyes darted around. They said nothing else, nodding to one another in silence and walking off.

Crap, they'll probably talk about that later. I really need to get a better handle on this. The hardest part of my new ability, I'd found, was controlling my voice. At least those girls were likely the only ones to have heard my appalled commentary. Whenever I focused on something, that seemed to be where my voice would come from, or near it, at least. It was not ideal, though it certainly beat shouting everything to the entire dormitory, including the commons area.

Sarah entered my room, likely preparing to serve me breakfast in bed. Not a typical routine, but since I'd had difficulties keeping anything down, it was a necessary precaution.

Thinking my flub over, I chuckled, remembering when my cousin Rina spat her tea out after I'd startled her a few days ago. Though in her defense, it startled *everyone* when I cursed after stubbing my toe.

An unfamiliar sound caught my ear, a mix between distress and bliss. Zeroing in on it, I learned that not every sound is worth exploring.

"What's wrong Anessa?" Sarah asked, "Your face just brightened like an apple. Are you feeling unwell?" She moved over to place her hand on my forehead.

"N-no, it's not that. You know the new maid we took on last week?"

Sarah nodded.

"I don't think she's going to work out," I said, and covered my face.

"Why not?" She asked and placed her other hand on her own forehead. "You do feel a bit warm."

"The smaller pantry to the side of the kitchen. Under the stairs?" With a nod from Sarah I continued, "Maybe go stand there for about... three minutes? You'll see what I mean. I think the guard there may also need to be dismissed."

"Reason?" She asked.

I waved her in, "A... d-dalliance, I guess?"

Sarah shot straight up and marched towards the stairs. "I'll be back," she said, pausing no more than a breath at my doorway.

Uh oh. Keeping an eye on her while avoiding the pantry wasn't too difficult.

The look on their faces when they saw Sarah there was priceless. Though her next move surprised me. She marched them straight to the library and closed the door.

Our love-struck maid was dismissed without back pay, and the guard had entered through the window near the kitchen.

Sarah's words surprised me. "You," she approached the guard. "Were it not for the magnanimity of our Imperial High Grace, Imperial Princess, Champion of the High Goddess of Craft, Anessa Carlyle…" Each title she stated caused his pallor to worsen. "You could be *executed* for trespass into the Imperial Princess's Gynaeceum. As it is, you will be dismissed and your sword hand branded, to be carried out in the nearby smithy by day's end." She tossed a small pouch onto the end of the table for each of them.

"You will not receive your *pay*, but this is for your silence. Take it of your own will. You may either depart by your power," her tone shifted down, "or ours. The Mother-Penitentiary will receive your confessions within the hour." Her gaze fixed on the guard. "The master of the guard will be in here shortly to take your livery badge and sword."

Neither of the blanched party said a word. Both picked up their pouches.

She left the two there in the room alone, but stationed two guards outside the door after locking them inside. The couple didn't even look at one another after that.

After that I couldn't bear to watch them. *I didn't think they'd brand his hand for entering.* I suddenly realized that in fact none of my guards had been male ever since I hit seven years old, and estrus hit me in full. *Why do I miss the obvious so much? Is it just a case of them having no need to tell me the rules unless it becomes relevant?*

Once Sarah returned to me, I gave her a frown. "I didn't know it would be that big of an issue."

She smiled. "You did nothing wrong, Lady Anessa."

"Will they really brand his hand?" I asked and rubbed the back of mine. "That'll hurt, and remind him of this mistake for life."

Her smile dropped. "That's the point. My lady, you hold a very high station. What if he was using her to get close to you?"

"I can take care of myself," I insisted.

"Maybe, but you still occasionally sleep, don't you?" she asked in a level tone.

The thought that accompanied her words made my frown deepen. "That's an…" I took a breath, "unpleasant thought."

"Right. We can't know his true intentions, and it's best we don't dig." Her eyes became distant. "Doing so would be far worse than a mark on his hand."

Tania entered with the breakfast Sarah was supposed to bring, causing her to cover her mouth briefly in chagrin as she realized her oversight.

"Ah, thank you Tania," she said. "Something of import came up and it required immediate attention."

Tania nodded. "So I've heard." Her failing to dally on the matter said more than gossip might have.

"Have we heard back from Sir Orris about my gift? He was supposed to provide a new draught, wasn't he?"

"When we described the full set of symptoms, he said he'd need to fine-tune it a little for your needs," Tania said while pouring some tea to go with the steamed buns.

Must be the newer chef. She cooks items closer to Asian cuisine. My mouth watered. *Not that I mind.*

"Also," Tania continued, "his gift isn't exactly the same as yours. You'll need to continue to adapt."

"But I'm able to return to classes today, right?"

Sarah answered, "If you manage to keep both breakfast *and* first lunch down. Yes. You've been absent for quite a while, so your class schedule has changed. You'll do a *light,*" she paused to look at me directly, "and I mean light, run after first lunch. Then…" she went on to describe my course load ad nauseam.

Later in the day I was finishing my "light" run at fifty miles an hour. Given I could go five times that without issue, it really was more of a jog for me. Slowing down, I walked for a few blocks to ease to a stop near my statecraft and leadership adviser's office. This was the latest addition to my coursework, and it was new to me.

I knocked on his door, and he beckoned me to enter.

"Lady Anessa, I presume?" he asked.

"Yes, sir."

He was sitting at his desk reading a paper in front of him. The air he gave off was the polar opposite of Dean Donovan. Whereas one was orderly and everything had its place, here there were stacks of paperwork, books opened to specific pages, and a general mess to navigate to even approach his desk.

"This came for you today," he said, pulling a letter from a tall stack at his side. He waved the envelope for me to retrieve without even looking my way.

After I'd taken it, he added, "I've seen these before, you can read it over there," he pointed to a small nook in the corner that had just enough space to sit without fear of being buried.

Though the envelope was a plain ivory, the front of it was just my name in the cleanest handwriting I'd ever seen. *I would say a girl wrote this, but there's something methodical about the lettering.* Its seal, though, was a pitch-black motif of a dragon chasing and biting its own tail, embossed in gold.

The bottom right of the envelope was debossed with G.M.G., which told me it was from Yukirei's father.

"To her Imperial High Grace and Imperial Princess of the Westwood Empire, Anessa, High Duchess of the Imperial Carlyle Duchy:

Know that by the Grace of His Imperial Majesty and the Imperial Ruler's Seal, on Finday, Mankae 4th, 1741, we hereby Appoint and Order Anessa, Imperial High Duchess of the Imperial Carlyle Duchy, to the office of Field Marshal of the Northern Marches of the Tulip Kingdom with command of the forces assigned thereto; for a term of at least two years, or so long as hostilities plague our northern frontier.

This conferment is made not only to prepare you as a future Imperial Duchess, but to recognize your contributions to our Empire, even those which cannot be credited to your name.

Your appointment is mandatory. Should you choose to exercise a wish to self-exclude, you will not only bring shame to your family, but you will be stripped of your titles and disinherited.

May Her Goddess Eloria guide any who stand in your way to the next life.

-Eugene Truval

Grand Master-General of the Westwood Empire"

As I read the letter my palms began to sweat. *A minimum of two years, with no definite end.* Heat roiled in my gut and despite my senses calming down, I wondered if I would be sick.

"Are you okay, Lady Anessa?" asked one of my guards.

"Yeah," I said. "I just need a minute."

My statecraft adviser cleared his throat. "I can tell you won't be of much use today. Why don't you come back at the same time tomorrow?"

I nodded and left. The walk back to the Imperial Royal dormitories was a blur.

Entering my dorm Gideon's solemn face worried me further. I'd been clutching the letter in my hand since the adviser's office. Despite my strength it wasn't even wrinkled, even though I know I squeezed it a few times.

His eyes locked onto it and he held up one of his own.

Approaching him we sat across from one another in silence for a few minutes.

"Do you want to read mine?" he asked in a hoarse voice.

I nodded and pushed my envelope over to him.

Gideon had also been appointed to a field marshal position. Though he had been assigned to a safer area, near our southern neighbor, the Tanis Region. Worse, his term would start within the year, instead of three.

Sitting his down on the table between us I cried silently with my hands on my forehead.

He quietly sat to my side and pulled me to his chest. "It's going to be okay."

Grabbing his jacket, I said, "Mmm." Tears were easier than words, and I once again wished for the ignorance of reading about the war on a mobile phone, instead of taking part. It was one of the few times I hated being a noble.

CHAPTER TWENTY-EIGHT
REASONS

"WE'VE GOT OUR work cut out for us," my statecraft adviser said grimly. "To be frank, you're not ready for a field marshal position." Waving his hand he said, "I wouldn't expect you to be, as a sheltered child."

His assertion made my right eye twitch. *Seriously? I know I'm a little sheltered, but he doesn't need to say it so bluntly.*

"Of course, it's normal for nobility to cut their teeth in upper military ranks to prepare them for the 'wonderful,'" he snorted, "life as a noble."

Trish intruded long enough to say, *"He doesn't have a high opinion of nobles, does he?"*

I silently nodded to her in agreement.

"Come back next week. I need a little time to plot out your next two years. We'll go over some options on who can train you up."

Who? He's not going to train me himself? Though I wanted to say it, he shared Dean Donovan's penchant for rank and rigor, so I refrained. "Yes, sir."

"That will be all for today," he said and looked up at me. "Dismissed."

When the door closed behind me, I let out a groan. *He's more difficult than Dean Donovan.* Near my dormitory I saw Yukirei and sped up.

"She's going to your dorm suite, you don't need to hurry," Trish jeered.

My motion stalled for a second and I smiled at myself. *You're not wrong I suppose.*

But thoughts of a happy meeting evaporated when I got close enough to hear her.

"I can't believe Daddy!" Yukirei shouted from within my dorm.

Uh oh.

Gideon was trying to console her with his hands on her shoulders as I entered. We locked eyes for a second before he let go and sat down.

Yukirei looked back at me, her eyes reddened. It was clear she'd been crying.

"What's wrong?" I asked.

On the table between Gideon and Yukirei was a letter addressed to her. It looked much like my own.

"You too, huh?" I asked with a sigh.

Gideon pursed his lips and shook his head.

What?

When I picked the letter up off the table to read it, my mouth fell open. There was a very big difference in her appointment. *She's set to be on the front lines.* As I kept reading, I fought back the bile that rose in my throat again, like when reading my own. *Within the week!* Tears bit at the corners of my eyes, and I knew what it meant to be so angry I could cry.

"Is there anything we can do?" I asked.

Yukirei shook her head. "No. Daddy won't even talk to me right now." She gripped her arm. "I actually haven't been able to get an audience with him for a few months."

"Why are they involving us in the first place?" I said throwing the appointment letter onto the table. "We're just kids!"

"Anessa." She placed her hand on her chest. "Gideon and I are adults by law."

I scowled. "Maybe, but you're both still awful young."

"It's our stations," she said. "An Imperial High Duchess, her Imperial Marquess *husband*," she said narrowing her eyes at me.

It earned Gideon a glare, which he dodged less than gracefully by looking at the table.

Her voice shook, "And the Grand Master General's brilliant Striker daughter. Together we represent a solid *third* of Westwood's upper echelons in Imperial rank." She closed her eyes and pressed her lips together in a thin line. "Leaving us out would invite rumors of favoritism, despite the nepotism of placing us so high in command."

No training for Yuki, I guess. Perhaps she's been trained most of her life anyway, considering who her father is.

Gideon spoke up, "It's not fair that they're putting you on the front lines, though, Yuki."

She smiled and took his hand for a moment. "It's okay. Loi d'Equilibre should balance things out. I won't engage any mortals directly."

I wanted to hold my hand up and say that wasn't what he meant, but the gaze they shared for a moment said I'd just be intruding.

Loi d'Equilibre, I thought, *Law of Equilibrium.* Based on how she said it, she wouldn't need to worry about facing mortals head on. *Lucky for* them.

"Daddy has always told me my real training would be on the front lines," she said. Her voice took on a mocking tone, "'It's what's best for you,'" she snorted. "He's avoiding me because he knows I'd knock him in his big nose."

Her threat of violence reminded me why we'd butted heads early on. She had a little bit of a temper, but I found myself smiling.

"What if a mortal uses a weapon that could hurt you?" Gideon asked. It was the question on the tip of my tongue as well.

Yukirei shrugged. "It's their funeral. I'm not required to die a fool's death. If they take up arms towards me, even if it would bounce off of my protective artifacts," she gave us both a glare that made our breaths hitch. "I can and will defend myself."

Gideon and I both sighed, then we looked between one another and laughed for a second. It didn't last long, but it was oddly nice.

"Otherwise, unless it's a secret mission or of grave importance, the law applies." She looked at me. "I can usually tell mortals and those in the Nascent Realm apart from those in the Ascended and Sky Realms."

Is she looking at me because I'm harder to tell apart? She did say my control over essence sucks.

I took my own letter from my storage ring and offered it to her. She read it over. Gideon did the same.

Afterwards we just sat there, each of us looking at our new orders in an awkward silence.

A few minutes later Yukirei shot up and raised her hand in the air. "Let's go do something."

"Like?" I asked.

"Something we can all do together. Not a restaurant though. I ate a few days ago, so I'm not hungry," she said and put her hands on her hips. "Hmm."

"Horseback riding?" Gideon offered.

She snapped her fingers and pointed to him. "Yeah, that's perfect!"

"I haven't ridden in a few *years*," I admitted.

"That's okay, riding a horse is like r–" She snickered. "Like riding a horse!"

The Anfangian equivalent of "riding a bike" is silly. Though since we don't have bikes, it's not far off. As we walked to the stables, it reminded me, I hadn't actually ridden since I was nine. *This might be nice.*

At the stables, along with the usual beast noises you'd expect, there was an occasional light buzzing that reminded me of spot welding. Even stranger, the moment we stepped inside, every horse seemed to back into the corners of their stalls.

"They seem spooked," Gideon noted.

"That they do," Yukirei said and shot a glance at me.

Since I was facing away from her, I turned to her, and asked, "What?"

"Hm?" she said, blushing suddenly.

"You looked at me," I said.

"But how–" she started and arched a brow.

"Right," I said. "You probably don't know." I ushered her toward me and spoke in a quiet tone. "My vision is all weird, I can see all around me at all times now. Even above and below me."

Gideon moved up to my side. "And through things," he said and covered his chest, batting his eyes at me.

"Hey!" I said and batted his arm. "Preface that with some context! I didn't have control over it at the time. And I didn't see anything…" I lowered my voice, "indecent." Thinking to myself, *I'm not telling Gideon I saw his bottom.* The intrusive thought made me shake my head.

It was Yukirei's turn to act appalled, and she unconsciously mirrored Gideon's cover-up gesture.

"Really?" I said, my cheeks turning apple red. "I can't see anything unless I try!"

She closed the distance between us, smirking and bumping my hip with hers. "So you could if you wanted to?"

I held my mouth open and stared at her, unsure what to say. "I–" my flushed cheeks heated further, "haven't tried," I pouted, "so I really don't know."

Gideon lowered his voice and leaned in. "*I* have nothing to hide."

The uncharacteristic behavior made me gape up at him.

"Neither do I," Yukirei said innocently, and held her hands out to her side as if inviting trouble.

"You," I growled and took his arm, "are a bad influence on Gideon!"

She smiled with her tongue between her teeth. "Maybe," she rushed forward and took my arm. "But you like me anyway."

The further we walked into the stables the noisier the horses became. I approached one of the stalls and the horse within started to buck toward the entrance throwing hay and other *stuff* in my direction.

"Whoa there, little lady," the stable master said. His hand went out in front of me and he gestured for me to move back. "Maybe just back away a little."

My head guard coughed, and the man quickly retracted his hand, making me realize he was only about an inch from my chest.

Remembering the male guard from my dormitory, I thought, *Ah, I'd hate to think what they'd do had that gone differently.*

"Sorry Lady…" he said, expecting my name I'd guessed.

"Anessa Jean Carlyle," I said, motioning toward Gideon I said, "Gideon Ignotus." Toward Yukirei I said, "Yukirei Truval."

His voice cracked, "Right, thank you."

Though I chose to omit our titles, it seemed that he recognized at least one of us. *Maybe all of us.*

He took a second to reset, and coughed. "It seems the common horses are a bit agitated right now. If it would please you, we have some high beasts that may be a better fit?"

The horse in front of me was still trying to escape its stall by pushing against the far wall. Its eyes were wide and bloodshot. A new smell coming from it said it was more than afraid.

Why is it afraid of me? I wondered. "It's okay buddy," I said quietly. "I'll look elsewhere." Turning to the stable master I said, "Show us, I don't know what I'm doing that's spooking them, but I don't want to cause trouble."

He gave me a short bow, "Very good. Please, this way."

We looked at various sturdier beasts. Most were horses, but not all. One was even a giant pig, which didn't react to me, though my guards rejected it outright.

Yeah, the optics there would not be pretty, I thought. Imagining myself atop a large sow made me chuckle. My encounter with the dire boar made me doubly cautious of the creature.

"These guys are beautiful," Yukirei said and approached the four remaining "horses."

Their fur was a mid-blue, smooth near their backsides yet a bit goatish near their face. They appeared to be a mix between an ox and a horse, but far stouter, with piercing red eyes.

One of them approached the clearly reinforced steel gate to its stall and leaned in toward me.

Curious, I put my hand up toward it. Behind me I noticed the stable master turning toward me, in slow motion, his eyes widened comically as I touched the animal.

"I wouldn't–" he started but by that point I had already placed my hand on its muzzle, which was cool to the touch. Half a second later I was rewarded with a nasal discharge right in my face. Thankfully my mouth was closed.

Ew, I thought as I closed my eyes and backed off a few paces, frozen, hoping it wouldn't drip on my clothes.

Gideon, thankfully, rushed to me and began to wipe my face.

"Yeah, I was going to warn you, he's been sick for a few days," the stable master said. "Additionally, they're pretty dangerous."

As if on cue, I heard the buzz from what I thought was a welder again. It was actually the beast itself. An arc of electricity trailed from its nose to Gideon.

"Griblin's Giblets!" he yelped.

"Gods, are you okay?" I asked and pushed us away from the animal.

There was a half-dollar sized hole in his shirt and a mean welt on his skin underneath.

"Geeze, that really got you," I said.

"My entire arm is numb," he complained giving the animal a dirty look.

A laugh erupted from the stable master, "I'll bet it is. Our little lady here," he gestured toward me, "seems to be immune, or else she'd have burned her hand something fierce when she touched it."

My head guard approached him and peppered him with questions about why such a dangerous animal would be available for just anyone to touch.

"Do you want to ride one?" Yukirei asked.

Rubbing my cheek I said, "As long as I don't get snotted on again."

She covered her smile. "That was pretty funny though."

"Was not," I frowned.

Gideon added, "I'm not sure I could ride one." Shaking his numb arm ruefully, he said, "I'm clearly *not* immune."

"Yeah, you'd end up as a naked welted wonder," Yukirei teased.

It was my turn to hold back a smile. I failed as poorly as she had, then sobered as I realized the electrical discharges would probably stop his heart before they singed away his clothes.

"Oh," the stable master said, "We have a special outfit you can wear to ride."

Gideon said, "That would be great, thank you."

When the master brought it out, however, Gideon's smile faded. "Seriously?"

It looked like a puffed-up lineman's suit with a diamond metal pattern around its form.

"Come on," Yukirei said, not even trying to hide her smile, "I'm sure it's the height of fashion."

While those two were goofing off, one of the beasts nudged me with its nose.

"You're not going to sneeze on me, are you?" I said.

While it didn't, it did blast my face with hot air.

I deadpanned, "I'll take that over the other."

"Find one you like Lady Anessa?" the master asked while opening the stall door.

His answers must've appeased my guard, I thought. "I guess."

Yukirei asked, "Ready to mount up?"

With a nod I asked, "What do you think scared the horses?"

Holding out her hand for me to step up, she said, "You did."

CHAPTER TWENTY-NINE

SOULAR WHATSIT? / NEGLIGENCE

"I SCARED THEM?" I asked.

Yukirei nodded. "Your essence control is frankly terrible. You also have far more than you should for being in the Nascent Realm."

"That doesn't explain why that's scaring them," I said. "I didn't have this effect when I went hunting."

"Your essence is a lot more chaotic than it was even a short while ago." She leaned in and whispered, "It might be related to whatever ability lets you see all around you." Her voice returned to a normal volume, "Mortal humans don't have the ability to sense cultivators," she gestured to the horses. "However, that doesn't apply to animals. To them you're a predator."

I patted the thunder ox beneath me. "So why isn't this guy scared?"

She smiled. "Because he's in a higher Realm than you are." Placing her hand near its skin, we watched arcs of electricity trace harmlessly between the beast's body and her palm.

"That's pretty."

"It is, and–"

"I'm having second thoughts," Gideon interrupted gruffly.

We both looked at our tall diamond-tufted beekeeper, and stifled a laugh.

"You look great," she said through gritted teeth, and assisted him in mounting his own high thunder ox.

Before we set out we heard a snap coming from Gideon. While I could see all around me, I sometimes had to focus to pay attention to my immediate surroundings.

A few seconds later, another pop.

Yukirei and I finally burst out laughing, unable to hold it in.

"You're like the [cereal] elves, crack, popple and snap."

My companions both looked at me like I'd grown a second *and* third head.

Did I remember it wrong?

Trish's laughter came through a few seconds later. *"Yes, but your confident delivery was brilliant."*

Triday, Runariae 7th, 1740

"Okay," Gideon said, "breathe in," he paused, "and out, and clear your mind of unnecessary thoughts."

We had our eyes closed and were sitting across from one another with a fair distance between us.

"You know the essence you draw in as usual?" he asked calmly.

I nodded, then said, "Yes," with a smile.

"Draw some in and trace it to your dantian. Then ask your dantian for some of it back."

Arching a brow I tried to do as he asked. "Okay," I said, stretching the word. When I pulled essence in, I always weaved it into tiny strands. The hour-to-second pill I took a while back tripled my intake. Giving the essence around me the tiniest of pull made me light-headed, and I heard a nearby vase crash to the floor.

Crap. I thought and cracked open one of my eyes.

Gideon was leaning back on his hands with wide eyes.

"That might explain it," I said aloud and sighed. "My Thrusense increased my pull by ten times, I think."

"More like a hundred times," Gideon said shakily, "at least. The draw was trying to pull *me* in."

Sarah had already called another maid in to clean up the mess I'd made.

"Was it really that bad?" I asked Sarah, then remembered to look her way.

"I'd say closer to eighty times," she mused. "Our Lord Gideon may have felt it was pulling him in because he was caught unaware," she pursed her lips, "or perhaps because the second vase hit him in the head."

"Oh, sorry Gideon," I said and dipped my head.

Deuday, Totharae 6th, 1740

Reeling in my drafty essence took the next two months. I hadn't really done any cultivating meditation since my Thrusense "turned on" so I hadn't realized I was a constant chaotic outpouring of essence.

Sir Orris finally responded to my missive a month into the process, saying he *forgot* to mention that it can boost your essence draw.

Thanks for nothing, Sir Orris.

My power had always been unpredictable, a combination of strength and weakness caused by my constantly fluctuating essence draw. It started to make real sense on why Dean Donovan wanted me to get it unter control.

Years ago, I went to an outdoor eatery with my friends to celebrate a false victory over one of the Blackwood brothers. He'd toyed with me in the ring, but then my odd pink essence destroyed his shield, which turned out to be an artifact he didn't have permission to use. The shield's destruction demoralized him, and I won by simply pushing him out of the ring. Narrowly snatching victory from the jaws of defeat.

One day, I was told to meet someone important.

"Heath?" I asked as I approached an older gentleman sitting at one of the tables.

"And you must be Lady Anessa?" he countered. Despite being retired, he wore his full uniform and decorations of service. From the near armor of pins, on both sides of his jacket, he appeared quite accomplished.

"Yes, sir."

"Call me General Emerson."

I nodded.

"Follow me," he said and walked in front of me with his arms behind his back.

Dad walks like that. Strange. Is it a military thing?

After five minutes of walking, we approached a clearing where there were already a five-by-five block of people standing at attention. Though the final row had only four people.

"Seems we're missing someone," he said in a level tone.

"Sir, Cadet Chaya is presently absent," called a man that was standing to the side next to the block of cadets.

"Very good, captain, at ease. I'll take it from here."

The man saluted General Emerson and took a seat to the side.

Right, he's not leaving because General Emerson is retired. This is more training for me, than these cadets.

"Lady Anessa," General Emerson said. "This is a good opportunity to learn what a good discipline for such a transgression is." Waving his hand he said. "You might not think this is a big deal, but if they were preparing for a battle, or a mission? You get left behind, or worse," He regarded me for a few seconds, "killed."

"Killed for being late?" I asked, startled.

"No, killed because your mission started without you, your team left you behind, and you're surrounded by the enemy. Not all missions start on friendly ground."

All I could do was purse my lips and nod. *Kind of makes me want to be sure I'm never late again. Yikes.*

Scratching my cheek, I leaned in and whispered, "What do I *do*, exactly?"

He straightened up and arched a brow at me. "Hmm."

His silent glare made my stomach somersault. *Crap.*

"Captain," General Emerson said, "What do you do?"

The man that was relaxing to the side shot up and said, "Sir, I follow orders, and see that my orders are followed."

"Good, at ease," the retired General said. "Lady Anessa."

"Yes, sir?"

"First, begin, not end with 'Sir.'" He began to pace around me. "Second, I gave you a dossier, didn't I?"

"Sir, you did, but I'll admit, I did not read it." I sighed. "I assumed my Lady Maid would tell me what was important."

"Third: sealed dossiers are not read by servants, as a general rule. If it's for *you*," he stepped closer to me and said clearly, "I fully expect you to read it."

"Sir, yes sir," I replied, not intending to mirror the stereotypical soldier response. "Sorry, sir."

"Fourth, never apologize," he continued, and I winced inside. "If you mess up, learn from it, but don't try to appease your superiors with platitudes or they'll eat you alive."

Got it. Start with Sir, read dossiers immediately, and learn from my mistakes without making excuses. I sighed. So far, I was zero for three.

"With that said, we will start with basic marching drills." He gestured to the squadron and added, "Pick one of the cadets here and follow what they do. Tomorrow I'll correct anything you don't pick up."

"Sir," I said, my face red from shame. *Damn it. I screwed up.*

"One of the good things about being a noble," Trish said.

What's that, I thought back.

"You have access to very good teachers. Dean Donovan, Ban, and now a certain retired General Heath Emerson," she noted. *"He's polite but firm, and doesn't accept anything less than excellence from you. When you realized your mistake, you were upset at yourself, not at him."*

Except for my statecraft and leadership adviser. He's kind of useless.

"Is he? Some people are good at connecting others. Even if he didn't know General Emerson directly," she corrected me, *"he knew someone who did."*

"Before that, though," Emerson said. "We'll begin with an introduction. You will introduce yourself," he said then moved in to whisper, "As callous as it may seem, do not remember anyone's name." He gestured toward the group.

Why wouldn't I remember their names? Won't they have a better opinion of me if I do?

"*Anessa, how many miles are the Northern Marches of the Tulip Kingdom?*" Trish asked.

Right, it's pretty large, isn't it? What's that have to do with—

"*Twenty-four hundred miles. That entire span is your territory once your appointment starts. How many people do you think it takes to patrol such a distance?*"

I didn't have a response for her, so I waited for her to tell me.

"*Close to a hundred thousand,*" Trish said. "*If you fill your brain with the names of your foot soldiers, it will just weigh you down.*"

It made me a little dizzy. *And here I thought,* I looked over the cadets, *that this would be easy if I just received a little training. How do you know all of that?*

"*Your Thrusense is handy. When you're about to fall asleep I've used it to peruse the library,*" Trish said, and a smug smile came through. "*A little finesse with how much you peer through things and you can actually read books—while they're still on the shelves—just fine.*"

Her information on the scale of my future was sobering, and I took a step forward. "I am Field Marshal A. Carlyle."

Several of them tensed upon hearing my last name, standing a little straighter, returning their focus forward.

Guess Dad's a big deal? He is their prime striker, after all. It reminded me of when he'd scared literally half of Westwood when he blasted across the sky, too low to the ground. Many had feared the gods were angry, and domestic animals throughout the empire were terrified. *Zooming along at a hundred and thirty thousand miles an hour will do that. I'd never want Daddy as an enemy.*

Right as I finished introducing myself a cadet approached in a sprint from our side, wheezing coughing as they slowed down.

General Emerson clicked his tongue upon seeing them.

As they calmed down and stood up, our eyes met for a brief moment. With short wavy brown hair and purple eyes, a surge of heat through my body reminded me that my estrus was in full swing.

Gods damn it. Not now. Who is this idiot, anyway?

Since I faltered and covered my stomach with one of my arms, instead of me addressing the cadet, General Emerson stepped forward.

"Cadet, give your name and reason for being late."

"Sorry sir. I was caught up by the school's disciplinary committee for running too fast," he said, his voice neither high nor low.

"And your name? Where is your badge?"

"Ah, right. My name is Chaya. I forgot about my badge, then remembered," he brought up the bag he had slung over his shoulder, "I'd sewn it into my bag."

The old general pursed his lips. "Cadet Chaya, your badge should be in hand, or on your person. Not sewn into a sack. It was a test to see if you could be bothered to keep track of it." His tone shifted down half an octave, "Since you affixed it onto your bag, you clearly cannot. I fully expect you to remove the stitches and clean its edges up after you have done so. Is that clear."

"Ah, okay."

Emerson chided, "You are to respond, 'Sir, yes sir.'"

"Ok–"

"'Sir, yes sir,'" the general repeated as ire crept into his voice.

"Sir, yes, sir!" Chaya said, finally getting it right.

"Field Marshal Carlyle," Emerson said, making me jump.

"Sir?"

"What punishment do you think would fit the cadet's tardiness?"

I need him to be away from me sooner than later, I thought as our eyes locked for a second and had to look away. "I think they should run ten laps."

"Around what?" Chaya said.

Thinking about what would get them far away I said, "Ersta's minor track."

What hadn't occurred to me was that someone needed to make sure Cadet Chaya completed the laps.

Thanks to my poor judgment, I decided to run the laps with him, since my focus was drifting between not looking like a fool, and chasing the cadet.

What the hell is wrong with me? I thought furiously as we completed the final lap.

Halfway through the laps my lower back, upper glutes and core ached. I'd completed a run like this hundreds of times. Far longer runs, in fact, but this time it took everything I could manage to maintain an upright posture. My body seemed to be fighting me the whole way.

I don't understand what's going on with me today. It's like I want to run on all fours.

Turning my attention away from the cadet's posterior was the hardest act of all. *Damn being a cat-kin.* What pissed me off more than anything that I was objectifying someone. It wasn't how I was raised.

As we rejoined the other cadets and Chaya rejoined the other cadets, General Emerson called me to the side.

"Are you okay?" he asked.

"I'm okay," I said despite the aches and tremors running through my muscles. It required me to close my eyes for my Thrusense to stop eying the now extra sweaty cadet.

"Are you sure? You know as the ranking officer, when you give an order to complete a disciplinary action," he dropped the volume of his voice, "you can assign someone else to make sure it is completed."

I kept my distance from Emerson, because I knew I was a smelly mess. "That would have been handy to know three hours ago," I said and laughed, which caused my lower abdomen to ache, making me groan.

"You say you're okay, but you're visibly panting. Are you a little out of shape?" He took a step forward and I held up a hand.

"I'm fine, it's... girl stuff," I said, and tried to clamp my mouth shut, since I hadn't noticed my panting.

Now I'm panting like a common house cat? Almost immediately, I had to open my mouth again as I felt light-headed, and I was much, much hotter for trying to stop it.

"I think I should stop here today," I admitted.

The old general nodded silently and barked orders to the cadets which I missed entirely.

I took off in a rush toward my dorm suite, panting the entire way.

Upon entering the Imperial Royal dormitory grounds I saw a collection of guards off to the side lounging.

"What are you doing?" I snapped, still a bit lightheaded.

They all snapped to attention and their smiles faded.

"Your Imperial High Grace, we were doing as we were instructed, and taking a break while His Imperial Highness spends some quality time with his family."

Their admission that the breach of etiquette was an order made me angry, but they were not the right people to take it out on. I did not have the authority to countermand an order given by my cousin. "Carry on," I said in almost a growl.

Watch, that vile idiot is going to do something and blame me. I shook my head at the thought, it was far darker than my thoughts usually tread.

Entering my dorm suite I rounded the corner and spotted Gideon. I froze.

He was sipping tea and he sat it down. His pupils flared and he stood, crossing the room toward me. I followed in kind.

Before we were within a few feet of one another, Sarah interposed and said, "Anessa, please, your bath is ready."

Showing my fangs to her I growled and she turned me around and nudged me forward. When she'd closed the door behind us, I took her arm and, to my surprise, bit her hand as she passed by me.

"Lady Anessa, that hurt," she said calmly, but firmly.

Despite that I bit her hand a few more times, and she only patted the top of my head, giving me a bit of solace. The bath wasn't actually ready yet, but she rang a bell and instructed them to run one, all the while I had her hand in my mouth.

What the heck is going on? Everything's so muddled and foggy!

Once I let her hand go heat rushed through me and my strength faded. I fell forward onto Sarah and she prepared to get me ready for a bath.

Why am I biting Sarah's neck? I thought as I lost all sense and reason.

Every muscle in my back ached when I woke up a few hours later.

"Ow," I said and turned onto my back. "What happened?"

As the fog lifted, I noticed someone's hand in mine. Recalling how I'd nearly pounced on Gideon, my heart rate increased and I lifted up my head to get a better look.

It was Sarah.

"Oh thank the gods," I muttered aloud.

"Hm?" She said and stirred. "Good evening, Lady Anessa."

"Can I ask a silly question?"

She nodded. "Of course."

"Why are you in my bed?"

"You had a bit of a spell earlier." Swinging her legs over the side she added, "We had the local doctor look you over, and he said you were simply exhausted."

"What did I do? I don't remember anything after you told someone to run me a bath, and even that's a bit hazy." I sighed. "I haven't lost control of myself like that since I was nine years old."

"You returned from your first training exercise with General Emerson and seemed to be beside yourself." Standing she moved to her truckle bed at the foot of my own. Something she'd started doing during my issues with my Thrusense arose.

She started to pick up the bedding and I asked, "Are you leaving?"

"That was my goal. You seem to have regained yourself, and your god-given gift is now under control," she stood there and looked back to me. "Would you prefer I stayed for a little longer?"

Patting my own mattress I asked, "If it's okay I'd like to continue talking about what happened earlier. There was this cadet, Chaya that was late. When he arrived and our eyes met, things went sideways…"

After explaining it to her, she went quiet for a few moments.

"Soular Kinship, most likely," she finally said. "A strong case, at that."

"The last thing I want to think about is *another* connection like that," I said with a groan.

"Just having kinship doesn't mean it must be fulfilled. The fact that it took place outside of an Awakening Ceremony most likely means they may have a future connection to you."

"Still not something I want to worry about," I said. "Future or not. I have everyone I want in my life with me," I grabbed her hand. "That includes you."

Sarah smiled. "It pleases me to hear that. As a bonded, I'll always be with you."

Her reminder that she was a slave made me frown. "If I can ever do anything about that, I will."

"I know, and I thank you."

"Then because I was around Chaya during estrus was the issue? That's it?"

"You spent three hours running behind him. Where was your mind during that time?"

At her question I suddenly found the floor rather interesting. "Somewhere it likely shouldn't have been."

"Three hours of that, followed by smelling your mate, Gideon, pushed you over the edge."

Sarah calling Gideon my "mate," didn't help my mood any. "I'd prefer to call him my husband."

"Maybe so, but when you're dealing with animal desires from your beast heritage, you need to be honest with yourself. It might be best if you stayed in for a few days."

"I *just* started my training! It would look bad for me to bow out this soon."

"You said Chaya was late, and the running was punishment?"

I nodded.

"Maybe if he continues to be late, you should give him tasks that take him far away from you? You should be out of the worst of your heat by tomorrow."

"Yeah, that might work." I laughed. "Assuming they're late again."

Thinking of disciplinary action reminded me of the guards from the entrance of the dormitories. "Right, I was meaning to tell you. Lukas ordered the Imperial Royal family's guards to wait outside the commons area."

"Really?" Sarah asked.

"I think we should report it."

"To whom?" she asked, tilting her head. "I doubt His Imperial Majesty, Jorin Q'Tar would take kindly to you tattling on his son."

She's not wrong, I thought and frowned. "Perhaps not, but at the very least we should tell my parents, so there's a record of it. If it ends there, so be it. But if it leads to a problem later, it may be important to document."

She bobbed her head. "I'll do so in the morning."

On the desk in my corner, I saw the black dossier General Emerson had sent me. *I suppose I should read that, see what I missed by leaving a bit early because I was busy supervising Chaya's discipline myself.*

Picking the black folder up, I opened it and smiled. The paper inside included the location, date and time of when to meet him, and nothing else.

Touché, general.

CHAPTER THIRTY

BANNED DIRE TUSKS / "CHAT"

"CADET CHAYA IS late again, it seems," General Emerson said.

I laughed.

"Something funny about that?" he asked.

Shaking my head and holding up a hand I said, "Not for the reasons you're thinking. My Lady's maid called it, is all."

He snorted. "She has good instincts."

"While we wait for the cadet to arrive, can you give me some ideas on how to keep our tardy Cadet busy?"

"Asking an old, retired, *general* for ideas on administering punishments for delinquency?" He smiled. "That's almost evil."

"Well, when you put it that way," I said and motioned for him to continue.

He had a fierce grin. "For starters…"

Chaya was late every day for the next week. As Sarah had guessed, once my heat passed, the cadet was no more interesting to me than anyone else. It made me wonder if it was really soular kinship, or just hormones because he had pretty eyes.

At the end of the week, I decided I needed to take a detour, and headed to the Boar's Head Inn. Just like the first time, my presence stood out thanks to my retinue of five guards.

"Can you help me with something?" I asked the keeper behind the bar, setting a small silver down as I did so.

The barkeep was different from the one I remembered during my first visit. Though since we'd bought the place and then returned it to the owner for free, it's possible the old owner had retired with what we paid. "You thirteen?" he asked, then looked at my head guard.

"Y-yes," I muttered, "that's not my question though."

Once my head guard nodded, he poured and set down a full mug, walking off with the silver in hand. All before I could clarify the misunderstanding.

That wasn't helpful. Curiosity struck me and I sniffed the drink. I wasn't sure if it was my cat-kin heritage or my Thrusense's enhanced smell, but it bit at my nose with notes of citrus and a yogurt-like sourness. The combination made me wrinkle my nose.

Pushing it away I thought, *Yeah, no.*

When he'd finally come back around, he noticed I hadn't touched it.

"Not to your liking?"

"I came to ask you a question, not for ale."

"So ask."

"I'd like to know how to contact Ban, Master of the Hunt and his party," I asked.

He shook his head. "Not possible."

Ah, right, they moved on to another town.

Placing a small gold onto the counter, I repeated my intent. "If they come back by, can you ask that they reach out to me?" Setting a placard on the counter with my name and information, I started to rise.

The man's lips thinned, and he shook his head, reluctantly pushing the gold back across the counter toward me. "Lass, it's not that I don't want to, or I don't know where they are. I can't. Nobody can."

This statement made me retake my seat, and turn toward him.

"A month after they left town, we received word that they were wiped out by bandits," he said neutrally.

For a few seconds I was speechless.

"Survivors?" I asked.

He shook his head.

Before I got a few steps away from the counter, I caught him saying, "Strange that you're asking the same kinds of questions as that other guy."

"Hold on," I said. "Who else asked about them?"

"They were popular, so a lot of people asked," he said. "But the one that stuck out the most was a shady-looking guy with great gear. He wore a cloak, so I didn't get a good look at his face," he tapped the back side of his hand, "but he did have a distinctive golden dragon insignia on his glove."

"Was that before, or after their party was wiped out?"

The barkeep tapped the counter thoughtfully. "I'm pretty sure it was before."

Placing the small gold back onto the counter, I said, "Thanks. You've been a great help."

Exiting the inn, I blew through my teeth. *I can't believe they're all gone.* It left me numb, and my chest ached. *Sam gave her life for me, and they encountered bandits only to end up the same way.*

Walking aimlessly, I saw the vexing Chaya ahead of me.

He looked around, and slipped between two buildings when he spotted me.

As I walked by, I just looked at him. "Chaya, are you trying to hide from your C.O.?"

He sighed and stepped out. "Sir, yes, sir. Sorry sir." Dusting his front off he said, "It just seems like you hate me. I've been doing menial chores ever since we met!"

"You've been late to every single cadet training session," I said flatly. "To be clear, I don't hate you, it's standard discipline."

He scratched his cheek. "I just thought you'd be nicer."

"Nicer?" I said crossly.

"You have a reputation of generosity," Chaya said and saluted at my tone. "The trust my tuition comes out of is in your name." He pulled out a condensing ribbon from the bag he was carrying. "As are my books, and uniforms." With his smile, I blushed, and he continued, "Plus, you're the champion of the Goddess of Craft, so I suppose these fall under that umbrella."

I scratched my cheek. "I'll be honest, I did that more for my own sake than anyone else's. It felt wrong to be the only one with up-to-date books."

"Oh," he laughed. "That makes sense, too."

His smile and laughter made me feel a bit guilty at snapping. "If I seem on edge, it's because I just got bad news, and I'm worried about my upcoming appointment."

One of my guards on my tail made a face and gestured to some of the others. They discreetly moved over.

Crap. Am I not supposed to talk about my appointment?

We continued to walk and talk about the bad news, and I told Chaya about Ban and the hunting party. Hoping to contain my slip up, and get more confirmation, I asked, "Would you mind sharing a meal in my Dorm Suite for second dinner?"

He said, "Sure, I could eat."

One of my guards dashed off almost immediately, and I immediately realized my mistake. *Crap. I just invited a boy to my room.* My stomach did a somersault. *And I just told Sarah I wasn't interested in having anyone else. She's going to tease me for this, even if I had different intentions.*

Nearing my dorm suite, the Imperial Royal family's guards were once again collected outside.

Chaya started to ask a question, but I held my hand up and we continued past them.

Inside the commons area, I saw Lukas and his family. He was moving fluidly through sword forms. His competence was leagues beyond my own, and may even have been near my Dad's.

Why is someone like him so talented, and given so much? It made me shake my head looking at Chaya, who was likely thinking the very same thing about me. *Jealousy comes in many forms, and they're all ugly.*

Nearby was Gobza, playing a flute, matching Lukas's motions.

Despite my reservations, seeing Rina smile at her brother was something I never thought I'd see.

A chill ran down my back remembering the copper smell, and ichor that trickled down my *everything* a little over a year ago. *Please let it be genuine.*

Just before I entered my dorm suite, he stopped his movements long enough for me to glance at his dominant hand. He'd always worn gloves, but I'd never paid them much attention. In that briefest of moments a chill gripped me as I saw a golden dragon insignia, and the barkeep's words surged in my mind.

That's a coincidence, right? Tears entered my eyes as I thought of Ban and almost knocked into my guard in my distraction. It was the same one that had dashed forward after I'd invited Chaya to my dorm suite for a meal.

"Excuse me, Lady Anessa," said my guard.

"Yeah."

"Is everything okay, Lady Anessa?" Sarah asked. "You're white as a sheet."

"I'm okay," I lied. "Sarah, would you be so kind to prepare an extra spot, for dinner, for my guest, Cadet Chaya?"

She bowed. "Of course." Another of my maids walked forward and took his bag, taking it into another room, for some reason.

Is there something wrong with his bag?

"So Chaya," I started. "Are you from Ersta?"

He stood across from me, and dusted off his breeches before sitting. "Yes, our family has been here my entire life." Pulling an item from his side, he brandished an ornate knife and held it sideways in his hand. "Pa's a blacksmith, like his pa before him."

Several people around us shifted when he pulled out the knife.

Chaya will need to learn not to brandish a weapon in front of a noble, in their own domicile. Seeing everyone relax after I took it from his hand, I looked it over.

The blade edge had an intricate filigree pattern, filled with what I assumed must be copper, since I doubted they'd give their son a gilded weapon based on his patchwork attire.

"This is beautiful." I ran my finger down the spine of the blade, which itself also had a purple pattern on it that matched Chaya's eyes. "Your family must do well," I said, knowing that probably wasn't the case.

"Pa's one of the best," he said with a laugh. "Or so he says. Our family had an agreement with the Ersta town guard a few decades ago, but when we lost their favor, our major source of income left with it."

"Well, your dad does excellent work," I said, hefting up the knife.

"Oh no! Please don't use that blade to gauge his work. That's just one of my apprenticeship blades," he waved his hand. "Pa's on a whole different level."

I motioned for Sarah to come over and handed it to her. *She'll have a better idea than I do, and I know she'll assess it.*

Chaya held out his hand tentatively as though we'd taken something precious as it disappeared from view.

"They'll give it back when you leave," I reassured him. Leaning in I whispered with a wink, "For future reference, don't pull out a bladed edge in noble company. It made everyone nervous."

As we talked about Chaya's past, I found myself smiling, then the why hit me. *He reminds me of Earth!* Someone socially ignorant about nobility, just trying as hard as they can. I found myself smiling at the epiphany.

"I've been wondering. Why *have* you been late every single day?"

With a sigh he said, "My bosses don't seem to respect me enough."

Bosses? Plural? I asked, "What do you mean?"

Sarah returned and stood a few paces further than normal behind me.

Chaya continued, "I've told them time after time that I need to get to my Cadet training, but they always seem to find last-minute things for me to do."

I leaned back. "Have you considered finding a different job that does?"

He nodded. "It's difficult, though. We're up against a mountain of debt and every minute I'm not working, we risk losing our shop."

"It's weird that you have more than one boss. Do they micromanage too much?"

Knitting his brows together in apparent confusion, he said, "I have four jobs."

Oh. That's why he signed up to be a cadet. Career military men make a lot more than unskilled labor. With my Thrusense, I noticed Sarah holding her hand over her nose behind me. *Is she feeling okay?*

As the maids delivered another round of food for me, I called Sarah over.

"Is everything okay?" I whispered.

"Yes, it's just that our guest has a…" she paused and added, "unique scent."

Turning my attention to Chaya I thought of using my extended sense of smell near him, but decided against it. *The last time I tried to sniff at a distance, I ended up sniffing inside the toilet.* The resurgence of the smell made my stomach turn. Standing, I leaned forward and lightly sniffed the air around Chaya.

Only to immediately realize how that looked when Sarah coughed.

Good job, Anessa.

His scent was musky, and a little sweet. However, that was mostly overpowered by the incredibly putrid scent of the sewers.

Chaya blushed and said, "Sorry. I am on Ersta's sanitation crew. It's difficult to avoid brushing up against the walls or ceiling when I work."

"Sarah," I called and turned to her. "Prepare a bath for our guest."

Chaya held up his hands in protest. "No, that's okay! I wouldn't want to impose."

"I insist," I said with my hand on my chest. "It was indelicate of me to do that, for one, and two, it will do wonders to relax after pushing yourself so hard."

He nodded. "Okay."

Sarah had delegated the task before I even finished. "Please, this way," she said with a smile.

Oof. At least let him finish eating.

"The food was great," he said. "Honestly I haven't eaten so much before in my life."

As Sarah guided him away, I heard her ask him about the apprentice knife.

Guess she's trying to make amends, too.

When Sarah returned, I said, "Do you think we should look into their blacksmith? If Chaya's blade is an apprentice's level, I'd imagine the master is even better, right?"

Sarah nodded and pulled out an S-ROB. "Indeed. Chaya being an above-grade cultivating smith means their shop will soon be very busy."

"Above-grade what?" I asked.

"The purple on the spine is High Grade Fourth Rank Steel, and Chaya said the shop's master can work yet higher."

"Wait, Third grade is what they use at the Sky Realm. What even is above that?"

Sarah didn't say anything and merely tapped the obscuring barrier cube.

She can't say? Wasn't Uncle Jorin a half-step in the Otherworldly Realm, which I guess is my answer to that question. I wonder why it's such a secret, then. Then I realized: the shop's master must be able to work with a steel higher than that. *No one's even talked about the fifth or given it a name.*

"One thing I can say," Sarah said, "You will not have to worry about Chaya pestering you any longer. I really imagine that they'll invest heavily in the master's smithy, as well as the apprentice."

"Why would they invest in Chaya personally?"

"He's a smith that works above their Realm. Usually, the higher the smith's Realm the higher the steel. If a smith at the Nascent Realm is working Otherworldly steel..." she didn't finish the sentence.

Right. A level beyond the master smith. I shook my head. *That sounds like dangerous stuff. I'll let the adults figure it out. You can buy cities for the Sky Realm artifacts Dad uses, I can't imagine what sixth Realm artifacts would go for.*

One of our maids had quickly laundered Chaya's entire bag and brought it into the commons area.

No sooner had she bowed and went back upstairs then Chaya entered in nothing but a towel.

I face-palmed and blushed to my ears. *Gods man, get a clue. I know you're not used to etiquette–*

He had walked over to his bag and stopped. Before dropping the towel.

She then unzipped her bag, bare to the world, and squatted to pull out her school uniform, dress and all.

I blinked. *How the hell did I miss that Chaya was a girl!?*

I'd been covering my face, but Thrusense made it as though my hand wasn't even there, something it tended to do from time to time, as though I wanted to watch, which made it worse. Because I did.

Sarah sported a half grin and shook her head.

"Chaya," I said. "I know we're all women, but it is very uncouth to undress in my lounge."

Trish chose this most inopportune time to intrude on my thoughts, and said in a mocking tone, *"You peeked."*

Really? You're going to tease me, now?

"Now is the perfect time to intrude. Let me know if you want a playback."

"Sorry," she said and smiled. "Someone set out a pink dress for me, but pink's not really my color."

As if to prove my point, Gideon opened the guest room door and froze on seeing the bare Chaya, who hadn't yet put anything on.

Though she did seem to have at least some sense of modesty as when the two locked eyes she covered herself with her shirt and blushed deeply.

Gideon had been reading a book, which tumbled from his hands when they saw one another. For far longer than he ought to, he just stood there, then picked up his book silently and held it forward. He said, "Excuse me," then retreated to his room and shut the door.

Why did Chaya drop her towel in the first place? Is she daft? Was she trying to get my attention?

"Commoners bathe communally, they have a different sense of modesty," Trish explained. She paused, and sent over the image of a lit light bulb. *"Remember gym locker rooms and showers? It's like that, except with a big bath instead of a shower."*

Her skin was deeply tanned. In fact it seemed that it wasn't a tan at all, since there were no tan lines. I thought, after seeing her blush, *Pink would* definitely *suit you.*

CHAPTER THIRTY-ONE

TIMING OF A LAST LAUGH

A WEEK AFTER my embarrassing encounter with Chaya, I was on my first-lunch break alone. Gideon had drill training, and Yukirei was serving on the front lines already.

"I should have invited Sarah," I thought aloud.

Behind me, down the street, I caught a glimpse of a blond man with golden eyes wearing a toga. His stroll and pace were measured and graceful. He looked as though a Classical Roman statue had been brought to life. Well-defined–but not bulky–muscles, a chiseled chin, and porcelain skin that would make any man or woman jealous.

My heart skipped a beat when he turned in my direction and smiled, despite the fact that I was not looking at him. It seemed that my curiosity about his appearance had not gone unnoticed, despite the fact that I wasn't facing him with my physical eyes.

Okay, that's unnerving, I thought as he headed my way. The closer he tread, the harder my heart pounded. *He's just a pretty boy, why am I freaking ou–* My thoughts stalled and my brain reset. Once he stepped within a hundred feet, a wave of essence crashed into me. Each ten feet he came closer, it was as though the essence multiplied tenfold.

When he got within five feet, the pressure made me feel like I was going to pop.

As though my body were trying to protect me, my Thrusense collapsed in on itself and my vision snapped back to my previous normal. The sensory underflow gave me a light sense of vertigo, but it was quickly replaced with the panic of turning around to greet my "guest." *At least I can breathe now.*

A glance at my guards showed they were all frozen. My main guard had moved a hand towards her weapon, but she was shaking. I wasn't sure if it was due to fear, or something else was preventing her from moving. Either way, it told me I was alone. "Greetings senior," I said and bowed my head with my fists pressed together. It was a greeting Dad taught me before coming to school that if something about someone was intensely off, like it was now, I should treat them with respect.

"Well met, child," he said in a honeyed voice. Looking to my guards he added, "You may relax."

They all instantly fell to the ground.

Crap. Who is this person?

"How may I help you?" I asked as evenly as I could.

"You don't have anything I need anything in particular. I noticed something here that was interesting, so I decided to take a look. I'm in town to buy a blacksmith's shop, and noticed someone I couldn't get a reading on."

Buy a blacksmith's shop? Odd thing to do, though I suppose my family bought an inn to give me a bath, so I can't argue the logic.

"Tell me," he said, making me jump. "Do you have a god's protection?"

My eyes darted side to side, and though it was the simplest request, I drew a complete blank for a second. "Yes, senior."

He nodded. "May I ask if you're a champion, and if so, of what?"

"Yes, senior. I am the champion of craft," I said in a trembling voice.

"Ah, that explains so much," he said. "I won't bother you any further." Looking into the distance he continued, "It seems I've drawn some attention by stopping to talk, so I'll be leaving now." With that, he vanished.

My guards woke up and jumped to attention, surveying the area warily.

"I'm going back to my dormitory," I said. "I'm not feeling so well."

I couldn't help but run. None of my guards muttered a word of complaint. They were equally in a hurry to get out of there.

At the gated entryway, my main guard said, "Lady Anessa," she saluted. "We must report this incident immediately. It is by the grace of the gods that we are alive, but if there are powers like that on the move…" Her voice quaked. "May Eloria guide us."

Parroting her prayer back to her, I walked slowly to the entrance to the commons, shaken further. My Thrusense was still on the blink. The stench of alcohol coming from the Imperial Royal Family's guards to my right made my stomach churn. Clearly they weren't just hanging out on the sidelines today.

My usual urge to chastise them wasn't there, so I just sighed and walked past them. The liquor was stamped with the Royal Seal of Approval, a pair of dragons biting one another's tails. Distinct from the Ruler's Seal of authority, since there were two dragons.

When I picked up the faintest smell of copper I paused. *Did they redecorate inside with plants?* Then a muted earthy undertone came in and I shivered unconsciously. *The hell is that smell?* I wondered and opened the door. Despite having several gigantic windows to let in natural light, the room remained pitch black.

The combined effects made my teeth ache when the prior smells slammed me in the nose like a mallet. *Something's wrong.*

It was concerning, but I desperately just wanted to return to my room, so I plunged in further.

"Rina?" I said aloud to pure silence, the tinny echo the room had was gone. "Iana?" I called, hoping her sister would reply.

As I stepped down the stairs toward my dorm suite, I used the railing in the darkness, but it was slick, wet, and warm. I held my hand up to the little bit of light entering the room through the door to find a crimson red covered my palm.

Oh gods. Quickening breath made me dizzy and I noticed the door was creeping shut. To my side I saw the outline of a figure on the floor.

Why can't I see very well? My Thrusight isn't working because of that weird senior, and why aren't my eyes kicking into low light?

"Hello?" I said toward the person lying on the ground. "Are you okay?"

Before I could reach out and see if they were okay, a condescending and razor-sharp voice cut the air, "Oh yeah. I almost forgot about you."

While turning toward the voice, my god-given gift suddenly returned, and the room snapped into horrific clarity. I'd never wanted to be wrong more in my life than I was about my cousin's intentions.

Before me was the Imperial Royal Prince, Lukas Q'Tar, apparently now the last of his imperial line, save for his father, because the rest of his family lay dead on the floor.

And the walls.

I couldn't purge the images around me from my sight, even with all my muster.

Seeing the blood on the blade resting against his shoulder, I snapped and lunged forward toward him as tears failed to blur my vision.

My punch was little more than a wet snap as he caught my fist and jerked it to the side, taking me off balance.

He sighed and his contempt-laden voice said, "I suppose you are probably a backup." He hefted his sword into the air. "There shouldn't be any harm in taking out the trash."

Lukas paused as if to show me he was in no hurry to finish what he started.

His tendons flexed on his sword arm.

I pushed the deleterious essence and Will quicker than I ever had.

I needed ten full seconds to deal with the dire boar, but here I had no more than the blink of an eye.

Hitting his collar bone as hard as I could, I was rewarded with a crisp snap as my wrist shattered. He didn't even budge.

I'd put everything into that strike, and it hurt *me*.

Knowing he had his sword primed to strike, and feeling I was out of options, I closed my eyes tight.

When I was pushed down to the floor, and his weight fell on top of me, I feared the worst. However, when I pushed him off of me as hard as I could manage, I was met with no resistance.

Putting weight on my broken arm made me fall back to the floor in pain. I rolled over to stand up. It took all my energies to focus on avoiding rolling into a pool of someone's blood, which had already started to cool.

Rushing away from my attacker, I backed into a half-height partition and looked back at him. It took me a moment to realize that he wasn't moving, beyond opening and closing his mouth, like a fish out of water.

I wasn't going to stick around to figure out what he was doing. Fearing he was toying with me, I ran out of the commons building and screamed, "Help! Please help!"

I found all of the guards bending a knee to a man I didn't expect to see, touching down in the courtyard. Tanned skin and eyes that had seen it all, and that he was done with it. His brows were furrowed and his posture cross.

"What happened?" Jorin, the Emperor of the Westwood Empire asked without preamble.

Grabbing my wrist and bowing, I said somewhat incoherently, "Please, help. The commons was dark when I entered, I don't know if any of them are..." I tried to explain what I saw. But either I was rambling, stumbling over my words, or both. He held up his hand to quiet me. He glanced at the Imperial Royal Family's guards, "I will deal with you lot later." He then continued forward and walked right past me.

Following behind him, I worried that the room was no longer dark as he navigated it with ease.

I wondered if the effect had vanished and thought, *Please don't think I was lying.*

It took me a moment to process the full scope of Lukas's transgression. Rina lay huddled with her sister and their mother, the Empress who laid before them. Her arms were out as though she were trying to protect the girls. Jorin's two other consorts and their sons were there as well. As I looked over the carnage, I fell to the floor and sobbed.

Rina has only ever been nice to me. Seeing her glassed-over eyes was something that flashed inside my head, and I knew it would haunt me.

"Anessa," Jorin's cross voice called.

I'd been curled up against a half-height partition and hugging my knees. "Yes?"

"What happened here?" he barked.

Swallowing at his evident ire, I tried to organize my thoughts more clearly. "W-when I got here, the room was pitch black. I smelled something worrying. I was trying to get back to my dorm suite," I recounted the events as I knew them. "I came back from classes early because a powerful cultivator met me in Ersta when I was on my first-lunch break…"

Jorin listened patiently and didn't interrupt.

His small mercy allowed me to recount all the rest as best as my shaken mind could.

"I came when their life tablets broke," he said and gestured toward his family. "This 'senior' you mentioned might be someone I know of. If it is, it *would* explain why they all broke at the same time."

I waited silently. It felt like I was standing next to a ticking bomb that might go off at any second.

The intensity in his next words made me jump. "The timing of his visit couldn't have been fucking worse!" With a swift kick Jorin split one of the partitions into two. "If it weren't for that, I could've saved at least one of them…" His voice trailed off and he floated from person to person, keeping his feet away from the ocean of blood and bodily fluids, checking them for a pulse.

Lukas was no longer moving at all, and the color had drained from his face.

I just killed an Imperial Prince, I realized, and broke out into a cold sweat.

When he had arrived, Jorin's face was already stern and unforgiving. As he touched down next to each of his kin, his lips pressed thinner and thinner, his brows knitting more each time. He would shake his head and take a breath.

While the senior from before could have crushed me like an ant, the essence Jorin was bleeding in his silent seething rage was nothing to sneeze at either.

Not even Daddy put out that much energy when he was angry about Oliver being poisoned.

The emperor examined everyone but Lukas. Once he'd checked all of his fallen, he laid them neatly into a line. Lying them flat and closing their eyes.

Then, with a broad wave of his arm, they all vanished inside his storage ring. He brought his hand up in a fist and blew through his teeth. "Damn it."

"What?" I asked cautiously.

"I was hoping I might be wrong, about at least one," he said in a defeated voice.

Right, storage rings won't permit living things within them. It means they were, without a doubt, dead.

Then he looked at the prince for the first time. "You said you took out Lukas yourself?" Jorin asked.

"Yes, sir. I hit him in his collar bone, but my attack broke my wrist, and he collapsed onto me shortly after. I was attempting to use a skill that 'deletes' whatever it touches. I was too panicked to check on him after he fell on me, and I just pushed him away."

Jorin nodded and stepped over to his son, turning him onto his side. "Yes, that would do it," he said flatly.

"What?" I asked and approached, without rounding around Lukas's body to see what Jorin was looking at.

"You severed his spine. There's a three-inch hole where his vertebrae should be."

Stretching my lips imagining it, I stopped in my tracks. *I don't need to see that.*

He then made my stomach sink when he waved me over. "Come take a look."

My frown deepened but I did as ordered. The sight made a lump form in the back of my throat, and I made a mad dash toward one of the interior plants and lost my first-lunch. *I did not need to see that!*

Once I'd finally stopped, I turned back to my uncle. And I screamed, because he wasn't alone.

"What?" he asked, genuinely puzzled.

I pointed behind him and shrieked, "What in the Nether is *that?*"

It was a skeletal figure clad in black. The only way I could describe it is a *reaper*. As if on cue, it held out its bony appendage and a scythe formed as though it materialized on the spot, like it was being taken out of a storage ring.

Jorin turned, "What are you talking about?" He shook his head and turned back to me. "Did you hit your head in your scuffle with Lukas?"

He can't see it?

The reaper held the weapon back and struck at my uncle, but the blade merely bounced off his neck.

Is it just a ghost, or did *I hit my head?*

The specter looked at the weapon then held out its hand, creating a tether to Jorin. It thrust that same hand into my uncle's chest, and only then did he react by lurching forward and coughing out a mouthful of blood.

Crap! I'm not seeing things!

A taffy-like substance emerged with its hand, drawn from my uncle's back. The creature chopped at the extraction with the blade and a tiny layer splintered off from its surface, bringing Jorin to his knees.

He swung toward his back trying to fend off the unseen assailant. The taffy substance didn't seem to react to his movement, and remained fixed on his center, now appearing from his chest. His hands merely phased through his attacker.

Only then did my brain finally kick into gear. *Gods, what am I doing just watching* him die?

I picked up a nearby bench and threw it at the apparition. It went right through it, though the blade did nick a plank's edge, shearing the bench into two.

OK, so it's incorporeal. Fantastic. How do you fight such a thing?!

My attack didn't go unnoticed, and it turned to face me, letting go of the white mushy goo from Jorin, which snapped back into his body.

Taking aim, it swiped at me, in slow motion. It was so easy to dodge.

Is it used to being unseen?

Looking at the remains of the bench I threw at it, I realized the planks were all cut at different angles that didn't match the two halves. *It's like it was deleted.*

"Are you seeing something girl?" my uncle asked, coughing up more blood.

"Yes, sir. It's some kind of floating skeleton with a black cloak." I picked up a rock from one of the planters nearby. *Maybe I should fight fire with fire.* Pushing Will and essence into the rock, I threw it at the reaper.

While the rock phased through it, the essence I'd imbued the rock with must have left a mark. The monster screamed in a voice I could only describe as ghastly nails on a chalkboard.

Oh, gods that was awful! I thought hastily covering my ears.

The ghost's chest now contained a circular hole that was slowly closing up.

Taking another stone, I did the same thing again, pressing more essence and will into it, aiming for its head this time. But it used its blade to block my throw, and the rock merely vanished on touching its edge.

Crap. I need to watch its weapon.

Hoping to confuse it, I aimed for the floor, thinking it would bounce, but instead my effort deleted part of the floor in a cone about ten feet long.

"Sorry!" I shouted to no one.

"Use your Will, child," Jorin said. "I can't see what you're seeing, but I don't think you're trying to kill the floor. That screech earlier made my bones ache. Whatever it is, you can obviously hurt it." He clutched his chest. "Imagine the rock bouncing off the floor into your target, if that was your aim."

Huh. Can it be that easy?

Turns out, no. My second attempt only dug a deeper hole onto the once-pristine floor, exposing the dirt beneath the foundation.

"Keep trying," he said in a fit of coughs, while I dodged another of the reaper's slow attacks.

It had moved a fair distance from its starting point, and I now saw the thinnest of tethers from its ghostly tail to a bracelet on Lukas's wrist.

"I'm sorry," I said. "I think I can see the source. I'm going to attack it, but Lukas may lose his hand."

"Do it," Jorin said flatly.

As though it sensed my intent, the thing turned to me and sped up.

Instead of attacking the spectral tether near my late cousin, I attacked his wrist directly, wiping out his wrist and a section of his leg by mistake.

The wraith, reaper, or whatever it was called let out another wail and began to break up, although the weapon in its hand clattered to the tiled floor. Soon, nothing remained but the scythe.

Curiosity got the better of me and I hefted the blade. It weighed nothing. Not a feather's weight, but literally nothing. I asked, "Can you see this?"

"Yes, the moment it fell to the ground it appeared out of the air. Store it," he coughed. "We'll figure it out later."

Doing as he asked, I came over to his side and helped him sit down. "You really don't look so good."

"I'm dying, that's why," he said matter-of-factly.

"Were you sick?" I asked in shock.

He shook his head. "Whatever that was, it's mortally wounded me. It attacked me in a way I can't even wrap my head around. My cultivation foundation is crumbling." He coughed blood into his hand. "Go to your lady's maid. Have her make a report to the Imperial Carlyle Duchy, while I take care of a small task outside. After that, I am taking you to Aspwood."

Before I could ask why, it dawned on me: *I just became the sole heir to the empire itself.* Rushing to my dorm suite, I felt chilled to my core, remembering the soothsayer's words about what I would inherit: *"It depends on who you kill."*

Entering my room usually doesn't turn many heads, but when you are covered in blood from the chest down people tend to notice.

"Anessa," Sarah said, aghast, and ran over to me. "Are you okay?"

"Y-yeah," I said and frowned. "The blood isn't mine," I whined, "Lukas, he…"

Sarah didn't ask more than that. In minutes they'd drawn me a bath, and I explained the situation to my Lady's maid while I washed my family's blood off my skin.

After I got out of the bath, Sarah pulled me into a hug. "I'm so glad you're okay. I'll send a missive to your parents, so don't worry about any of that."

As Tania finished dressing me with Sarah's help, I asked, "Will you two join me in Aspwood?"

"As soon as we're able," Sarah said.

We entered the sitting area to finish getting me ready, but my uncle entered before they were ready.

"What's taking so long?" The Emperor demanded.

Everyone froze in an instant as I gulped.

"That was my fault," Sarah said and gave a deep curtsy, holding it in place. "It wouldn't do for Her Imperial High Grace to appear in the palace in a bloodied dress."

"I must correct you, Sarah Knecht von Anessa," he said. "Anessa Q'Tar is Her Imperial Highness the Crown Princess of the Westwood Empire." He sighed. "Given the circumstances, it's a forgivable offense. So do not take alarm."

Tania brought forward the semi-sheer sleeves on my outfit, but the rest of the gown had never been worn and was still mostly packed away.

Jorin started to cough into his hand and held his off hand up when someone approached him.

"We're out of time," he said. With a wave of his hand, I lifted off the chair I was sitting on, one sleeve half-attached, the other still in the box.

I wasn't sure how to react, so I just froze and waved to my lady's maids as he walked out of my dorm suite, with me floating behind him like a distressed balloon.

We were in the air seconds later and blasting toward Aspwood.

"Death's curse," Jorin said and flexed his hand. "We have records of it through history, but I never knew there was anything to it. Cultivators, like myself, dead for no reason against opponents they should have no challenge against." He gave a grim smile. "I'm probably the only one to not die immediately."

I was sitting beside him on my knees, on a "floor" of air. It was rather unlike my experience with my father, since he had carried me on his arm. I was fine with this arrangement though. It seemed inappropriate to be carried around by the emperor himself.

"Usually the one who dies is the person who lands the final blow, or so we thought." He glanced at me. "It seems the trigger might be touching the body after death, perhaps. I'll let the investigators figure that out." He laughed. "Though you did sorta destroy the evidence."

"Sorry," I said and bowed my head.

"Don't apologize. You saved my life, even if only for a brief while."

"How certain are you to die?" I asked.

"Dead certain." We sped up. "Pun intended," he intoned. "Whatever that did to me has fractured my cultivation base. It's faltering as we speak. By month's end I'll exit the Sky Realm and drop into the Ascended Realm. Once that happens, I'm afraid I'll live only a couple days."

"But that just means you'll be a mortal, right?" I pleaded. "Can't you persevere?"

"You have a good heart, Anessa. I'm sure of my prediction because the others struck with such a curse," he paused and said finally, "have *all* died."

CHAPTER THIRTY-TWO

MOURNING TRANSITIONS

OUR FLIGHT TOOK an hour to travel over a thousand miles. Jorin was every bit as fast as my Dad, but there was a clear urgency in his effort that day. As though he were running out of gas, despite an unwavering sense of determination.

I could see that the essence rolling out from him–to permit our flight–was irregular and would occasionally nearly sputter out entirely. At one point I was actually afraid we might fall. Though I knew we were in no real danger, even at our speed and height.

As we approached Aspwood, I was surprised to see a vast clearing and a well-used pathway that seemed to disappear into a hillside.

When we neared the clearing's center, we slowed to a stop and Jorin said, "Sorry for this minor indignity, but we are in a hurry." He then motioned to place me on his arm, like my Dad had done years ago.

We descended toward the ground, but instead of slowing down we sped up. I couldn't help but close my eyes and bury my head in his shoulder. Instead of crashing into the ground, though, we passed straight through it. I realized we'd entered a tunnel built specifically for vertical descent.

Smacking his shoulder I said, "That scared me! You could've warned me."

He sighed. "In my experience with carrying others beneath my Realm, all a warning does is increase anxiety and... thrashing." He looked down. "We'll land soon. Do not speak for a while. You are an uninvited guest, and I just bolted out of a high-profile meeting claiming the death of the Imperial Royal Family."

Got it. So they'll be cautious of me.

We must have descended at least ten miles beneath the planet's surface. Even so, the temperature was steady. It brought many questions to mind about what the planet itself really was. On Earth we would've boiled alive by now.

I've always wondered about this planet. Either something's strange about this world in general, or physics isn't as I remembered it on Earth.

Upon the tunnels giving way to an open chasm, I realized, *It's like we're bypassing several layers of security.* Then I saw the Imperial Royal Palace. A building so grand I could only gasp. It had *side buildings* large enough to fit our Imperial Royal dormitories.

We landed in a courtyard smack in the middle of a "smaller" building. Guards stood in every archway wearing halfmail armor with steel helmets. Based on the sensation I got from them, every one of them was a match for my lead guard, or a hair above.

Jorin's Sky Realm Reaction lifted me from his arm and sat me on my feet.

Each of the guards fixed on me and slowly approached, their hands ready to draw steel.

Uncle Jorin raised his hand, which was now covered in his own blood from his coughing fits.

"She's with me," he said, and they halted their advance. "This is Anessa Q'Tar, formerly Carlyle, the only qualified heir of Westwood as the sole surviving heir to the Imperial Royal family. See to it that she is–" his coughing fit flared up again. "–taken care of," he said in gasps.

The female guards among the many dashed forward toward me and they collectively moved me to the Imperial family's gynaeceum.

"Matron Pan," the guard that met me first said. "Dame Lorenvald reporting with orders."

An older woman approached. "Yes, Dame Lorenvald?"

"Please see to Her Imperial Highness, Crown Princess Anessa Q'Tar."

"That title can't be correct," Pan said. "Word is His Imperial Majesty is to extend the crown to Her Imperial Highness Rina Q'Tar within the week."

The dame shook her head slowly. "Lady Anessa is all who survives."

An image of Rina's face flashed in my mind's eye and her lifeless glare made me tear up. *Gods, I'll never forget that face.*

Pan and several maids behind her gasped.

The matron took a step back and her hand went to her chest. "Are you certain? That can't be right. That would mean–"

Dame Lorenvald put her hand on Pan's shoulder and whispered, "By His Imperial Majesty's own word."

Pan merely thinned her lips and curtsied to me, then gestured forward. "Your Imperial Highness, please, come this way."

Everyone behind the matron mirrored the curtsy and made a path for me.

The guards saluted before departing, but two remained at the entryway as the door closed.

Walking forward through a row of people on either side, I was reminded of the day Gideon and I were to announce our engagement. *I felt like a prize pig then. Now I'm just* empty.

"What do you need me to do?" I asked after I entered a large bedroom.

"You do not need to do anything you do not wish," Pan said. "We will take care of everything." She gave me a weak smile. "Though I might ask you to raise an arm or two."

I smiled despite myself. "Okay. I'm just a bit unfocused, my mind's elsewhere."

"One would imagine that being picked up and whisked off in the middle of the day is a bit surprising," she said.

"Yeah, not so much that," I said and shook my head. "Seeing Rina," I started.

Pan's eyes widened, but she didn't intrude.

"And everyone else like that was–" Recalling it made me freeze.

After a few seconds Pan just hugged me. "I hope you'll forgive my forwardness," she whispered. "I didn't know you were there. Go ahead and cry as much as you need."

"Mmm," I said and followed through. *I didn't even know I was. Everything about this feels wrong.* I asked, "Why did Lukas do that? To his sister? His mother? Children?" Each word was a sob and came as a whine. "I don't understand." I pulled away and looked Pan in the eyes. "Am I no better than him because my hand–" I sobbed and hiccupped, "ended his life?"

She guided me to the bed and sat across from me. "It's going to be okay," she said and patted my hand. "You can tell me anything you want." Her voice softened. "I won't repeat it to anyone, okay?"

I nodded, and unloaded everything on her. About the ghastly reaper, Jorin saying he would die soon, and even how I feared Lukas had Ban killed and that none of his motives made any sense to me.

"Your Imperial Highness," said another older woman who had entered. "I'm the court physician, Mala," she added with a curtsy. "Would it be okay if I offered you a draught to calm you?"

"Okay," I said.

She prepared something and brought it to me, but before I could take it another woman poured a small amount into a different cup, then tasted it herself.

Huh, Sarah said the tasters do that, but it's odd seeing someone show me my food or drink isn't poisoned. I didn't usually see the process. In my dormitory they usually tested it in front of Sarah, instead of myself.

The taster nodded, and Mala handed me the draught. "This should calm you down," she said.

I took it, but the cup slipped right through my limp fingers, tumbled to the floor and broke. "Oh yeah, I suppose I did break it after all."

"What did you break?" she asked.

"My wrist."

She held out her hands. "May I?"

With a nod, she took a hold of my arm, and I winced a bit when she felt up and down my arm. It was uncomfortable, but that was all.

Why do I feel so detached? It should hurt more than that.

"Please fetch physician Horace, we'll need to apply some essence pins."

Pan curtsied and rushed off.

"I'm going to prepare you another drink, now," Mala said. Once she'd done so they repeated the same testing process, using a different taster.

The new taster's eyes widened in swallowing the drink, and her face flushed in seconds. She sat down and gave me a thumbs up.

Did she make this one stronger because of my wrist? I didn't much care, and downed the offered liquid. Within a minute my vision collapsed in on itself and returned to "normal." *The longer I have this god-given gift the more normal seems to stray.* The potion then hit me with a wonderful almost null state that made my distant emotional state fall away. *Wow, that's the good stuff.*

"*Don't expect they'll give this to you often,*" Trish said.

Where exactly have you been?

She sent an image of shrugging. "*I don't make the rules, I just follow them. Crises like that are hard for me to poke into.*"

I could've used you, for emotional support at least.

"*I know, I'm sorry,*" she said.

A shaky voice caught my attention. "Hello Your Imperial Highness," an elderly man said. "I'm Horace, would you it be okay if I took a look at your arm?"

Holding it up I said with dreamy detachment, "Okay."

He palpated my wrist.

My wrist–I now realized, with a head that was ironically clearer while high–had already ballooned up to about half an inch thicker all around.

The older man nodded on occasion. "You're lucky," he said. "The bone shards missed your arteries."

Yeah, I'd be dead otherwise, right? I wanted to say but decided not to, though I did have to ask, "How are you able to tell that when you're closing your eyes?"

Horace smiled. "The same way I'll fix your wrist. I'm using essence to see inside, then I'll use essence pins and glue to secure everything. You'll wear a cast for three days and be good as new. But you'll still need to wear a cloth wrap for a few weeks to remind yourself, and others, that your wrist is healing. The pins will degrade on their own, so I'll only have to pester you once."

The hell? If what he's saying is true, it's the closest any cultivator's efforts have come to magic.

He pulled out a gray stone the size of a golf ball that, with its lackluster appearance, cast a soft light on the palm of his hand.

Pan held out a leather bar with flared ends and said calmly, "You might want to bite this."

Crap, I thought, and promptly forgot about how magical it all seemed.

I was not exactly singing the physician's praises during my operation, because even being out of it as I was, having your shrapnel-like bone fragments being moved around inside your soft tissues hurt like crazy. Without the relief of the narcotic potion, I would've passed out.

Either the man was very strong, or he secured my arm with a form of Reaction, because despite my strength being enough to shatter my own arm, it was rooted in place the entire time, to the point where I almost dislocated my shoulder from all my thrashing.

When he finished, he wrapped my arm in some cloth, then they lathered it in a pine-like varnish paste.

After they finished all I could do was fall back on the bed and be glad the ordeal was over. I was out in seconds.

I woke hours later to a sight that made me smile.

"Hi Sarah," I said. "Is it strange that I missed you?"

She said softly, "Not at all. I got here as quickly as I could."

"Is Tania here?" I asked, sitting up.

Sarah helped me up and patted my forehead with a cloth. "Tania and several others will be about a month out. I'm only here by your mother's grace. As the empire mourns, any from your staff will need to be vetted."

"That's a shame," I said.

"Are you up for a bath?" asked Sarah.

I nodded.

Unlike in the dormitory, no fewer than four maids rushed me. Tania seemed like a stickler for the rules back home, but her behavior was the norm here, and no part of my skin—arms included—was uncovered for even a second even as they changed me into the cloth I'd wear during my bath.

This seems excessive.

"Just imagine them as birds or animals changing you like they would a princess," Trish said.

The image made me laugh and there was a brief pause in their motion as though they were making sure I was okay.

That was awkward.

My arm was held above the water at all times. They'd even tasked one of the girls with holding a cloth that was wrapped around my cast so it would stay above water. Well, I say "girl," but the woman was stout and built like a brick house. Despite that she seemed to struggle.

Guess the cast isn't waterproof?

"Swelling," Trish said flatly. *"The heat will make it worse and crack the cast from inside. They could replace it, sure, but they're trying to see to your comfort. It would hurt quite a bit."*

Since when did you become a medical expert?

"Since ever, what was I studying for?" Trish quipped. *"To understand how modern stuff is better, you gotta know the past."*

Huh.

After my bath they ushered me to bed, and gave me another sedative, a weaker one this time.

Before Sarah could retire, I asked, "Please stay here?"

She nodded and departed behind a privacy screen before returning in her shift. "Please excuse me," she said and laid down by my side.

Taking her hand into mine, I started to talk to her.

Startling awake in the middle of the night I was glad that I wasn't alone. Sarah's platinum blond hair was lit calmly by Fandar's blue moonlight.

Am I a bad person for asking her to stay? I wondered to myself.

"You could do worse," Trish poked.

What?

"You still miss some jokes," she said with a sigh. *"I was teasing you for waking up next to her."*

Gods, don't make it weird.

"Yeah, Yukirei would've been better," she and sent an image of the scene before me as if it were Yukirei.

Don't do that! I chastised. My eyes burned. *I just killed my cousin, and after he killed seven other members of his family,* my *family, now isn't the time for jokes!*

"I'm sorry," she said solemnly.

I needed you and you weren't there. Now all you can do is tease me about Yuki, Sarah, and act like this is some big game to you.

"I'm so sorry," she said frantically, *"I didn't mean—"*

What did you mean!? What even are you? You seem to phone it in when it's convenient for you. I'd sat up and started sobbing.

Sarah held me without saying a word and I eventually fell back asleep.

In the morning I woke to Sarah calmly rubbing my back calling my name. No fewer than six people surrounded my bed. They had me ready in under ten minutes, with a bath, *and* changed my cast.

"Please tell me this won't be my morning every day," I said to Pan.

She smiled. "Not *every* day, no."

My right eye twitched. *She didn't say it wouldn't be the only time.*

"Now then," Pan clapped twice. "In thirty minutes, His Imperial Majesty, through a herald, will announce to the empire proper that the royal family has passed away," gesturing toward me, she added, "but the backup remains." She held up a gloved hand, with a single finger extended. "You will sit on the lower throne at his side." Another finger extended. "Do not speak." She raised another one. "You will look down and to the side until your name is called, then you will look into the orb that the herald is speaking into."

A knock came at the door and an older gentleman dressed in a pure black suit and undershirt entered. He held a black lacquered box with gilded inlay. Its surface was filled with a filigree that was reminiscent of the flow the ouroboros on the Imperial Ruler's seal gave.

He stood before me and opened the box, presenting a ring with a copy of the ruler's seal.

Pan picked it up and gestured for my hand, sliding it onto my pointer finger. It was a perfect fit.

How the hell did they get the size right?

"Please sign here, Your Imperial Highness," the man said and offered a scroll.

It noted I was taking charge of a copy of the Imperial Signet for the day or until it was released back to the state. Seeing no weird clauses, I did as asked.

He signed it after me, then offered a small jar barely larger than the head of the ring. "Make an impression, and stamp the scroll."

Doing as he asked, I pressed the waxy substance into a box I'd assumed was intended for the test impression. "What's this for?" I asked as Pan then signed the overly-airtight document.

"Don't lose the ring. That's your provisional copy of the Q'Tar dynasty ruler's seal." The man smiled. "You'd make several old men rather unhappy if you lost it." His tone hardened and his smile vanished. "Myself included." He nodded to us and left the room.

"Charming," I whispered after the door closed behind him. "He didn't even give us his name."

"Lord Quinby is an ass," Pan said. Winking at me she added, "But I'll deny saying it."

"My day has just started," I said with a sigh, "and I'm already weary from what kind of pomp and pageantry is in store for me."

Pan sighed. "It's not going to get easier. You're about to find out the difference between an heir whose readiness isn't priority, and an eminent heir."

"Speaking of that," I said and dropped to a whisper. "Do we have word on how His Imperial Majesty is doing?"

Pan held up a finger to her mouth, and produced an S-ROB. After she activated the sound barrier she said, "Quiet or not, if you need to ask questions like that. Say so first." Her eyes drifted to some of the maids in the corner of the room. "Not everyone is in the loop yet."

Looking over to Sarah, she just smiled at me.

I wonder why she wouldn't tell me that? Remembering that she'd often pull a cube out, I wondered if she had, and I just ignored her.

"Okay, is he doing okay? Is he really…" I quieted, despite the barrier, "dying?"

Pan looked down. "He is. Doctors say a little over two years, if he stops using his cultivation base. He's diminished to the Ascended Realm already. They're stuffing him full of tonics, but that timeline is including their best efforts."

▼ ▼ ▼

Entering the throne room, I was surprised to see *ten* chairs set up. Two larger prominent thrones sat in the front, with four on either side were slightly smaller.

My personal insignia of a teal dragon with flame-colored hair was on a silver banner above the smaller throne to Jorin's right. Since each of the others had a symbol of their own, I realized, immediately, these were the chairs of those who had fallen.

To the far reaches of the room was a sight I didn't expect. There were tiny copies of the 'remote viewing box' hardware that all tethered to a central box. It was a cultivator version of a television production. Instead of cables here and there, the devices seemed to use hard sleeved lines. *They'd have to design the room around this technology.*

While it was modern-looking in many ways, the hard-wired aspects of the enchantments gave an impression of how a medieval production studio might look.

This was not at all what I pictured.

There were even sections of the floor taped off in different colors. I saw someone taking a string and stretching it from the orb or camera and adjusting the tape accordingly.

Oh. Are they taping out the field of view?

Several people dashed around in headsets. It was quite the sight, seeing maids run about with the contraptions on. Were it under different circumstances, I might even have found it funny.

A maid came forward holding a clipboard with a feather quill in her hair. "Name?"

I raised an eyebrow. *It's unusual that some people don't know me, though kind of nice.*

"Anessa Jean C…" I paused and bit my lip. "Q'Tar." I thought, *That they took my family name from me will take some getting used to. I don't like it.*

She scribbled it down on the page, dipping the quill in a tiny inkwell at the tip of the clipboard, only enough to write my name down. "Okay, go take your seat. His Imperial Majesty will be here shortly." The quill went back to its clear resting place, leaving a small dab of black ink in her brown hair.

As I took my seat, I noticed the lighting was no better than in any other room. *How do their "cameras" have such great optics? I remember YouTubers would need to pump the scene full of light to get anything usable out of a broadcast.*

While I waited, another maid came up to me and curtsied. "Lady Anessa," she took to my side and pointed out in front of me. "During our broadcast…" she went on to explain the same sequence of events that Pan had, but the maid gave me visual landmarks to track so I knew *exactly* where to look.

Five minutes later the far doors opened, and a parade of people entered. Led by an ancient man that could've been my uncle Jorin's grandfather, with a pronounced hunch and dull black-gray hair, they guided him by the arm up onto the stairs of the dais.

My breath hitched as they led *"grandpa"* and sat him next to me, and I realized who he was.

"Surprised?" the elder's voice quaked.

"Uncle Jorin?" I said, forgetting my honorifics.

"That's me," he said and gave me a weak smile. "If my steward hadn't watched me enfeeble before his eyes," he laughed the best he could. "They might assume I was a terrible pretender."

I asked tentatively, "Is it as hard for you as it is me to not cry?"

"Harder, I imagine," he said and sighed. "Mortality," he said and held up his withered hand, "I don't mind. Being forced to follow my family in death is the worst. With mortal children, I'd come to accept that I would leave some of them behind, but..." his voice trembled, "Not all of them."

We sat in silence for several breaths.

I can't imagine what it must be like to have cultivator children, let alone knowing I'd outlive them if they're mortal.

Uncle Jorin continued, "From your reaction, I take it you haven't thought of children much, have you?"

When I shook my head, he added, "Love them. Regardless of their talents. Their faults. And find a way to forgive the darkness in their hearts." His voice hardened, "But don't be blind to it, like I was."

A light horn at our side quieted the room.

"We're remoting in five... four... three..." one of the maids with a clipboard said and stopped speaking at two. She then stepped out of frame.

Once the shock of the tech wore off, the herald began his declaration. As the names were read off, a silver cloth was lowered over each of the thrones to represent their fall.

It took all I had to not bawl hearing Rina's name. The herald proclaimed at the end, "The Imperial Royal Family has fallen, survived by His Imperial Majesty," he gestured to my uncle, "Jorin Q'Tar, and his niece, Anessa Jean Q'Tar."

No pressure.

CHAPTER THIRTY-THREE

WEDDING BELLS AND HER TELLS

AFTER THE BROADCAST, I was approached by the "fun" Lord Quinby. He presented me with the signet ring box once again, and we returned the valuable item to his custody. He locked the box and immediately remanded it to the guard he brought with him. A separate piece of paper was signed for each.

This is a bit much.

Before he left, Quinby said, "Lord Olafur requests your presence," then pointed to the far end of the throne room.

And he can't be bothered to come here and talk to me himself?

Before the man walked off, a squirrelly man wrote down some things in a book and the three departed together.

With my Thrusight I noticed that what he wrote down was the time, date, and the fact that Lord Quinby asked me to talk to Lord Olafur.

Approaching the older gentleman, I realized he may have opted to stay at the entrance because he was particularly frail. He was barely more vigorous than my enfeebled Uncle Jorin. It ablated my annoyance until he spoke.

"Your Imperial Highness, Chancellor Helios demands your presence in the Imperial Royal Council chambers to discuss a matter of importance," he said and gave me a wrinkled smile.

Couldn't Lord Quinby have told me that? Instead of unloading on a seemingly senile old man, I nodded and sought Pan, who could tell me where the bloody chambers were.

It took me no more than ten minutes for me to fetch Pan and us to reach the chambers. However, when we arrived, we were denied entry.

The guard said, "I am sorry Your Imperial Highness. I was instructed that no one is permitted entry unless they have their personal token." He handed me the token I'd just given him. "This one is for an Imperial High Duchess named Anessa Carlyle, of which you are neither."

Before saying another word Pan pulled me to the side and pulled out an S-ROB to communicate.

"It seems that Chancellor Helios is up to no good. He knows full well you haven't been assigned your new token."

"So they're playing games?"

She nodded.

I sighed and crossed my arms and thought. Using my Thrusense I tried to peer within the room and heard the Chancellor Helios comment, "Her Imperial Highness is late, it seems."

Quinby laughed and shook his head.

Gideon sat to the side, with his hands folded in his lap. Looking as though he'd been called to the principal's office.

Why is Gideon there, and these assholes find yanking my chain funny?

"Griblin's Giblets," Olafur said and stood from his chair as quick as his frame would allow. He hobbled toward the side door and said, "I'll be right back, this infernal bladder of mine."

"You should get the healers to look at that," Quinby quipped with a laugh.

"Bah! The last time I did that the cure was worse," as he toddled down a side hall he said, "It burned for three weeks!"

The older man entered what I'd assumed was a restroom. Looking at the layout, I saw a door to our side. "Am I allowed to go in there?" I asked the guard.

"Yes, Your Imperial Highness, you are. The only thing through there are restrooms and vacant meeting rooms."

Giving him a smile I said, "Perfect, thank you."

Pan whispered to me, "Do you need to use the restroom? A lady should be discreet about that."

My cheeks flushed. "No. Just follow me, please."

Through the door and around the corner, the door he exited from leading to the council room was guarded. Knowing I'd get the same denial I ignored the man stationed there.

Holding my hand up about waist high, I peered through the restroom wall and was thankful to see no cursed imagery. *He's still there.*

Waiting near the entrance, when Olafur exited the room I said, "Lord Olafur!"

He jumped and held his chest with wide eyes. "Ahh!" He waved his cane's head in my face. "Don't do that!"

"Sorry," I said while leaning back and stifling a laugh. "I was hoping to catch you."

His eyes narrowed and he sighed. "Oh, were you?"

"It seems I'm having a bit of an issue with the guard," I said and hiked a thumb at the nearest one to the council chambers.

"I should be able to help you with that," he said in a flat tone.

We entered the chambers using the same door he'd departed from and the jovial atmosphere flatlined the moment the council members saw me. Though my uncle gave me a barely perceptible smile.

Why would they not expect me to show up when summoned? I thought ruefully.

"So good of you to join us," Chancellor Helios said and gestured forward toward the floor beneath them. "But you are rather late."

"I am, aren't I. It seems someone neglected to grant me the appropriate token needed to gain access. Since you, Chancellor Helios, requested my presence, I'm certain you will be following up to figure out who made the error that inconvenienced you."

He nodded once stiffly.

"Lord Gideon," the Chancellor said. "Please rise and take to Anessa's side."

After Gideon had done so, the Chancellor continued, "Now then. Your coronation has been set for the date you turn sixteen. At that time, your marriage will be made public through ceremony. Gideon Ignotus's honorary Imperial Marquess title will be elevated to an official position within the week." He coughed. "Since several… vacancies have occurred in the imperial ranks over the last few years, his appointment won't present any issue."

Yeah, sorry for finding out several of your imperial nobles are corrupt. Though I never received proper credit for the removal of several imperial nobles some time ago, I didn't mind. It was incidental, but it seems when you're higher nobility, just being involved grants you the right to take credit.

The Chancellor flipped over a page in front of him. "During that time, you will be seen often with Lord Gideon, so that you rise in familiarity together."

"Then I'm just supposed to do everything you say?" I asked crossing my arms. *I'm not about to let these strangers think they can steamroll me.*

"Yes," Jorin said. "At the very least, the empire needs stability right now since they have just lost eight members of the ruling family, and will soon lose another in me." He frowned at that. "Further, it takes time to prepare for your ascension to empress. That little time is the only grace I can grant you, niece."

It was all he could give me. Accepting the time with good grace was all I could do in return.

▼ ▼ ▼

Finday, Lokandae 22nd, 1741

"Here you are," Sarah said, handing me the talisman for Anessa Q'Tar, Imperial Crown Princess of the Westwood Empire.

The Imperial Royal Council spent the past two full years continuing the games they'd played right after I arrived in the palace.

The time had not softened the council's attitude toward me, and while they couldn't directly attack me, the elaborately rigid protocols of the court gave them plenty of tools to make my life difficult. But if they were finally giving me the talisman, it meant they were going to announce my status as crown princess.

Two years doesn't seem like a very long time. But I'd spent those two years being jerked around by a bunch of old codgers. It felt like an eternity.

Uncle Jorin had been withdrawn from everything during those two years, not that I could blame him. His entire family had predeceased him. That's a nightmare that you *never* wake up from until the bell rings in your name.

It took everything in my willpower to not crush the talisman in my hands. Though I suspect that might be what they'd want.

"Finally," I said, and thought about how dodgy the men had been. "Any ideas how they adapted to me so seamlessly? We didn't tell anyone about my Thrusense but my parents."

"Well…" Sarah began, and her voice trailed off. "It might be their use of money. When you explained that they were able to start avoiding you so expertly, despite your abilities, I contacted your home estates. There were several retirements in rapid succession, which raised some flags. They may have literally bought into rumors around your god-given gift."

My mouth hung open. "And you're just telling me now?!"

"Yes. It's not out of malice, I tend to only operate on concrete evidence. Would you have preferred that I interrogate them?"

"No," I shook my head. "I wouldn't have. That's not who I am." A dark thought weaseled its way in, *Lukas sure would have. Thankfully I'm better than he is. Though that's a pretty low bar for comparison.*

Sarah had turned away, but raised a finger and spun back around. "Word is, your banners have been distributed since late Zenthriae," Sarah said.

"Just how much work goes into a coronation?" I asked. "The team involved must be enormous!"

"Jorin's was a few hundred thousand, I hear," she said nonchalantly. "I'd imagine yours would be much the same."

Her casual declaration made me stand and shout, "*How* many?"

She repeated herself and added, "It might be a bit more in your case, since they're rolling your marriage into it. With them having," she moved her head with her body, "*also* delayed the announcement of your heirship until last week, they're really working overtime."

"That's insane! Why does it take so many people?"

Sarah said, "They'll have an equally elaborate celebration in each kingdom across Westwood. That's forty-one celebrations in all."

Before I could ask why there were forty-one, when the empire only has forty kingdoms, I remembered Aspwood's special status. It was its own territory, distinct from the kingdoms.

That's a bit more believable. It made a fire burn in my chest. *Which is why the council isolating me for so long is so infuriating!*

They'd made me spend two years studying etiquette and diplomacy. They also had me busy meeting crowds in no fewer than fifty parades, with such scant reception it may as well have been a dress rehearsal.

The six Imperial Ball Dances they'd put on kept me so isolated from those in power, I may as well have been a… Ruminating over their efforts, I realized they were worse than I thought. *They want a figurehead. A puppet.*

It helped me make up my mind, and I realized my plan for my coronation had to go ahead. A little surprise I'd been planning for everyone that would help me cut some of the strings they'd placed around me over the time I'd known them.

Tania knocked and entered. With a curtsy she said, "Your Imperial Highness, we are ready if it pleases you."

Let's get this show on the road.

Moving from two to four maids helping me took some getting used to, but it was second nature now. Pan had retired and moved to training Sarah. The older chief lady's maid had long served the late empress. She'd expressed her desire to retire, and she received zero push back from me and mine.

Flutters of indecision made my stomach churn. "Why am I so nervous? I wasn't even this nervous when Gideon and I wed," I said aloud.

"I don't know what you're talking about," Sarah said and winked.

Right, don't admit that we're already married in current company. Not that it'll matter in an hour, since we'll have our public ceremony. It then made the butterflies even more active as I asked, "Wait. We won't need to repeat that silly, er…" I paused and avoided eye contact, "ceremony will we?"

Sarah nodded and smiled.

Crap. I thought and followed up, "Is that why they waited until the day *after* my birthday?"

Sarah gave a faint nod but didn't say anything beyond that.

Those sly bastards, waiting for a heat. They're trying to push things along just like last time. Thankfully I'm in better control this time. I'd had time to work on improving my self-control over the past two years. Remembering my near-slip with Gideon after my run behind the cadet whose name I forgot, I amended my thought, *Hopefully.*

Gilded glittering sequins filled my outfit, and I was reminded of Lady Vivian, late queen of the Rhinebur nation. *She would have approved of this outfit.* Every time we met, she was always dressed to the nines or tens.

"Is this real gold?" I mused aloud.

"Yes," came three responses, causing a quiet round of giggles.

Stepping out onto the public platform, I briefly waved at the thousands in attendance. The imperial royal guard was out in full force. Circles formed around performers who had paused at my arrival. Those closest were of noble blood and were starting to shuffle in. There were commoners as far as I could see. Although I didn't know these people, they cheered when they saw me.

It wasn't time for my announcement to the crowd, so I dipped back into the palace and headed to the grand hall for my coronation.

"That was so nerve-racking," I said, pausing to catch my breath.

My attendants ushered me forward, reminding me of the brisk pace the day was to have.

With practiced finesse, the coronation itself was a blur. Only the highest nobility was permitted within the hall. I was sure I did everything right, but my nerves made the experience largely forgettable. Since I'd run through the procedure at least a hundred times, due to the orders of those old cretins, I wasn't worried about a slip-up.

As the layers were shed, I breathed a sigh of relief. "That's much better," I said. "I was so worried about ripping it."

"You did," Sarah teased.

"What?" I said, and a blush nipped my ears.

She showed me an under-layer with the tiniest tear near a rivet for its lace.

"Don't scare me like that!" I said and batted her wrist. "I thought I'd embarrassed myself."

"You were flawless, my empress," she reassured me.

Registering my new title made me thin my lips out. "Empress, huh." Shaking my head I added, "I don't feel like one." I grinned. "Though part of that I hope to resolve in my speech."

REBORN IN THE PERFECT FANTASY WORLD

Sarah narrowed her eyes. "Anything I should know about?"

Shaking my head I said, "No." I paused, and my voice raised in pitch a little bit, "Maybe?"

"Your Imperial Majesty knows best, I'm sure." she sighed. She tapped my nose with the fixing agent, making the blue makeup on my face tingle. "Done."

We headed straight to my wedding ceremony in an adjacent, equally grand hall. There was no grandstanding from Eloria this time, and I may have allowed my kiss with Gideon to linger a bit longer. Since I wasn't eleven any longer, my reservations about the whole thing had diminished.

Our kiss calmed the fluttering and made my head spin, but I had to disengage when the Father of the Scripture's children coughed.

Instead of mama-Krissi it was Uncle Jorin who handled the ceremony itself. It tugged at my heart strings to hear his voice, which was now a weak monotone.

He's all but given up, I thought sadly.

While Gideon took his oath as emperor consort, I thought about my upcoming first proclamation. The ache starting in my teeth made it clear I was more worried about this than the formal events proceeding around me.

The brief focus on my husband permitted me a silent prayer, *Eloria, Mother Goddess, please let this go without a hitch.*

Upon exiting back onto the balcony, the heralds at our sides blasted their horns, bringing silence and attention.

Gods, I want to throw up, I thought as I approached the railing.

"It is our great honor that we are able to welcome you as Empress Anessa Q'Tar and Emperor Consort Gideon Q'Tar of the Westwood Empire," I started, and swallowed my nerves. What followed was a carefully rehearsed series of empty platitudes offered up by the Imperial Royal Council.

Despite my bitter mirth at the council, they knew how to play a crowd. When the crowd ate the words up I had to tip my proverbial hat to those old men for their carefully-crafted empty words. I *almost* felt bad about going off script.

"Many of you know, I am the goddess of craft's champion," I said, dampening the fervor. I could tell that my deviation had immediately caught the attention of the council, and they were not smiling as they listened intently. "What is not widely known, is that I am Her Goddess Eloria's True Champion of Craft…"

The crowd's intensity reached a fever pitch at this announcement, and I held up my hands to quiet them. "…and her True Champion of Death."

Despite the teeming audience of thousands, you could have heard a pin drop. In a second, a quiet rumble from the "sky" above us punctuated my words. This, even though we were miles underground. A glance at the council showed they would definitely have liked to flay me alive, had they dared. But the continuing thunder in the air, a not-so-subtle endorsement by Eloria herself, left no room for doubt.

With a smile I thought, *Their days of toying with me are over.* I was going to be a bigger problem than they thought.

Thanks for making it this far!

Ratings and reviews are the lifeblood of a series. If you have time, please take the time to leave one.

This series will be releasing often, so look forward to the next book, and follow me on Amazon for updates!

Thank you to Alice Waites (Damson) for the illustrations in this story. It wouldn't be the same without her help. Her Bluesky account can be found @damsonfox.bsky.social
Another thank you to Danny DeCillis, my editor. For making my words not trip over one another.
Thanks to the talented Ashley Gatti for her voices in the audiobooks.

My website is cristoph.net and my X account can be found @cristoph_a_t

ESTAR TRANSLATION GUIDE

Days of the week:
Unday - First day of the week.
Deuday - Second day of the week.
Triday - Third day of the week.
Quattoroday - Fourth day of the week.
Midday - Fifth day of the week (midweek).
Hexoday - Sixth day of the week.
Septaday - Seventh day of the week.
Octday - Eighth day of the week.
Finday - Ninth day of the week.

Month names (and their English equivalent):
Runariae - January
Crotariae - February
Totharae - March
Evantaiae - April
Lokandae - May
Jothariae - June
Mankae - July
Ylldriae - August
Hanvarae - September
Fandariae - October
Polarae - November
Zenthriae - December

While Runariae is positionally equivalent to January, that's where the similarities end. Months are 27 days long (three in-world weeks).

Äneaca is Anessa's name in Estar.

UNITS / CONVERSIONS

Standard minute - Sixty-four seconds.
   Standard hour - Sixty-four Standard minutes.
   Standard day - Twenty-four Standard hours.

   Anfang day - Forty-eight Standard hours or two Standard days.
   Anfang Week - Nine Anfang days.
   Anfang Month - Twenty-seven Anfang Days or Sixty-one & 11/25 Earth days long.
   Anfang Year - Three-hundred-twenty-four Anfang days, twelve Anfang months, or six-hundred-forty-eight Standard days. With one leap Anfang day every nine Anfang years.

"Days" are Anfang days, but they're 54.6 hours long as noted in some chapters. A year is a Standard year. This is clarified as needed in the text. There are two Standard years per calendar year. So Anessa ages twice per year.

CHARACTER GUIDE

Anessa Jean Carlyle / Q'Tar - Our protagonist. Her death on Earth is somewhat of a mystery. She thought at first it was her best friend that took her life, but things might not be as simple as that. Early Nascent Realm. She is the new Empress of Westwood.

Eloria Kirzington von Addenal - Anfang's goddess of Death. She was once viewed as the goddess of craft.

Eugene Truval - Grand Master General of the Westwood Empire, Yukirei's father.

Evan Q'Tar - Heir to the Redwater Empire. Late stages of the Ascended Realm.

Jorin Q'Tar - His Imperial Majesty, the Emperor of the Westwood Empire. Sky-Realm, half-step in the Otherworldly Realm.

Julilah Carlyle - Roland's first wife. Veronica's on-pa. Anessa's step-mother. Mortal.

Lily Carlyle - Anessa's mother and Roland's third wife.

Lukas Q'Tar † - Anessa's cousin. Heir presumptive and Imperial Prince of the Westwood Empire. Middling Sky Realm.

Max Winnie - Portia's fiancé, son of Baron Min Winnie. Middling Ascended Realm.

Gideon Varn / Carlyle / Q'Tar - Son of the Varn Baronet from Rhinebur. Anessa's husband. Early Ascended Realm.

Oliver Sil Carlyle - Anessa's older twin brother. Former heir of the Carlyle Imperial Duchy. Was in the late Sky Realm, but due to poisoning he is now a mortal.

Portia - A commoner-turned-gentry from the Maaka Institute of Cultivating Juniors. Anessa's friend. Max's fiancée. Commoner. Mortal.

Rina Q'Tar † - Was slated to be the Imperial Crown Princess, but was slain by her brother, Lukas Q'Tar. Anessa's maternal cousin through Jorin Q'Tar.

Roland Carlyle - Anessa's father and the patriarch of the Carlyle family. Late Sky Realm.

Rufus - Anessa's sentient sword that she received from her brother when she was eleven years old. Seems to be malfunctioning.

Sarah-Knecht von Anessa - Anessa's lady's maid. Bound to Anessa for life through a slave contract.

Trish - Anessa's friend from Earth. Talks into her mind at times.

Veronica Nu Carlyle - Anessa's not-sister. Kristine and Julilah's daughter.

Yllia - Head maid of the Carlyle family.

Yukirei Truval - Gideon's second fiancé. She was antagonistic to Anessa when they first met, but has since warmed to her in realizing her mistakes. Somewhat of a tsundere. In a acp hoth with Anessa Carlyle. Early Sky Realm.

† - Deceased.

CULTIVATION TERMINOLOGY

Realm - A major steppingstone for cultivators to differentiate between one another.

Stage - A portion of a Realm necessary to advance. Typically, a Realm composes many stages.

Step - Denotes an even smaller portion of a Realm and subdivides Stages.

Dantian - A means for a cultivator to store essence within their body.

Divine Link - A connection with a god or goddess during an Awakening Ceremony.

Meridians - Similar to how veins and arteries carry blood, meridians carry essence.

Nexus - An organ within a cultivator that is used to control essence. It's similar to how your heart pumps blood, a nexus pumps essence. Different in that it helps you enact control *external* to your body.

Mortal - A non-cultivator. Equivalent to a normal person on Earth.

Nascent Realm - A cultivator who is in the first Realm. The weakest Nascent Realm cultivator is stronger than the average mortal (usually).

Ascended Realm - The second Realm. Most consider this Realm to be the real start of someone's cultivation journey. The Nascent Realm is like being on training wheels.

Sky Realm - The third Realm. At this stage, cultivators start to understand basic gravity and learn to counteract it. This is done innately, and they slowly move to temper their bodies for what comes next.

Ring of He - An enchanted ring which is capable of providing female couples with the means to have children. Cannot be used by someone under the influence of a Ring of She. Can be used by Mortals.

Ring of She - The opposite of the Ring of He. Cannot be used by someone under the influence of a Ring of He. Can be used by Mortals.

On-ma - The mother of a child in a female-female relationship.

On-pa - The father of a child in a female-female relationship.

S-ROB - Short-Range Obscuring Barrier. A device used to keep conversations clandestine. Comes in a few varieties.

Will - A necessary component to cultivation. Without Will, essence carries no form.

www.ingramcontent.com/pod-product-compliance
Lightning Source LLC
Chambersburg PA
CBHW070647180626
46817CB00006B/2264